WRITTEN AND ILLUSTRATED BY

CORNELIA FUNKE

2 Palmer Street, Frome, Somerset BA11 1DS

Text © Cornelia Funke 2021
Cover illustration © Laura Ellen Anderson 2021
Inside illustrations © Cornelia Funke 2021

First published in Great Britain in 2021
Chicken House
2 Palmer Street
Frome, Somerset BA11 1DS
United Kingdom
www.chickenhousebooks.com

Chicken House/Scholastic Ireland, 89E Lagan Road, Dublin Industrial Estate,
Glasnevin, Dublin D11 HP5F, Republic of Ireland

Cover design by Steve Wells
Typeset by Dorchester Typesetting Group Ltd
Printed and bound in Great Britain by CPI Group (UK) Ltd, Croydon, CR0 4YY

1 3 5 7 9 10 8 6 4 2

British Library Cataloguing in Publication data available.

ISBN 978-1-911077-98-5
eISBN 978-1-913696-25-2

For Danny and Kat, Laurel and Larry,
the real Mary and the real Alfonso,
who all helped me find the real Malibu.

A FEATHERED FLOWER

In New Zealand January is a summer month. But this particular morning was quite crisp, and Guinevere Greenbloom spotted eleven dew elves as she followed her father to the boat that would carry them out into the bay. Dew elves love cold mornings. Of course they had made sure that they couldn't be spotted easily – all fabulous beings are masters of camouflage and Guinevere was quite sure nobody else noticed the tiny elves – neither the men loading their boats along the pier, nor the three fishermen who were sitting side by side on the wooden boards dangling their lines into the water.

'It's incredible. It almost feels as if the world is younger here!' Guinevere whispered into her father's ear. 'Dew elves, fishmen, gullings, wind riders . . . I've never seen such an abundance of fabulous creatures!'

'And once again, we seem to be the only ones who detect them!' her father whispered back. 'How can people be so blind?' He cast a glance at the fishermen. 'I guess the fabulous friends we brought may have drawn the others.'

Guinevere heard voices in the small wooden suitcase he was carrying. But before she could ask her father about its inhabitants, Barnabas stopped in front of a boat, its name written on the white hull with blue paint. *Kaitiaki.* That was the name of the sacred Guardians of the Māori.

'You are right, by the way, my love,' said Barnabas Greenbloom, stepping on to the narrow gangway, 'the world *is* younger in New Zealand. Its two islands are the most recent large land masses to rise from the sea, and humans probably settled here no earlier than 900 AD. It is also the only place on Earth where many of the native birds walk on foot.'

'Which can prove to be quite deadly a habit.' The man who appeared behind the railing wore the traditional tattoo of the Māori on his dark face, along with a wide smile. 'Our birds didn't foresee all the predators that would come to these islands by ship one day, along with lots of white men.'

He was a bear of a man, and the fierce hug he gave Barnabas had Guinevere worried for a moment that he'd break her lanky father in half.

'Guinevere, may I introduce you to Kahurangi Ngata?' Barnabas said, when the Māori finally let go of him. 'He is, as far as I know, the only human who speaks the dialects of thirteen whale species.'

'Which were far easier to learn than the three tortoise languages I speak, not to mention the kiwi dialects I barely manage to utter with my leaden human tongue.' Kahurangi Ngata held out a hand to Guinevere, a hand that was covered in swirling lines and patterns of leaves. 'Very honoured to meet you, Guinevere Greenbloom, protector of the last Pegasi, friend of moss fairies and mermaids.'

His T-shirt showed the kiwi, the most famous of the walking birds of New Zealand. Guinevere would have loved to see one, but sadly they never showed up during daytime, and were famous for their shyness.

Guinevere and her father had originally been on the way to the Himalayas to visit her brother Ben and thirteen freshly born dragons. Why they had taken a detour to New Zealand Barnabas had only explained in very vague terms, but Guinevere was too busy taking in the beauty that surrounded them to ask and New Zealand had always been a place she had yearned to visit. But while Kahurangi was steering his boat through an archipelago of islands that drifted on the glassy water like mossy green turtles Guinevere began to wonder about the purpose of this expedition. In the past months her parents had often discussed buying a farm in New Zealand. MÍMAMEIÐR, the sanctuary they had founded in Norway, by now could barely host all the fabulous refugees who came to them hoping for shelter and safety. Many had lost their homes to roads or dams. Others had been driven away by farming, deforestation or human wars. MÍMAMEIÐR granted them all safety, but for many of them the north of Norway was too cold. So when Barnabas had told Guinevere about the detour to New Zealand, she had assumed the search for a second sanctuary to be the reason. But when she had suggested that, Barnabas had only muttered: 'No no, my love. We decided to go somewhere else for that. But there's just something I have to quickly check on.'

The clear water around them was even more densely populated with fabulous creatures than the small harbour. One of them was a green seahorse, a creature so rare that her father normally wouldn't have been able to rein in his enthusiasm, but Barnabas cast only an absent-minded glance at it. He seemed distracted and worried, and he lowered his voice when he talked to his Māori friend – a behaviour Guinevere wasn't used to from either her father or her mother, as they usually didn't keep secrets from their children.

Something to check on. What *had* they come for? This detour was becoming more and more mysterious.

Hothbrodd wouldn't tell either. The troll, as always, was their pilot. (He had also built their plane.) 'If your father hasn't told you, it's not on me to do so, Guinevere Greenbloom!' he had growled. 'And if it's any comfort to you, he didn't tell me much either.'

Two flying fish jumped over the boat, their tiny nixling riders waving at Guinevere. *Ben will be so jealous when I tell him about this place!* she thought. *No, Guinevere,* she corrected herself, leaning deeper over the railing so as not to miss anything, *your brother isn't jealous of anyone or anything at the moment. For he's probably holding a young dragon on his lap right now.*

That thought – she had to admit it – filled her with jealousy. She was glad her father had promised that after this they would head straight for the valley in the Himalayas where the last dragons had found refuge from her kind. It was only fair, of course, that Ben had met their offspring first – after all, he had helped the dragons to find the valley. And then . . . he had become her brother. *Your* foundling *brother*, she could almost hear Ben say.

Guinevere missed him. She always did, when they were separated for too long, and it had been more than a month since he'd left for the Rim of Heaven, as the dragons called their valley.

Kahurangi slowed the boat down and let it drift towards the steep shore of an island that was still wrapped in morning mist. A sign next to the wooden pier announced that it was a bird sanctuary, and Guinevere spotted traps for possums and rats between and in the trees. The walking birds of New Zealand were easy prey for the predators that had been brought to their islands by humans.

'I guess we can all agree that birds who prefer to walk shouldn't become extinct,' Barnabas said in a low voice as they followed Kahurangi up a path that was lined by tropical trees and views of the sea and other islands. 'But as you know, your mother and I despise traps, so she suggested bringing the suitcase you're carrying. Let's see whether my old Māori friend likes it.'

He winked at Guinevere and stopped under what looked to Guinevere like a Kauri tree.

'Kahurangi!' Barnabas called. 'I forgot to tell you. We brought a gift. I hope you'll like it.'

He placed the suitcase on the ground and carefully opened it. Kahurangi frowned when he saw the two dozen small men and women inside. They were as blue as cornflowers and stood barely higher than a can of beans.

'What is the meaning of this, Barnabas?' the Māori said. 'You know we don't like creatures from outside to be brought to our islands. They cause nothing but harm!'

The gnomes frowned back at him as they climbed out of the suitcase.

'You aren't a native of these islands either, my friend,' Barnabas replied. 'May I remind you that the Māori arrived here barely seven hundred years ago? These are bluelings, and I think your birds will be very grateful to have them around for a while.'

'The possums will chop off their heads!' Kahurangi exclaimed.

The bluelings burst into laughter. One of them turned to the suitcase and tapped his finger against it. It disappeared.

Kahurangi stared incredulously at the spot where it had lain just a second ago. Then he bent down and picked up a suitcase as small as a grain of rice.

'That's what they'll do with your bird-eaters,' Barnabas said. 'I guess even flightless birds can eat predators that size?'

The Māori stared down at the gnomes. 'Well, I suppose the Greenblooms' methods always were a bit different!' he murmured.

'I hope so!' Barnabas smiled. 'We'll pick them up in a month. Treat them nicely – they're in high demand. But now, show us what we've come for!'

The path they followed ended on a wooden platform, rising on stilts from a thicket of the high ponga ferns that only grow in New Zealand. It granted a magical view over dozens of islands. Thousands of birds swarmed above the turquoise waters: albatrosses, petrels, shags, prions, gannets, skuas . . . Guinevere quickly gave up trying to name them all. More and more of them were landing on the water, forming a shape with their bodies that resembled a flower, a huge flower

drawn by feathers and beaks.

'Look familiar?' Kahurangi handed Barnabas his binoculars. 'I'm sure it reminds you as well of the tale you and I were once quite obsessed with.'

Guinevere's father took the binoculars and trained them on the birds.

'What tale?' Guinevere asked, but her father had forgotten about her as he stared through the binoculars at the swarming birds.

'It could be nothing but a coincidence,' he murmured. 'There need to be four of these.'

'Oh, I remember. *Four to announce her, four to receive her.*' Kahurangi was also staring at the birds. 'But what if this is the fourth announcement?'

Barnabas lowered the binoculars.

'*In times of need . . .*' Kahurangi said. '*That's when she will rise* . . . We definitely live in such times, don't you agree?'

Barnabas sighed. 'Yes. Yes, we do. But do such things really happen? It feels like a very foolish hope.' He pointed the binoculars at the birds on the water again. 'It can't be,' he murmured. 'We're too used to chasing dreams, Kahurangi.'

'Can you please stop talking in riddles around me?' Guinevere gave her father a friendly punch in his bony back. 'Even sphinxes make more sense than you two!' She had met a sphinx once, and had found her very exhausting.

Her father put his arm around her. 'Sorry, it's just an ancient Māori tale, my love. Kahurangi and I came across it in our twenties, when we were both studying sea monsters. But there are many tales like that.'

Guinevere noticed the warning look he cast his friend, but Kahurangi only had eyes for the birds as another swarm of gulls arrived. The world seemed to be made from beaks and feathers.

'Let's hope you and I are the only ones who remember that tale,' the Māori said. 'Though we both know who would be very interested in this.'

'Yes,' Barnabas replied. 'And I have little hope he won't hear about it.'

'He hasn't done much damage since you saved the sky serpent from him. How long ago is that? Five years?'

Guinevere's father nodded. 'No damage *that we know of*,' he added. His face was grave.

'I hope he still feels her poison.'

'Maybe.'

At times Guinevere lost her patience with grown-ups, even when she loved them as much as she loved her father. Of course, he noticed her frown. He always noticed when she or Ben were upset with him. He was as good a father as he was a protector of fabulous beasts.

'I'm sorry,' he said. 'We need to be on our way. We have far more important things to attend to! Right?'

He winked at Guinevere.

Yes, they did! How much did freshly born dragons grow in a day? She had missed more than thirty days by now! She had been in Greece tending to the torn muscle of a young Pegasus when her brother had left for the Rim. It had been Chara, one of the foals they had saved a few months ago.

Her father handed the binoculars back to Kahurangi. 'Even if this proves to be just about old memories, thank you for calling me. But now we have to visit a few young dragons, or I will lose my daughter's love.'

Kahurangi gave a deep sigh as he turned his back on the swirling birds. 'Young dragons? Shame I find it so hard to leave these islands behind. I fear I was a tree fern in a former life.'

'I'm actually quite sure you were a three-eyed lizard,' Barnabas laughed. 'I'm glad you took human shape in this life. It's sadly too dangerous to send you photos of the dragons, even across our FREEFAB network. They're our best kept secret, of course. But hopefully one day this world will be a place where dragons can travel freely and unharmed. I'm sure they would love these islands.'

'We're a long way from that world,' Kahurangi replied. 'So maybe the old tale really is coming true.'

They walked back to the boat in silence. Guinevere was thinking of the dragons, but she was quite sure Kahurangi and her father still had other things on their minds. *He hasn't done much damage since you saved the sky serpent from him.* Did she want to know? Not really.

As the pier was coming into view, Kahurangi suddenly bent down and picked something up from the path. A tiny possum sat in his tattooed hand.

'I'm not sure about this, Barnabas,' Kahurangi said as he released the beetle-sized creature on to a leaf. 'This may cause other problems we can't foresee.'

'I know,' Barnabas sighed. 'But you need them to stop eating the birds, and I want to give your possums at least a small chance of survival. And I really despise traps.'

Guinevere loved him for the disgust on his face. Her father was no good at killing, but he knew everything about preserving lives.

When they came back to the boat two bluelings were sitting on the steering wheel.

'No way, Barnabas!' one of them exclaimed. 'Far too many birds on these islands. We request to be taken back to MÍMAMEIÐR. Or wherever you're going.'

'Yes, definitely,' the other one piped. 'Give me snakes. Give me raccoons. But birds? No way!'

Kahurangi cast Barnabas an amused glance as he plucked the two bluelings from the steering wheel and placed them into Guinevere's hands. 'Well then, New Zealand is definitely not the right place for you two,' he said. 'We are very proud of our birds here.'

CHAPTER TWO

ABOVE THE CLOUDS

Hothbrodd was not only a strikingly big and strong diurnal troll. He could talk any tree into growing just the piece of wood he needed, whether it was to build a house, a plane . . . or a suitcase for bluelings. Hothbrodd had built many things in his long lifetime, but he was especially proud of the plane whose tanks he was filling with sea water when the Greenblooms came back from their expedition. The troll had built the whole thing himself – with the help of (as he put it) ten dim-witted wood-drill gnomes, whose stubbornness, Hothbrodd claimed, had made a substantial amount of his green hair turn grey. Hothbrodd found most creatures exhausting, including other trolls, and Guinevere felt very flattered that he made an exception for her family. She was extremely fond of the grumpy troll.

'Ah, so we're finally heading where we intended to go?' Hothbrodd growled as they waved a last goodbye to Kahurangi. 'Or was there another phone call from an old friend? Thor's hammer on your head, Barnabas! How many old friends can one man have! You'll have to find yourself another pilot if you're

planning more detours, for I'm determined to see those young dragons before they are taller than Guinevere!'

'Yes, yes, next stop is the Rim of Heaven,' Barnabas confirmed. 'Holy Greenbloom promise!'

He was quite silent for the next few hours as Hothbrodd navigated the plane through the clouds. He wouldn't even tell Guinevere more about the sky serpent or the Māori tale. 'You just overheard two middle-aged men remembering old times, my love,' was all he would say. 'Kahurangi and I met when I was very young and completely obsessed with the beasts of the sea. I barely knew your mother then!'

Guinevere couldn't imagine her father without her mother, but of course there had once been a Barnabas who'd neither been a husband nor a father. Beasts of the sea, though?

'You don't even swim!' she exclaimed as they flew over clouds that looked like mountains made from the foams of the ocean. 'I thought you didn't like the sea?'

'Oh, I was very fond of it once,' her father replied. 'I was even a quite decent diver. Do you know that to this day we have only identified about fifteen per cent of the species that live in our oceans? And that doesn't even include the fabulous beasts.'

Guinevere scrutinised her father as if he had revealed merman scales on his arms. 'So what happened?'

He fell silent and looked down at the clouds for a very long time.

'I nearly drowned trying to save a friend,' he finally said, 'and what is worse, I failed. Since that day I can't bear to be underwater. It's very annoying, as your mother loves it so much.'

He wouldn't say more. And as Guinevere loved her father very much, she respected his silence. She was sure her brother would find out more about those old tales. Ben was very good at making her parents talk about their past, maybe because he had joined the family so much later. They often felt obliged to make him feel a part of it by sharing memories.

Her father made several calls to MÍMAMEIÐR during the flight. He asked Gilbert Greytail, FREEFAB's genius rat cartographer, to prepare a world map – for what purpose, Guinevere didn't quite understand. FREEFAB was the secret organisation her parents had founded to study and protect all the fabulous creatures of this world. Barnabas told Gilbert to inform all the members (who of course included Guinevere and Ben) to look out for bird formations like the one they had witnessed. Then he talked for a long time in a low voice with Lola Greytail, who – apart from being the only flying rat in this world – was Gilbert's cousin and FREEFAB's best scout. Lola was quite talkative, and Guinevere was not surprised when her father was soon mostly just listening, apart from mysterious remarks like: 'No, don't take that risk!' and 'Just look out for any travel preparations.'

Finally Guinevere gave up on trying to make any sense of her father's murmurs and joined Hothbrodd in the pilot's cabin.

'I know you don't want to tell me,' she said as she moved the suitcase with the two bluelings from the passenger seat. 'But Dad really looks worried. Don't you think his daughter should know what that's about? Who did he save a sky serpent from? And what does all that have to do with those birds? Please, Hothbrodd!' She gave him her most encouraging smile.

'Don't use that smile on me, Guinevere Greenbloom!' Hothbrodd growled. 'Cadoc Eelstrom. That's who he saved the serpent from. He's an old enemy, and as evil as they come. I understand why your father doesn't want to tell you about him. He knows Cadoc from school, and has fought him many times over the years.'

'*Fought?*' That was not a word Guinevere associated with her father.

'Well, yes!' Hothbrodd grunted. 'Your father may not like swords or guns, but Barnabas Greenbloom is a fierce defender of all those he loves and treasures. Cadoc is everything your father is not. Greedy, cruel, selfish, and without any scruples. Certainly not someone you want your children to meet. So forget about him, and let me concentrate on flying this plane, or you will

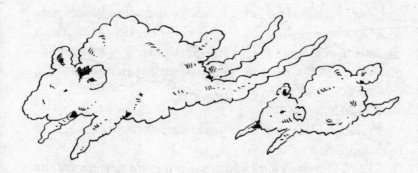

never see those young dragons!'

'But what does he have to do with those birds?'

'Just pretend you'd never seen those birds,' Hothbrodd growled. 'The fewer know about them, the better. Now close your eyes, and dream of young dragons. We have nine more hours to go. I really hope those little ones aren't flying yet! If we've missed that part, I'll roll your father into a ball and feed him to the night trolls.'

That sounded like quite a nasty fate. But Guinevere had grown up with troll threats, and she certainly didn't have to close her eyes to dream about the young dragons. She even saw them in the clouds that drifted by. Sky sheep and cloud dragons . . . her mother Vita had often told her tales about them, and Guinevere had sworn at the age of five that one day she'd ride a Pegasus through the clouds to look for them. The next day her mother had put a tiny dragon, felted from white wool, on to her breakfast plate.

'To make sure you remember that wish,' Vita had said. 'Your father likes to stand on solid ground, but I've always been drawn to the water. Maybe you'll be the Greenbloom who explores the skies and the element of air one day.'

The woollen dragon was not white any more – Guinevere had held him too often in her hands for that – but he still came with her wherever she went. He was in her bag right now. Air . . . was that her element? Hadn't her dragon-riding brother earned that by now? Or was fire the more appropriate element for Ben?

Four to announce her, four to receive her.

Who was 'her'?

'I promise I'll explain once we are sure,' her father had replied to that question.

Cadoc Eelstrom. That's who he saved the serpent from. He's an old enemy, and as evil as they come. Hothbrodd's words followed Guinevere into her dreams; and she dreamed that as she slung her arms around a young dragon, a shadow bent over her and stole him away.

CHAPTER THREE

TOO GOOD TO BE TRUE

When Cadoc Eelstrom was a boy, his grandfather used to take him to the zoo. One day – his grandfather didn't like to remember it – they'd been sitting on a bench at the tiger enclosure, and Cadoc was wondering what was supposed to be so interesting about watching a very bored huge cat when he realised that his grandfather wasn't watching the tiger.

'Do you see him?' his grandfather had whispered. 'They are very good at hiding.'

'Who?' Cadoc had asked, and his grandfather had pointed at the tiger's water bowl.

'You have to watch very patiently,' his grandfather had said softly. 'They are so good at fooling our eyes.'

So Cadoc had stared at the bowl. And then, after what felt like an eternity, he had spotted one for the very first time. A fabulous creature. A gnome, shorter than his thumb, skilfully stealing tiny shreds of meat from the tiger.

'Isn't he wonderful?' his grandfather had sighed. 'They are everywhere, but most people don't notice them.'

Cadoc had realised even then that he didn't consider them wonderful. Not at all. He detested them, all those goblins, elves, dwarves, nixies . . . they disgusted him. His grandfather had soon realised that, and had regretted making him aware of the gnome in the tiger enclosure ever since. But Cadoc was grateful, although they still disgusted him, for he had soon realised that one could exploit their magic – to get richer, more powerful, even to stay young . . . Cadoc was forty-five years old now, but no one would have guessed that. Life hadn't drawn one wrinkle on to his pale skin, and all those years hadn't left a hint of grey in his short pale-blonde hair. No. Cadoc Eelstrom had the slender body and the smooth face of a fourteen-year-old boy. He owed his youthful appearance to a rare kind of fairy – the moss fairy, to be exact. Their magic melted age like butter in a hot pan. It only worked as long as one avoided sunlight, though, so most rooms in his vast fortress were underground. Who wanted to be outside anyway? The outdoors was dirty, most times either too hot or too cold and filled with furry, feathery, filthy things . . .

Cadoc frowned at the mere thought of it and stared at his computer screen. It showed the floor plan of the newest extensions he was adding to his underground quarters. He liked to walk down the long well-lit corridors, lined by fully climatised storage rooms, filled with artefacts from the fabulous world that were supposed to perform some kind of magic. Some he hadn't figured out yet, but it never hurt to have them. There were paintings (very large paintings) in every room of his house, showing him catching fairies, kelpies and other monstrosities. It was nice, from time to time, to remind himself of how successful he had been stealing their magic.

Oh, yes, he was having fun.

Fun. What else was life about? Fun was the only thing that filled Cadoc's empty heart. For empty it had always been. All there was to be found in his heart was a hunger – to have, to take, to devour. And sometimes to destroy. Yes, that could also feel satisfying.

He put his feet on his desk and cast a fond glance at his very well-made shoes. What was the leather from? Kelpie? Waterman? He had forgotten. Whatever. They were absolutely waterproof. He pulled a small mirror out of his pocket vest and inspected his face. Yes. Fourteen. Not one year older. He smiled at himself – then frowned. Was that a trace of a wrinkle next to his nose? He would have to send Copper out to hunt for fresh moss fairies. He liked to look fourteen. It was the perfect age.

Talking about Copper . . . there was a metallic knock at the door.

'Come in.'

The man who stepped in barely fitted through the door of the vast windowless office room. The electric light made his rusty red skin shine like polished metal. They'd discovered him when they'd dug the southern corridors. Of course, Cadoc had been the only one who'd detected him, despite his enormous size. His true name was endless and a pain for any tongue, so Cadoc just called him Copper. He was incredibly strong and made a good body-guard, but more importantly all Coppermen were very inventive when it came to altering existing creatures. Their magic made them far more efficient and dangerous. That talent proved to be quite useful. Not to mention the fact that despite being a fabulous creature Copper was neither furry nor scaly – a quality Cadoc appreciated very much.

'Did you get confirmation on the birds?'

'Yes. They are forming a flower, as you anticipated.'

Cadoc took his polished shoes off his desk and got up from his white leather chair. *Curse it.* He still felt the sky serpent's poison in his bones whenever he moved fast.

They are forming a flower . . .

Was it really possible? She was rising, the creature he had never believed to be a reality. No more need for moss fairies! The greatest magic to be found on this planet would soon be his, and his alone. Cadoc the Immortal, the Ever-Youthful . . . Maybe they would build temples to him

What sacrifices would he ask for? That might prove to be entertaining. At least for a while.

'There is another thing, sir.' Copper clearly didn't like to deliver the next message. 'The guards spotted the rat again. The flying one.'

'Where?'

'In one of the northern corridors.'

Curse that filthy rat. He immediately felt the sky serpent poison burn his bones again – a reminder of the humiliating defeat he had suffered from the man the rat served.

Barnabas Greenbloom . . .

No! Don't think of him, Cadoc. If she was rising and he could steal her magic, that would be the end of everything Barnabas

Greenbloom loved. They would all disappear, the creatures he and his FREEFAB friends protected. Wiped off the Earth. It would be such a relief not to see them everywhere – see, smell, sense them – and there would be no need for them any more. For she held more magic than all of them together. After all, if the tales were true, she had brought them all into this world!

Oh, this was too good to be true!

Cadoc hummed the opening notes of *Puff the Magic Dragon* as he walked to the small cage that hung on a silver chain from the ceiling. It held six moss fairies, green-skinned, with rainbow-coloured wings. Cadoc pulled a pair of leather gloves over his fingers before he opened the cage. The fairies' teeth were sharp, but their dust would smooth the angry line the mention of that rat had dug into his skin.

He grabbed one by its thin green legs and pulled it out of the cage. The others attacked him, but their teeth didn't get through the gloves.

Cadoc shook the fairy until he had filled a small glass with her silvery dust. Copper watched him expressionlessly. He had warned him that one shouldn't shake them too often, as it took them several days to recover. Whatever . . . he could always find new ones.

Cadoc pushed the little thing back into the cage and let her dust trickle into a tea mug. Oh yes, he was sure the rat worked for Greenbloom. Who else would have such a filthy creature spying for him?

Cadoc had hated Barnabas Greenbloom from the moment he'd walked into his classroom. So clever and humble, all noble and smiling. Already, on his second day, he had protected that nerd with the thick glasses from Cadoc. And the ginger girl with the braces. Yes, those were the friends Barnabas liked. What was the name of that loathsome Māori? He was bound to have had told Barnabas about the birds.

Yes . . .

Cadoc poured hot water over the fairy dust. He'd been hunting for moss fairies near an abandoned house a few blocks behind the school when he'd found out that Barnabas Greenbloom was able to see them too. All those gnomes and fairies and nixies . . .

Greenbloom had once caught him pulling off a fairy's wing. So what? Their wings could make you fly! What else was the use of them? That redhead had been with him, Lizzie Persimmons. Cadoc still remembered the disgust and contempt in her eyes.

Well, Lizzie Persimmons was gone now. Because she had tried to save a mermaid he had caught in his net. The web between their fingers was supposed to enable humans to breathe under water. Thanks to Lizzie Persimmons he still didn't own any mermaid fingers. His prey had escaped with her help, but the propeller of his boat had sunk her saviour. Lizzie Persimmons had been swallowed by the waves and Barnabas hadn't been able to save her, although he had risked his own life trying.

But he has saved many others, whispered a voice inside him.

Cadoc took a sip of the fairy-dust brew. It didn't delete annoying thoughts, unfortunately. Unicorn blood did, but – well – the unicorns were gone too. He had killed the last one himself, only to find out their powdered hooves didn't grant invulnerability, as so many tales claimed. It had been quite a disappointment.

What are you doing? Can't you see how much you can learn from them, Cadoc? To this day he could still hear Barnabas's voice, so sharp with judgement and contempt. *Don't you feel honoured that you can see them? All the tales they inspire, all the magic, the joy and hope we find in dreaming about them. Wishing for them, imagining them . . . They are the translators between us and all the other creatures in this world.* Yes, that was the kind of nonsense Barnabas Greenbloom could go on about for hours, with Lizzie smiling at him, and so many of the others nodding in admiration.

Cadoc emptied the mug.

He was so much better than all of them. Better, smarter, richer – and if that was thanks to a ruthless father and equally heartless mother, well, who cared?

He walked back to his desk and playfully reached for the spray that always stood next to his computer. 'I want this rat dead, Copper.'

'Yes, sir.'

The shimmering eyes filled with fear. Coppermen were quite sensitive to salt, as well as to everything acidic. That's why Cadoc always had that spray can handy – to make Copper miserable when he wasn't pleased with him. Like now.

But right now his mind was too busy thinking about the birds.

'Go,' he said. 'There will be three more incidents like the one in New Zealand. Get me the exact locations.'

The Copperman nodded and left. Coppermen moved astonishingly swiftly and soundlessly for their size.

When he was gone, Cadoc walked back to the fairies' cage and watched them flutter anxiously as he ran his fingers over the bars.

She was rising.

Yes!

This would be his to take. No one would get in his way. He would steal what she brought from the deep and there was a chance that would also be the end of Barnabas Greenbloom and all his efforts to save his fabulous friends.

He shook the cage, and watched with delight as the fairies tumbled against the bars.

CHAPTER FOUR

WHAT COULD BE MORE IMPORTANT?

B en couldn't decide what had melted his heart more: the time when Firedrake's oldest son Silverscales (whom everybody just called Scales) had put on a very determined face and flapped his small wings so fast that they nearly came off? Or when his sister Moondance had chased her twin brother Thorny (full name Thorntail, the twins exactly three minutes younger than Scales) through the cave, both of them stumbling over their own paws?

Young dragons were definitely too much for a human heart.

'You do nothing but stare at them, dragon rider.' Firedrake put his warm snout on to Ben's shoulder as Maia – his mate – was pulling Scales from a crevice he'd got himself stuck in.

'I know!' Ben sighed. It was a very happy sigh. The sight of the young dragons brought back the memories of another enchanted day – the day he had met Firedrake for the very first time. How different his life had been then – so empty and lonely.

This past month had granted Ben more dragon time than he

had ever enjoyed before. Not even his first journey on Firedrake's back could compete with it. He'd been drenched in dragons – sleeping, playing, laughing, flying with them. Paradise – that's what it was. No, it was *better* than paradise. He wished it never had to end.

Ouch! Ben felt a sharp pain as Moondance crashed into him and dug all her claws into his chest. They were quite long and sharp, and Ben expected blood to seep out of his T-shirt. But when he looked under his shirt there was not even a scratch.

Firedrake noticed his bewildered glance.

'I always hoped it was true,' he said. 'But I was not sure. You remember when Tattoo's fire hit you by chance? Or when Scales bit you in the arm? Not a scratch.'

Ben looked at his arm. Yes, Scales had bitten him hard. They'd been wrestling, and the young dragons didn't understand their strength yet. He had expected his arm to be badly mauled, but . . .

'You're changing,' Firedrake said softly. 'Don't you feel it?'

Yes. Now that Firedrake mentioned it . . . Ben did feel different. How could he not, being surrounded by dragons? He felt fiercer, stronger, and even a bit wilder after these past few weeks. As for Scales' bite and Tattoo's fire . . . he ran his fingers over his skin. He didn't feel much of a difference.

Firedrake smiled. 'Don't worry, you won't grow scales. I should have told you long ago, but Sorrel said it's just a foolish old tale. Those tales claim that over the years all dragon riders take on certain traits of their dragon. A less fragile skin is one of the first effects. You've been a dragon rider for quite a while now, and lately we've spent much time together.'

Ben gave him an incredulous look. 'You mean . . .?'

'You will get stronger. Your muscles, your bones . . . they all will share part of my strength. Your eyes will see as well at night as mine. Your hearing will sharpen. Maybe it already has. Fire won't be able to harm you any more, and at some point you will begin to hear the others talk.'

'The others?'

'Animals, plants . . . the other living things.'

Ben looked up at the bats swarming under the cave ceiling. How would it feel to be able to hear them talk?

Amazing!

He looked up to Firedrake and smiled. 'So being a dragon rider even comes with a reward?'

'A reward that hopefully makes up for the dangers it brings.'

Ben playfully punched his fist against Firedrake's scales. 'You know I never mind the danger! As long as we're together!' He ran his hand over his dragon's shimmering scales. 'Will I be able to feed on just moonlight?'

Firedrake laughed. 'I never heard anything about that. And you won't grow wings, just in case you were hoping for that. Which I admit I'm grateful for, as otherwise I might lose my dragon rider!'

Ben flung his arms around his neck and buried his face in his warmth. 'Dragons never lose their dragon riders.'

'Firedrake!' a voice shrilled through the cave. 'Your offspring found another of my hiding places! What kind of dragons fancy mushrooms?'

Sorrel was standing in the entrance of the cave, her fur all bristly. Firedrake's brownie companion did not enjoy the company of the young dragons – quite the reverse.

'Calm down, Sorrel!' The brownie who appeared behind her had four arms and held a half-eaten mushroom in each hand. Burr-Burr-Chan had been their guide when they'd found the Rim of Heaven. But without Firedrake's will to find it, the last dragons would have perished in a Scottish valley. Instead they were raising a new generation amongst the sheltering peaks of the Himalayas.

Ben smiled. Life was good.

'You have to hide them better, Sorrel!' Firedrake caught a young dragon tumbling down his back. They liked to climb around on the grown-ups, tear at their tails or chew on claws and fingers. For human skin that could be quite painful. Ben ran his hand over his arm. *Over the years all dragon riders take on certain traits of their dragon.* Maybe his adventures had only just begun.

'Festering fungus, I *did* hide them well! Those little brats are worse than truffle pigs!' Sorrel grabbed one of the half-eaten mushrooms from Burr-Burr-Chan's fingers and held it up accusingly. 'That's a Golden Lion's Paw. Incredibly rare. Now covered in dragon's saliva! Disgusting! It tastes like sulphur!'

'Of course it does. They're dragons, Sorrel!' Maia, the mother of Firedrake's three children, stepped to her side. 'And they find your mushrooms because they have inherited their mother's sharp nose. I apologise!'

'Well, there will be punishment!' The half-eaten Lion's Paw hit Scales's head. 'I'll add stinking spotheads to my mushrooms from now on. Let's see how your offspring like those. *And* how much you'll all enjoy this cave being full of your babies' vomit!'

Firedrake sighed.

'I'm sorry,' he said, walking over to Sorrel. 'I really am. But they are so young. And there are quite a few of them.'

Yes, there were. Wherever you looked in the huge cave, a young dragon was stumbling out from behind the stalactites or fluttering off a rock. Thirteen. Thirteen young dragons! Nobody had expected such numerous and healthy offspring. The last dragons of this world, led by Firedrake all the way from Scotland, would not remain the last ones. They had written a new chapter in the long history of their species.

'Oh, by the way . . . you're wanted down by the lake, dragon rider.' Sorrel tried another of the half-eaten mushrooms Burr-Burr-Chan had dropped, then spat it out in disgust. 'Sulphur!' she murmured. 'My whole life tastes of sulphur!'

'By the lake? Why?'

A young dragon fluttered off a rock and tumbled over when he tried to land at Ben's feet. Was it Spark or Stargazer? Ben knew Firedrake's children very well by now, but the others . . . it wasn't always easy to distinguish them from one another. They all had their parents' silver scales and golden eyes, and chubby legs and chubby necks.

'The homunculus wants to talk to you.' Sorrel opened her

rucksack and threw in the sad half-eaten mushroom remains.

'Twigleg?' Ben put Spark back on his paws. Yes, it was definitely Spark. 'When did you talk to him?'

Sorrel shrugged her shoulders. 'A few hours ago. He said he has a message for Barnabas. He and Guinevere stopped somewhere on their way. But the Spiderleg said they should arrive any minute. He was quite excited about something, but you know he gets like that easily.'

'A few hours ago?' Ben exclaimed.

'I told you we should go and tell him!' Burr-Burr-Chan said to Sorrel, scratching his furry belly with two of his four hands.

'Well, we had to find new provisions!' Sorrel mumbled. 'Seeing as they keep getting eaten.'

Ben considered Sorrel one of his closest friends by now, but sometimes he still wanted to make her choke on her beloved mushrooms.

The mountain valley where the last dragons raised their young was also the place where they once – a long, long time ago – had all come from. Their ancestors, Sorrel had mentioned, had named the lake the Eye of the Moon. It was easy to see why, as it shimmered like a silver mirror between the snow-covered peaks that guarded the Rim of Heaven.

When Ben stepped to its shore, the reflections of heavy rain clouds were drifting over the calm surface of the water. Ben cast them a worried glance as he knelt down in the short yellow grass at its shore. What he had come for could only be achieved when the lake's surface wasn't troubled by rain or wind.

The Eye of the Moon always brought back dark memories. Nettlebrand, the deadliest enemy the dragons had ever known, had risen from its waters when Ben had seen it for the first time. More than two years had passed since Firedrake, Maia and some of the other dragons had beaten Nettlebrand, along with brownies, mountain dwarves, a homunculus and a flying rat, in the same cave that now granted shelter to their children. Only lately had they realised that this terrible enemy had left something very useful behind.

Ben bent forward and drew a circle on the icy water with his finger. It was only a few seconds until Twigleg's face appeared, as clearly as if he looked at Ben from a mirror. The homunculus had been Nettlebrand's spy before he had fallen in love with the boy who rode a dragon, and during that time he had always used water to contact his master. It had taken Twigleg and Ben many months to develop a method that imitated this form of communication. After a few setbacks it now worked quite perfectly – unless it rained – and Ben had been able to talk to Twigleg almost every day, even though the homunculus was far away in Norway at MÍMAMEIÐR. They'd never been apart for this long since they'd become friends. It felt weird, but Twigleg had had good reason to stay behind.

This reason was standing behind him as his small silhouette appeared on the water.

Twigleg had always believed that he was the last one of his kind. He had watched Nettlebrand devour his brothers, and had only been spared himself as his master needed someone to polish his scales. Only lately he had found out that his youngest brother had escaped the massacre.

Freddie (as he liked to call himself, although his given name was Fleahead) was waving at Ben with a wide-eyed smile. He had lost a leg escaping Nettlebrand's teeth, and like Twigleg he had believed for more than three hundred years that all his brothers had perished. They'd found each other again by pure chance – or serendipity, as Freddie preferred to call it. He had even written a play about the events, called *The Volcano Mission*, which he had staged several times already at MÍMAMEIÐR with a group of gnomes, dwarves and whoever else wanted to take part in it. Twigleg called the play a wild work of fiction, but the brothers had been quite inseparable since their reunion, and when Ben left to visit Firedrake's newborn children Hothbrodd had just carved a new wooden leg for Freddie. So Twigleg stayed at MÍMAMEIÐR, worried that his brother might find it hard to adjust to the new limb. Judging from Freddie's smile, Twigleg had underestimated his younger brother's resilience.

'Master! Finally!' Sorrel was right. Twigleg did get overly excited quite easily. 'I was sure that mushroom-munching brownie had forgotten to deliver my message!'

'I told you Sorrel would remember!' Freddie gave Ben another beaming smile. 'You worry too much, brother.'

Twigleg's face gave it away that he wondered from time to time whether life hadn't been easier without a brother. Freddie's optimism was quite a challenge for his worrying nature. But Ben also saw how much happiness even the bickering with Freddie brought into Twigleg's sometimes quite lonely life. It is very lonely to be the only one of your kind. Ben remembered that feeling from his orphanage days.

'Did your father arrive, master?'

Twigleg cast Freddie a strict glance as a Lilliput gnome crawled out of his collar. Freddie always had some tiny creature in his pockets. 'It's ridiculous!' Twigleg would exclaim. 'They are drawn to him like children to the Pied Piper!' Sometimes a whole dozen would peek out of Freddie's unruly red hair. Some of their smallest refugees were probably living constantly in his pockets by now.

'No, they're not here yet,' Ben said. The clouds reflecting in the water were getting worryingly dark. 'Sorrel says you have a message for him?'

Twigleg and Freddie nodded in unison. Their movements were often the same. Ben found that amusing, but Twigleg could get quite irritated by it. There are advantages to considering yourself the only one; everything you do is unique. Freddie reminded Twigleg that their creator, the alchemist Petrosius Henbane, had actually used the same recipe for him and his brother. 'I'm sure there were some variations,' Barnabas had comforted him, when he'd referred to himself gloomily as 'just a copy'.

'Your creator certainly didn't steal the same animal's life spark for both you and Freddie,' Ben had pointed out.

'True,' Twigleg had murmured. 'I still suspect mine was a cockroach, but Freddie's must have been a peacock spider. Where else could his irrepressible urge to dance have come from?' Freddie loved to tap-dance for hours on the long library table at MÍMAMEIÐR while his brother explored the books on the shelves.

'Yes! The message! Of course!' Twigleg looked at his brother sternly when he started humming to himself. 'Barnabas left instructions that we should inform him immediately if a similar incident as the one he witnessed in New Zealand occurs. It did. Please tell him we just received a report from the Sea of Okhotsk . . .'

'That's in Kamchatka,' Freddie added.

'A similar incident? What incident?' Ben asked.

But Twigleg and Freddie were dissolving in the circles drawn by a raindrop on the water's surface. The rain began to come down so hard that Ben had no choice but to hastily rush back to the dragons' cave.

'New Zealand,' he murmured as he dried his hair and clothes in the dragon fire that Firedrake was gently breathing in his direction. 'What are they doing in New Zealand?'

Whatever is was, he thought, it certainly couldn't be more important than thirteen young dragons.

CHAPTER FIVE

FATHERS

Indeed. What could be more important than thirteen young dragons? When Barnabas Greenbloom walked into the dragon cave he forgot what he had seen in New Zealand. He even forgot that he was forty-five years old. He was a boy again when the first young dragon looked at him – the boy who had drawn dragons since the age of five, and had always dreamed of some day meeting one. *One?* Now there were dozens!

Ben and Guinevere smiled at each other as their father got down on his knees and all the young dragons came to greet him, fluttering and tumbling over each other as if they knew how

much the fabulous creatures of this world owed to the man they were burying under their small bodies, sniffing and snapping and flapping their wings in his face. Of all the magical moments in his life, Barnabas Greenbloom would always consider this one to be the best. The best and most unforgettable.

'Which ones are the children of Firedrake and Maia?' Guinevere asked, holding her hand out to a tiny dragon who was less bold than the others, and was trying to hide from the newly arrived strangers behind Ben's back.

'That one's Scales, their oldest!' Ben pointed at a dragon who was licking Barnabas's nose. 'You can recognise him easily because he has a few blue scales around his eyes. No one knows where he got those from. The one chewing on Dad's shoe is Thorntail, the second son, who owes his name to his extremely pointed tail. And his twin sister –' he looked around '– has vanished, as always, and will soon show up on a dangerously high– Ah, there you are!' He pointed to a steep rock and a tiny but very fierce-looking dragon on top of it. 'That's Moondance.'

Firedrake had walked over to the rock and was looking up at his little daughter with an expression that was both worried and proud.

'Who is this one?' Guinevere smiled at a dragon who sniffed at her knee and growled when she tried to touch her.

'That's . . .' Ben scrutinised the young dragon so closely that she growled at him as well. 'Shimmertail's and Snowsnout's daughter Nightsong. I think!' he added, with a smile.

He had expected to favour Firedrake's children, but he loved them all, each and every one of them – even Spark, who had nearly taken his finger off with his sharp teeth when he had first tried to touch him.

'We have to talk!' Guinevere whispered, caressing the shy dragon baby's scales. 'Dad has been very secretive. Did you ever hear him mention the name Cadoc Eelstrom?'

Ben shook his head.

'It seems he is an old enemy of his. And that Dad's worried he will learn about those birds we saw in New Zealand.'

'Birds?' So that was what Twigleg had been talking about.

Guinevere frowned when Ben delivered his message.

'Kamchatka?' She held her hand out to Nightsong, who still wasn't sure whether she should allow the new human to touch her.

'*Four to announce her, four to receive her*,' Guinevere murmured. 'So it has already happened twice, then!'

Ben didn't understand a word, but before he could ask Guinevere what all this was about, another dragon landed in his lap. Twelveclaws! Very easy to tell apart from the others, as she had an additional claw on each front leg.

'Odin's ravens! Look at that!' Even the boldest young dragons hid behind their parents' legs when Hothbrodd's barky voice echoed through the cave. The troll stared at the dragon offspring with such disbelief, as if he was sure they would turn into nothing but thin silvery air in the next moment.

'Dragons everywhere! Nothing but dragons!' Hothbrodd boomed. 'Did they eat Sorrel and all those other brownie rascals? I don't even see one of those greedy mountain dwarves! Last time we came the cave was swarming with them! I wouldn't mind if they'd been eaten.'

Thorntail slowly approached Hothbrodd and sniffed at his hairy feet.

'The brownies are – of course! – hunting for mushrooms,' Ben explained. 'And the dwarves left a week ago to go mining for gems in the mountains on the other side of the lake. They find the young dragons annoying, as they constantly mistake them for toys or try to chew on them.'

Hothbrodd clearly liked that sort of behaviour. 'Chew on them! Ha!' he grumbled, bending down to Thorntail. 'I like those little ones already! Exactly what one should do with mountain dwarves.'

Guinevere cast him a disapproving glance, which the troll of course ignored.

'Sorrel pretends she doesn't like them because they eat her mushroom provisions,' Ben whispered into her ear. 'But I think she's upset because Firedrake doesn't have much time for her. If you ask me, it looks quite exhausting to be a parent!'

'Yes, but it's worth it!' Their father was standing behind them, his grey hair a wild mess, his glasses bent, his clothes covered in dusty paw prints, and his smile as wide as the sickle of the moon. 'I hear from Firedrake that Twigleg left me a message?'

'Yes. He—'

'It happened in Kamchatka too, Dad!' Guinevere finished Ben's sentence.

The smile on Barnabas's face vanished. He didn't look like a boy any longer, but like a man again – a man who had seen too many dark things in his life. Still, Ben didn't only detect worry in his father's face. There was something else. Disbelief. Excitement. Hope. But it was all mixed with fear – an emotion one did not often see on Barnabas Greenbloom's face.

'So the tale *is* coming true,' he murmured. 'Kahurangi was right.' He stared at the young dragons, who had finally all found the courage to gather around Hothbrodd.

'Tale?' Ben looked enquiringly at Guinevere, but she just shook her head.

'I told you!' she said. 'He's been very mysterious.' She cast her father a reproachful glance.

'I know, I know,' he said. 'There is a lot I have to explain. But first I have to know more myself!' He looked at his watch. 'It should be early afternoon in MÍMAMEIÐR. I'm sure Gilbert is already working on the map . . .'

'Greenbloom!' Sorrel pushed her way through the young dragons, firmly clutching a bag that smelled very strongly of mushrooms. 'Do those dragonlings annoy you as much as me?'

Burr-Burr-Chan's bag was equally stuffed and strong-smelling. Both of them were smiling in the way only well-fed brownies do. Barnabas smiled back, but his thoughts were clearly somewhere else.

'What's wrong?' Sorrel asked. Brownies are far more sensitive than they care to reveal. 'Barnabas Greenbloom! I am quite annoyed by the dragonlings, but if there is some kind of monster coming for them, I want to know.'

'I wouldn't call her a monster,' Barnabas replied. 'If the tales about her are true, she comes to *bring* life, not to take it. But . . .' He shook his head. 'No! This may all be a false alarm. And even if . . . No!' He shook his head once again. 'I still can't make myself believe this is happening in our lifetime.'

He cast a glance at the dragons and the brownies. Then he turned abruptly. 'I need to talk to your mother.'

'*I wouldn't call her a monster?*' Guinevere whispered as her father walked hurriedly out of the cave. 'That sounds like we're definitely talking about one!'

CHAPTER SIX

BROTHERS

*S*ea *birds forming flowers . . . Birds swarming above ocean in petal-shaped formation . . . mysterious bird gatherings . . .* Twigleg had spent hours typing these and other searches into his computer. Nothing! Absolutely nothing! It was very upsetting.

Twigleg's computer, barely bigger than a matchbox, was brilliantly tailored for his needs. His master had built it for him, in collaboration with his science teacher. Ben still frowned when the homunculus called him 'master'. 'Twigleg, we are best friends!' he didn't get tired of correcting him. But Twigleg would always think of him as his master – the master he had wished for during all those dreadful and unhappy centuries as Nettlebrand's slave.

Bird swarms in flower shape . . . strange behaviour of sea birds . . .

He could type as fast as he could write with a quill by now. He still preferred the latter, having used quill and ink for more than four hundred years, but yes, usually the machine had its advantages. Usually, but not today.

Nothing! Absolutely no results of any use! *Mercury and sulphur,* he thought, *that proves it once again.* When it comes to research, computers are NOT the best tools! NOT AT ALL!

Twigleg closed the tiny machine with such vigour that Freddie messed up his tap dance moves. His brother had been dancing on the library table for hours while Twigleg had been typing. Fortunately his master had also made some earplugs in just the right size for Twigleg. They still smelled a bit like red wine, as Ben had cut them from a cork, but Twigleg was immensely grateful for them.

Why did brothers demand so much attention? There: Freddie was moving his lips.

'What?' Twigleg pulled the cork out of his ears.

'I'm sure either Barnabas or Ben will soon tell us what this is all about, brother. Why not just wait? You know they are busy with the young dragons!'

The young dragons . . . of course. Freddie had put his thin fingers right into the wound! What on earth had given him the strange idea that his newly found brother needed his company, when instead he should have accompanied Ben to the Rim of Heaven? Why had it taken him so long to realise that Freddie was in fact much tougher than he?

It was that missing leg. The stump had given Freddie quite

a lot of trouble shortly before Ben had left. But since Hothbrodd had made him a new leg, he was absolutely fine! More than fine – he was dancing with it. Dancing! While Twigleg was far, far away from his master and still hadn't seen the young dragons! It wasn't fair. No.

The homunculus gazed through the huge windows of the library, a frown on his face. The birdmen who lived in the trees outside were repairing their nests after the last rains had badly damaged them. They were doing that for the twenty-third time this year, if Twigleg had counted correctly. His younger brother had the same irritating patience. And all those discussions over small things like how often to brush one's teeth or why Freddie always left his dirty socks lying around . . . Yes, Twigleg had completely forgotten about all that bickering when yearning for his devoured brothers!

Luckily Freddie didn't like to be in the library half as much as Twigleg did. In fact, most of the time he stayed away from it. Freddie enjoyed company much more than his older brother, and since his arrival at *the most fabulistic place on Earth*, as Freddie called MÍMAMEIÐR, he had become friends with every gnome, every mushroom-man – yes, even with the gloomy fossegrim who played his violin under the waterfall by the nearby fjord. He had founded a band with two green gnomes and a barkgnome, not to mention that play he had written and performed about their reunion – and he had learned all the traditional dances of the nixies and pixies. He had assisted Tallemaja, the huldra cook at MÍMAMEIÐR, so often in the kitchen that now she called him her *most talented little homunculus-chef*. And even Gilbert Greytail, FREEFAB's notoriously grumpy rat cartographer, allowed Freddie to watch him draw his magical maps. Three hundred and forty-two years of misery, hardship and loneliness . . . yes, to be honest, Freddie had had an even tougher life than Twigleg, and still he met the world with a smile! Had the alchemist who had created them both mixed something into Freddie's bottle that made him somehow immune to misery?

There! He was humming one of his silly tunes right now as he tried out another dance step on the library table. He used his new leg as if he had been born with one made from wood! And he was right, of course – although Twigleg would never have told him that. Why didn't he just wait until Barnabas was done cuddling young dragons and told them why all their scouts and FREEFAB friends were looking for swarms of birds doing strange things?

Only Gilbert seemed to know more, but he wouldn't say what the map Barnabas had asked him to draw was about. Ungrateful rat! How often had Twigleg done research for him? Or made sure that no gnome child walked over his precious maps?

Patience, Twigleg! But Twigleg could no more rein in his curiosity and his thirst for knowledge than Freddie could keep his feet from dancing. No, he would find out why Barnabas was suddenly fascinated by sea birds who had set their feathery heads on forming flower patterns. The only mistake he'd made was to rely on the accursed computer while he was sitting in one of the best libraries in the world!

Freddie stopped dancing when Twigleg began to nimbly climb up one of the huge bookshelves that lined the room. 'Brother?' he called after him. 'May I remind you how easily our limbs break? Please come down!'

But climbing felt as natural to Twigleg as dancing did to Freddie. Many inhabitants of MÍMAMEIÐR called him Spiderleg because of it – a nickname Twigleg hated, for one of his greatest fears was to end up in the web of a huge spider. Well, it wouldn't even have to be all that huge, considering his size! Luckily the Greenblooms kept dust-eating caterpillars on their shelves to protect their books, and those also fed on spiders' webs. Another reason why Twigleg loved the library.

'Sea birds . . .' he murmured as he walked along the shelf where the Greenblooms kept their books on flying creatures. It was the fifth shelf from the bottom. Would he find the information he was looking for in *Birds from New Zealand*? But then what about those in Kamchatka? Maybe it was better to search the books on *Mysteries of the Natural World*. Those were two shelves below.

Twigleg hastened down one of the rope ladders Ben had installed after he'd caught him swinging from shelf to shelf using a page marker dangling from a book. It was really touching how concerned his young master was about his safety. Twigleg hadn't found many friends in his long and so often lonely life, and certainly none like Ben Greenbloom. Oh, he missed him so very much! He really should have gone with him, instead of playing the responsible older brother.

With a sigh he climbed down another ladder and nimbly tiptoed down the shelf until he came to a book bound in black leather. It was so thick that the homunculus was barely able to drag it out, even though he had much practice in dealing with books made for human-sized hands. Usually his master helped him lift them off the shelf. Another sigh escaped Twigleg's narrow chest. What if Ben liked the young dragons so much that he stayed with them and Firedrake at the Rim? *Nonsense, Twigleg!* he told himself. *MÍMAMEIÐR is his home. And he has important duties and tasks waiting here!*

He had just managed to drag the heavy book out when

Tallemaja, the Greenblooms' cook, walked in to ask whether he and Freddie wanted some of the soup she had cooked for dinner. What great timing! Twigleg made her pull twenty-three books from the shelves before Tallemaja went back to the kitchen, announcing in her booming voice that one day his little head was sure to explode, leaving nothing but a mash of printed pages behind.

Well, just the twenty-three might be enough. Twigleg cast a satisfied glance at the long spread of books laid out on the library table. Yes, one of these was bound to give him the answer he was looking for.

Twigleg didn't notice Freddie slipping silently out of the room as he opened the first book. Soon only the sound of rustling pages filled the library – and the snoring of Gryfydd Longtoes, the leprechaun who had his workshop under the table and was sleeping off his exhaustion after repairing twelve pairs of greengnome boots. The night pressed its dark face against the windows, and the forest surrounding the grounds and buildings of MÍMAMEIÐR filled with the voices of owls and wolves.

Hothbrodd had cut a small door into the heavy library portal for all those who couldn't reach the handle. It was well after midnight when it was suddenly pushed open and Freddie forced a big notebook through the small door. Twigleg shuddered when he saw that his brother had tied some kind of rope around it and was dragging it across the floor like a sled!

'Freddie! That is not the way books are moved in this house!' Twigleg really made an effort not to sound like a patronising big brother or a know-it-all, but he wasn't very successful.

Freddie, of course, did not even notice the criticism in his words. He was far too busy dragging the book all the way to the table. 'Brother!' he called up to Twigleg, beaming with pride. 'I think I found out why Barnabas wants everyone to look for those bird flowers!'

Twigleg took a deep breath and looked at the long line of books he had studied in the past few hours. 'Really?'

Freddie freed the notebook from the rope. Wait! Was that one of Barnabas's ties? Yes, it was! Twigleg groaned as Freddie kicked it aside and opened the notebook at a page which he – and at this Twigleg felt so nauseous that he almost threw up all over the library table – had marked with a dog-ear fold!

'May I . . . hmm . . .' *Take a deep breath, Twigleg!* 'May I ask where you found this notebook?' From where he was standing, it looked like the book contained letters that had been glued to the pages, as well as lots of handwritten notes.

'In Master Greenbloom's bedroom!' Freddie replied cheerfully. 'I asked myself: *Freddie, where does Barnabas keep the books he thinks a lot of? The ones that talk about all the things he deeply cares about? In his bedroom, of course!* Mistress Greenbloom confirmed it. Wait!'

Freddie ran his finger along a handwritten line. He always did that when he was reading something.

'Here!' He lifted his finger as if an important discovery had flown from the notebook right up to the library ceiling. 'Here it is, brother! Listen!'

Twigleg sat down on the edge of the table and let his thin legs dangle in the air, looking down at his long-lost brother with a deep frown on his forehead. In Barnabas's bedroom! Twigleg would *never* enter that room without explicit permission, but it clearly hadn't even crossed Freddie's mind to ask for such a thing.

How could they be so different? Had their other brothers been equally different from them and each other? Were they maybe not brothers at all, but just the same species? An artificially created life form, each created from a different recipe? And which ingredient was it that caused that cheerfulness, as well as Freddie's complete lack of respect for rules and constraints?

'Twigleg!' Freddie gave the carpet a gentle tap with the silver foot Hothbrodd had attached to his wooden leg. 'Are you listening?'

'Yes, I am. But may I first enquire about the contents of this notebook?'

'Oh, yes, yes!' Freddie cast a glance at the label on the cover. 'Robert Louis Stevenson. *Notes and Memories from Samoa.*'

Twigleg's frown deepened. 'Stevenson? Impossible. It's just a notebook, some kind of diary maybe. Whose notes are those?'

Freddie shrugged. 'Why shouldn't they be Stevenson's? I know he was famous, but Master Greenbloom is famous too, isn't he? And he's filled many notebooks himself! I picked this one because it looks as if he studied it a lot. There are many Post-its in there. With exclamation and question marks!'

Twigleg hid a yawn behind his hand. It was late, and his head felt as if he had read far too many useless words. 'Why should this have anything to do with sea birds forming flower shapes? Robert Louis Stevenson was a poet! He made up stories. We're looking for something that really happened!'

He got up. It was time to get back to his research.

Freddie, though, wasn't discouraged that easily. His small heart was scarred by a lot of misery and hardship, but he had a spark of light in him that burned brightly, however dark the world around him was. And he was even more stubborn and determined than a leprechaun – even though leprechauns had the reputation of being the most stubborn fabulous creatures on this planet.

'This handwriting,' Freddie leaned over the notebook until his pointed nose touched the paper, 'shows a very distinguished personality. Look at the Ts! And the R! I studied graphology for years. One master of mine, a lawyer, wouldn't do business with anyone until I analysed the writing and found his client to be trustworthy. This is clearly the hand of a great artist, and I find this passage especially interesting.'

He cleared his throat and began to read out loud:

'*I came across a strange myth both in Scotland and Samoa, that features a giant sea monster who rises from the depths of the ocean in times of great need. Her coming – and yes, the tales agree that it is a she – is announced by swarms of sea birds, who gather to form the shape of the creature on the water. According to the tales, this happens in four places, which, being connected by two lines that mark where they cross, reveal the location at which the monster will surface to release four precious pods. And here it gets even more intriguing, my old friend! All these tales contain the same central line:* Four to announce her, four to receive her. *The first part, of course, refers to the birds and the four locations, but it took me a while to find out what the last part means. If I understood correctly, it is the instruction that the pods need to be welcomed by four fabulous beasts representing the four elements. They have to take the pods to their place of birth, so the seeds they contain will bring healing and new life to earth, air, water and fire.'*

Freddie looked up from the book. *'Four to announce her, four to receive her!'* he called up to Twigleg. 'That's why Master Greenbloom wants everyone to look for those bird formations – and that's what Gilbert's new map is about. To find the location where she'll release the pods!'

Twigleg closed his eyes. Was he happy about Freddie's discovery? No, he was jealous! Oh, he was so irritated with himself! All those lonely centuries had quite obviously made him incapable of being a good brother. His master, on the other hand, was an excellent brother and never jealous of Guinevere, although she could at times be very intimidating in her brilliance.

Freddie, of course, had no idea that his brother held such despicable emotions about him.

'But why the shape of a flower?' he murmured, still kneeling in front of the notebook. 'A giant sea monster that looks like a flower? That doesn't sound exciting!'

Exciting?! Who wanted it to sound exciting?

Both homunculi turned with a start as the library door opened.

'Twigleg. Freddie.' Vita Greenbloom rubbed the sleep from her brown eyes. 'One of the mushroomlings woke me because she was worried about the light in the library. What's so urgent that you're both working through the night? Or is Freddie having trouble with his new leg?'

'Absolutely none!' Freddie assured her with a wide smile. 'The new leg Hothbrodd made actually serves me even better than the one Nettlebrand devoured! The tap-dancing is so much easier with a silver foot. No, Gilbert wouldn't tell us, so Twigleg tried to find out for himself why Master Greenbloom has everyone looking for those sea birds forming flowers.'

Of course. Twigleg hung his head in embarrassment. What an impatient and nosy fool Vita would believe him to be now! *And* he had woken her in the middle of the night. His curiosity would kill him one day, he was sure. Curiosity? *That's a nice way of putting it*, he scolded himself. *Your urge to be a know-it-all Twigleg, more like!*

But Vita gave him an understanding smile.

'Yes, Barnabas has been surprisingly secretive in the past few days.' She knelt down next to Freddie on the thick red carpet, which fifteen tiny Moroccan genies had knotted to thank the Greenblooms for freeing them from a plastic bottle.

'You should know,' Vita said, 'that Barnabas only gets secretive when he's not sure he believes in a story. Or when he fears the arrival of dramatic events. Both may be true in this case.'

Freddie's eyes widened until they were the size of peas. Usually they were no bigger than the heads of pins.

Vita closed the notebook and cast a glance at its cover before opening it again. 'Robert Louis Stevenson? I was determined to become a sea captain after I'd read his book *Treasure Island*, and it even made Barnabas consider a career as a pirate. His great-grandfather was a friend of Stevenson's. And he obviously had no idea how famous his skinny Scottish friend would be one day. Otherwise there was no way he'd have glued his original letters into a cheap notebook. They would be worth a fortune by now if he hadn't! But Barnabas decided to keep them in his ancestor's book, including his great-grandfather's notes. One of them claims that Stevenson heard many of the stories from a selkie woman. Barnabas loves that idea, of course. And yes, he believes that some of the tales are connected to the bird formations.' She winked at Freddie and Twigleg. 'Well done. I'm sure you found the letter mentioning them?'

Freddie nodded and Vita leaned over the notebook.

'Yes, it's all there,' she murmured. 'Barnabas travelled all over Scotland and Samoa to study the tale at its sources. We had only just met and I didn't go with him. But two very close friends of Barnabas accompanied him: Kahurangi, whom he just saw in New Zealand, and Lizzie Persimmons. Both close friends from his schooldays, who, like us, believed in the existence of fabulous creatures. Lizzie drowned just a few months after that trip, and Barnabas has been afraid of the sea ever since. He doesn't like to talk about it.'

Vita stared out of the window, to where the darkness of the night swallowed even the trees growing close to it. 'They learned a few more details about Stevenson's tale on Samoa,' she murmured. 'Quite troubling details. Every story has a dark side, doesn't it?'

'Troubling?' Twigleg cleared his throat. He had a deep dislike for that word; it gave him heartburn. Freddie, of course, had exactly the opposite reaction. He jumped to his feet and looked up to him as if Vita had just announced that Christmas would be celebrated twice from now on.

'These details –' his feet made a few excited dancing steps '– they are probably a family secret, I assume? Twigleg and I do of course understand that we're not pa—'

'Of course you're part of the family, Freddie,' Vita interrupted him. 'Your brother is my son's best friend!'

Her words turned Twigleg's heart into syrup – and filled it to bursting with longing for his master.

'And no, these details are not a secret – at least not in this house,' Vita continued. 'I'm sure Barnabas didn't tell you yet because he still isn't sure what all this means.'

Well, Twigleg was definitely worried now. He cleared his throat once again. Why did fear always clog his vocal cords? 'The letter Freddie read from speaks of a "giant" sea monster. Can we define *giant*? Are we dealing with dragon size? Or a monster the size of a –' he gulped '– sea serpent?'

Vita shook her head. 'Nothing on the planet compares to this creature, it seems. As big as an island, so vast that a hundred whales would get lost in her shadow . . . those are the quotes Barnabas brought back from Samoa.'

Twigleg closed his eyes, but all he saw was a giant beast rising from the oceans, gulping down a blue whale as if it was a mackerel.

'Tales often exaggerate the size of fabulous creatures,' Vita comforted him. 'And as you both know, the biggest ones are usually not the most ferocious ones. No, it's not the size of the monster that's worrying, but what happens if it feels threatened. But those stories are hopefully just the kind of apocalyptic tales that are told all over the world.'

Apocalyptic. Now that word was definitely worse than *troubling*.

'So what *does* happen?'

There was nothing but curiosity in Freddie's voice. Unbelievable, thought Twigleg.

Vita closed the notebook, picked it up and rose to her feet. 'The Aurelia – that's what they call the creature in Scotland – only rises at times when life itself on this planet feels threatened and calls for help. She carries pods that contain seeds of new life, of fabulous creatures never seen before, creatures that bring healing for water, air, earth and fire. But if the Aurelia is received with violence, or someone tries to take her pods by force, she . . .' Vita stared once again into the night. 'She'll set the oceans on fire,' she murmured, 'which will destroy all the seeds she brought, and . . .'

'. . . it'll be the end of the world!' Freddie exclaimed excitedly, as if that was an event he had always hoped he would witness.

'No, not the end of the world, Freddie.' Vita shook her head. 'It says that all those she brought into this world will —' She hesitated and fell silent.

'You know what?' she finally said. 'Barnabas is right. We shouldn't talk about all this until we know for sure what it's all about. She smiled at the homunculi. 'Let's get some sleep.'

'Oh, no!' Freddie exclaimed in alarm. 'Please, Mistress Greenbloom! Both Twigleg and I have lived through many bad things in our lives. To know about them is always better than wondering what they are!'

Vita looked from one homunculus to the other. Both of them were staring at her, wide-eyed.

'Yes,' she murmured. 'Yes, I always found that to be true myself.' She pulled out one of the chairs pushed under the library table and sat down. 'Well . . . here it is. If the Aurelia is met with violence when she rises from the sea to deliver her seeds, it will not only be the end of those seeds. She will never return, and –'

Vita took a deep breath '– all fabulous creatures will disappear with her, as they were her gift to this world.'

Even Freddie's feet had forgotten how to dance. He looked up at Vita as if he was waiting for her to laugh and say that she had only told a joke. But Vita Greenbloom's face was grave.

'I'm sorry,' she said. 'Maybe it would have been better if you two hadn't been so clever. I don't want you to live in fear now. That's why Barnabas was so secretive about it, even with me. He knows how bad a liar I am – even worse than him!'

The library filled with silence. Only the leprechaun was snoring under the table, ignorant of the threat of doom that made the night suddenly look darker than any other. *All of them . . .*

Twigleg cast a glance at all the books surrounding them. Most of them talked about the fabulous creatures of this world. Would they be meaningless soon? Would he and his brother be nothing but a few dead pages in a book?

It's a tale, Twigleg, he tried to calm himself. *Nothing but an old tale. Those birds don't know what they're doing. It's probably all about some especially tasty fish.*

'You say "she",' Freddie said. 'What is she?'

Vita put him on her left shoulder and Twigleg on her right. 'The Aurelia is supposed to be a huge jellyfish, as beautiful as a flower blooming in the depths of the ocean.'

It got better and better. The deadliest creature in the sea was *Carukia barnesi* – a jellyfish.

One of the screens at the end of the room came alive. It flickered and hummed, and an image tried to take shape. There were, all in all, thirteen TV screens in the library of MÍMAMEIÐR, connecting it with FREEFAB members all over the world. When the image finally became recognisable it was still quite bad. Ben and Guinevere had tried several times to convince their parents that the technical equipment at MÍMAMEIÐR desperately needed an upgrade. But their parents always countered that there were too many fabulous creatures in need of food or shelter to spend money on cables, screens or speakers. Well, Twigleg thought – as Lola Greytail, the best of all FREEFAB scouts, emerged from the mists on the screen – maybe soon there wouldn't be that many. For how big was the chance that a huge monster rising from the sea would be received peacefully on this planet?

No, they were doomed. They were all doomed! The last Pegasi they had saved. The griffins. Even the young dragons that just had been born. Hothbrodd would fade, Tallemaja, the leprechaun and all those gnomes swarming MÍMAMEIÐR . . . the birdmen, the mushroomlings, the elves and fairies . . .

And the humans would probably not even notice! So many animals disappeared every day, so many fish, beetles, birds. Who cared if fairies, dragons and homunculi joined them?

Oh, what a dreadful night.

'Well, that's good luck!' Lola Greytail shrieked, her rat voice as energetic as ever. 'I was worried no one would be awake at this hour. How late is it in Norway? Two a.m.? I tried to reach Barnabas, as it should be daytime at the Rim, but no luck.'

'It's stormy over there,' Vita said. 'Both Twigleg's and Gilbert's last talks with them were interrupted by rain. And Barnabas has thirteen young dragons around him.'

It comforted Twigleg to see Lola's whiskered face, even though her image was blurry. No bad news could break Lola Greytail's spirit. She frowned at the mention of the young dragons, though Lola was not exactly the motherly type. The sound of a plane propeller melted her heart far more efficiently.

'Well, tell Barnabas that an albatross reports a third incident near the Chilean coast,' she shrilled.

Vita and the two homunculi exchanged a long glance.

'We need exact coordinates, Lola.' Twigleg was embarrassed to hear how hoarse his voice sounded. Fear, of course.

'I already sent them over the FREEFAB server,' the rat replied with a slightly insulted expression. 'Who do you think you're talking to, humclupus? A cheese-stealing house rat?'

'Three!' Freddie exclaimed. 'Then there's only one more missing.'

'I'm not done yet, humpelclus,' Lola corrected him. 'Another swarm was spotted in Newfoundland. And yes, I sent those coordinates as well.'

Four to announce her, four to receive her.

'There is something else, Vita,' Lola said. 'Cadoc Eelstrom knows about the sightings as well. He's getting ready to leave his underground lair.'

CHAPTER SEVEN

ENSLAVED

A thousand squid eggs and a glass of lobster offspring. All Copper had to do was to spit into the mix, and they would be ready to go within a day. They would grow to the size of an orca, their claws like metal, cutting and grabbing what his enslaver was after.

He was watching him.

Cadoc Eelstrom. His enslaver could not even pronounce Copper's true name. But of course he would claim to be the creator of the lobster squid – as he claimed to have made the starling drones and copper wasps that guarded his fortress, or the manticore who chased his enemies to their graves.

Of course he hadn't. The man who had stolen his freedom was not able to create anything. He was a deadly parasite that fed on the life and magic of others. A pale, ever-hungry maggot, despite the smooth skin and blonde hair he owed to the countless moss fairies Copper had caught for him.

It was the greatest fear of any Copperman to be seen by a human. For if one of them detected them, they were cursed to serve them for the rest of their lives . . . Copper had become Cadoc Eelstrom's slave in one of the wretched tunnels they were digging for his constantly growing fortress on the western coast of England. One glance from those pale-blue eyes and the Copperman had known his fate. He still felt the black despair that wrapped his heart and mind since then. He should have known! After all, it had happened to his grandmother too, but they'd all been so angry about them digging deeper and deeper. He had promised the others he would make the tunnel collapse, trusting that the humans he would come across would mistake him for a rock or a plate of metal, as they usually did. Instead he'd left as a slave, and that was what he'd been for the last three years. Three long terrible years, knowing he would never be free again. For only one thing could break that curse – dragon fire. And the dragons were gone. As were the wild woods and the silence in the world, both above and underground.

Copper spat into the mix of squid eggs and lobster and closed the metal can firmly before he shook it.

One two three. The number of creation.

'I'll release them tonight.' His voice had a slight echo. It rang like a bell when he wanted it to reach a long way. 'The moon will be growing, and so will they, with the help of her light. They will grow fast.'

'And you're absolutely sure they'll find the Aurelia?' Cadoc Eelstrom scrutinised him with his pale eyes. *I know how to hurt you,* they said. *So don't disappoint me.*

'Yes,' Copper replied, holding the pale-blue gaze. 'The birds told us where she's heading. So we also know where she's rising.'

'The Pacific Ocean is big.'

'They'll find her.'

Cadoc Eelstrom nodded. 'So she *is* coming?'

'Yes.'

Only a human could ask that question. They didn't know anything about this world, although they liked to pretend they were its master. The Copperman felt the answer in his bones and in his rusty-red blood. He felt it in the ground, in the air he breathed. The waves were whispering her name as they covered the sand with foam.

She's coming! they hissed. *She's rising. She's singing.*

CHAPTER EIGHT

THE OTHER DRAGON RIDER

Ben was standing in front of the dragons' cave, watching the morning mist weaving wet white veils between the mountains of the Rim.

The next adventure was about to begin. His mother was already on her way to the Californian coast – the destination Gilbert had worked out from the four bird sightings. Twigleg and Freddie would travel with her, and soon Hothbrodd would leave with Guinevere and Barnabas to join them. His father had by now unveiled at least some details about their mission, but Ben shared his sister's belief that there was still much more to tell.

He himself intended of course to travel by dragon. Firedrake would, as it had turned out, play a vital part in the mission, which made his dragon rider very happy. After these past weeks Ben had dreaded saying goodbye to Firedrake even more than usual. This was both an exciting and desperately important mission – of course! – but he knew already how much he would miss the dragons, the old and the new ones. He would miss them terribly.

'Ben? May I talk with you for a moment?'

Maia was standing in the cave entrance. Most times at least one of her children was crawling around on her back, but she was alone, and for a moment Ben thought she would tell him that Firedrake couldn't come, as he was a father now. He should have known Maia better.

'I am glad Firedrake will be part of this new adventure,' she said. 'He misses travelling with you, I know that, although he would never admit it. You've been his friend since long before I met him, and long before those rascals were born.' She cast a loving glance into the cave. 'They *can* be quite wild. And we agreed that once he is back, *I* will go on an adventure! I always wanted to see

MÍMAMEIÐR and the valley where Firedrake was born. But that's not what I came to talk about.'

She lowered her neck. And her voice.

'Sorrel was in Firedrake's life long before you and I became so important for him. I think she feels quite neglected and a bit sad. She's been so angry lately, and I fear she won't allow our children into her heart because she feels they stole the last bit of time Firedrake has for her. You know Sorrel even better than I. She bickers and complains, but she would never say what truly bothers her. Maybe you think it's a foolish idea, but . . . would you mind flying with your father and sister, while Sorrel follows with Firedrake, so she has some time alone with him, and can maybe let go of all that anger?'

As if to prove Maia's point, the brownie's voice could be heard inside the cave.

'Leave me alone! No! Brownies don't like children! They don't! Get away from me! Now!'

Ben exchanged a knowing glance with Maia.

'Of course, you're right,' he said, although he had been looking forward to the flight. Very much so, actually. 'I'll go with my family and I'll see Firedrake in California.'

Maia gave him a grateful smile.

'Sorrel may never warm to our children,' she said. 'But maybe this gives them a chance.'

'She'll come around,' Ben said. 'She just needs time.'

It had taken him ages to get on Sorrel's good side. And in some ways he understood. She had been Firedrake's only companion for so long – during all those years the dragons had hidden from his kind in Scotland, frightened to fly by day, just shadows of themselves. It had been Sorrel who had been by Firedrake's side to cheer him up and keep him alive.

'Stink morrel and sulphur spur!' her voice shrilled out to them. 'You'll be the death of me! Wait until I catch you!'

Ben laughed softly.

'Yes,' he said. 'I think it's a very good idea, Maia. Sorrel needs some Firedrake time. It's overdue. Otherwise she may poison us at some point with one of her mushrooms.'

CHAPTER NINE

DEEP, DEEP UNDER THE SEA

'Hothbrodd, please! Build a machine that can take us deep down under the ocean! To the merpeople!' The troll couldn't count the times Guinevere had come to him with that request. Especially after one of her teachers, thanks to mermaid blood from her mother's side, had lived in a merpeople settlement for a while. Hothbrodd was very fond of Guinevere, embarrassingly fond. But he had still shaken his head.

'How often do I have to tell you? It's too deep,' he'd answered each time. 'My submarines would get crushed like empty beer cans.'

Hothbrodd was right. No human could survive where Guinevere and her mother so wished to go. Down, deep down, where human lungs can't breathe even when they are helped by air tanks and diving suits. In the realm where neither day nor night exist, neither morning nor evening. Neither sun nor wind are felt down there, but nevertheless every second countless creatures are born in the depth of the ocean, living their lives and meeting their deaths – with names like the wolftrap angler, the glowing sucker octopus, the bloody-belly comb jelly, the threadfin snailfish, the hula-skirt syphonophore . . . Yes, they exist! All of them. Down where the sun is just a distant memory and life in all its shapes unfolds in a fading twilight that soon turns into darkness. A darkness as black as the ink of a black-bottle octopus. Well . . . not quite.

There are lights everywhere in the wet darkness of the deep sea, flickering with such brightness that they make the stars look pale: chains of oranges and whites, violets and blues lining fins and tails, fleets of jellyfish floating by like illuminated umbrellas plucking ghostly white snails out of the water . . .

The deeper regions of the oceans are filled with fireworks. Some serve as traps, some as warnings, but they've all been created by life itself, without any help from a distant fiery star. They draw the silhouettes of huge and tiny fish into the sunless darkness: crabs, jellyfish, snails, spiders, eels and creatures humans have never named, millions swarming above mountains and through valleys no human foot has ever touched, above fields of anemones and coral forests.

Right behind one of those forests a huge rugged cliff rises from the ocean floor, its stone so black that the dark waters make it almost invisible. It rises more than six hundred metres up, all the way to the surface, where over the centuries many ships have crushed their hulls on its sharp-edged surface, to sink with men and mice into the deep. The broken ships have scattered gold coins and jewels, broken barrels and treasure chests on to the ocean floor, where crusts of mussels and corals grow on their planks and cannons, their masts heavy with the nets of blinking spiders, and the rotten wood shimmers with the multi-coloured slime of rainbow snails.

From afar all this looks like nothing but a graveyard for

sunken ships. But the wrecks at the foot of the black cliff harbour one of the deepest settlements of the Moana merpeople. It is called Momi, and the broken ships are home to more than a thousand fish-tailed web-fingered women, men and children – not to mention all the lantern fish, dog crabs and cat spiders that live with them.

On the day when Maia was talking with Ben at the Rim of Heaven, two mermaids emerged from the wreck settlement, followed by six tiny merlings (that's what mer-children are called) and a huge lantern fish. They passed the guards who watch Momi from the crow's nests and headed for the open waters, passing through shoals of silvery fish. The lantern fish glowed like a pale-yellow

pumpkin swimming ahead, watching his surroundings with a grim frown on his wide forehead. Or like a small sun that had fallen into the ocean.

The six merlings had of course heard of the sun, but only the way human children hear about sunken cities. A huge fireball flying through a big dark empty space? Come on! Who would believe in such a thing?

The two mermaids who were herding them like swimming sheep had seen the sun and felt its warmth on their skin. One of them had even lived in its light for many years, which also explained why she looked so different from her mermaid friend. Laimomi, as her parents had named her, had the typical looks of the Hawaiian merpeople. Her green-scaled face resembled the face of a fish, with its wide eyes, pronounced lips and noseless features. Her companion's face, in contrast, resembled the carved figureheads staring from some of the shipwrecks. When asked about her friend's strange looks Laimomi usually frowned and replied that it was common knowledge that all merpeople in the North looked like that. But that was far from the truth. Laimomi's friend Lizzie looked that way because she had been human once. The two had met more than twenty years ago, when Laimomi had been trapped in the net of a human Lizzie knew all too well. Cadoc Eelstrom . . . They both still shuddered just thinking of him. Lizzie had almost drowned when she had come to the aid of the desperate mermaid,

but Laimomi had saved her by giving her one of her scales to swallow. The scale had transformed Lizzie into a mermaid, but ... well, she looked a little different.

Laimomi and Lizzie had called the settlement under the black cliff their home for many years now. They were running an orphanage in one of the biggest wrecks, as sadly many merlings lost their parents to sharks, squid or human fishing nets. Currently they had thirty-four orphans in their care, but only the six following them were old enough to swim in the wild waters surrounding the wrecks. Lizzie had promised to show them the old ruins that she and Laimomi had found just a few weeks ago at the bottom of a nearby ravine that cut deep into the ocean floor. Both Lizzie and Laimomi were quite excited about their find, as they believed the ruins to be one of the shell palaces left behind by a merpeople called the Goldscales.

The small group was exuding a soft red glow, as Lizzie had served them algae for breakfast that made their scales shimmer reddish. Underwater, that colour signalled POISON! to predators, so the algae were a very efficient way to protect the merlings from ending up as a snack for an octopus or giant squid. They were also surrounded by clouds of silverworm fish, which obscured their shapes and made them look much bigger. For their services the fish were in return allowed to build their cocoons in the masts of the wreck that housed the orphanage. It was a very useful agreement for both sides. Koo (as the lantern fish was called) made fun of all these precautions, as he considered himself a very dangerous and ferocious fish. But the two mermaids had seen too many dangers in their lives to trust the safety of their orphans just to him and his admittedly quite numerous teeth.

The merlings were very talkative on this exciting day, but they didn't chat with their voices like human children. The depths of the ocean are filled with sound as much as they are filled with light, but it is mostly the sound of the waves, the distant roar of a sea quake or the song of the whales. Many of its other inhabitants communicate without sound. Underwater (and that is the space which makes up most of this planet), electric signals are a very popular form of communication and . . . light.

'Light? No, no, no!' Twigleg would correct if he heard. 'Bioluminescence is the term! It is a very special form of light produced by the body.'

It is indeed a very special kind of light, and the six merlings were flashing with it like fireworks. But Laimomi shushed them with a few white lights from her tail as they approached the ravine, while Lizzie swam over the edge and watchfully gazed into the abyss below.

'I hope you remember what we taught you on our last excursion!' she signalled, lights dancing across her pale-green scales like a ripple of orange juice. 'Dim your lights before we dive down. By now the giant squid sometimes even hunt by day, and some of them may not be too worried about your red-flag colour.'

The kids answered with a flash of green. Oh, yes, the giant squid . . . they all knew about those. They had eaten one of the guards just a few weeks ago, and even the smallest merlings knew that squid were even more dangerous than the spotted octopus who also lived down there and sometimes reached up with his arms to grab whatever he found. But the octopus only hunted in the Black Hours, as the merpeople called their night, and so did the squid most of the time. Therefore the merpeople used the Silver Hours, as they called their days, to practise with their offspring how to dive down into the magical world the ravine guarded, without being eaten.

Lizzie and Laimomi had been on countless excursions like this with their protégés. They knew every creature and plant that lived below, and neither of them was afraid of the deep. On the contrary, they both loved the countless wonders one could find down there. 'The only thing you have to fear is fear itself,' Lizzie always taught the merlings. 'It'll paralyse your limbs and your mind and will make you feel small and fragile. But courage will give you an armour! A turtle shell for your heart!' *Sadly it won't always protect you from evil,* Lizzie was each time tempted to add. There would come a time when she would explain that to the merlings as well. For she had been courageous, and still she would have lost her life if Laimomi hadn't saved her. Good is not always stronger than evil, as she had learned that day. Laimomi had escaped Cadoc Eelstrom, but Lizzie knew how many fabulous creatures had been less lucky and had fallen prey to him. No. The threatening shadow of a shark or a stingray was nothing compared to the shadow true evil cast. Nobody had taught her that lesson more convincingly than Cadoc – even when he had been just a cruel and scheming boy. But Cadoc Eelstrom had also taught her that one had to fight people like him. And there was one protection against them.

Friends.

Very good friends.

Like Laimomi, everything Lizzie knew about life underwater she had learned from Laimomi. Yes, she was a wonderful friend. And Koo pushed his nose gently against her forehead – of course! Koo was a very good friend too. Lizzie ran her hand tenderly over his golden scales.

'Ready?' she called, while the lantern fish cast his light into the ravine. 'What do we say?'

'May Nāmaka be with us!' the merlings flashed.

'Good!' Laimomi signalled. 'One after the other. Lizzie shows the way. No excursions on your own. *Ho'ohiki?!'*

'Ho'ohiki! Promise!' came back sixfold.

'Okay! Makana! Haimi! Bane!' One by one the merlings followed Lizzie as she let herself slowly sink deeper, Koo by her side.

'Kona! Leilani! Ahonui! . . . Ahonui!?'

The last merling was mesmerised by yellow tang fish, but Laimomi chased him over the edge and after the others.

It was a long way to the ruins, and taking the merlings on an excursion felt always like herding a flock. But Lizzie and Laimomi loved these expeditions. There was so much life down here, still unharmed by the world above, and although there was danger, there was also peace and abundance and the feeling of being surrounded by life as it had been for thousands of years.

'Did you ever dive all the way down, Lizzie?' one of the merlings asked. 'Some say the ravine has no bottom! And that the water goes on for ever, until one reaches the realms of Death.'

They all stared at Lizzie and Laimomi, wide-eyed.

'Well, we all know that's nonsense,' Laimomi mocked. 'What did we teach you? All bad things come from above.'

They all cast a glance up. High above them a huge octopus drifted by, its long arms covered with glow fish. They looked so beautiful that one almost forgot how deadly those arms were. Laimomi's mother had been killed by an octopus. Yes, danger most often came from above. Nets, anchors, submarines, birds diving deep with razor-sharp beaks . . . The six children who followed the mermaids would still have to grow a few centimetres before Lizzie and Laimomi would take them up to the surface to teach them that the sun actually existed and glowed even brighter than Koo. And that the most dangerous enemies walked on two legs, built metal boats with deadly nets and filled the ocean with plastic and poisons.

One day. But not today, Lizzie thought, while she waved the merlings onwards. No, going down was the safer way. Always.

But suddenly she slowed down and looked at Laimomi.

'Do you feel that?' she signalled.

Laimomi nodded. The water was buzzing like the fins of an electric eel. The two mermaids exchanged a worried glance. Below them the skeleton of a blue whale appeared from the dark, its bones covered with glimmer snails. They made the water shimmer with a thousand colours and lights.

'I have a strange feeling,' Laimomi signalled. 'Maybe we should turn around.'

Lizzie grabbed two kids who'd dashed off to chase a blubber fish. 'Agreed.'

Even Koo was flickering nervously, although he was trying to look very fierce and not worried at all.

And then suddenly there was a sound, deep deep below them, in the vast velvety darkness. A sound as soft as the fins of a huge ray parting the waters.

Light poured up from below, like a sea cow's spilled milk. It revealed the silhouette of a gigantic body. Oh, yes, it was gigantic, although it was far, far below, so deep that Lizzie almost believed in the tale of a bottomless abyss. A million lights were dancing around the shape. Lizzie couldn't recognise whether they were part of the body, or other creatures surrounding the monster. For a monster it must be, as huge as it was. And was it singing? The whole ocean seemed to hum with a sound that resembled no other, not even the songs of the whales.

'Up! Go up! Go, go, go!!!' She saw Laimomi pushing the

merlings upwards, away from the light and the song, tumbling up past fish and crab and eel and snails. Lizzie grabbed Ahonui, who was once again trailing behind, but the others were eager to get away from what they had spotted in the deep, and were swimming as fast as their tiny tails and arms allowed.

The edge of the ravine was a black cliff above them. They were shaking with exhaustion when they finally reached it, and saw the comforting masts of Momi in the distance.

'What was that?' the merlings all flickered.

'Let's not find out!' Laimomi replied. 'Off you all go! Back to the wrecks. We'll have another excursion very soon.'

Lizzie was still staring over the cliff into the ravine.

'I think I know what we saw, Laimomi,' she signalled. 'I need to send someone a message. Now.' She looked pleadingly at Koo. 'Can you use your strongest vibes? This message has to travel a long way. It's very, very important!'

Koo cast a disapproving glance into the ravine, but he raised his scales until he resembled a hedgehog pumpkin. Yellow sparks began to sizzle on the tips of the scales.

'*Naia to Fufluns*!' Lizzie signalled, very slowly, to make sure Koo caught every letter. '*She sings where Momi sleeps! Heading hikina*.'

Koo released a shower of sparks for every syllable. They drifted away in all directions, glittering clouds carrying Lizzie's words. She followed them with her eyes until they faded in the dark, then she turned to Laimomi.

'Can you watch the merlings for a while? I have to go back into the ravine.'

Koo sent very disapproving signals.

'I didn't ask you to come with me!' Lizzie signalled back. 'Laimomi will need your light on her way back.'

'You can't go down there alone!' Laimomi's lights were red with alarm. 'What is this all about, Lizzie?'

The merlings all gave off nervous flickers, clinging to Laimomi's arms and tail. But Lizzie was already swimming over the edge of the ravine.

'Don't worry!' she signalled. 'She's not evil. It's quite wonderful that she has come! But I have to make sure she is safe!'

And with a last wave to the merlings she dived back into the ravine.

Koo looked more like a tomato than a pumpkin as he followed her.

CHAPTER TEN

THE WRONG COAST

'Oh, no,' Ben heard his father murmur. 'This is bad.'

Barnabas Greenbloom dug his toes into the cold sand and uttered a deep sigh as he stared at the waves, dyed black by the night. A few rocks covered with sharp-shelled mussels broke the tide, and a waxing half-moon spotted the beach and the sea with silver.

'So this is the beach she is heading for?' Ben heard his father utter another deep sigh. 'Any chance Gilbert Greytail made a mistake with the map? Not that that ever happens.'

His mother shook her head. 'Maybe she'll rise a hundred metres further east or west, but this will be the beach.'

Vita wrapped her arm around Barnabas's shoulder. 'We still have time.'

'Not that much.' Ben pointed at the moon. 'Seven days, if the Aurelia always arrives on a full moon, as you say.'

He turned and gazed up the steep cliffs that lined the beach. He spotted far too many houses up there. Houses, wooden steps and a path down to the sand. Not to mention the freeway, whose noise Ben could hear even now, at 11 p.m.

They had, of course, hoped for a wild stretch of coast, a beach humans weren't interested in. It would be difficult enough a task to keep the appearance of a vast sea monster unnoticed! And now this. Malibu, California. Ben was sure that Hothbrodd would have uttered his whole arsenal of troll curses, but he was busy setting up camp about thirty miles further south-east. It hadn't been easy to find a place where both the plane and their tents and activities would go unnoticed. Luckily an old friend of Barnabas had suggested just the right spot.

His father cast another gaze at the houses above and sighed.

Ben wondered whether he was asking himself where he would find the other three fabulous beasts who'd receive the pods. The last time the Aurelia had risen, far more fabulous creatures had been available for that task. But now . . . so few were left, especially when it came to the big ones! Firedrake had been an easy choice for the element of Fire, but who would be the couriers of Water, Earth and Air?

He and Guinevere had discussed that, and so many other questions on the long flight to California. His sister's company had made it so much easier to accept that he was on a plane, and not on his dragon's back.

What did the Aurelia look like? That was a question they had discussed in great length. They had looked at every jellyfish the web had info on, and then of course a few only the FREEFAB network knew about. 'Yes, she'll probably look quite similar to those,' their father had commented at some point. 'Just a thousand times bigger.'

'Probably more like a million times?' Guinevere had added.

'Yes, probably.'

Ben stared at the ocean, closing his hand protectively around

Twigleg, who was sitting on his arm. Freddie stood on Guinevere's. Twigleg's brother ('younger brother' Twigleg liked to add) almost never just sat somewhere. His feet were always on the move, and the rhythm of the waves inspired him to do some wild dancing on Guinevere's shoulder. She had prevented him twice already from tumbling into the sand. Twigleg and Freddie had passed the border controls in a doll's house that Hothbrodd had built for their travels. It was as big as a suitcase, and quite heavy, but worth the effort of bringing it along. The Customs officers were usually so enchanted by the troll's woodwork that they didn't even wonder whether there was anything or anyone inside. For the baggage scan the homunculi had only to hide inside a closet that Hothbrodd had built from the wood of what he described as a 'very special' alder tree.

Four Greenblooms, two homunculi and a troll . . . they all had agreed that they had to keep the welcome committee for the Aurelia small, so as not to draw the attention they were trying to avoid. But there would be a few more helpers necessary.

'The friend we'll meet here tonight will make things much easier,' Barnabas had said as they'd climbed down the sandy steps to the beach. 'He was the one who suggested the place where we'll set up camp. No one knows this coast better, as he is able to speak to the animals who call it home.'

That sounded quite promising.

When Alfonso Fuentes emerged from the night, his steps gave away the fact that he preferred dry ground to the wet sand under his boots. He was barely taller than Ben and Guinevere, but he was a great man, taller than most. One look into his eyes made that clear to anyone who could see the true shape of things.

'¿Cómo estás, Barnabas?' he asked. The glance he cast at the night-black ocean was at the same time respectful and very aware

- 77 -

of its dangers. Alfonso Fuentes loved the earth, the mountains and all its creatures, Ben would soon come to know that. 'We all have a preference for one element,' Barnabas had once said to him. 'Some of us are water, some air, some earth, and then there are of course the ones who are fire.' That would probably be him, Ben had thought. Alfonso Fuentes was Earth.

'*El Brujo.*' Barnabas bowed his head with a smile. 'May I introduce my wife Vita and my children Ben and Guinevere.'

'*Encantada.*' Alfonso smiled at them. 'May I also be introduced to your tiny friends?' He pointed at the homunculi. 'They have a slight resemblance to the gnomes that live in avocado trees. But their skin is not as green, and I don't see flowers growing from their heads.'

Flowers. From their heads. Twigleg clearly found that thought slightly disturbing.

'My brother and I are homunculi, *Señor* Fuentes,' he said. 'Artificial creatures, made by a man who considered himself also a *Brujo*. That means Magician or Witcher, master,' he whispered into Ben's ear. Twigleg spoke fluent Spanish, of course.

El Brujo . . . As Barnabas had uttered that title like a compliment, Ben was sure Alfonso Fuentes practised White Magic, in contrast to Twigleg's creator, who had preferred the Dark Arts.

'Our creator made us in bottles!' Freddie announced that fact as if there was no better way to be born. 'It took twenty-three days to grow us.'

'Twenty-three? Ah, *Magia*!' Alfonso Fuentes clearly found the world as enchanting as Freddie. 'But you two should beware of the pelicans. They often hunt near the beach, and you are exactly the right size for their beaks, and a tasty snack for their young.'

'Pelicans?' Twigleg cast a nervous glance at the sky, and Ben closed his hand more firmly around him.

'Alfonso saved me once from a Nahual, a Mexican shapeshifter,' Barnabas explained, with a smile. 'He introduced me to many fabulous creatures of the Americas, and we couldn't have a more knowledgeable helper. The troll who brought us here is very happy with the spot you suggested for our camp. He says it looks like a place for dragons, though sadly they never existed on the American continents.'

Alfonso smiled. 'There are tales about a tribe of giant flying lizards in the mountains of Veracruz.'

'Really? Maybe we can find them together one day!' For a moment Barnabas had forgotten why he was standing on a beach in California. But the waves brought the memories back, rushing on to the sand as if they were whispering about the creature to come.

'Yes. I guess we have more urgent things to do, my friend,' Alfonso said. 'I already talked to the coyotes, the hawks and the snakes. They're not at home in the ocean, but they listen to the wind and to the waters underground. Something is coming, they all agree on that. And that it's huge, and will arrive when the moon is full. So nothing new there. But I asked a friend to join us, who lives in and from the sea, and speaks with almost every creature in it. I think he has already arrived.'

Just a few steps behind them a man rose from the waves, his long black hair dripping with the salty waters of the ocean. Watermen are usually olive-green, and merpeople have the colour of the waters they live in. But the skin of the man who rose from the waves and waded with calm steps on to the beach shimmered like pale gold in the moonlight and was patterned with dark spikes. He had a dozen arms that looked very strong, most of them ending in pointed tips instead of hands. His face, though, looked quite human, despite the two breathing slits he had next to his nose.

'Elewese,' Alfonso introduced him. 'These are the friends who are here to make sure the Aurelia delivers her sacred pods safely.'

Elewese scrutinised each one of them so thoroughly it was as if he could read their whole life history from their faces. His eyes were as golden as his skin, and they widened slightly as he beheld Freddie and Twigleg.

'It seems many are coming to these shores to help with that,' he said with a voice made from water. 'Merpeople, kelphorses, shoals of whispering anemones . . . there are more fabulous creatures in these waters than when the white whale came to rub the shell-men off his flanks. Which happened almost four hundred years ago.'

'Some may have come because we called them,' Vita said. 'We'll need help to shield the Aurelia from boats and other humans who could get in her way.'

'Yes, you will.' Elewese cast a glance over the waves that left their white foam on the sand. 'She who lives for ever, that's what the whales call her. The Great Aurelia, the Singer from the Deep, the Bringer of Life. Or Death, if she chooses. I hear she hasn't risen for more than two thousand years.'

'And she is really a jellyfish?' Guinevere asked.

'That's what I hear,' Elewese replied. 'With a thousand arms and a hundred eyes.'

'Master Elewese?' Freddie piped from Guinevere's shoulder. He seemed utterly fascinated by the man from the sea. 'Excuse my curiosity. May I ask what kind of merman you are? I've met quite a few, but none of them looked like you.'

Elewese smiled at the homunculus. His dozen arms constantly moved in the air as if they were looking for the water. 'I was once human like your friends, little man. I was born into a tribe of fishermen and canoe builders, who lived on this coast long before the white men came. We arrived here from an island. One of our goddesses, who gave us a rainbow as a bridge, told us not to look down, but I was never good at listening. Which is how I got this body!'

'Then you're one of the legendary Chumash!' Freddie exclaimed. 'I listened on audio to the traditional tales of your tribe on the plane. The story about the rainbow bridge was one of them! But didn't the Chumash who looked down and fell into the sea turn into dolphins?'

'Well, all the others did. But I –' Elewese lifted his arms '– I turned into a starfish! It was quite confusing in the beginning to have eyes in the tips of my arms, not to speak of the fact that I have so many! I'm very good at cracking things, though, and my skin is as firm as an armour. But I still wish I had at least turned into a horn shark or a garibaldi.'

'That's the state fish of California,' Twigleg whispered into Ben's ear. Of course. He was embarrassed that his brother proved to be more knowledgeable than him.

'I will do my best to recruit as many additional helpers as I can find,' the Chumash said, his arms painting waves into the night. 'The Greenblooms have quite a reputation amongst fabulous creatures, both on land and sea. Very much in contrast to most humans. I have to get back now; I can't be out of the water for too long. But Alfonso knows how to call me.'

His feet left human footprints in the sand as he walked back into the waves. They all couldn't take their eyes off him. Elewese was a reminder of how different a world the Aurelia would come from.

'How long ago did he become a creature of the sea?' Guinevere asked. 'I didn't know that was possible!'

'There are many ways to change your body,' Alfonso said. 'Though most of them are forgotten. Elewese doesn't count the years, but we believe that he left his human body behind more than three thousand years ago.'

Three thousand years . . . Ben followed a spider with his eye as it crawled over the sand. How did it feel to live that long? The spider had an unusual shape. It looked like a coin with legs. A copper coin.

'Everything will be fine,' Alfonso Fuentes said. 'Together we'll make sure of it.'

Barnabas nodded, while the waves whispered, as if they knew about all the secrets in the world.

'Yes,' he murmured,' we'll make sure of that. Somehow. We have to.'

CHAPTER ELEVEN

HIGH ABOVE THE SEA

Twigleg was woken by the sound of a zip. His master was closing his jacket. Where was he going? It was still dark, wasn't it, and they were in a dangerous country! Far more dangerous than the woods around MÍMAMEIÐR. Or even the mountains surrounding the castle of his old master Nettlebrand. It reminded Twigleg of the jungles they had crossed to find the griffins. Though there were not as many trees – which Hothbrodd wouldn't like. Rattlesnakes, coyotes, mountain lions, scorpions, black widows... when Vita had named all the animals even humans had to watch out for here the list had been endless! And there were so many more who weren't dangerous for humans, but would prey happily on a homunculus! Hawks, gopher snakes, raccoons...

Twigleg sat up. 'Master? Where are you going?'

'Oh, sorry, I didn't mean to wake you!' Ben whispered. 'I really wish humans could move as silently as you or Sorrel. Even Hothbrodd is less noisy! I'm just going for a walk. I can't sleep.'

Freddie was sleeping as peacefully as if they were at home, in one of the beds in the doll's house. He was snoring like a cricket, and didn't even wake when Twigleg pulled his coat from under his head. Freddie had turned it into his pillow. Of course: he didn't have a clear concept of 'mine' and 'yours'. 'I am sorry, brother,' he had once said, when Twigleg had caught him wearing one of his shoes. 'I had to steal and lend for centuries to survive. It's an old habit. This shoe is really nice!'

The sky above the tents they had put up last night was indeed still dark. The tents were actually tent-lice – very useful fabulous creatures, who were small enough to fit a dozen in a matchbox. They transformed into quite spacious lodgings in the roughest territories, rain- sun- and windproof, and all in return for just a few breadcrumbs and some apple pips.

The grounds of their campsite were surrounded by huge rocks that looked like strange beasts in the dark, and Twigleg was quite relieved when Ben put him on his shoulder before he climbed on to one of them. They were high up in the mountains overlooking the Pacific Ocean. From where they had camped, one could see all the way to Catalina island (yes, not all of Twigleg's research had been in vain) and to the Channel Islands. Rows of white and red lights drew the shoreline into the dying night below them. Humans in their cars – they looked so much more beautiful and mysterious from a distance, and without the treacherous light of the sun. But the stars above them were already fading, and soon the fireworms would be nothing but endless rows of metal and exhaust. On the horizon the morning light was already separating the ocean from the sky, and Ben uttered a deep and happy sigh.

'Oh, what a fantastic view!' He kept his voice low, as if he didn't want to help the day to chase the night away.

'Look at this place, Twigleg! The mountains and the sea! And those rocks!'

Oh, Twigleg had missed him so much. It was of course nice to have a brother again, after all those centuries of considering himself the only survivor of his kind. But Freddie didn't quite fill his heart the way his human master did.

'It is really beautiful here,' Ben murmured. 'But I'm glad Firedrake will join us soon. And I miss the baby dragons. I got so used to them.'

And I missed you, Twigleg thought. *So much.*

Behind them a bird began to chirp a welcome song for the new day – a warbler, if Twigleg was not mistaken. A rustling at the foot of the rock made him cast a nervous glance down, but he only spotted a young rabbit, furry and long-eared, the kind that could be found nearly everywhere in the world. Good. Rabbits were amongst the few creatures homunculi didn't have to worry about – as far as he knew, anyway . . .

The sky above the ocean turned an early morning yellow and Ben gazed at the islands in the distance. 'Do you think the Aurelia is as big as one of those?'

Twigleg very much hoped she was not *that* big! He so wished he hadn't studied all those ancient sea-monster maps . . . they were quite terrifying, especially Sebastian Münster's very upsetting *Monstra Marina & Terrestria*! What if all those monsters did indeed exist? Horned sea devils, huge crabs, bull fish, man-eating sea pigs . . . one map showed a beast that devoured whole ships! If the tales were right, the Aurelia was certainly big enough to do that. Well, probably she'd wrap all her thousand arms around a ship and just pull it under the water! *She'll wrap her arms around all of you, Twigleg. Around all the fabulous creatures in this world, and down you'll go. Deeper and deeper. To wherever she'll take you.* The homunculus shuddered.

'Don't look so worried. It'll be all right. We'll make sure of it. Together.' Ben gave him a comforting nudge with his finger. 'We can't think too much about what might happen. It'll drive us all crazy. Think of the magic instead! Isn't it incredible that the Aurelia has come in our lifetime? What kind of creatures will spring from her seeds? Maybe she'll even bring back some of those who were lost – the unicorns? The flying whales? Or the elf horses . . . you could ride one of those!'

Two coyotes appeared from the sumac bushes surrounding the rock, staring up at them with amber eyes. Twigleg dug his fingers into the fabrics of Ben's jeans. 'I'm really not sure I like this so-called New World, master!' he said with a slight tremor in his voice. 'It may be a bit *too* new for a homunculus who is more than four hundred years old!'

The coyotes, luckily, didn't find their scent appealing. They turned and disappeared as swiftly as ghosts down the bushy slope that descended to the distant shore, where rocks and trees gave way to houses and streets.

'Yes, we'll have to watch you and Freddie closely here!' Ben cast a glance at two red-tailed hawks drawing wide circles above them. 'I don't think the two bluelings like to be watched. Hothbrodd says they immediately went on an adventure. You have no intention of doing that, right?'

Twigleg shook his head. No. He still felt exhausted from all the adventures in Indonesia, where they had looked for the griffins. Couldn't the Aurelia just head for MÍMAMEIÐR? And he would wave at her from the library?

He was glad Lola would be here soon. Lola Greytail had a very calming effect on his nerves, though there had been that night in Indonesia when she would not have been able to save him from the teeth of that binturong . . .

and she would insist on bringing that devilish plane of hers and taking him for a flight over these mountains in it. Twigleg sighed. Why was life so exhausting at times?

A spider came crawling up the rock. Was it poisonous? Twigleg had read very worrying things about the black widows. But they were black and shiny, as round as a pea with a red cross on their bellies. This one looked like a copper coin with eight spindly legs.

'Oh, this is the most exciting place!' Freddie appeared so suddenly next to Ben that Twigleg nearly slipped off his master's knee. 'I already met a gopher snake, a black-collared lizard and a scorpion! The lizard and the snake were still stiff from the cold morning air and I got the impression that the scorpion doesn't like foreigners. The hawks, on the other hand—'

'Freddie!' Twigleg interrupted him. 'Those are all deadly creatures. Have you lost your mind?'

'But I'm armed, brother!' Freddie triumphantly held up a fork. It was almost as tall as he was.

Ben laughed. 'I can see I don't have to worry about Twigleg as long as he has his brother by his side.'

Twigleg was just going to remind him that *he* was the older brother, and therefore quite capable of taking care of himself, when Hothbrodd's shell horn boomed its wake-up call behind them. The troll stood on another rock, that rose from the sumac and toyon bushes, as if it had always waited for the day it would carry a Norwegian fjord troll. Hothbrodd was holding not only his shell horn (and the story of how that had came to him would fill another book), but also a stone the size of Ben's head.

'Barnabas! Vita!' the troll yelled in the direction of the tent, from which right at this moment the head of Ben's adopted father emerged. 'Look at this stone! I'll be damned in Helheim if it isn't proof that there were dragons in these mountains once!'

Barnabas Greenbloom got to his feet and scanned his surroundings with a very pleased and admiring glance. 'Those rocks do indeed look like petrified dragons. But I fear they never existed in this part of the world . . . Alfonso!' he called up to his friend, who was getting out of his truck high above them, at the top of a rocky slope that did indeed look like a dragon's back. 'What kind of fabulous creatures are at home in these mountains? I only know of the Coyote People and the Invisible Geckos.'

Invisible Geckos . . . Twigleg suppressed a sigh.

'Those rocks,' Alfonso pointed at a row of sunbleached stones lining the slope above him, 'are called the Stone Warriors. There's a tale that claims they were petrified by a huge beast that wakes on full-moon nights. But I watched many full moons rise here and never met it.' Alfonso Fuentes sounded quite disappointed.

As he came down the steep path that led to the grounds where the Greenblooms had raised their tents, three dogs followed him – dogs who, as Twigleg realised with a start when they came closer, were actually coyotes. Twigleg felt their amber gaze like fire on his skin. Alfonso, Ben and Barnabas were inspecting the stone Hothbrodd had found.

'Remind me, what do coyotes eat?' he whispered to Freddie, who was tap-dancing in front of the doll's house where Ben had left them.

'Oh, almost everything,' his brother replied. 'They probably wonder what we taste like, as they definitely won't have ever seen a homunculus before! You should wear a red jacket, brother. I always do. It sends the signal that you're poisonous.'

A red jacket? Twigleg wiped a few ants from his sleeve. The mere thought made him shudder. But . . . the coyotes were still looking at him!

Guinevere and Vita were not that interested in Hothbrodd's stone. They had discovered a Stone Stilt's cave and a bush with Singing Flowers. The spot Alfonso Fuentes had suggested as their base enchanted them all in very different ways, and even Twigleg had to admit that he felt strangely young among these mountains, despite his 457 years.

They finally all gathered between the tents to have some coffee and the breakfast tamales Alfonso had brought – though not before they'd checked the grass for rattlesnakes, at Twigleg's request.

'Alfonso, I forgot to ask: did you hear about any strangers arriving here lately?' Barnabas did his best to sound casual, but Guinevere cast Ben a knowing glance. They both could hear from their father's voice that the answer to this question mattered very much to him.

'There are many strangers who come to rent the houses on the beach,' Alfonso replied. 'What is his name?'

'He may be using a different name . . .'

Barnabas turned abruptly as a buzzing sound grew louder and louder. It sounded like a massive hornet.

'Here comes the raaaaaaat!'

Lola flew her plane so closely past the coyotes that one of them nearly dug his teeth into its wing. Then she looped the little flying machine swiftly between the tents and landed right next to the tamales and the coffee mugs.

Ben saw the concern on his father's face melt into a smile.

'Alfonso, may I introduce Lola Greytail, our best scout and spy?' Barnabas broke a tiny bite off his tamales while Lola climbed out of her plane. 'She has had a very long flight. She came all the way from England – and she may have an answer to the question I just asked you.'

He handed the tamales to the rat and filled one of the homunculi's mugs with coffee for her.

'He is here. I guess that was the question?' Lola took a bite of tamale and a sip of coffee.

Barnabas took off his glasses and polished them with his shirt – a gesture that always showed he was deeply upset.

'Come on, Dad,' Guinevere said. 'We all know his name by now. Cadoc Eelstrom. What are you worried about? That we'll all turn to stone if we say it?'

Her father sighed and pushed his glasses back on his nose. 'You're right,' he said. 'Your mother always warned me that making him a secret may be dangerous one day.'

'And you never keep secrets from us!' Ben said.

'No, I don't,' Barnabas replied. 'And I kept this one only because it brings back many sad and terrible memories. But you're both old enough to hear about them.'

CHAPTER TWELVE

A SHADOW FROM THE PAST

Twigleg had heard the name Cadoc Eelstrom long before Barnabas had told his children about him on a mountain overlooking the biggest ocean on earth. The homunculus had heard that name for the first time on a foggy winter's day about two years ago. Barnabas had come back from the fjord with his face pale from distress, his fists clenched in anger. Twigleg had never seen him like that before.

He had walked past him without a word, the same man who always had a few friendly words for everyone. Twigleg had followed him, although he had been embarrassed about his nosiness. But he had been so worried! Barnabas had disappeared into his study and then – Twigleg hadn't believed his ears! – he'd heard him break things in there, and shouting over and over again: *Curse you, Cadoc! Curse you!*

Barnabas hadn't come out for dinner. He never missed that meal, as he loved to listen to the tales all the guests of MÍMAMEIÐR told at that occasion. But then Vita had shown up, with a plate filled with blueberry pancakes

(Barnabas's favourite dish).

She had knocked three times before her husband finally opened the door. Still shaking with anger. And yes, he had been crying.

'He killed two kelpies, Vita! What did he think to gain from that? More strength? Riches? Oh, when will I finally be able to stop him?'

Vita had stepped into the study and they'd closed the door. But homunculus ears are sharp, and Barnabas's words had made Twigleg only more curious and worried. So he had crept to the door and had pressed his ear against it. That was the day he had learned about Cadoc Eelstrom.

Twigleg learned that Eelstrom had been Barnabas Greenbloom's enemy since their schooldays. And he heard another name for the first time through that locked door: Lizzie Persimmons. It seemed that something terrible had happened to her when she tried to protect a mermaid from Eelstrom – and that Barnabas had tried in vain to save her. Twigleg learned about so many things that day that made him shudder: fabulous creatures killed or mutilated for their magic, chased to their death, their offspring stolen, their hearts ripped out . . .

'Oh, Vita, all those legends and myths I collected when I was young!' Barnabas had exclaimed. 'How could I write it all down? What a fool I was to reveal their secrets instead of

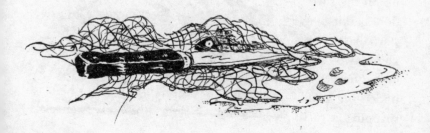

guarding them! I'm sure Cadoc still has the notebooks he stole from me. All the things he learned from them! The heart of a sky serpent makes you rich. The heart of a dragon makes you invincible. The dust of moss fairies keeps you young for a hundred years . . .'

'. . . the webs between the fingers of a mermaid make you invisible,' Vita had softly added. 'I know. But it is not your fault. You wrote all those things down because you wanted to learn about them, understand them, protect them . . .'

'But I didn't protect them!' Barnabas's voice had shaken with despair. 'My scribblings . . . they betrayed them! What a terrible species we are! I just wish I wasn't human.'

'Barnabas!' Vita had stopped him. 'It's not only humans who are cruel! The wasp who lays her eggs into a living caterpillar doesn't feel compassion when her children eat their host. Compassion, I fear, is quite a new sentiment in this world.'

'But Cadoc doesn't do it for his offspring! He does it because he always wants more, Vita! Does greed allow us to harm other creatures? Are we allowed to cause pain and despair for more money, power or a more comfortable life? No! Not even for more knowledge!'

That was the last thing Twigleg had overheard. Hothbrodd had shown up on the corridor, barking Barnabas's name, two crab gnomes under his arms snapping at each

other with their claws. And Twigleg had hastened back to the library, where the books had soon made him forget Eelstrom. He had always found shelter from evil in books.

But sadly they couldn't keep it away for ever.

CHAPTER THIRTEEN

THE SONG IN THE DEEP

Lizzie had never before swum so deep into the ravine. She had long passed the ruins, but the song led her on, the song she heard below her. It filled her from head to tail now, with so much joy and light that Lizzie wouldn't have been surprised if she had dissolved in it like a pebble fish in the poisonous ink of a spotted eel.

Oh, it was so beautiful. Almost too beautiful to bear. It had all the glory and the sadness of the world in it, all its stories from the very beginning to this day. But that's of course who she was: the Great Aurelia, the Singer from the Deep. She was the memory of the world, its hope and soul. And she had come in Lizzie's lifetime! Lizzie could still not quite believe it.

Oh, how she yearned to talk with Barnabas about it!

In all those years since they'd last gazed at each other through layers of salty sea water, she had missed Barnabas on so many occasions, but never quite as much as now. They had talked so often about the magical being that was singing below her. What would the fabulous creatures look like that her seeds would bring into the world? They'd spent countless nights discussing them! Would her seeds bring the unicorns back? The three-headed dragons? The birds of paradise?

Underneath her the huge silhouette was moving in the light she was spreading, a majestic translucent shadow. The Aurelia didn't move fast, but if the tales told were true, she would reach the coast and deliver the four pods when the moon was full.

Oh, Lizzy so hoped Barnabas had received her message! Was he even alive? Down here one didn't hear much about the world above. Did he have children by now? If yes, what were they like? Did they look like their father? Lanky and always smiling, polishing his glasses, letting mud gnomes and moss fairies ride on his shoulders?

She made Koo repeat the message every hour. The lantern fish was quite upset with her. But although he blocked Lizzie's way over and over again, flashing his warning lights and even snapping at her tail, he couldn't convince her to turn around.

No.

Even if this would be the end of her, and even though she felt the pressure of the water like a fist now, she couldn't turn back.

She had to keep the Aurelia safe. She had to somehow watch over her. For *he* might hear about her too. No. She wouldn't even think his name! The mere thought of him made the cold waters around her feel even colder.

She passed the ruins of another underwater palace, that seemed even older and more magnificent than the ones they had set out to show the merlings, but the moving silhouette was still far beneath her. Would the water squash her body? Would the pressure kill her? Lizzie didn't know. After all, she hadn't been born as a mermaid, and as far as she knew, none of the merpeople ever dived this deep.

She could see the thousand arms now, floating around the Aurelia's body like a web made from all the colours of the rainbow.

Swim, Lizzie!

Oh, her arms felt heavy, and her scaled skin hurt from the cold and the weight of the water.

Koo pushed his nose into her shoulder. What? Was he trying again to convince her to turn? No. He snapped a floating alga out of the water, that was covered with tiny red flowers, and chewed on it, signalling for her to do the same. Lizzie tried. It tasted terribly sweet, but she immediately felt the cold and the pressure less and she gave Koo a grateful pat on his yellow scales. He loved to be patted. He was sometimes almost like a huge dog, though he would have been very insulted to be compared to a pet. Lantern fish were actually quite wild. They even picked fights with sharks if they had to, and Lizzie felt very honoured that Koo had followed her into the ravine.

They could see the Aurelia quite clearly now. And yes, she was huge, even more huge than she and Barnabas had imagined. How often had they discussed whether she was bigger than a grey whale. She was at least ten times that size. Without her arms. Each of them trailed through the water for over a hundred metres. And there! Lizzie felt her heartbeat like a drum inside. There was something glowing. That must be one of the pods.

'What do you think they look like, Lizzie?' she remembered Barnabas's voice. 'Like fruit? Like a sponge? Or an egg?'

'Maybe like a turtle's egg?' she heard herself say.

They had both been wrong. The pod Lizzie saw shimmering on one of the Aurelia's arms was bright blue and fuzzy and looked more like a plant seed.

'I will protect you!' Lizzie whispered. With all the lights on her tail. 'I will not let Cadoc Eelstrom get you. Holy holy mermaid promise.'

Beneath her the dark was humming with beauty and joy and life, and a thousand eyes opened like flowers on the Aurelia's skin.

Oh, Barnabas, please! Lizzie thought while she felt her song and light engulfing her. *Please answer my message. We have to protect her.*

Or there would be no more merpeople in the shipwrecks of Momi. And she would fade with them.

CHAPTER FOURTEEN

ENCOUNTERS ON THE BEACH

In the afternoon Vita drove down to the beach and Ben decided to go with her. He had spoken to Firedrake before he and Sorrel had left the Rim. It would take at least two more days until they'd arrive. So there was not really much use for a dragon rider. Which left far too much time to think about the threat the Aurelia brought along with the promise her pods held. When his father had finally told them all about it, he had tried his best to sound optimistic, but Hothbrodd hadn't made that effort.

'Let me spell it out, Barnabas,' he had growled. 'If this Eelstrom lunatic harms the big jelly, she'll set the oceans on fire and we'll all disappear with her: trolls, dragons, brownies, homunculi – even Lola, as she is a talking rat . . . *det var som pokker!* I admit I don't envy you humans being left behind in such a boring world.' Then he'd turned around and checked on his plane.

Trolls, dragons, brownies, homunculi . . . mermaids and

Pegasi, gnomes, fairies, elves, kelpies . . . No. No, Ben couldn't allow himself to think about it. He saw in Guinevere's face that she felt the same. As did his parents. 'Let's just not think about it. We need to focus on the task ahead,' Barnabas had said that quite a lot by now, but of course none of them could stop thinking about it. While pretending all was fine . . . Twigleg had a hard time doing that, and it cut Ben's heart in two that he couldn't just tell him it was all not true.

'Does Firedrake know?' he had asked his father. 'Yes,' Barnabas had replied. 'That's another reason why he insisted on being the Courier of Fire. We will also secure the future of his children if we succeed in protecting the Aurelia.'

Let's just not think about it.

So . . . Yes. Plenty of reason to go to the beach. To explore how they could best protect the place where the Aurelia would rise was certainly better than staring at the sea wondering whether he would ever feel happy again if there was no more Firedrake in a few days. Hothbrodd was setting up communication at the camp to stay in contact with MÍMAMEIÐR and all their helpers. Barnabas and Guinevere had stayed to help him, along with the bluelings and Freddie. Twigleg, though, had insisted on coming with Ben to the beach, despite the threat of seagull and pelican beaks.

'Master, please! I can always hide under your jacket!' he had pleaded, his eyes so frightened and sad. Seven days . . .

No. Ben definitely didn't want to live in a world without dragons and homunculi. He would just fade with them – after he had killed Cadoc Eelstrom!

Of course he had given in to Twigleg's pleading eyes. But as he stood in the sand and saw swarms of seagulls hunting above the waters and two long-legged cormorants turning their heads towards him, he regretted bringing the homunculus with him.

Seagulls, cormorants, pelicans . . . this coast certainly swarmed with magnificent feathered creatures. But their beaks definitely spelled danger – at least for a homunculus.

'Stay in my pocket!' he told Twigleg. 'It's not safe.'

The beach looked quite different in the daylight. Two people were walking their dogs and a squadron of pelicans swooped over their heads. They looked glorious, but they definitely had enough room for several homunculi in their beaks.

Both he and his mother had been quite silent on the drive down. Usually they chatted in the car, but Ben was sure that Vita was, like him, going through the list of all the fabulous creatures she loved, trying to imagine how life would feel without them. Her friend Raskervint, for example, who was a centaur . . .

'Did you ever meet him?' Ben finally asked, as he walked side by side with Vita down the beach. Guinevere had looked Eelstrom up, but they hadn't found anything. No photos. Nothing about his business, his private life, his past . . . It seemed that Eelstrom was hiding his activities from the eyes of the world as well as the Greenblooms did. What did he look like?

'No,' his adopted mother replied. 'I first heard about him after he'd caused the death of Barnabas's friend Lizzie Persimmons. Barnabas only mentioned her briefly, because it is still too hard for him to talk about her. Lizzie was a very good friend of his, and he still can't forgive himself that he didn't manage to save her. They were protecting a mermaid from Cadoc. He was after the webs between her fingers, as they are supposed to make humans invisible. Lizzie got into the draught from Cadoc's ship propeller and suddenly she was gone. It's no comfort for Barnabas that he nearly drowned too. He owes his life to our friend Kahurangi, who alerted him to the gathering birds in New Zealand.'

Ben took a step back when a wave licked at his shoes. 'What happened to the mermaid?'

'Cadoc didn't get the webs, which would have been the death of her. The rest we don't know.' Vita sighed. 'I hope Lola finds out where Cadoc is staying. If he's really here.'

She looked up at the houses overlooking the sea and at the many footprints in the sand. 'They close the beaches at night, but I'm sure some of the people who live nearby come down nevertheless after dark. Let's pray the Aurelia arrives late in the night. Your father is right: this is the wrong coast. Maybe the Aurelia doesn't know how much the world has changed in the past two thousand years.'

A few cliffs rose from the water, their surface dark and sharp-edged. Ben saw tide pools shimmering in the crevices, and between the rocks, as they came closer, he saw most of them filled with anemones, mussels and starfish. Was one of them Elewese? he wondered. If yes, the Chumash didn't show himself.

'Master!' Twigleg climbed out of his pocket and pulled at his sleeve. 'There! Ears of the Ocean!' His curiosity was the one thing that overruled Twigleg's timidity. Ben closed his hand protectively around the homunculus as he stepped closer to the rocks he was pointing at.

'Yes, you're right, Twigleg!' Vita whispered, leaning over the dense assembly of shells that covered the wet stone. 'Some of these are definitely not the regular mussels one finds here.'

The cliff the tide had laid bare was jagged and they had to be careful to not cut their feet and hands walking over the rock. To Ben the shells all looked the same, but Vita bent over half a dozen clinging to the stone just a hand's length above the water, and began to hum a melody as joyful and temperamental as the dance of the waves. The shells stirred after just a few notes and opened like flowers yearning for the sun.

'Voila!' Vita stepped back with a smile. 'Now they listen. Twigleg, do you think you can talk to them?'

'Let me try,' the homunculus replied. 'I'm only fluent in ten mussel dialects. Let's hope one is familiar to them.'

He cleared his throat while Ben cast a watchful glance up and down the beach, but as it was cold and cloudy now, they were the only humans as far as the eye could see. The mussels covered the rocks so densely that it was not easy to place Twigleg between them. Their dark shells reached up to his hips, and he almost cut his fingers on their sharp edges as he tried to hold on to one of them.

'No worries, master!' he said, as Ben immediately reached down to pick him up again. 'I'm fine! I assume the inhabitants of these shells . . .' he tried his best to sound fearless and not worried at all, 'are as soft and wobbly as regular mussel-dwellers?'

'Yes,' Vita replied. 'They eat nothing bigger than a sand flea.'

'And I'm watching the seagulls,' Ben added while Twigleg once again cleared his throat.

'Greetings, most honourable Ears of the Ocean!' the homunculus called in his best sing-song voice. 'All mussel species appreciate poetic phrasing,' he added in a low voice. 'We were wondering whether you'd heard anything unusual lately,' he continued, 'in the salty realms of your kingdom?'

The Ears of the Ocean were clearly pleased with this opening.

They began to chatter so rapidly with their shells that Twigleg had to make sure they didn't take off his hands.

'They say . . .' he listened intently, '. . . there is a strange message. Someone has been sending it out every hour.'

'A message?' Ben exchanged a glance with his mother. 'What does it say?'

Twigleg once again listened to the shells' rapid chatter. '*Naia to Fuf-luns!*' he translated. '*She sings . . . where . . . Momi sleeps! heading hikina.*'

Vita looked at Twigleg in disbelief. 'Naia to Fufluns? You must be wrong.'

The homunculus leaned over the mussels. 'Please repeat!'

The mussels began to chat again, even faster than before. The homunculus frowned and looked up at Vita. 'That's what they say.'

Vita stared at the ocean. 'Impossible,' she murmured.

'What is it?' Ben asked. 'Do you know those names from somewhere?'

'Yes,' his mother replied. 'Your father called himself Fufluns when he was at school. It's the name of a Roman god who protects plants and animals. As for Naia . . . that was Lizzie Persimmons' nickname.' She shook her head. 'Sorry, Twigleg. Could you repeat the last part of the message?'

The homunculus did – while the Ears of the Ocean kept on chatting about the other things happening on these shores, about the orcas who were hiding in the nearby marine trench to hunt the grey whales' calves, about a strange disease amongst sponges and a ship pouring poisonous waste into the sea.

'*She sings where Momi sleeps! Heading hikina.*' Vita drew a piece of paper from her jeans pocket and wrote down what Twigleg had translated. Then she stared at it for a while.

'No,' she finally murmured. 'It doesn't make more sense in writing. I have no idea what this means. But hopefully Barnabas does.'

'Well done!' Ben said, lifting Twigleg carefully back into one of his jacket pockets. 'Although we don't understand it yet. Freddie may be the better dancer, but you certainly have the superior translation skills. They still amaze me.'

The homunculus gave him a wide and grateful smile. Ben was of course aware how hard it was at times for Twigleg to match Freddie's enthusiasm.

'You shouldn't believe a word they say. Only fools trust the chatter of mussels.' The creature who emerged from under a pale-blue anemone was only slightly bigger than Twigleg, with hair resembling seagrass, black fish-eyes and fingers that ended in sharp black thorns. One of the mussels snapped at her, but the mermaid – for a mermaid she was – dived into a tide pool at the foot of the rock before the shell could grab her thin blue arm.

When she reappeared, Ben could for the first time see her tail. It resembled a braid, woven from eight strands of rainbow-coloured scales. They untangled the moment she pulled herself out of the water and turned into legs that carried

her up the rock as swiftly as the legs of a spider. When she reached the top she stared at them with so fierce an expression that Twigleg returned quickly to Ben's pocket.

'You're the humans the starfish talks about.' Her voice was a strange mix between a snake's hiss and the waves' whisper. Four more of her kind appeared behind her and gave them as hostile a stare as the first one.

Vita knelt down in the sand to make herself smaller and less threatening. Ben quickly followed her example. 'Incredible!' he whispered. 'Mermaids with legs! I wish Guinevere could see them!' He was terribly tempted to take a photo with his phone, but it was a FREEFAB rule never to document the existence of fabulous creatures, as others could find out about them too easily.

What had his father's notebooks looked like? Ben would have loved to page through them, as Barnabas had been his age when he'd filled most of them. But Barnabas had burned those that Cadoc hadn't stolen.

'What kind of merman is he?' One of the mermaids pointed her thorny finger at Twigleg, who was peeking out of Ben's pocket. 'Did he lose his scales?'

'Scales? I never had a scales!' Twigleg called up to them. 'I am a homunculus!'

The mermaids whispered with each other as if they were not sure what to make of that answer.

'Thank you so much for showing yourselves to us,' Vita said. 'I'm sure this beach poses many dangers for your kind.'

The mermaids exchanged a mocking giggle.

'Danger? *We* are the danger,' the one who had appeared first snarled. 'We're braidmaids! The dogs fear us as much as those deeply annoying seagulls. We heard you're gathering helpers to shield a creature who'll come from the deep.'

'Yes, we are.' Vita couldn't take her eyes off the mermaids. She loved all fabulous creatures, but if Vita had had to choose one Ben was quite sure it would have been mermaids.

'Would you be willing to help?' he asked. 'We would be very grateful. And it might serve you as well. It might serve this whole world.'

But the five braidmaids suddenly disappeared with a splash into the open sea, their legs weaving back into a tail before they vanished in the water.

'I guess you know that braidmaids are almost as dangerous as a Japanese pufferfish?' a deep voice behind Ben remarked. 'The poison is in their tail fins. And they are much less trustworthy than ear mussels.'

Ben pushed Twigleg deep into his pocket as he rose to his feet.

The man, who was standing just a few steps away from him

and Vita, was surprisingly short considering his dark voice. Ben towered at least two heads over him and he was not very tall for his age. But the height the stranger was missing, he made up for with a very sturdy and muscular build. Every wrestler would have envied him for his shoulders, and his gloved hands would have fitted a man twice his size. The eyes he was scanning them with were shaped like a cat's and as green as the leaves of a beech in spring. Ben knew those kind of eyes very well. Gryfydd Longtoes, the leprechaun who lived and worked under the library table at MÍMAMEIÐR cast him exactly the same green gaze when Ben brought him a leaky boot or delivered another warning that killing rabbits to make leather from their skin was forbidden on MÍMAMEIÐR grounds.

Yes, the stranger who'd scared away the braidmaids was unmistakably a leprechaun, although he had coloured his wiry green hair black and covered his clawed fingers with gloves. The dog by his side resembled a bulldog, but there was something odd about him. The teeth he bared when Ben gazed at him were sharp ivory needles, set neatly in three rows.

'No need to get rude, Mannanan,' his master said, patting his head. Then he bowed, first to Vita and then to Ben. 'What an unexpected pleasure to meet someone who knows how to start a conversation with the Ears of the Ocean. May I introduce myself? Derog Shortsleeves. I know these mussels have the reputation of being dumb. But in fact they're just very gossipy, like domestic geese, who can spend all day discussing the quality of dried worms. I therefore usually seek information from less talkative sources like selkies and merpeople. Both can be dangerous, but who isn't? One just needs to know how to bribe them.' He winked at Ben, as if those strategies were usually a male domain. 'What kind of creature is hiding in your pocket, my boy, if I may ask? Is it a greengnome? I was sure there weren't any on this so-called new continent.'

'You're right. He is not a greengnome,' Ben answered. 'He is not from here. We are all just . . . tourists.' A leprechaun. On the Californian coast. His mother tried to hide it, but Ben saw how much Derog Shortsleeves' presence irritated her at this place and time. Gryfydd Longtoes had taught them all how much his kind liked dark jokes, and Ben's parents had threatened him with exile several times. Once he had almost tricked Tallemaja, their cook, to put a few sleeping mushroomlings into a stew, and Gryfydd was only a Dwarf leprechaun, whereas Derog Shortsleeves was clearly one of the taller line. They were known for their devious nature, not to mention their greed for gold and their passion for really mean pranks.

'I detect a Southern Irish accent, Mr Shortsleeves.' Vita managed to give the leprechaun one of her nicest smiles. 'From Cork, I would say? Are you also spending your holiday in Malibu?'

The leprechaun revealed needle-sharp teeth as he returned her smile. 'Not exactly. I'm here for business. My lodgings are actually nearby, as I like to watch the seals and sea lions. Especially the ones who sometimes take off their furry skins. They love the rock over there.'

He pointed at a cliff rising from the waves a hundred metres or so away from the sand. Ben detected half a dozen seals on it, drying their wet fur in the sun. They looked like regular seals from afar, but Ben doubted that Mr Shortsleeves was lying about their nature. Sometimes a selkie swam down the fjord that cut into MÍMAMEIÐR grounds. Guinevere and Vita liked to talk to them, but Ben kept his distance, since one had nearly taken off his hand when he'd tried to protect a mud nix from it.

'Well.' Derog Shortsleeves turned up his collar against the

cold wind. 'I'm sure we'll meet again.' He pulled a small golden case out of his pocket and handed Vita his card. 'I don't think I asked for your names yet.'

'Tonnesen,' Vita replied. 'Vita Tonnesen, and this is my son Ben.'

Ben loved the fact that both Vita and Barnabas used the last name he had been born with as their incognito when they were travelling. And it still warmed his heart to be called their son.

'Tonnesen.' The leprechaun smiled as if he knew that was not really Vita's last name. 'Watch over your little friend,' he said to Ben. 'He is a very rare creature. Or how do you call it? Endangered?' He called to his dog. 'Let's go, Mannanan.'

One of the seals barked after him as he walked away over the wet sand. It sounded quite human. Mannanan cast them a sinister glance and followed his master, while Ben eyed the seals on the rock. Yes, indeed. Two of them had the patterns on their backs that he knew from the selkies in Scotland.

'Selkies and a leprechaun in California? This place holds many surprises indeed.' Vita didn't take her eyes of Derog Shortsleeves until he had disappeared behind some rocks.

'Do you think he is here for the Aurelia?' A leprechaun would be thinking of only one thing, if he had indeed come for her: how much gold one could make with her pods.

'I hope not.' Vita stared at the rocks behind which the leprechaun and his dog had disappeared. 'It would also be his end, if it's true what the tales say about the Aurelia's anger.' She put her arm around Ben's shoulders. 'Come. Time to get back to the others. We have plenty of news to deliver!'

Not forgetting that mysterious message the Ears of the Ocean had chattered about. Sent by someone his father thought to be dead.

CHAPTER FIFTEEN

AWAKE

The sun was already setting as Vita and Ben arrived back at their camp in the mountains. Hothbrodd and Barnabas were standing high up on a rock that rose into the darkening sky, like two grim gorillas who had guarded these stony lands for thousands of years. Hothbrodd was gesticulating, while Barnabas was inspecting the grey surface at his feet.

'I wish I had come with you!' Guinevere sighed when she welcomed them back. 'They have been climbing around on those rocks for hours, and I had to listen to the wildest theories. Maybe there once were dragons in America. Maybe the rocks are petrified sea monsters . . . at least we set up the transmitter and the antennae, but the reception is still quite shaky!'

'Wait until we tell you whom we met. You'll wish you'd come even more!' Ben teased.

On the horizon, far out above the sea, the setting sun turned a caravan of clouds into a herd of pink sheep grazing above the glittering waves below. How he yearned to climb on to Firedrake's back and fly out to them! He couldn't wait for him to arrive, although part of him was always slightly worried when Firedrake left the safety of the Rim. 'Dragon rider,' the dragon had stated when he'd last admitted that, 'I'll never again be the prisoner of a place. I'm not willing to pay with my freedom for my safety. And neither will my children just hide in the Himalayas. What a miserable life would that be? I want to show them the world! Yes, we'll be careful, but maybe there will come a time when dragons roam the skies freely again and humans greet them as bringers of luck. Who knows?' Ben cast a glance at the darkening sky above him and imagined Scales, Moondance and Thorny drawing circles around their parents like the hawks he had spotted in the morning. He really hoped Sorrel would be less grumpy when she arrived, so his sacrifice getting on Hothbrodd's plane instead of his dragon's back had not been in vain. No, he told himself smiling, Sorrel wouldn't be Sorrel if she wasn't grumpy. But he was glad he had done it for her nevertheless. Bickering, swearing, mean-tongued Sorrel . . . in some ways she was as much his sister as Guinevere, although there was no way he'd ever tell her that.

'Barnabas!' Vita called. 'Come down! We have news!'

She was scanning the surrounding rocks with a worried expression as her husband and the troll began their descent.

'Do you two also have the strange feeling that someone is hiding here?' she asked. 'And I'm not talking about ancient dragons. I think we should move our camp to another place.'

Ben knew what Vita was talking about. He felt a strange discomfort as well. As if something was stirring under his feet. Well, this was earthquake country, but . . .

'Maybe it's just the night coming,' Guinevere said. 'These rocks cast strange shadows. They look almost alive.'

They did.

'I'll check on Twigleg and Freddie,' Ben said and walked over to the doll's house, where the two homunculi were having dinner at the table in their dining room. Hothbrodd had really done a fabulous job with the house. It had a functioning kitchen, as Freddie liked to cook, a bathroom with a proper tub, two bedrooms and even a small library. The woven table mats under the blue plates were presents from a grassgnome woman whom Freddie had saved from a rat. He was quite a fighter, in contrast to his brother. Ben read it at times on Twigleg's face that he secretly wished to be a bit more like Freddie.

'Where are the bluelings?' Ben asked while he knelt down next to the small house. Their wooden suitcase was empty.

'Another of their expeditions!' Twigleg didn't hide his

disapproval. 'I told them they'll end as coyote snacks, but they just laughed at me.'

'They're very brave,' Freddie said, digging his fork into his pasta. 'I think next time I'll go with them.'

'No, you won't!' Twigleg snapped.

Freddie smiled at Ben. *Yes, I will,* the smile said.

Barnabas and Hothbrodd had reached the foot of the rock. Would his father be able to decipher the strange message? Ben very much hoped so. Vita and Guinevere were just walking towards him when Twigleg jumped up from his chair. The tiny blue porcelain plates Guinevere had bought in a toy shop were moving over the table as if they were coming alive. The ground under Ben's feet was shaking and he saw Vita pull Guinevere protectively to her side.

'Get away from the rocks, Vita!' Barnabas yelled. 'This is not an earthquake!'

He started running, while Hothbrodd cast an alarmed look at his plane. Around them the ground was coming alive. It felt as if it was breathing.

'Stay where you are!' Ben yelled at the homunculi who stared up at him with wide eyes. He hastily closed the two doors Hothbrodd had built to seal the house and pushed the lock in place. Behind him a scaled back broke through the grass, and huge claws emerged from the soil.

'Run!!!!' Hothbrodd yelled. 'All of you! To the plane!'

But it was too late.

The monster that had emerged from the ground was cutting them off from the plane. Its pointed tail was covered with spikes, and when it opened its jaws it bared a row of stone-grey teeth. Cloudy eyes stared down at them, as if the creature wasn't fully awake yet. But then it shook its massive head and gave off a growl so deep that it seemed to rise from the centre of the earth.

Ben stepped protectively in front of the doll's house. He tried to pick it up, but the monster opened its jaws and wrapped them all in a cloud of dusty hot breath. Ben fell on his knees. He could feel his limbs stiffening. He threw himself protectively in front of the small house as the monster drew breath once again.

A few steps away his mother was trying to shield Guinevere, but her face turned as grey as stone as the beast wrapped them all in its breath again.

Ben saw his own hands turn grey as well. He saw his father and Hothbrodd fall to their knees, and then the whole world was made from stone.

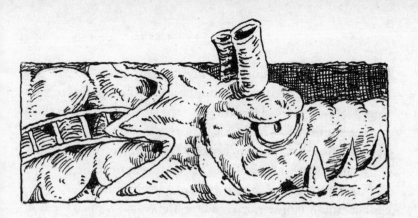

CHAPTER SIXTEEN

A MORE PERMANENT SOLUTION

Twigleg was trembling. He was shaking like a leaf in the wind. But Freddie pressed his hand so firmly on to his mouth that he couldn't even moan or call Ben's name. Freddie had pushed him under the table when his master had locked the house. And so far the walls Hothbrodd had built kept them safe, but there was no window to peek out of when the house was locked this way! No no no! Twigleg's thoughts were racing. He would tell Hothbrodd that they needed some kind of outlook for emergencies like this! If they got out of this mess alive he would! What had happened to his master? Was he okay?

Okay? How can your master be okay, Twigleg? a cruel voice whispered inside him. *There is a monster stomping round out there.*

Oh yes, he had caught a glimpse of it before Ben had shut the doors. A terrifying glimpse! Was it still there? Maybe he could somehow peek through the boards. But Freddie pulled him back when he tried to crawl out from under the table, shaking his head violently. And suddenly Twigleg heard it too. Steps. Steps in the grass. But not from a monster's paws. They sounded two-legged. Shoes, yes . . . Humans?

'Look at this!' he heard a young male voice. 'Well done, Copper. Very efficient. Yes. This looks like a more permanent solution.'

Twigleg heard a knock. Like knuckles against stone.

'Amazing. So perfect that they picked this spot. I guess you can't summon monsters everywhere, right?'

'No. Though there are many of them.'

Twigleg had never heard a voice like that before. It sounded like it was made from metal – metal that was alive.

'They all want to wake,' it said. 'But one needs to know how to call them.'

'Well, you clearly do. And it is very useful that you also know how to make them go to sleep again. Can you wake it again?'

'No,' the metal voice replied. 'Even I can wake such a monster only once. The effort takes years off my life.'

His companion seemed not to care about that price. The steps came closer. Oh, no! They would discover them. Would the metal man crush them? How big was he?

'Heavens,' he heard the human voice mock. 'So Barnabas's son plays with dolls' houses. Well, I'm not surprised. His father was always childish.'

The steps left – and stopped again.

'And there he is!' the voice said. 'Do you remember, Barnabas? I warned you not to get in my way again. I am sure you would be delighted to hear that I still feel that sky serpent's poison in my bones. But it is hard to listen with petrified ears, I guess.' He laughed. Yes, the speaker was clearly human, but there was more warmth in the metallic voice. It had to be him. Cadoc Eelstrom. Twigleg shuddered. What would he do with him and Freddie?

At least they didn't have wings he could pluck out!

'So who are the others? I guess your wife and daughter?' he heard Eelstrom say. 'They will never age now. Isn't that generous of me? After you ruined so many attempts of mine to preserve my youth.'

The cruelty of his mockery was too much. Twigleg tried to free himself from Freddie's grasp, but his brother was too strong.

'Nice idea to plant those spiders on the beach,' Cadoc Eelstrom said. 'They took them up without any idea that we planted the perfect tracking tools on them. Not bad, Copper.'

'Thank you, sir.' There was something in the metallic voice. Twigleg knew it very well. His own voice had sounded like that when he'd talked to Nettlebrand. The metal man hated his master.

What does that matter now, Twigleg? He did something terrible to Ben and to his family. While you were hiding under a table!

'Why are you still staring at that boy? Come over here, Copper!' he heard Eelstrom call. 'It's a day troll! Can you bring him back to life? They are disgusting, but a powder made from their tongues is supposed to give power over trees and their magic.'

'No one can bring that troll back,' the metal voice answered.

'Neither him nor the others. Not for the next hundred years. Wasn't that what you wanted?'

'Yes. Yes, I guess I did. Let's go.'

The steps passed the doll's house once again. But then they sounded more and more distant. Until all Twigleg could hear was an owl screeching and coyotes yelping in the distance.

'I think they are gone, brother!' Freddie finally let him go. 'But we can't be out there! Not before the sun rises! I don't have my fork. The coyotes will get us. Or the owls. And I don't think there's anything we can do for the others.'

No. It didn't sound like it.

No one can bring that troll back. Neither him nor the others. Not for the next hundred years.

Twigleg felt his heart crack. But it didn't break – that was a good sign! No homunculus survived his master's death, if he loved him. And oh, he loved his master so very much! He pressed his hand to his chest. Yes, his heart was still beating. Ben Greenbloom was still alive.

'I don't care about the coyotes. Or the owls,' he said with a shaking voice. 'I have to find out what happened to them. There must be a way to get out of here!'

It was pitch-dark in the house, so he couldn't see his brother's face. But Freddie's voice was full of admiration when he finally spoke.

'As you wish,' he said. 'There is actually a trap door. I asked Hothbrodd to install it in my bedroom.'

The trap door opened without effort when Freddie pushed back the carpet he had covered it with. But underneath there was solid ground, dusty and baked by the sun. Twigleg got down on his knees and started digging, tears running down his face. Freddie knelt down beside him and started digging as well.

CHAPTER SEVENTEEN

ON MARY'S MOUNTAIN

Of course, Freddie was the first one to get out.

'Oh no!' Twigleg heard him whisper. 'Oh, no, oh, no!'

Twigleg felt fear like a stone in his stomach, and for a second he considered staying under the house and sparing himself the sight that made his brother utter such terrified words.

But he had to find out! Even if that sight would break his heart. After all, it was still beating.

Freddie pulled him on to his feet the moment he emerged from the tunnel they had dug, and flung his arms around him.

'We'll get them back!' he whispered into Twigleg's ears. 'I don't know how, but we'll get them back!'

The first thing he saw was the monster. Or what it had become again. It was a huge rock, its bared teeth just a pattern on the stone, its eyes holes in the moonlit surface. But then he saw what Freddie tried to shield him from. His master had thrown himself over the house that had kept them safe. He had wrapped his arms around it and his face was pressed against its walls. Twigleg approached the silent figure with trembling knees. One of Ben's hands had dug into the ground, each finger grey as stone. Twigleg was glad he couldn't see his face, for that would surely have made his poor heart burst into a thousand splinters. A hundred years. Twigleg sat down between his master's petrified fingers and pressed his hands on them. He could wait a hundred years. Why not? The coyotes would drop dead if they tried to eat him, from all the hatred and rage he held inside. Cadoc Eelstrom. Yes, they would drop dead taking just a bite of him.

Behind his master's petrified body he saw Vita and Guinevere, melted together, and behind them Barnabas and Hothbrodd, each nothing but a lump of stone, their faces stiff with terror. Well, in Hothbrodd's case stiff with rage.

A hundred years. They would pass. He had served Nettlebrand more than three centuries and survived it.

Freddie had found his fork. He held it like a spear while he was walking towards Guinevere. He stared up at her for quite a while. Then he bent and picked something up. And came back to Twigleg.

'Look, brother.' He pointed his tiny flashlight at a piece of crumbled paper. A flashlight, a knife, scissors . . . Freddie always

had those tools on him. He believed in being ready at all times for all kinds of situations. Maybe that wasn't so foolish after all. 'That's Vita's handwriting, isn't it?'

'It's the message.' Twigleg murmured while more tears were dripping from the tip of his nose. 'The message from the sea.' What did it matter now?

Freddie folded the paper nevertheless, until it fitted into his pocket. 'We'll get them back, brother! There's bound to be a way, and we'll find it.'

'What are you talking about? Didn't you hear that metal man? There *is* no way!'

The sound of his own shrill voice made Twigleg stir. It pierced the silence of the night with despair. *Well done, Twigleg! Tell the coyotes and the owls there are two desperate homunculi to snack on!* He pressed his hands on his face and began to sob. But that was no comfort either. His hands were slippery with his tears, as he pressed them against Ben's cold hand.

'Barnabas? Vita? Where are you?'

It took Twigleg's paralysed mind a few moments to recognise the voice, that was calling from somewhere above them. Alfonso. It was Alfonso Fuentes' voice!

'Here! We are here, *Señor* Fuentes!' Freddie yelled with his cricket voice. 'Down here!!'

The owl came for them immediately. Twigleg saw her white feathers lit by the moon. Freddie pushed him under his master's petrified body and aimed his fork with a grim expression at the attacking bird. Her sharp claws could tear them both to shreds like pages from a book. Twigleg closed his eyes. But instead of feeling the claws he heard Alfonso Fuentes' voice and then the voice of the owl, as if she was answering him. Twigleg opened one eye and saw the white wings high above him head for the stars.

'*Ah, pequeños Señores!*' Alfonso Fuentes sighed as he knelt down next to them. 'I fear I suggested a very dangerous camping ground. What a fool I was! A friend of mine told me many years ago that there was a monster sleeping amongst these rocks. But I thought she was just telling me a tale the tribes in these mountains used to tell. Just an old tale! But don't we all know they carry grains of truth in them?'

He lifted Freddie on to his shoulders and reached for Twigleg.

'No!' The homunculus pushed the helping hands away. 'I am staying with my master. He will wake. In a hundred years. And I will be here!'

Alfonso looked with great sadness at Ben's silent silhouette.

'*Señor* Twigleg,' he said. 'Your master wants you safe. Nothing can harm him at the moment, but the owls will eat you long before those hundred years have passed. Please come with me. I'll take you both to a place where you will be safe. And maybe we can come up with a plan to bring your master back much sooner than in a hundred years. *¡Vamos!*'

He once again held out his hand to Twigleg.

'Please, brother!' Freddie piped. 'You know Ben wouldn't want you to be owl food. They rip their prey's head off, did you know?'

Twigleg cast a glance at the sky. That was quite a troubling information. Well, his master probably didn't want that to be his fate. Twigleg slowly got up and touched Ben's hand one more time, before he climbed into Alfonso's.

'*Una noche oscura.* This was a dark night,' their saviour murmured as he walked from one Greenbloom to the other and finally stopped in front of Hothbrodd's petrified body. The troll had lifted his fist in anger as the monster's breath had enveloped him.

'We will find a way,' Alfonso said softly. 'A hundred years are far too long a time without one's friends.' He gently wiped the tears from Twigleg's face. '*Siempre hay esperanza.*'

He cast an encouraging glance at Twigleg on his left and Freddie on his right shoulder. 'Barnabas Greenbloom didn't come all the way to California to be a rock and stare down at the Pacific Ocean. Though I'm sure there are not many views that can compete with this place.'

He looked one more time at the petrified faces. Then he turned and walked with heavy steps back to the path that led up to his truck.

'It was Eelstrom!' Twigleg sobbed when Alfonso placed them on the passenger seat. 'I am sure! Cadoc Eelstrom and some kind of metal man. Lola was right! He's here!'

Lola! He had forgotten about her! Barnabas had sent her off to find out where Eelstrom was staying. Where was she? And what about those foolish bluelings who'd just wandered off? Whatever! He had other things to worry about.

'Everything will be fine, brother!' Freddie whispered, while they were both trying not to slip off Alfonso's truck seat. He took the curves of the road that was winding ahead of them through the night with breathtaking speed.

Everything will be fine? How could not even this night change Freddie's naïve belief in happy endings? *Well, Twigleg,* he heard Ben's voice calmly state, *your old master Nettlebrand tore off Freddie's leg and almost ate him. But he is still alive – and dancing! How could he not believe in happy endings?*

'Your brother is right, *Señor* Twigleg.' Alfonso Fuentes took the old truck around another bend as if he was driving a racing car. '*Todo será bien.*'

Twigleg tried really hard to believe him, but all he could

think of was his master's cold hand.

'We have to let the others in MÍMAMEIÐR know,' he mumbled. 'Oh, why didn't I try the communication system Hothbrodd installed?' *Because it was all trampled by a petrifying monster, Twigleg.* A tear stole down his nose.

'Is there by any chance a pond or lake nearby, Mr Fuentes?' Freddie asked.

'Yes! The friend I am taking you to has a wonderful pond,' Alfonso replied. 'It saved her and her dog during the big fire that burned these mountains in 1993.'

He put his foot on the brake and turned left on to an unpaved road that led to an open gate and past a withered wooden sign. The name on it was written in bold and colourful letters: *Mary Bright*.

'I really don't like it that we left my master and the others all alone at that terrible place, *Señor* Fuentes,' Twigleg whispered.

'*No se preocupe.* I'll send some of my men to watch over them,' Alfonso replied. 'But you and your brother will stay at Mary's.'

The narrow road led up through a rocky gorge. Twigleg spotted fossilised shells in the rocks – a reminder that millions of years ago the mountains around them had been on the ocean floor. When the road came out into the open the moon showed Twigleg fruit trees and a simple house, surrounded by a wide wooden porch and old oaks and sycamore trees. Far in the distance, like spilled liquid silver, the shimmering surface of the ocean met the night sky at the horizon

Alfonso parked his truck and put them both back on his shoulders.

'You will like my friend, *pequeños señores*,' he said, while he walked towards the steps that led up to the porch. 'There is no one quite like her.'

He knocked on the glass door that led into the house and peeked through the pane. 'Mary? *Lo siento!*' he called. 'I know it is late, but I need a safe place for two *amigos pequeños*.'

They didn't have to wait for long. Twigleg saw the lean figure of an old woman through the glass of the door. She wore a blue morning gown, and her grey braids reached all the way down to her hips.

'Alfonso!' she said, with a smile both for him and the two homunculi, as she opened the door. 'You bring magical guests, I see.'

Twigleg guessed Mary Bright to be about seventy years old, but her smile was the smile of a girl. (Mary was actually ninety-two years old, as he learned later.) She had a face tanned by a life under the southern sun, and it was lined by a thousand smiles. Mary Bright reminded Twigleg of Vita's old centaur friend Raskervint, though Mary seemed totally human. Her face showed the same wisdom and the same curiosity about everything life and the world brought her way.

'That sounds indeed like the tale the Chumash women shared with me, when they warned me of the rocks in these mountains,' she sighed, after Alfonso had told her what had happened. 'They told me about a huge monster that turned their warriors and many creatures into stone. But they always said it had been sleeping for at least a thousand years!'

'He woke it!' Freddie said. 'The metal man who serves Barnabas's old enemy. I don't know how, but he did!'

His words made Twigleg bury his face once again in his hands.

'The *pequeños señores* would like to use your pond, Mary,' Alfonso said. 'They want to inform their friends of what happened. I'm not sure I understand how they intend to do that, but would you mind?'

Mary didn't ask for further explanations. She placed Twigleg and Freddie on her shoulders and instructed them to hold on to her long grey braids. Then she carried them through the night, past wild cacti and coyote bush to a huge pond that reflected the stars amongst stone oak and rocks.

'Mary and I will keep watch while you do whatever you need to do,' Alfonso said, while Mary set the two homunculi down at the edge of the pond. 'Mary talks to the coyotes, but I don't trust them to listen, in case they consider you two for a meal.'

'Thank you!' Freddie said. 'I've been eaten before and it's really not a pleasant experience!'

Twigleg read from both Mary's and Alfonso's face that they would have loved to hear that story, but they took a respectful step back, as he approached the water.

A few tiny water nymphs were sitting on the lily pads, their wings catching the moonlight, and a froglike creature, its head resembling a coyote's, jumped from a stone into the water. Mary obviously shared her mountain with many creatures, some of

them clearly fabulous ones. His master would have loved her place! Sadness drowned Twigleg's heart as he stepped so close to the water that it soaked the tips of his boots.

'MÍMAMEIÐR!' he called. 'MÍMAMEIÐR! Twigleg calling!'

The pale face that appeared on the water belonged to one of the mushroomlings Gilbert had given the task to watch the water radio.

'Mouldy, get Gilbert! Fast! It's urgent!'

Mushroomlings don't do anything fast. But it actually didn't take that long before Gilbert Greytail's pointy face appeared. He looked quite annoyed, but MÍMAMEIÐR's rat cartographer got annoyed quite easily.

'It's about time you called!' he muttered. 'I've tried for hours to check in with Barnabas or Hothbrodd! I—'

'Gilbert!' Twigleg interrupted the rat. 'We have bad news!'

'Well, I have news as well,' Gilbert snapped. 'Though I don't know whether it's bad. I'm getting reports from everywhere, that somewhere in the Pacific Ocean someone is sending mysterious messag—'

'We received that message too!' Freddie piped. 'We were just going to decipher it, when—'

'They are stone!' Twigleg cut his brother short. 'Stone, Gilbert! All of them. My master, Vita, Barnabas, Guinevere and Hothbrodd!'

Gilbert Greytail nervously brushed his ears with his paws. That gesture always gave away that the usually very calm white rat was stressed. 'Stone? What do you mean?'

Freddie did a few sad dance steps. 'I fear those words describe their current state of existence quite precisely, Master Greytail.'

Gilbert feverishly brushed his white whiskers. 'Does that mean, you two are the only survivors of the FREEFAB team?'

'*Lo siento, Señor Rato.*' Alfonso knelt down next to the homunculi. 'Alfonso Fuentes,' he introduced himself. 'I am an old friend of Barnabas Greenbloom. We will do everything to bring him and his companions back to life.'

'Yes, we will!' Mary confirmed.

Gilbert scrutinised her and Alfonso with unveiled distrust.

'It seems you two made a lot of new friends over there,' he said to Twigleg. 'I hope you're not being too trusting.'

Twigleg cast Mary and Alfonso an apologetic glance. It was not in Gilbert's nature to be polite. 'This was not just bad luck, Gilbert! Do you know about Cadoc Eelstrom?'

The rat straightened up. 'What about him?'

'He's here!' Freddie exclaimed. 'He is the one who did this! He and some kind of metal man who serves him!'

'He is a Copperman,' Gilbert grimly replied. 'Lola can tell you more about him. Or was she turned into stone as well?'

'No. Barnabas sent her out to find out where Eelstrom is staying,' Twigleg said. 'We so hope she is still alive!'

'Well, I wouldn't worry too much. Lola is by far my toughest cousin,' Gilbert said. 'And I have three hundred and two of them. I'm glad, Firedrake is on his way to be the Courier of Fire – though he won't be pleased to hear about his dragon rider's fate! Shrii, one of the griffins, just agreed to represent Air. Eight, the Great Kraken who helped us a few times, is supposed to represent Water. I couldn't reach him yet, but hopefully with him there is more help coming your way.'

Firedrake. Of course! Twigleg had completely forgotten that Sorrel and he were on their way! He felt such a relief. Everything would be fine. The dragon always gave him that feeling.

His brother uttered that sentiment, of course, in his very own Freddie way.

'Firedrake!' he exclaimed, while his feet were dancing a thousand patterns into the wet ground. 'How could we forget he's coming, brother? Maybe dragon fire can break the stone spell? Or Firedrake can fight that metal man and force him to take the enchantment back. Or . . .'

He came up with another dozen foolish ideas, but Twigleg didn't listen. He only relished the relief and hope he felt. Yes. Everything would be fine. With Firedrake around it always was. Always!

Alfonso straightened up. '*Un dragón*. Did you hear that, Mary?' he said. 'Days of magic!'

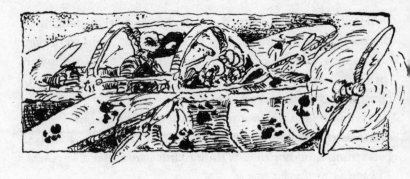

CHAPTER EIGHTEEN

HIS ALONE

Lola was alive, and she hadn't been turned into stone. But she had got herself into a different kind of trouble.

She had found the house Cadoc Eelstrom had rented without much effort. It was by far the hugest mansion looking down on the beach where the Aurelia would deliver her pods.

'He is such a boringly predictable villain!' Lola muttered, while she flew past the huge glass sliding doors that faced the sea, keeping a safe distance from the surveillance cameras she spotted everywhere.

She was just wondering whether she should try to get in, when a spotless white Land Cruiser pulled up in front of the house, and the Copperman and Cadoc Eelstrom climbed out. Lola didn't like the look on his face. No, she didn't like it at all. Cadoc Eelstrom looked triumphant.

Since Lola worked for FREEFAB, Barnabas had asked her often to check on his old enemy – not always an easy task, as Eelstrom liked to hide underground like a pale-blonde mole – but Lola had always found a way. Thanks to her reports they

had saved a sky serpent
in Guatemala, a fossegrim
in Sweden and a swarm
of will-o'-the-wisp in
England from him and
Lola had had the pleasure to
see Eelstrom's freakishly boyish face look quite
sullen and brooding over his failed endeavours.

But not today!

He walked towards the pompous mansion he'd rented, as if
the world was his. His alone.

'That's not good,' Lola murmured. 'Not good at all. What did
the little slime-head do?'

The Copperman cast a glance at the roof she had landed on,
while he was following his master. Not even Barnabas and Vita
knew much about his species. It was a very mysterious one. How
was their hearing? Their sight in the dark? Could they read
thoughts like some basilisks? The Copperman's stare always
reminded Lola of those abominable creatures. But there was
sadness too in those eyes – and anger.

Too many thoughts, while hiding on a dangerous enemy's
roof! She should have known better.

Lola suddenly heard a hum behind her. No, not one, hundreds.
They were all around her plane. Wasps or something that
resembled them. But they weren't striped. They were solid
copper and they were swarming so densely around her plane,
that her propeller sputtered when she tried to start her engine.
Their compact little metal bodies pressed against her windows,
their wings beat against the glass and several shiny stings pushed
through her ceiling like sabres.

Done! Lola thought, as she once again started the engine in vain. *Killed by a swarm of copper wasps. What a stupid way to die, Lola Greytail!*

Below her the Copperman was still standing in front of the house, while his master had long disappeared inside. And yes, he was staring up at her. *You got past my starlings far too often, rat,* his eyes said, *so I had to come up with other guardians.*

Oh, yes, the starlings in Eelstrom's English fortress . . . they weren't much fun actually, with their sharp beaks, but these wasps were much more annoying.

The humming around her was deafening by now and more and more stings pushed through the chassis of her plane. But just when Lola wondered whether she should jump out and fight them all, her engine finally answered her desperate efforts, and the propeller kicked in.

Oh, how she loved her plane! Her fierce and fearless indestructible plane! It chopped through the wasps and carried her up, although it was still surrounded by their humming bodies. The wasps followed Lola like a shimmering cloud, the moonlight reflecting on their wings and bodies. They pushed her towards the open sea. Of course – they wanted to drown her! She tried to turn the plane, but the wasps didn't give her a chance, and soon she found herself above the ocean, the waves breaking underneath her against the rocks and shore and Cadoc Eelstrom's mansion sitting on the cliff above, all windows darkened by blinds except for one. Was that silhouette behind the sliding glass door his or the Copperman's? The wasps blocked Lola's view, before she could tell.

Her engine began to sputter and her propeller stopped to spin, crushed by all those wings. Down her plane went, down towards the rushing waves. Oh, this would be a rough emergency landing! The wasps withdrew as she hit the water, and Lola saw the swarm heading back to their master's lair, while her plane was helplessly bopping up and down on the waves like a message in a bottle – with a rat inside instead of a letter.

The water began to seep in through the holes the stings had punched, salty and cold.

No. No, this was definitely not the death Lola Greytail had wished for! Drowned? The only flying rat on Earth?

She kicked the door open and pushed herself into the open. What now? Should she try to swim? She cast a glance over the water, scanning it for shark fins, when a head appeared from the waves, right in front of her. The eyes looked human, but the skin certainly did not. It resembled the surface of a starfish. As did the three arms that emerged from the water and gently grabbed her plane.

'You look to me like a friend of the Greenblooms,' her saviour said. 'Am I right? I admit I've never met a pilot rat before. But neither have I seen a swarm of copper wasps on this coast until tonight and I've lived here for several thousand years. I have to say I didn't like the look or sound of them.' Another arm emerged from the water and shook Lola's paw. 'Elewese. Formerly Chumash. Currently starfish.'

'Lola Greytail. Much obliged!' Lola called into the roar of the waves.

'I can carry you and your plane to the beach, if you like?' Elewese carefully pushed a few crushed wasps off the windscreen. 'I fear it is not in shape to get you there. Looks like it needs some serious repairs.'

Lola sadly had to agree with the starfish man's verdict.

She cast a glance at the wings and bodies the ocean was carrying away.

Yes, they definitely resembled copper.

CHAPTER NINETEEN

TOO LATE?

Yes. Firedrake would arrive, and all would be fine. Twigleg had repeated it so often, while he was sitting on Mary's porch, that it was a constant murmur in his head by now. The bluelings had come back unharmed from their expedition, and Twigleg had to admit that it was quite impressive how they had tracked them all the way to Mary's. They were resilient fellows – and as arrogant as peacocks! Freddie had given them a vivid report of what had happened, but they had listened with unimpressed faces. 'Well, it's a wild world,' one of them had murmured. 'Shame you didn't bring our suitcase. And then . . . they had asked Mary whether they could build themselves a cabin under her porch. Twigleg could hear them hammering down there right now.

Shame you didn't bring our suitcase! He and Freddie hadn't even brought their own house! Why hadn't those bluelings made the monster small, as Barnabas claimed they did with rats and possums? 'We were on a hike when it came, have you forgotten?' the smaller one had snapped, when Twigleg had asked.

No, Twigleg didn't like them. He wouldn't have minded at all if they'd been turned into stone as well!

Alfonso had left to check on his men and Mary was making breakfast in the house – after she'd asked them what homunculi liked to eat. *Twigleg, make yourself useful,* he told himself, *or all you'll think about will be* . . . No! He wouldn't go there!

Freddie had left the note that Vita had written next to the plate of pancakes Mary had brought. Twigleg climbed on to the table and smoothened it with his hands. Maybe he could at least prove himself useful by deciphering the mysterious message!

Naia to Fufluns! She sings where Momi sleeps! Heading hikina.

Fufluns was Barnabas, as Vita had told them on the beach, and Naia was Lizzie Persimmons, the friend Barnabas believed to be dead. Which she clearly wasn't, unless someone had stolen her nickname. *She sings* . . . that probably referred to the Aurelia. But who was Momi? And *hikina*?

Freddie was dancing between Mary's geranium pots, of course. He had been dancing since sunrise. 'It helps me think, brother!' he had replied softly, when asked how he could still dance in a situation like this. Twigleg yearned for his ear corks. But suddenly a very familiar sound drowned out Freddie's relentless tapping: the sound of a plane propeller.

It sputtered and stopped, and a voice, that brought almost as much comfort as the knowledge that Firedrake was on his way, called:

'Humclupuuuses! Where, tigered cats and howling dogs, are you?'

Freddie shot out from between the flowerpots as fast as a lizard.

'Lola! You're alive!' he shrilled. 'Where have you been? We were so worried!

How could he yell all that while jumping down Mary's porch steps? With a wooden leg?

'Well, it is even a surprise for me that I am still alive, humclopus brother!' Lola announced, while she climbed out of her plane. It looked . . . different. Patched up, and with a shiny new propeller.

'I was brought down!' she said, after she'd escaped Freddie's hugs. 'Brought down by a swarm of wasps. It was quite something! And then a Chumashed starfish-man saved me from drowning and sent out a seagull to let Alfonso know I needed a few parts to repair my plane.'

She climbed up Mary's steps and sat down on the edge of the porch with an exhausted sigh.

'I admit I was glad, when I didn't see that beach any more and that mansion with Eelstrom and the Copperman lurking in it! Rat-murdering lowlifes!'

'So you found the house, where Eelstrom stays?' Twigleg asked, his voice shaking.

'Of course! Alfonso told me what those brutes did last night! That's why those rat-killers looked so damn pleased with themselves when they came back to their beach palace!'

Mary stepped out of the house with a breakfast tray.

Lola smiled up at her. 'Hello. Do you by any chance have any coffee for a rat who has just narrowly escaped a wet grave? Lots of sugar, no milk?'

'Of course,' Mary said. 'I assume you are Lola, the rat my guests were quite worried about. I'm glad you're safe.'

'So am I!' Lola sighed, lying back and closing her eyes as Mary walked into the house again to get her a coffee. 'Heavens, I'm really not myself,' the rat murmured. 'Those wasps nearly sank me! One of their damn stings actually scratched my shoulder. Maybe that's why I can barely keep my eyes open.'

'Lola,' Freddie sat down next to her, 'what is a Copperman?'

'No one quite knows,' Lola muttered. 'They're quite elusive. But this one is a deviously inventive creature, that's for sure. No idea how he made those wasps.'

Mary came back with a shot glass filled with coffee and placed it by Lola's side. The rat opened her eyes and gave her a grateful smile.

'And he was able to wake an ancient petrifying monster!' Twigleg took one of the tiny toast pieces Mary had served them with home-made jam. But he couldn't get it down. His stomach was filled with too much sadness.

'Firedrake is on his way and Lola escaped!' Freddie spun around with outstretched arms and added another pirouette. 'So we have no reason to lose hope!'

That was one dose too much of his relentless optimism.

'Well, what if Firedrake is turned into stone as well?' Twigleg exclaimed. 'And if we couldn't protect ourselves from Eelstrom, how are we supposed to protect the Aurelia from him? We didn't even manage to decipher that ominous message . . .'

Lola sat up and took a sip from the shot glass. 'What message?'

Freddie climbed on to the table and came back with Vita's transcript.

Lola read it first with a frown, then a smile. 'Freddie, carry on dancing! That's all good news. Very good news and totally unexpected!'

Freddie cast Twigleg a triumphant look, as if Lola had just delivered the final proof that his optimistic approach to life was always right.

'So . . .' Twigleg couldn't quite hide his irritation as his brother began to tap-dance all along the porch. 'Would you enlighten us, Lola? What does it mean?'

Lola took another sip of coffee. 'Well, first of all, we now have proof that Lizzie Persimmons is very much alive! Which is amazing news. Although I have no idea how she can be so deep underwater that she can watch the Aurelia.'

The rat stuffed two bits of toast between her teeth and licked the jam off her nose. 'Barnabas never stopped blaming himself for her death. He will be very happy to have that guilt off his conscience. Well, at the moment he probably doesn't feel it, being stone and all, right?' She giggled.

Lola's humour was something Twigleg found hard to appreciate at times.

'Anyway . . . the rest of the message is as clear as water,' she continued. 'The Aurelia is on her way! She's passed Momi, near Molokai, one of the Hawaiian islands. And *hikina* means east, of course. In Hawaiian.'

Of course. Twigleg blushed in embarrassment. His Hawaiian had always been flawed.

'Your brother is right, humplucipus!' Lola punched his shoulder with her grey paw. 'I'm alive. Lizzie's alive! And the Aurelia heads in this direction, as we predicted. This is all excellent news! Now we just have to un-stone our friends.'

Mary was leaning in her doorway behind them. She had listened to Lola's last words with an unusually grave expression on her face. 'When does your dragon friend arrive again?' she asked softly.

Twigleg looked at her in alarm. 'In about two days. What is it?'

'Oh, nothing.' She turned. She knew she was a bad liar.

'Mary! What's wrong? Please!'

Mary gave off a sigh and looked up into the trees surrounding her house as if she hoped for help from them.

'The Chumash,' she finally said, 'believed the spell of the monster could only be broken within forty-eight hours. By then it reaches the heart and lasts, as you said, for a hundred years. I just hope your dragon comes in time.'

She gave Twigleg a sad smile. *By then it reaches the heart . . .*

Twigleg jumped up and down the porch steps.

'Where are you going?' Freddie called after him.

But Twigleg was already running past the coyote bushes and gopher holes, through the dry grass and over the sun-baked ground towards Mary's pond, its water shimmering under the blue sky. The red-tailed hawks were circling up there, but what did it matter if they or the rattlesnakes ate him. His master was lifeless! Well, actually, Twigleg thought, while he was jumping over a lizard's tail, he would prefer an owl to just tear off his head to a snake.

'Hey! Humpclumpulus!' Lola's voice shrilled behind him. 'What do you think you're doing? Don't exploit the fact that this rat is tired from fighting murderous wasps! This is not a place where small creatures like you can stroll around alone!'

Small? She was smaller than he! But yes, Twigleg had to admit that Lola's fighting skills were far superior to his. He, in fact, didn't have any skills of that kind.

'Brother! Wait!'

Of course. Freddie had come too. And he probably didn't worry at all about being eaten.

'Didn't you hear what Mary said?' Twigleg called over his

shoulder. 'No, you were probably too busy dancing and drinking coffee!'

'I heard her loud and clear.' Lola had almost caught up with him. How could she be so fast, although she was quite a stout rat? Twigleg jumped over a gopher hole. Someone should tell Mary to pour peppermint oil into these holes. *They are everywhere! There must be thousands of them.* Twigleg ran faster. Mary's pond looked even larger in daylight, and he froze as he saw the slender white silhouette of an egret standing in the water. His beak was almost as long as Twigleg measured from head to toe. But Lola flapped her arms and shrieked so loud that the huge bird spread his wings and flew away.

'Firedrake!' Twigleg was terribly out of breath as he leaned over the water. 'Firedrake!' he gasped. 'Sorrel! Anyone! Helloooooo! Please! Please! Can anyone hear me?'

The pond flickered in the sun, and a red dragonfly flew up from a reed.

'This is not how it works, brother,' Freddie put his hand on his shoulder. 'Remember? You can talk through water from anywhere to MÍMAMEIÐR because of the device we built. But without that, just from pond to p—'

'Nettlebrand was able to do it! Why not us?' Twigleg exclaimed. 'Maybe it just needs some practice! And . . .'

An image formed on the water. Furry, with pointed ears.

'Twigleg?' Sorrel's eyes narrowed with surprise. 'What, death caps and puffershroom? Can a brownie not wash her face in peace without you showing up?'

'Sorrel!' Twigleg had never been so happy to see the brownie. In fact, he usually wasn't, as they were not too fond of each other. 'It works! I made it work! You can see me, right? And hear me?'

'Loud and clear. Sadly.' Sorrel blew her nose in a leaf. 'What do you want? Firedrake is asleep. It's a long flight and I have to make sure he gets his breaks. So don't . . .'

'Who are you talking to, Sorrel?' Firedrake's head appeared behind her on the water. 'Twigleg! Did something happen?'

'Yes!' Freddie yelled over Twigleg's shoulder. 'Someone petrified the Greenblooms. A terrible human! His name is Cad—'

Firedrake pushed Sorrel aside. 'Where is Ben?'

'He's all grey and cold!' Twigleg sobbed. 'And soon the stone will reach his heart and then all is lost for a hundred years!'

He couldn't get any more words out. Lola gently pushed him aside. 'They hope your fire will help. How soon will you get here, Firedrake?'

'Day after tomorrow,' Sorrel said. 'He shouldn't fly by day, and he needs to take breaks, so . . .'

'Tonight,' Firedrake corrected her. 'I'll be there tonight.'

Sorrel scowled at Twigleg. *Your fault!* Her cat-eyes said. *Your fault if humans see him, or the flight exhausts him.*

'Tonight,' Firedrake repeated. 'Get on my back, Sorrel.'

CHAPTER TWENTY

WOULD HE DARE?

Light. Damn, there was too much light. It seeped through the white walls of the house Cadoc had rented – for an absurd amount of money – through the blinds and the cracks around the doors. Why didn't they have basements in this miserable part of the world?

He rubbed another portion of sunblock into his white skin. Ah, it hurt! That expedition into the mountains had burned him like a lobster. But to see his enemies reduced to a few pathetic rocks had been worth the sunburn, and he'd drunk two extra portions of fairy dust, although he had to shake them very hard by now to get anything out of them. Cadoc touched the birthmark behind his ear. His nanny had once told him that fairy spit had planted it there, and that such a mark was proof he was a changeling. For quite a while he had therefore considered himself an abandoned, and of course immortal, fairy offspring – until his father had learned about it and ridiculed him. Since then he had somehow accepted he was human. And mortal. But that might change soon. He dipped some sunscreen on to the mark and smiled at his reflection. The thought of being a changeling still intrigued him. They were considered quite devious, cunning creatures, weren't they?

He smiled one more time at his reflection and turned his back on the mirror.

Beaten. Barnabas Greenbloom was beaten and gone. Well, at least for the next hundred years. He would have to deal with him again, if the Aurelia's pod really made him immortal. But who cared? Copper would be his slave for eternity and he would be sure to come up with something if his old enemy should stir again. Now he could finally concentrate on the Aurelia. Underwater preparations were on the way, and the beach would be ready soon. It would be a walk in the park. Shame he hadn't gotten that troll's tongue, but maybe in a hundred years. Something to look forward to!

Cadoc chuckled while he inspected the braidmaid he had ordered Copper to catch for him. He had spotted quite a few interesting creatures as he had walked the beach last night to give Copper instructions on how to secure the Aurelia's arrival. For a moment he had even suspected the seals on the rocks to be selkie. But that was highly improbable in such warm waters. He had always wished to get his hands on one of them to find out exactly how that skin worked, but they were fierce and evasive.

The braidmaid bared her teeth when he knocked against the glass of the aquarium Copper had dropped her in. He would have him catch more of them. The magic of their ingeniuous tails was supposed to make rope or any kind of fabric unbreakable. One of the many useful things Barnabas Greenbloom had written about. Cadoc walked over to the table by the window and affectionately ran his hand over the three notebooks he had placed next to his computer. They looked so shabby and faded on the white marble desk, and still they were his most treasured possession. He had managed to steal four of Barnabas's notebooks. The fool had always kept them under his school desk – to scribble into them, when he thought no one was watching.

Oh, Barnabas. He was too good for this world. He always had been.

That son of his though . . . there was something about him. Copper had noticed it too. He felt strangely interested in the boy . . .

Cadoc rang the bell he called him with. Just a small copper bell. That's how one kept them close and on alert.

'Sir?' His strangely flat face had patterns on the cheeks and forehead that looked as if someone had drilled them in. Swirling lines that resembled ancient patterns on withered Druid stones. That face rarely gave anything away, but up on that mountain Cadoc had seen something there. Something resembling hope. Hope for what?

'That boy – Barnabas Greenbloom's son . . . Why did you stare at him the way you did? Up on the mountain?'

Copper lowered his gaze. But he had to answer him. He couldn't lie to him, could he?

'He was so young. I pitied him.'

Nonsense. Coppermen were astonishingly sentimental. But *that* much?

Cadoc walked towards him until he stood right in front of him. Copper was such a giant that he had to look up to him, but that made the feeling of having power over such a mighty creature only more exhilarating.

'You shouldn't lie to me, Copper. I always find out,' he purred. 'I can order you to step into that ocean down there and you will have to do it, although it will burn your skin. Don't tempt me. What did you sense about that boy? Although he was solid stone?'

'It is as I said.' The metal eyes met his gaze. 'I pitied him. I lost a brother at that age.'

Cadoc held him with his gaze. Maybe he told the truth. Copper was not a fool after all.

'Go,' he finally said. 'Catch me a few more of those braidmaids.'

CHAPTER TWENTY-ONE

DROPPING BY

The sky was still so blue. It just wouldn't turn dark. Would Firedrake keep his promise? What if Sorrel convinced him that it was too dangerous to fly during the day? Twigleg looked over to Mary, who was telling Freddie and Lola how to best talk to rattlesnakes. And how to make pancakes from the wild buckwheat that grew on her land. All very useful, he was sure, but right now he could not think of anything but his master so cold and lifeless, just another stone bleached by the sun. By now the hatred Twigleg felt for Cadoc Eelstrom and his copper-skinned helper burned inside him like a fever.

Mary came over to the bench he was sitting on, her face soft with compassion.

'How about a little road trip, Twigleg?' she asked. 'Alfonso went into the mountains to meet someone he believes to be the perfect courier for Earth, and his men are watching our petrified friends. Why don't we make ourselves useful and drop by the house where this Eelstrom resides?'

'Drop by?' Twigleg gave her a look both desperate and

hopeful. 'And then?'

Mary smiled. 'Freddie and I have a few ideas on that. They know Lola, so I suggest you stay with her hidden in my car while Freddie and I execute our plan. Are you ready, my little friend?'

'Ready!' Freddie confirmed, while his feet began tapping expectantly.

'Good,' Mary said. 'Let's get in the car!'

Freddie wouldn't reveal what he and Mary had in mind as they drove down to the sea. Lola navigated Mary to a narrow street where the houses on the left all overlooked the ocean. The house she pointed at was a huge modern block where all the windows were closed by blinds. Mary parked just a few metres further down and Twigleg and Lola watched from the backseat, as she got out of the car with a basket in her hand and walked towards the massive entrance door.

Twigleg had foolishly expected the Copperman to open the door. But he did not of course show up. After all, most humans didn't even know about his existence. It was a young maid who opened up when Mary rang the bell, with raven-black hair and a guarded smile. She clearly didn't know what to make of the old woman with the long grey braids, who was suddenly standing in front of her employer's door. Twigleg could hear Mary say that she was collecting donations for the California Wildlife Centre (something Mary actually did quite often). The girl shook her head. No, her evil master certainly didn't make any donations for injured wild creatures. But Mary kept her in the open door by chatting about wounded seals and owls sick from rat poison . . .

What was this all about?

As Mary pointed at the sky to distract the maid from what happened below, Twigleg watched alarmed as Freddie quickly sneaked out of the basket that Mary had set down on the doorstep. He slipped so closely past the maid's legs that Twigleg's heart nearly stopped, and the next moment he had vanished into the house.

No, no! This was far too risky. But of course Freddie had been all for it! What if the maid closed the door before he was back? What if the Copperman caught and squashed him? Freddie knew very well, why he hadn't told him about their plan. Twigleg would have strongly opposed such recklessness! After all he was quite fond of Freddie – very fond, actually, and he really didn't want to be without a brother again!

The maid was laughing about something Mary said about baby skunks. *Good. Keep that door open.*

Freddie was taking an awfully long time, wasn't he?

Because they had caught him! Yes! Of course! And he would be without a master *and* without a brother. Curse this place! Curse the New World and all its wildness! Even the Indonesian jungle felt tame compared with it!

Twigleg felt Lola's paw on his shoulder. She sensed, of course, how close he was to a heart attack.

The girl laughed once again, and there! Something scurried past her legs and disappeared into Mary's bag.

Just in time.

The maid's face froze and she looked over her shoulder. A dark silhouette had emerged in the hallway. She closed the door very abruptly, and Mary picked up her bag and walked back to her car.

With a smile.

'That was terribly reckless!' Twigleg whispered, as Mary opened the car door and set the bag on the back seat. 'What if she'd closed the door?'

'Well, she didn't,' Mary replied with a smile and got behind the steering wheel, while Freddie crawled out of the bag.

'Mission accomplished?' Mary asked glancing at him through her back mirror.

'Mission accomplished!' Freddie beamed. 'Twelve of Lola's listening bugs on the loose in Eelstrom's house. And, Lola! Did you know Eelstrom has a manticore in there? Luckily he didn't see me! But I nearly felt his whiskers as he walked past me.'

He smiled a wide smile.

'Good to know!' Lola said. 'I was not sure Eelstrom had brought him. Well done, Freddie. You are excellent spy material!'

'You were not sure?' Twigleg exclaimed. 'A manticore is not to be trifled with! And you didn't even warn Freddie of the possibility?'

'Relax, humclipus,' Lola purred while she winked at Freddie. 'Your brother handled it.'

She climbed up the passenger seat and waved at the mansion while Mary was driving away from it.

'Take this, Cadoc Eelstrom!' Lola hissed with a grim smile. 'You will regret the day you set those copper wasps on Lola Greytail!'

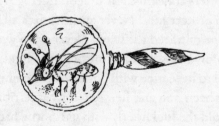

CHAPTER TWENTY-TWO

FIRE AND STONE

The moonlight reflected brightly on Firedrake's scales as he landed in Mary's yard. The sight of him took even the bluelings' breath away, and Alfonso and Mary smiled at the dragon, as if he had brought proof that there would always be magic and light in the world. Firedrake greeted them all: Mary and Alfonso, Twigleg and Freddie, Lola and the bluelings, while Sorrel climbed off his back. But there was only one person on the dragon's mind. Firedrake's wings were aching from how fiercely he had fought the winds. He had taken no breaks, despite Sorrel's concerns. His dragon rider . . . he hadn't been by his side to protect him! Never again! That's all he'd been thinking while he outraced the wind. Never again would he allow the boy to go on a mission like this without him. Yes, it had been wonderful to have time with Sorrel, to remember the years when it had just been him and her. But at what terrible price?

'Why did the fool not fly with us?' Sorrel had exclaimed after they'd received the bad news. Firedrake had of course not told her the truth. It would have devastated her, for although she teased and challenged Ben all the time, she loved him almost as much as Firedrake did.

'Where is he?' He cast a glance at the mountains surrounding Mary's humble house. They were little more than hills compared to the mountains he came from but nevertheless they felt almost as wild.

'Yes, where is he? Fool of a boy!' Sorrel stretched her tired limbs. 'I'm sure we broke the record for dragon speed. Twigleg!' She waved the homunculus impatiently to her side. 'I guess you want to come with us?'

Twigleg nodded and ran towards her.

'Don't you two need a rest?' Lola asked. 'You've just flown around the world!'

'I need my dragon rider, Lola,' Firedrake replied. 'I promise you, he's all I need.'

The homunculus knew how he felt. Firedrake saw it in Twigleg's eyes. His small heart felt as sore as his own with longing. And anger.

'Okay!' Lola gave him another concerned look. 'Who contradicts a dragon? And I'm sure you won't need the help of a tired rat. We planted spy bugs in the house of the enemy we're dealing with. Freddie and I will be listening to their reports, while you go and unpetrify the others. Once they are back, we'll hopefully know more about Eelstrom's devious plans and can jump into action!'

Once they are back . . .

Mary still couldn't take her eyes off Firedrake as Alfonso walked to his truck to show him the way. Dragons have that effect. Maybe because there is so much light in them. And so much kindness paired with strength.

Firedrake followed the truck, flying high enough to hide in

the night. It comforted Twigleg to hear the dragon's wings softly beating the air, while he clung to Sorrel's fur. Firedrake's mind though was racing. What if his fire didn't work? It hadn't freed the dragons they had found at the Rim, encased in stone, because they'd been without moonlight. *That's different, Firedrake!* he told himself! *They were stone for hundreds of years!*

Still . . . the question burned in his mind. What if his fire didn't work?

Alfonso was still making his way down the steep path when Firedrake landed among the rocks that had once been his friends. Alfonso's men backed away from him in awe, but their faces showed the same enchantment as Mary's as Firedrake walked past them to find his dragon rider.

The beast that had turned Ben to stone was nothing but a lifeless lump of rock. Firedrake smelled that it had returned to a sleep as deep and old as the mountains around him. What if Ben slept as deeply as that?

Firedrake barely dared to bend over his hunched figure. The sight was terrible. But his heart melted with relief as he sensed life in the petrified body.

'He tried to protect me and Freddie!' Twigleg had climbed up his neck. 'He put himself between the beast and us. Please! You need to bring him back.'

The homunculus knelt down between Firedrake's horns and began to sob.

'I will try my best, Twigleg!' the dragon said while he lifted his head to look at the others. They were still alive as well. Firedrake sensed that especially strong from Guinevere. Vita and Hothbrodd seemed fine too. The monster's breath had hit Barnabas the hardest.

Firedrake turned once again to Ben's crouched body. It

seemed long ago that he'd told him in the safety of the Rim that his body was changing. Would that help – or would it prevent his fire having any effect on him? There was only one way to find out.

Firedrake's mighty shadow fell on his petrified rider and wiped the moonlight off Ben's grey features.

'I should have been by your side,' he whispered. 'Let's take this as proof that a dragon rider and his dragon should never part ways.'

He let Twigleg climb back along his neck and on to Sorrel's shoulder. Then he took a step back and stretched his neck. He breathed his fire very softly on to the body of the boy he held so dear. It was merely the blue shadow of a flame that escaped his mouth and enveloped Ben with dancing sparks. They dyed the night blue and attached themselves one by one to the boy's body, while Firedrake's scales caught the light of the moon and shone like a thousand stars that had taken the shape of a dragon.

A hint of colour emerged from the grey on Ben's back. Then his fingers suddenly looked like human skin again. Firedrake spread his wings to give the flame more breath and power and his light filled the night.

'See?' Sorrel whispered to Twigleg. 'No need to worry when you have a dragon on your side!'

A sigh of relief escaped Firedrake's chests when Ben moved his right hand and he rose to his knees with a moan. There was still some grey in his face but it disappeared as soon as he flung his arms around Firedrake's head and pressed his face against the dragon's.

'Sorrel thinks you were a fool for not flying with us,' Firedrake whispered into his ear. 'So no more foolish ideas like that. And now get up, dragon rider. We need to take care of the others.'

Firedrake gently pushed Ben until he stood on his feet and stared at the house he had sheltered with his body. 'The others!

Of course!' he murmured. 'Twigleg! Freddie!'

'We're fine, master!' Twigleg climbed down from Sorrel's shoulder as fast as a spider. He flung his arms around Ben's leg and looked up at him with the widest and most relieved smile his face had ever worn. 'How are you?'

Ben lifted him up and nodded like someone who'd woken from a very bad dream. 'I guess I'm fine.' He looked around and froze again when he saw . . .

'Guinevere! My parents! Hothbrodd! What happened?'

Firedrake's fire brought Guinevere and Vita quite quickly back to life. Hothbrodd stirred the moment the first sparks hit his petrified skin. But Barnabas had stepped right in the monster's path to protect Vita and Guinevere and though the dragon fire broke layer after layer of greyness, he still wouldn't stir.

'What is it, Sorrel?' Ben asked, while Firedrake kept wrapping his father's silhouette in blue fire. 'Why is he taking so long?'

Sorrel put her furry arm around his shoulders. 'He took part of the petrifying spell that was meant for Vita and Guinevere. As

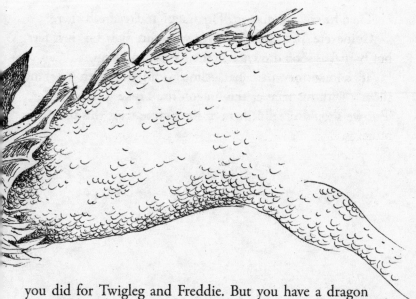

you did for Twigleg and Freddie. But you have a dragon rider's strength now. Your father doesn't. He only has the biggest heart. Which sadly doesn't grant much protection in this world. On the contrary.'

Firedrake breathed another shower of sparks.

'I'll kill him!' Hothbrodd growled, while rubbing his skin as if he needed to get the last remains of stone out. 'I'll tear him apart like a beetle. Hear my words. Cadoc Eelstrom is dead.'

'I'll help you,' Ben said. Firedrake saw an anger on his face that he'd never seen there before.

'There!' Twigleg exclaimed. 'There! His face!'

'Yes!' Guinevere, still leaning on her mother, gave off a deep, deep sigh of relief. And then she laughed. 'Of course! He heard us talk about killing! He doesn't like that!'

Barnabas gave off a deep moan while he lifted his hands. He stared at them as if he had never seen them before. 'Kill who?' he said hoarsely. 'What happened?'

Then he saw the dragon. 'Firedrake? You're already here?'

Guinevere, Ben and Vita were still quite slow on their feet, but Barnabas soon drowned in their kisses and hugs.

'It's a long story, Barnabas,' Alfonso said; he'd been watching silently with his men as the dragon fire broke very old magic. 'But we shouldn't tell it here. I don't quite trust this place any more.'

CHAPTER TWENTY-THREE

SOMETHING NEVER FELT BEFORE

Copper felt something strange. He had sensed it for the first time when he had seen the petrified boy. But near him it had just been a faint scent . . . the scent of fire magic, so bright and powerful that only one creature on earth had ever been able to wield it. He'd called himself foolish to even allow the thought that this kind of magic still existed – and with it the hope that one day he might be free. Hope was twice a terrible thing. Terrible when one had to live without it, terrible when it was crushed. But then last night there hadn't been just a faint scent. Oh, no. It had been a storm. The stars had turned into silver scales and he had dreamed of blue fire. Could it be?

No. The dragons were gone.

'Haven't the squids found the Aurelia by now? Copper! What's wrong with you? Maybe the sea air is eating your brain.'

His master had grabbed another fairy and was squeezing her like a dried-up lemon. They wouldn't last much longer, and it wouldn't be easy to find new ones. Moss fairies had been rare before his master had taken a fancy to exploiting their magic. Soon none would be left and Cadoc Eelstrom would begin to age. Stolen youth vanished fast. A month, maybe two, and his skin would reveal all the lines his greed had drawn. His hair would turn grey or fall out. Copper had to admit he would have loved to watch the years his enslaver had stolen melt away. But in less than a week the Aurelia would arrive, and he would have to help Eelstrom steal immortality from her. And make himself a slave for all eternity.

Cursed. How that word bit and hissed. No dream of blue flames or a boy's strange fiery scent would save him.

'No,' Copper replied. 'No, the squid are still looking for her. But they will find her.'

The pale-blue eyes covered his skin with frost. 'The consequences will be severe for you if they don't. What about the beach?'

Copper detected a few lines around the thin-lipped mouth. They looked strange on the boyish face. He was ageing. Which made him of course even more impatient. If only he could tell the squid not to find the Aurelia! But he had to follow his orders. Although they meant eternal misery for him. Like a copper puppet on a string . . .

'It's too early to release the worms,' he said. 'They dig themselves deep into the sand, and I don't want to lose control over them. But I'll do it soon.'

How he stared at him. He was still not sure whether his slave was able to betray him. *Do you really think I would still be here if I could?* he thought. *Do you think I would live with your foul smell and serve your rotten heart, Cadoc Eelstrom?*

'The Greenblooms are gone,' he said. 'Who else should get in your way? No one knows about the Aurelia. This world is blind.'

'I am tired of waiting.' Eelstrom pushed the moss fairy back into the cage and cast a disappointed glance at the dust he had extracted. 'This is the one fabulous creature who can't escape me! Yes, she may get angry, but who cares. Those pods are worth the risk. I'm sure those tales about what she'll do are just the usual apocalyptic fantasies, told to discourage bold endeavour.'

He pulled the gloves from his boyish hands and turned his back on Copper.

'Not sure if you know the grisly details of those tales,' he said over his shoulder. 'They claim that the Aurelia will take you all with her, if someone tries to harm her or steal her pods. Every fabulous creature still in existence. As I said . . . apocalyptic non-sense. I look forward to having you in my service for eternity. After all, I instructed you to build those squid in a way that they can snip those pods off the Aurelia's arms before she even notices they are gone.'

His laugh always gave away how pleased he was with himself.

Copper stared at his enslaver's back. *They claim that the Aurelia will take you all with her.* Take them where? Would they just disappear into the ocean with her? Or dissolve in thin air? *All of them, Copper. And you will have helped him.* There was only one comfort in that thought – that he would disappear too.

He closed his eyes.

Outside the waves were whispering about the Aurelia. And Copper sensed it again: fire magic. So strong it was as if he could feel its warmth on his skin. Where did it come from? Not from the ocean. No. It came from the mountains.

CHAPTER TWENTY-FOUR

AN UNLIKELY ALLIANCE

The morning after the night of stone and dragon fire was as foggy as if Firedrake's flames had filled the air with wet white smoke. It drifted up from the sea and hid the mountains and Mary's house looked as if it had been lost in the clouds. But Barnabas was determined to finally reply to Lizzie's message.

'She'll think I didn't get it!' he said. 'I have to go to the beach.'

But when he tried to go down Mary's porch steps his legs proved to be as stiff as if they were still made from stone.

'I understand, Barnabas,' Vita said while she helped him back to the bench at Mary's table. 'But you're not well! Let Ben and Guinevere go to the beach and find a way to answer Lizzie.'

Ben had never before heard his father utter troll curses, but on this morning he did. He used Hothbrodd's complete arsenal.

'My feet seem to weigh a ton each,' he exclaimed. 'Damn it! Damn! Damn! Damn! It seems like this time Cadoc has beaten me.'

'No, he hasn't!' Guinevere corrected him. 'You are alive and so are we, and Ben and I have sworn that we'll make him regret he ever came here. You shouldn't show up at the beach anyway.

Let Eelstrom think he succeeded!'

'Nice try. But for the same reason, you two shouldn't go there either,' Barnabas replied with a frown.

'It's so foggy that not even the seagulls will spot us,' Ben said. 'This fog is heaven-sent! And anyway – should we really hide? I want Eelstrom to know that his plan failed, and that we'll make sure the Aurelia is safe from him!'

Ben still felt the hatred this new enemy had stirred in him like a poison in his veins. This was worse than fighting Nettlebrand, the dragon-slaying monster built by an alchemist, or Kraa, the grim griffin who had locked them in a cage. Cadoc Eelstrom was human, and like them he knew fabulous creatures existed. But all they inspired in him was greed. Ben had only once felt this kind of hatred – at the orphanage where he'd been sent after his parents had died. There'd been several bullies there, older boys who liked to exploit and torment the younger and weaker ones. Ben had fought them many times, in the yard or on those dark corridors filled with the smell of loneliness and fear. Most times they had beaten him black and blue. But one had to fight them – the bullies of this world. Otherwise they only got meaner. And more powerful with every boy or girl who feared them.

No, he wouldn't hide from Cadoc Eelstrom. Ben's only worry was that he would find out about Firedrake. His dragon was exhausted from breathing fire so extensively right after the long flight. He was fast asleep under Mary's old trees, with Sorrel snoring by his side. The morning fog was hiding him still, but once it lifted he could be spotted easily from above and Lola had described the wasps that had chased her all too vividly.

'I may know a way how to hide your dragon.' Mary had noticed Ben's worried glance. 'I'll work on it while you go to the beach. And I'll have a few mushrooms waiting for Sorrel, when she wakes. I hear she likes them.'

Mushrooms. Yes, Sorrel would need lots of them after the adventures of last night! Hothbrodd had gone to check on his plane and had asked Lola to help him. 'I'll stay with your father,' Vita whispered as Ben and Guinevere got ready to get into Alfonso's truck. 'He is really not well, though he won't admit it!'

Both Ben and Guinevere were glad to get down to the sea. There was something about that wide horizon and the endlessly moving waves. They made them almost forget the house, hiding in the fog above them.

'According to Lola's description I would say it's the third house on the right.' Ben murmured.

Guinevere nodded. 'Yes. Huge and lots of glass. Blinds down. Definitely.'

'I wish we could just send the police up there,' Ben threw a handful of pebbles in its direction. 'Don't policemen in this country have plenty of guns?'

'With what reason?' Guinevere pulled him with her. 'That man turned us into stone, officer? He wants to steal the pods of a giant jellyfish?'

They both had to laugh. It felt good. Ben wondered whether Guinevere still felt the cold of the stone inside, like him. But he didn't want to talk about it. 'Let's deliver that message,' he said, 'and hope that Lizzie Persimmons is indeed still alive.'

'*If* she is, how does she manage to live underwater?' Guinevere stared at the waves. 'She is human!'

Ben detected a longing on her face that he hadn't seen there before.

'Let's go behind those rocks,' he said. 'Maybe one of the braidmaids can help us get that message out.'

'And I'd watch out for those wasps!' piped a fine voice.

Guinevere spun around. 'What are you doing here?' she hissed at Freddie, who was peeking out of her rucksack. 'I thought you were sleeping in the doll's house with your brother!'

Freddie smiled, pulling the fork that he had been carrying around to protect himself lately out of the rucksack. 'Our alchemist creator didn't say many wise things. But he had one motto I always liked: *You can sleep when you're dead!*' he announced, climbing on to Guinevere's shoulder.

Ben almost told him to go back into the rucksack. But he was sure Freddie didn't like it any more than he and Guinevere when people constantly worried about him, just because he was smaller than them.

The tide pools were well filled on this foggy morning, but although they searched them all, they could neither find a braid-maid nor Ears of the Sea amongst all the anemones and mussel shells. It almost looked as if someone had chased them away. Or . . .

Ben looked up at the mansion hidden by the white wet veils of the fog.

Had Eelstrom taken them?

Alfonso had told them to slap the water to call Elewese, but although Guinevere tried several times, the Chumash didn't show up. Not even when they called his name. Ben sat down on a rock and pulled out the paper with the message his father wanted to send. Guinevere sat down by his side, while Freddie climbed on to the rock behind them to explore its crevices with his fork.

'What now?' she said. 'Dad is already worried stiff that he hasn't responded to Lizzie's message yet.'

'My selkies could help,' a dark voice behind them said. 'I know your Chumash friend doesn't trust them. But that may be motivated by the fact, that they are interested in the same hunting grounds.'

Freddie raised his fork so abruptly that he nearly pierced Guinevere's ear.

Both she and Ben knew all too well how silently leprechauns moved. Gryfydd Longtoes made their hearts stop almost every day by showing up from nowhere. But Ben was nevertheless surprised by how silently Derog Shortsleeves managed to walk even on sand. The leprechaun was standing just a few steps away, his dog by his side, the mist wafting around them, as if they'd emerged from another world. How long had he been standing there? Ben wondered.

'So we meet again, Mr Tonnesen.' The leprechaun greeted him with a mockingly deep bow. 'I guess this is your sister? Or girlfriend?'

'No!' The answer came from both Ben's and Guinevere's lips at the same time.

The leprechaun granted them a sharp-toothed smile, and his dog barked at them, but his master bent down and silenced him by firmly placing his hand on his flat snout.

Guinevere rose to her feet. She was glad Hothbrodd hadn't come with them. He despised leprechauns. Gryfydd Longtoes had only made that worse when he'd stolen one of his boots to make shoes for himself from it. 'Leprechauns would sell their best friend for a decent piece of leather or a gold coin,' Hothbrodd liked to growl.

'*Pokker!* They're about as trustworthy as a basilisk.'

Guinevere had to admit they weren't her favourite fabulous creatures either. But their parents had taught them always to be polite to strangers, so she managed, like Ben, to greet Derog Greensleeves with a smile.

He returned it, but his green eyes seemed to know about Guinevere's thoughts on leprechauns. 'I would be delighted to help with the message you intend to send,' he said and held out his gloved hand invitingly. 'Selkies are very fast swimmers.'

Ben looked with unveiled suspicion at the outstretched hand and Guinevere took a step back. 'Thank you for the offer, Mr Shortsleeves,' she said. 'But we are aware that a leprechaun's help always comes with a price. What is yours?'

The leprechaun frowned and withdrew his gloved hand. One could spot the claws under the leather. 'I could say the same about humans, don't you think? But I assure you two, that in this case I don't expect any payment for my help. I offer it because –' he pointed at the house on the cliff '– we have the same enemy.'

'You know Cadoc Eelstrom?' Freddie piped.

The leprechaun cast him a thoughtful glance.

'Oh yes, I do indeed, homunculus,' he replied. 'And I'm sure Eelstrom has everything in place for the Aurelia's arrival. Can the same be said about you? It seems you can't even get a message to whoever you are working with underwater. But there is not much time left. Maybe it would be wiser to accept my help.'

He stretched out his hand once again, but this time with unveiled impatience.

'I won't offer it a third time.'

Ben exchanged a quick glance with Guinevere. She nodded, and he handed the paper to the leprechaun. Derog Shortsleeves unfolded it.

'*Fufluns to Naia*,' he read. 'Fufluns? I once met that god. Long time ago. And I know several Naias. It's quite a common name amongst merpeople.' He looked at the paper again. '*So glad you're alive. Preparing arrival. Three couriers on their way. CE is here too.*'

Derog Shortsleeves nodded and slipped the note into his pocket. 'The message will be on its way within hours,' he said, silencing his dog once again as he growled at a seagull emerging from the mist. 'I hope the popularity of the name Naia won't make the delivery difficult.'

'Her real name is Lizzie,' Guinevere said. 'Lizzie Persimmons.'

The leprechaun nodded once more. 'That information may prove to be helpful.'

He reached into his pocket. 'In case your mother lost my card,' he said, handing Guinevere another card. 'Once again . . . we have the same enemy. And here's a warning for you, homunculus, free of charge,' he pointed at Freddie, 'you'd better not underestimate the seagulls. They are much faster than you think. And to their eyes you look like a crunchy delicacy!'

He turned. And turned once more.

'As for your dragon, boy,' he said, 'I'm sure you know that Cadoc Eelstrom would be very interested in his heart. But I guess your silver-scaled friend can look after himself. I haven't felt a dragon's presence for many centuries. It is quite a pleasant sensation.'

CHAPTER TWENTY-FIVE

WATER MAGIC

What was the Aurelia feeding on? Lizzie had been following her for so long now, but she hadn't seen any of her shimmering arms catch prey. It almost seemed as if she was filtering life itself from the water. Lizzie kept a safe distance from her arms nevertheless. The only ones who dared to get close, and even swam between her arms, were tiny fish she had never seen before. There were thousands of them, as tiny as pygmy gobies, and with a strong resemblance to the soap bubbles she had loved to blow into the grey English sky when she had walked on human feet, breathing air and eating chocolate bars. Those she missed, she had to admit, but Laimomi had shown her a sea mushroom that tasted almost the same. Almost.

Laimomi.

Lizzie touched the shell necklace she wore. Her friend had made it for her. It felt strange to be without her. In all those years since she'd left the human world behind they'd always done things together. She would probably have died within hours underwater without Laimomi teaching her what to eat and what not, whom to stay away from and whom to seek. She had trained her to swim faster, dive deeper and most importantly, she had taught Lizzie how to speak underwater, with her hands and her lights, with a flip of her tail.

Stop it, Lizzie! she told herself. *Laimomi can't be here. Someone has to take care of the merlings!*

Below her the Aurelia was spreading her arms and pulling them back again, as slowly and graciously as if she was dancing. At times her transparent body looked like a ballgown drifting in the water, without purpose or direction, but she was heading east. North-east, to be precise.

Why didn't Barnabas reply to her message?

Maybe Cadoc had killed him by now? It had almost happened to her, after all. Why had she not tried to make contact with him years ago?

Because you forgot about the world above, Lizzie!

Koo swam to her side and pushed his fin gently against her green scaly arm. Lizzie was sure he could read her thoughts and moods. Fish were very tender with each other, she had learned. They loved to touch each other, and their senses were so much sharper and better than humans'. Of course, she had forgotten the upper world! Everything felt richer down here: the colours, the lights, the scents – yes, fish and merpeople were able to smell! She had been very surprised about that. Humans were so ignorant about life underwater.

Lizzie looked down at the Aurelia and let her song fill her heart. But it couldn't chase away her worries. Was Barnabas alive? And if yes, maybe he still didn't know about the Aurelia! And she would be the only one to protect her!

Koo gave her a frown. *What about me?* his eyes asked.

'Of course!' Lizzie signalled. 'You are right, I am not alone!

And you're a very strong and dangerous lantern fish. But still – just you and I . . . that won't be enough, Koo! Can you send the message one more time?'

Koo still looked slightly insulted. But he pushed up his scales and sent his sparks out.

Even if Barnabas waited at the beach the Aurelia was heading for . . . would he be able to find the four couriers? There were so few fabulous creatures left and those four needed to be big and strong to be able to protect and carry the precious pods the Aurelia had brought up from the deep.

Lizzie saw them glowing on four of her arms. They were blue, red, violet-brown and green, all perfectly round, and slightly fuzzy like plant seeds. The size Lizzie could only guess from afar. They were probably as big as Koo – well, a very flustered Koo! She was so tempted to swim closer and make her way into that maze of floating arms, but Lizzie had had close encounters with jellyfish and remembered the burn their arms gave all too well. *No, Lizzie, keep your distance! Be careful for a change!* That's what Laimomi would have told her.

Maybe she could swim just a little closer? Just . . .

Something grabbed her from behind.

She flashed all her lights, but the arms that held her were strong. And now they were tickling her!

When she finally managed to free herself she looked into Laimomi's face.

'Hello!' the mermaid said with her most mischievous smile. 'We decided, this is not the time to leave you be on your own down here.'

Behind her another eight merpeople appeared and waved at Lizzie. Most of them were her neighbours. They had all come!

'But what about the merlings?' Lizzie signalled.

'What about them? Did you forget how many good friends we have in Momi? They are looked after well. They'll probably behave much better when we get back.'

Probably. Lizzie had never been good at disciplining them, and neither was Laimomi.

They all laughed when Koo greeted them by ramming his head not too gently into backs and tails. Laughter underwater is yellow and orange. It wrapped Lizzie in light. She had never known a true family in her human life. She had no siblings and her parents had sent her to boarding school at the age of eight. She'd been quite lonely – until she'd met Barnabas and Kahurangi.

'You're a pretty fast swimmer now,' Laimomi said. 'It took us a while to catch up!' The others had teased Lizzie for years about

how slowly she swam. Only Laimomi had known it was because she was adjusting to a new body.

'She is so beautiful!' Laimomi's lights were soft whispers in the dark as she looked down at the Aurelia. 'She is so different from what I imagined. And her song!'

Yes. It filled them all with so much joy and beauty. The Aurelia seemed to embody life itself floating through the ocean – so effortlessly closing and opening like a flower. Lizzie was sure that the pods she was carrying would hold that same joy and beauty. They had to make sure, they were safe. And she was so glad she wouldn't have to try that all alone. So so glad! She looked at the others and smiled. They had all become friends, although she was so different and still didn't know everything about merpeople and the life underwater. Friendship . . . was there a stronger magic in the world? Lizzie looked down at the Aurelia. Maybe. But in her experience friendship could even compete with the magic of the shimmering creature who had risen from the deep to bring hope and new life.

She so hoped that Barnabas would be waiting at the beach. And that she could introduce her new friends to him.

CHAPTER TWENTY-SIX

BUGS AND LEAVES

Ben could hear Firedrake breathing, folding his wings, stretching his limbs. But he still couldn't see him! It had been three hours since Mary had cooked him a brew that in Sorrel's opinion tasted quite disgusting. But . . . it had made Firedrake disappear. Limb by limb, scale by scale, so completely that Ben was still worried he might never see him again!

Twigleg though seemed much relieved.

'I am so glad this gives us a chance to hide him!' he sighed. 'He may have to wait for hours on the beach to receive the Aurelia's pods. And even here,' he cast a glance at the sky, 'the invisibility will make it so much safer for him!'

True. But still . . . it was eerie. Sorrel had been invisible for only a few minutes, as she'd spat out the first sip she had taken from the brew, while Firedrake had emptied the whole pot Mary had filled.

'How do you feel?' It must have been the tenth time Ben asked that question, and once again Firedrake answered with a purr.

'I feel very well, dragon rider. It even makes my wings feel less tired from the flight. It's quite amazing. I must take some of those leaves with me. Remind me, Mary, what did you use?'

'White sage, buckwheat and a herb the dragonfly nymphs in my pond suggested.' Mary was sitting on the steps of her porch, while Freddie was tap-dancing next to her. The withered wood planks were making quite a perfect sound, as he had announced. 'That one may sadly be hard to find in the Himalayas, and I fear the same may be true of the sage and the buckwheat. But I'll pack you a big portion of the mix.'

'Humpumclupus!' Lola pulled the earphones off her head that transferred the signals of the spy bugs they had released in Eelstrom's house. 'How am I supposed to concentrate while you're making more noise with your feet than a typewriter?'

'Oh, sorry, Lola!' Freddie added two more steps and sat down next to Mary. 'Have they reported anything interesting yet?'

'No, it's quite disappointing so far,' Lola snapped, while she pushed the earphones back on to her ears. 'Our enemy seems to have nothing on his evil mind but fairy dust, the smoothness of his face and the question how best he can steal the magic from the braidmaids the Copperman caught for him. It seems he has left them alone so far, as one of them bit him. But he intends to take them to his underground fortress and I am sure they won't be so lucky there. He obviously believes he can make indestructible nets with their magic. He is indeed disgusting! I want to fly over right now and make a net from his skin!'

'Of course! We have to free the braidmaids!' Guinevere exclaimed.

'Yes, but we may sadly have to wait until the Aurelia is safe!' Her mother was leaning over a map that showed the coast, the ocean and the route the Aurelia was taking. 'The full moon is in four days.' She cast a worried glance at Barnabas who was walking up and down the porch stiff-legged. 'How do you feel?'

'Like the big bad wolf in *The Three Little Pigs*,' Barnabas gave back. 'I'm sure someone has filled me up with rocks! Mary, is there any brew that can make me feel a few hundred years younger than this? I promise I'll drink it, however bitter it is!' He sat down with a sigh and looked at his hands. 'They're clearly not made from stone any more, so why do they feel like it still?' He beat his fist on the table. 'I should just go over and punch Cadoc in the face with the stone fists I owe him!'

Ben and Guinevere exchanged a glance. They had never before heard their father fantasise about punching someone.

'Well, we're working on getting you that chance,' Lola said. 'Though I still like the fact that he believes you're all stone for a hundred years. That may make him reckless.'

She was adjusting her earphones when Ben suddenly jumped up.

A few silvery scales had emerged from thin air. And there was a paw, huge and clawed. And a leg, so strong . . . even after all these years Firedrake still took Ben's breath away, especially when appearing like this, scale by scale, until he stretched out his once again visible neck and smiled at them all.

'How long did it last?' Sorrel was laying out mushrooms on Mary's porch railing to dry them in the sun. 'King bolete, oyster mushroom, amethyst deceiver,' she murmured while placing her booty on the wood. 'Shaggy mane, deer mushroom, pungent slippery jack . . . excellent!'

Ben checked his watch. 'Three hours and thirteen minutes.'

Of course, they had considered using Firedrake against Eelstrom. But they all agreed that it was too dangerous as they didn't know what kind of magic the Copperman was able to use. So far the bugs hadn't revealed anything on that. *I'm sure you know that Cadoc Eelstrom would be very interested in his heart.* The words of the leprechaun made Ben's heart miss a beat each

time he recalled them.

'Here we go!' Lola pressed her earphones more closely on to her grey ears. 'It finally gets interesting.'

Barnabas rubbed his stiff hands and looked at the rat with a mixture of worry and hope. They all did. Except for Sorrel, who was spreading out her mushrooms.

'Come on, rat!' she snapped, while sniffing an especially big specimen. 'What is the bug report?'

Lola was listening with a frown. 'Eelstrom is talking about squid. But not the normal kind. The Copperman has altered them like the wasps who chased me.' She listened again.

'Have you found out more about him by now?' Vita whispered to Twigleg.

The homunculus shook his head. 'Gilbert and I checked all our sources. Just a few vague mentions of Coppermen, without any details. It's quite worrying I have to say.'

'Lola, what about those squid?' Ben asked.

The rat was still listening, but finally she pulled the earphones off her head. 'He gave them lobster claws.'

'Claws?' Barnabas went pale.

'Yep. To cut the pods off the Aurelia's arms.'

'Curse him!' Barnabas let both his fists come down on the table so heavily that the bluelings stopped hammering underneath the porch. They were building quite a palace for themselves down there.

'Curse him, curse him, curse him!' Barnabas got up, and then sat down again with another curse. 'This is exactly what we feared! Even if those squid don't manage to steal the pods – the attempt alone will anger the Aurelia! And everything will be lost!'

Vita was still staring at the map, running her finger down the Aurelia's predicted route. 'Where are those squid now?'

Lola shook her head with a grim frown. 'It sounds like they're already quite close to the Aurelia.'

Vita looked at Barnabas. 'We cannot just sit here and wait for her to arrive! What if it will be too late by then? We need to get out there – and warn Lizzie of the squid.'

'But how?' Guinevere asked. 'We can't dive that deep!'

'No?' Her mother got up, her face stiff with determination. 'Well, I think I'll have a talk with that leprechaun. After all he seems to be friends with some selkies, right?'

Barnabas looked at her with alarm. 'Oh, no! No, Vita! I don't like that idea, Not at all.'

'What are they talking about?' Ben cast his sister a questioning look.

Guinevere gave him a wide smile.

'We just divided the tasks, brother. You all take care of the beach. Mum and I will take to the sea.'

CHAPTER TWENTY-SEVEN

THE LEPRECHAUN'S LAIR

Leprechauns don't live in houses. The Greenblooms knew that, of course. So neither of them was surprised that the cards Derog Shortsleeves had given to Vita and Guinevere didn't list a street address.

Derog Shortsleeves
Shoemaker and tailor of fine leather
La Piedra Beach parking lot
3rd garbage can on the right

That was all it said.

The car park was empty except for two cars when Vita turned on to it. The owners were probably walking on the beach. There was no one in sight, but Guinevere cast a worried glance to the right, where behind a few houses the darkened windows of Eelstrom's mansion were reflecting the setting sun. Did he still believe they were all lifeless stone? From what Lola had learned through the bugs the answer was yes. Eelstrom seemed only to have his mind set on stealing from the Aurelia. But whether he knew it or not . . . it was time to talk to the leprechaun. Guinevere pulled her hoodie deep into her face before she followed her mother to the third trash can on the right.

Vita wore big sunglasses and a baseball cap – quite an unusual outfit for her. 'Gnomes and nymphs, not even I would recognise you!' Barnabas had exclaimed when he had seen her. 'Good!' Vita had replied. 'I must admit I'm having fun playing the secret FREEFAB agent.'

As Guinevere followed her mother across the car park, Freddie climbed out of her rucksack and on to her arm. By now it didn't even surprise her any more when he showed up so unexpectedly. 'I think you have your own homunculus now,' Ben had whispered at breakfast, when Freddie had had his coffee next to her plate. Guinevere liked that idea. She was very fond of Freddie, and had actually envied Ben over Twigleg's company quite often.

Her mother cast another watchful glance across the empty car park before pulling a bottle of French mustard out of her coat pocket.

'Here we go,' she whispered and threw it into the trash can. 'It was the best one I could find. Let's see whether Mr Shortsleeves considers it an appropriate knock at his door. Your turn, Freddie!'

Leprechauns only allow entrance to their lairs when addressed in Gaelic, and Freddie spoke it far better than any Greenbloom.

'*An bhfuil cead agam teacht?*' he called into the big bin. '*Is cara mé.*' Which roughly translates as: *May I come? I am a friend.*

The car park vanished the moment the homunculus had pronounced the last syllable, and Guinevere and Vita found themselves standing in a wide windowless vault, decorated with carpets and illuminated by dozens of candles. There was a long dining table, set with three beautiful Chinese plates, silver forks and crystal glasses. As they stepped closer it filled with jams, breads and butter, scrambled eggs, grilled fish and a small raisin and chocolate cake – Guinevere's favourite. Leprechauns are very good at sensing human desires.

'Ah, see who's here, Mannanan.' Derog Shortsleeves appeared in the chair at the top of the table, as if he'd been sitting there all the time. Maybe he had. Leprechauns are known for their ability to appear wherever they like and often quite unexpectedly. Mannanan appeared on the chair on his master's left, baring his teeth.

'How can I be of assistance? For I assume that's why you are here?' Shortsleeves waved invitingly at the food on the table. 'Please sit down and serve yourselves.'

Rejecting a leprechaun's food is considered a severe insult, so Vita and Guinevere filled their plates.

'We are here, Mr Shortsleeves –' Vita said helping herself to a slice of cake '– to ask you for two selkie skins.'

Derog Shortsleeves leaned back and gave her a mocking smile. 'That is quite a wish, Mistress Greenbloom. I guess we should drop the camouflage and call things and people by their true name?'

'Yes, that is always a good idea,' Vita replied, while Freddie sat down next to Guinevere's plate. 'And I know my wish is substantial. But we are willing to pay for the skins. Thanks to a few mountain dwarves, who believe themselves indebted to us, we can offer you a diamond for each skin.'

The leprechaun raised his eyebrows.

'Very tempting!' he replied. 'But as I told your children, we have the same enemy, and supporting your efforts to protect the Great Singer also suits my goal, so there is no need for payment.'

'What goal?' The question passed Guinevere's lips before she could remind herself that it might be quite rude. She found it very hard to trust Derog Shortsleeves.

'It's a very old-fashioned one, Mistress Greenbloom,' Shortsleeves replied. 'You may be too young to understand it. I've been looking forward to it for quite a while now and the arrival of the Aurelia will offer the perfect opportunity. I am here to take revenge on Cadoc Eelstrom.'

Guinevere exchanged a glance with her mother. Leprechauns were known for their unwillingness to forgive but revenge was not a word lightly used by a Greenbloom.

'May I ask how Cadoc Eelstrom made a leprechaun his enemy, Mr Shortsleeves?' Vita asked.

Derog Shortsleeves pulled a silver flask out of his vest pocket and poured a splash of whisky into this coffee.

'A little more than a year ago he caught my youngest brother Clad. With quite an ingenious trap, I admit. I suspect the

Copperman made it for Eelstrom. One has to say in in his defence that he has no choice. Eelstrom came eye to eye with him while extending his vast underground mansion in the South of England. So the poor sod has to serve him for the rest of eternity. It's the curse that haunts his kind.'

Guinevere cast her mother a surprised look.

'I've never heard about this curse,' Vita said. 'Coppermen are quite a mysterious species.'

'They are indeed.' The leprechaun took a sip from his cup. 'And there are very, very few of them. Anyway – Eelstrom locked my brother in a cell, he had equipped with all the tools and materials we need for our trade and promised to let him go if he made him five pairs of shoes.'

'Shoes made by a leprechaun a hundred years old,' Guinevere quoted, *'make life's paths to success and riches unfold.'*

'Exactly.' Derog Shortsleeves closed his eyes, as if he was delving back through his memories. 'We had just celebrated my brother's hundredth birthday when Eelstrom trapped him. My brother made the shoes, hoping his captor would be pleased with the result and release him – Clad was very young, and very naïve. Eelstrom was pleased with the shoes, but when my brother had finished the last pair he sent message to my father that the price for Clad's freedom would be all the gold we owned and—'

'—your father's leather knife?' Vita completed Shortsleeves's sentence.

'Yes indeed.' Derog Shortsleeves opened his eyes. They were as green as fresh spring grass. 'It seems you know all about leprechauns. Owning a leprechaun's leather knife vastly reduces a human's need to sleep. You just keep it under your pillow and a few minutes a day will suffice. We threw the gold and the knife into a hole Eelstrom had told us about. The next morning both were gone, and our brother lay in the hole. Clad was very frightened, and his hands were bleeding from all the work he had done, but he was alive. My father died exactly sixty-six days later. We never told my brother that he had paid with his life for his freedom.'

The leprechaun gazed at Guinevere. 'The handle of a leprechaun's leather knife . . .'

'. . . holds his life force,' Guinevere murmured. 'While the blade holds his skills and magic. A leprechaun can neither work nor live without his knife.'

She looked at her mother and saw the same sadness on Vita's face that she felt herself.

'We'd better not share this story with your father,' Vita said. 'Cadoc may have learned about the knife from his notebooks.' She looked at Shortsleeves. 'Eelstrom stole four of my husband's notebooks when they went to school together. Barnabas still blames himself for writing down all his observations and research on fabulous creatures. He had every tale about their magic recorded in those books, and if he were here, he would apologise for that to you. But he was young and didn't under-stand yet that writing down such secrets meant great danger for all those creatures he loved and admired. The tongue of a sky serpent makes one rich beyond measure, a dragon's heart makes one invincible, the webs of a mermaid make a human invisible, the dust of moss fairies keeps a person young for a hundred years . . . there are many more secrets like this and I fear Cadoc learned about many of them from Barnabas's notes. He will always blame himself for his deeds, although he has devoted his life to pro-tecting the fabulous creatures of this world from men like him.'

'But Barnabas Greenbloom still believes in kindness and hope, am I right?' Derog Shortsleeves leaned back on his chair and cast Vita a mocking glance. 'Those are quite foolish beliefs and surely don't make a man fit to fight evil.'

Freddie had been silently nibbling on Guinevere's cake, but those words brought him abruptly to his feet. 'Barnabas Greenbloom is not kind because he is blind to the evil in this world, Mr Shortsleeves!' he exclaimed, jabbing Guinevere's fork at the leprechaun. 'He is kind because it is his nature! And I am sure he has done much more in his lifetime to fight the evil in this world than you. So you'd better watch your words!'

Guinevere took the fork from Freddie, but she also gave him a very fond smile.

The leprechaun grabbed his napkin and wiped a hint of cream from his lips. 'Well, it seems Barnabas Greenbloom has friendship and love in his life. Which usually measures the quality of an existence.' He put the napkin on his plate and leaned once again back in his chair. 'I guess we all know, why Cadoc Eelstrom is here. The pods of the Aurelia are said to grant immortality.'

Guinevere cast her mother a surprised look. But Vita had clearly not known that either.

'So that's what Cadoc is after,' she murmured. 'We suspected that he just wants the pods because they're so powerful.' She looked at Shortsleeves. 'Immortality? You're sure?'

'Yes, but it's not a fact mentioned by any human tale. So your husband's notebooks are not the source of Eelstrom's knowledge in this case,' the leprechaun replied. 'I heard he caught a KnowItAll, a very old creature that lives underground. It didn't live long enough in captivity to tell him all the secrets they know, but this may have been one. Anyway . . . Eelstrom cannot take the pods before the Aurelia is very close to the shore. They won't be ripe. But I'm sure he'll try to steal them. Unless we all manage to prevent it.'

'What about you?' Freddie was still watching Shortsleeves suspiciously. 'Do you want to steal her pods as well, leprechaun?'

Derog Shortsleeves laughed out loud. 'I really like you, homunculus. Maybe I should make you my prize for the selkie skins?'

Freddie looked at Guinevere in alarm.

'The Greenblooms don't sell their friends, Mr Shortsleeves.' Guinevere's voice was shaking, as she placed Freddie on her shoulder.

The leprechaun chuckled, clearly amused by her anger. 'Neither do leprechauns, Mistress Greenbloom. Don't worry. You can keep the homunculus. And no, I don't intend to steal the pods. For did you forget? To anger the Aurelia would be the end of me too. No.'

He took another sip from his cup and put a slice of ham on Mannanan's plate, which his dog devoured with great pleasure.

'I'll get you the two selkie skins,' he said. 'Be at the beach tomorrow, shortly before midnight. But not where Eelstrom gazes down on us. I'll let you know the exact location.'

He raised his hands. One clap would bring them back to the car park. The leprechaun at MÍMAMEIÐR had once expelled Guinevere from the library that way. But she still had one question to ask. She knew her father would want to know the answer.

'Usually death is the punishment, when leprechauns take revenge for the ones they love. Do you plan to kill Cadoc Eeelstrom, Mr Shortsleeves?'

The leprechaun smiled. It was a small smile, but his fangs pushed over his lower lip.

'No, Mistress Greenbloom,' he purred. 'I give you my word. I will neither kill Cadoc Eelstrom nor will I steal the Aurelia's pods. But I will have my revenge. Be assured.'

CHAPTER TWENTY-EIGHT

A POND FULL OF DRAGONS

Mary's pond was filled with young dragons when Guinevere got back. Sadly with only their images, of course. But that was definitely better than not seeing them at all! Maia had brought them all down to the lake, Thorny and Scales and Moondance.

'You see how big they already are?' Ben whispered as Guinevere knelt down next to him. 'Maybe it was not a good idea to make Firedrake the courier. It will take so long to bring the pod all the way to Scotland and then fly back to the Himalayas!'

'Yes, it *is* a good idea, dragon rider,' Firedrake called from the other side of the pond, where he was trying to have a calm conversation with Maia while his offspring fluttered around her – and Mary's lily pads. 'Our children would want their father to do this, for it may give them a better world to live in.'

His offspring honestly seemed not to care at all about the state of the world or their parents. They were flying so fast already! And they were so wild with each other, snapping at the

others' wings and paws, bumping their snouts into each other's bellies . . . all the inhabitants of Mary's pond were watching the spectacle on the surface with great alarm.

For did you forget? To anger the Aurelia would be the end of me too.

Guinevere followed Firedrake's offspring with her eyes, while her heart was torn to shreds by the thought that in a few days they might all be gone, if they failed to protect them. And so would be Freddie and the nymphs on the lily pad and . . . no! Her father was right. They couldn't allow those thoughts, or they would just drown themselves all in Mary's pond!

'What's wrong?' Ben had been her brother for only a few years, but he knew her so well.

'Nothing,' she murmured.

'Nothing, as in . . . they may all be gone soon?' Ben slung his arm around her. 'Nothing, as in "Cadoc Eelstrom would love to cut my dragon's heart out of his chest"? Nothing, as in "Our father still feels the stone in his veins and we don't know how to get rid of it"? It's a lot of nothing at the moment, right?'

Guinevere nodded. 'But . . . I will soon have a selkie skin! The leprechaun will get them for us.'

Ben's eyes widened with both disbelief and admiration. 'So you're really looking forward to that? Another body – and one that lives underwater? The mere thought makes me want to throw up!'

Guinevere laughed, watching a tiny water nymph disappear under a lily pad with a gracious stroke of her tail.

'I can't wait, brother!' she said. 'I can't wait!'

CHAPTER TWENTY-NINE

WHO IS AFRAID OF
THE DARK?

Four more days until the full moon. Four days and nights until the Aurelia would be here and bring eternity. What would he do with it? Cadoc had no idea. But he liked the thought of being like one of the gods they had bored him with at school. They'd mostly entertained themselves with wars. Maybe he should try that? Well, he would have all the time in the world to decide. Would he continue to live underground, although he wouldn't use the fairy dust any more and would therefore be fine with the sun? Yes. He liked the darkness and his underground fortress.

It was very strange. He missed Barnabas. Cadoc was very surprised about that emotion, but it was undeniably there. Nothing was more challenging and entertaining than such a virtuous do-good enemy. Maybe he'd ask Copper to create one. Yes! He would tell him to make him look exactly like Barnabas, so he could beat him over and over again.

Fun.

So much fun.

That boy . . . Barnabas's son . . . he had dreamed of his petrified figure last night. He hadn't liked the dream. It had been one of those, one he couldn't get rid of. The petrified body had stirred the moment he had bent over it. Then the boy had stood up and he'd been exactly his height. And while he'd stared at him, wings had grown from his shoulders and silver scales had covered his skin. And then Cadoc had woken up, his heart racing, his bed wet with sweat.

Since then he had told himself a hundred times how ridiculous that dream was and that the boy was gone like his father, for the next hundred years. But the feeling remained. The dream had left a residue like soot in Cadoc's mind and heart: that Barnabas's son was much more of a threat than his father. Foolish. The dream had for sure been inspired by his schooldays, when he'd so often felt outshined by Barnabas. The boy had that light too, even his petrified face hadn't concealed it. The glow of unselfishness,

devotion to a good cause, all that noble nonsense.

Good riddance! One had to pull out the weed before it grew too high. How old was he? Fourteen or fifteen maybe?

Cadoc despised children and teenagers and everything that looked young. They made him feel old inside, despite his face.

He'd actually never felt young inside. He'd never seen much of his parents. A family photo for the Christmas card, in clothes tailored for the occasion. Frowns or smiles twice a month, yawns hidden politely behind well-manicured hands when he had to report on his school affairs. His father had been prone to fits of rage, but they'd been mostly aimed at his mother. Cadoc remembered the relief when he'd finally reached an age when he was as tall as them. He didn't even know whether they were still alive. He didn't really care. He had been fond of his grandfather . . . as fond as he was able to be of others. But he had died long ago. Most people accepted that fate. But most people also believed mermaids and unicorns just to be a fairy tale.

Cadoc gulped down another sip of fairy brew.

'You shake them too often,' Copper had warned him again this morning. His metal slave was getting quite impertinent. Time to refill those spray cans. He had sent Copper back into the mountains to take photos of the Greenblooms' grey stone faces – especially that of the boy. No, that dream had definitely not been a good one. Very annoying.

He looked forward to having his petrified enemies all framed on his walls. Those photos would also make a nice Christmas card – happy holidays and never make Cadoc Eelstrom your enemy.

'I have news, master.' Copper was back. Heavens. He looked even more gloomy than usual.

'What? Don't tell me there are problems with the squid.'

Copper shook his metal head. 'They should reach the Aurelia today, latest tomorrow.'

'What is it then? You look like I dumped you in the ocean.'

'The Greenblooms are gone.'

Cadoc set the empty mug down. 'You told me the spell lasts at least a hundred years.'

'Someone broke it.'

'Someone who?'

Copper gave him a glance he could not quite read. 'I don't know, Mr Eelstrom.' There was something in his face. No, he wouldn't dare to lie to him, would he?

'Find them!' Cadoc yelled. 'And whoever broke the spell!!'

Coppermen have very sensitive ears. Yelling was an easy way to punish them. One could see the pain distort Copper's patterned face. He really looked as if a demented goldsmith had decorated his skin with spots and lines.

'Yes, sir.' The hatred made Copper's voice sound hoarse. Hatred and helplessness.

'The Aurelia arrives in four days! I don't want any surprises. Unless you want me to throw you chained into that ocean down there and watch how the salt water eats your skin!'

Copper stared at the floor. 'Yes, sir.'

Cadoc pulled his mirror out after he left. He brushed his forehead with his flat hand, but the frown Copper's news had inspired wouldn't leave, and he spotted fine lines between his eyebrows and around his mouth. *Someone broke it?* Who could break a petrifying spell? Probably one of Barnabas's filthy furry friends!

Four more days.

No. His old enemy wouldn't get in his way! Four years had gone by since their paths had last crossed, on that foul day when his former schoolmate had saved that accursed poison-toothed sky serpent from him! Cadoc could still see her gliding towards him, after Barnabas had freed her from the trap he'd set for her. Four years and her poison still circled in his veins. Barnabas had of course not allowed her to kill him off in all his foolish goodness. He had grabbed her by the tail, and she'd let go of her prey for just a moment – which had given Cadoc the chance to escape. He would accept any bet that Barnabas had regretted that act many times since then. Cadoc had seen it even then on his face, but the fool couldn't help it. Cadoc felt a grim smile on his lips. Each time he grabbed or killed a fabulous beast he also stabbed Barnabas Greenbloom's heart. For he could have let that serpent kill him and thereby would have saved them all.

Yes. The pods of the Aurelia were his. And if the self-proclaimed saviour of fabulous creatures tried once again to get in his way, he would order Copper to kill him. And that son of his too.

Cadoc saw fear on his face, as the memory of that dream came back. He angrily pushed the mirror back into his pocket.

He had to admit, he was also scared of death. He actually expected all the creatures he had harmed to be waiting there (wherever there was) – to do to him all the things he had done to them.

Yes, he wanted those pods. He needed those pods.

And he always got what he wanted. *Unless a Greenbloom got in his way,* a voice whispered inside him.

And in his mind that boy rose to his feet again and grew wings from his shoulders.

CHAPTER THIRTY

GOOD AND BAD NEWS

The Aurelia's song was drawing legions of creatures by now. Creatures of any size, kind and colour. Most of them followed her just for a little while, but more and more came to stay – like Lizzie and her friends. Maybe it was the Aurelia's size, but Lizzie had the impression that her song also kept aggressors away. Those who came near her made no attempt to attack her. Schools of sharks followed and left, as if the song was enough of a gift, and even the giant squid, who usually liked to pick a fight, just gave the huge jellyfish a deferential bow and kept their distance.

Yes, all was going well so far! Wasn't it?

Laimomi suddenly signalled in alarm. She pointed at a silhouette that was heading straight for Lizzie.

Was that . . .?

Yes, it was a male selkie! The pattern on his back gave him away. And the fact that no other seal was able to dive that deep and swim that fast. But what was he doing here? Selkies liked cold oceans. Lizzie had never met one in this part of the Pacific.

Laimomi rushed to her side, and so did Koo. He was a fierce guardian despite his pumpkin looks, and the selkie slowed down when the lantern fish bared three rows of razor-sharp teeth. He didn't look too scared though. Selkies are very confident. In her human days Lizzie had studied their history for a while. And the magic of their skins.

'I have a message for Lizzie Persimmons,' the selkie signalled with his flippers. They usually communicated that way, but they were also quite good at telepathy.

Lizzie felt so fierce a joy that it pierced her heart.

'I am Lizzie!' she signalled back. 'Is the message from Barnabas Greenbloom?'

'Yes,' the selkie replied, while his eyes were fixed on the Aurelia. 'It says: *Preparing arrival. Three couriers on their way. CE is here too . . .*'

Laimomi exchanged a long glance with Lizzie. Oh, this was bad news. Very bad news.

'Thank you,' Lizzie said to the selkie while fear and joy fought each other in her heart.

'Did Barnabas give you that message in person?' Lizzie signalled to the selkie. 'I know these are not your home waters, and that selkies and merpeople . . .'

'. . . usually fight each other?' The selkie shrugged his shoulders. 'The leprechaun who asked me to play the messenger is an old friend. I did it for him, not for you, mermaid.'

A leprechaun? Barnabas didn't like leprechauns. But Lizzie decided to not mention that. 'Thank you!' she just signalled once again. 'The message you delivered is very important. For us all.'

But the selkie had forgotten about her. He was looking at the Aurelia with his big black eyes. All the merpeople, even Laimomi, were watching him suspiciously. Selkies and merpeople had fought many wars in many places of the world. But from time to time there were legendary friendships between them. There was even a city they had built together, famous for its beauty, not far from the northern shores of France.

CE is here too.

Lizzie could still feel the chill that had grabbed her as the selkie's flippers had written those words into the water. Should they tell the others about the threat that posed for the Aurelia? Lizzie saw the same question on Laimomi's face. Did they really have to ruin the joy the Aurelia was inspiring in everyone?

'What is the use of telling them?' Laimomi signalled to her, as the others were all staring at the selkie. 'They will do their best to protect the Aurelia anyway! You know that. I don't want them to all live in fear. And if we fail . . . well . . .'

They looked at each other.

Say it! Lizzie thought. *If we fail, the ships of Momi will be just rotten wood. There will be no merlings laughing, no guards in the crow's nests, no herds of seahorses . . .* Who else would die? Was Koo a fabulous creature? Probably. And the whales singing in the deep? Would there be anyone left except humans? Who would they tell their stories about, if Cadoc erased everything else with his greed?

Lizzie looked at the Aurelia. By now they swam at the same height. All that magic – how could Cadoc just want to grab and destroy it?

'The pods are useless until the Aurelia reaches the shore.' Laimomi wrapped an arm around her. 'We still have time.'

Yes. But Cadoc had that time too.

The selkie showed no intention of going back. He had joined those who were following the Aurelia, enchanted like them by her song, wrapped in her lights and colours. Lizzie, though, still couldn't move, numbed by the message the selkie had brought. What would Barnabas do? His message hadn't said anything about that.

Because he doesn't know, Lizzie.

'Stop worrying!' Laimomi pulled her with her, towards the others. 'We've beaten him before. We'll beat him again.' She had deep scars from the net Cadoc had caught her in. She had tried so desperately to free herself, before Lizzie had come to her aid. There were days when Laimomi could barely leave the settlement, because she felt the wound in her tail fin that the boat propeller had caused. But Cadoc hadn't caught Laimomi. *We'll beat him again* . . . They had to. All their lives depended on it.

Koo pushed his nose into her back. He was glowing dark orange – always a sign that he was worried or upset.

He pointed his fin at a shoal of pearl gobblers. Behind them Lizzie made out a pack of five strangely-coloured squid. They seemed to make sure the Aurelia's light didn't reach them, but a swarm of shimmering shiver fish gave them away.

'Have you two ever seen squid shaped and coloured like that?' Lizzie asked.

Koo and Laimomi shook their heads.

'You think . . .?'

'I don't know. Let's keep an eye on them.'

Koo bared his impressive teeth in agreement.

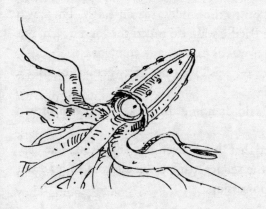

CHAPTER THIRTY-ONE

A NEW SKIN

T he night sky was studded with stars as Vita and Guinevere
stepped on to the beach where the leprechaun had promised to meet them. A crow had delivered the location. Sharp-
edged rocks made it hard to get to the sand, but the beach where
the Aurelia would arrive was miles away. As was Eelstrom's house.

Rogelio, one of Alfonso's men, was already waiting with a
small pontoon boat to bring them to a cruiser, whose lights they
could see in the distance, a boat sturdy enough to take them out
a few hundred miles on to the wildest sea on earth. There was
good reason why the Pacific was also called the loud ocean, but
on this night the water was as calm as a sleeping beast.

Derog Shortsleeves was waiting between the rocks,
Mannanan by his side.

'As promised,' he said, handing them each a greyish brown
bundle.

Guinevere stroked her hand over the silky fur. The leprechaun clearly had the selkies' trust to be allowed to lend out
their most precious possession.

'To shapeshift just push your left hand into one of the flippers, and the skin will do the rest.' He was clearly amused by the delight he saw on Guinevere's face.

'How do we take them off?' she asked. 'As we won't have hands.'

'Clever girl. Pull the skin off the right flipper with your teeth, and the rest will follow. At least, that's what I've been told. I never felt the slightest temptation to become a seal. I sometimes feel the wish to use their skin for an especially charming pair of boots, but I guess I wouldn't have many selkie friends if I did. So I only make pigs and cows my enemies. Good luck!' He bowed at them as usual and turned.

'One more thing before I go . . .' He turned back to them. 'How do you know where to find the Aurelia?'

Guinevere saw her mother hesitate with the answer.

'An old friend of ours is following her.'

'Of course!' The leprechaun smiled his most sharp-toothed smile. 'Lizzie, or Naia, whom I helped deliver your message to. How could I forget? I hear her way to communicate is by lantern fish.'

Guinevere exchanged a quick glance with her mother.

Derog Shortsleeves frowned and uttered a deep sigh.

'I see . . . you still don't trust me. Well, why should you? Humans have told stories about treacherous leprechauns ever since they learned how to use their tongues. I would accept any bet that humans have betrayed my kind more often than the other way around. But . . . you don't listen to our tales, right?' He once again turned to go. 'Take good care of those selkie skins,' he said over his shoulder. 'I had to work hard to convince the selkies that they can trust two humans.'

Mannanan growled at Vita and Guinevere, as usual, before he followed his master and soon they both vanished between the jagged rocks. But the leprechaun's words had stayed behind.

'He is right, isn't he?' Guinevere murmured. 'We don't know their tales. But they know ours.'

'Yes,' her mother said as they walked towards the boat that was waiting for them. 'All fabulous creatures do. Because they have to know them. As those tales are often the reason why humans fear or kill them.'

CHAPTER THIRTY-TWO

THE BAIT

It was quite silent on Mary's porch except for the hammering underneath where the bluelings were fortifying some of Mary's support beams. They'd been doing quite a lot of work on her house. They really liked Mary, even though she'd told them not to shrink all the black widow spiders.

Barnabas was sitting at the big table on Mary's porch, where they had gathered so often by now, and was worrying about Guinevere and Vita. Ben could read it from his face. They all did, although of course his father agreed that Lizzie needed to be warned about the squid. He still didn't feel well. It worried Ben how breathless he got after just a few steps.

'Your father protected your mother and sister from the full impact of the stone curse. I'm sure he gladly pays the price for that,' Alfonso had answered, when Ben had voiced his concerns to him. 'A dragon rider,' he had added with a knowing smile, 'does of course feel the dark magic that has planted the stone in your father's flesh much less.'

Dragon rider . . . Yes, Ben sensed it more with every day. He was getting stronger. And Alfonso was right: he hadn't suffered any effects from the petrifying spell. On the contrary. Since Firedrake had wrapped him in his fire, he felt as if it was burning inside him.

'Did you learn any more about those squid, Lola?' Even Barnabas's voice sounded tired. If only he would rest! 'There is no time,' he replied when anyone suggested that.

Lola shook her head. 'Those bugs are proving to be quite a let-down. I fear the manticore ate some of them. Such a shame! The others are quite upset and are hiding or just looking for food in Eelstrom's kitchen. There was some talk about worms, obviously in case the squid plan doesn't work. I guess there's no doubt by now what that plan looks like. The only question is when those squid will try to grab the pods. And whether our underwater friends can stop them.'

That made them all fall silent again. And feel terribly useless. There had to be something they could do!

'The Copperman hates Eelstrom,' Twigleg murmured. 'I heard it in his voice.'

'Which slave doesn't hate his master?' Barnabas said. 'But the curse the leprechaun told Vita about sadly also means that the Copperman will have to do whatever Eelstrom tells him.'

'Like catching moss fairies,' Lola said. 'Eelstrom seems to have quite a demand for them. Braidmaids, moss fairies . . . I'll need a flying bus to free them all. That rescue mission is high up on my To Do list. But for now it would draw too much attention.'

'The poor things!' Freddie exclaimed. 'What if they die before we get to them?'

'We survived more than three hundred years of slavery, brother!' Twigleg stated. 'They'll be fine. Lola is right. We can't endanger the Aurelia mission.'

Freddie was clearly not convinced. But Ben sadly had to agree with Lola and Twigleg. And so did the others.

'Don't look so worried, Freddie!' Mary tried to comfort him. 'It's just three more days. We'll try to free them as soon as the Aurelia's pods are safe.'

As soon as the Aurelia's pods are safe . . . They all looked at the horizon, where the ocean was meeting the blue sky.

'Any news from Eight?' Hothbrodd asked.

'Nope.' Lola replied. 'Gilbert still hasn't heard from him.'

And once again they all fell silent. If the Great Blue Kraken didn't show up, who would be the Courier of Water? The merpeople? No, the pod would need a far stronger fabulous protector.

'Alfonso says the Courier of Earth will arrive tomorrow,' Ben reported.

'Then I'm sure he or she will,' Barnabas said. 'How about the griffins? Any news from Shrii?'

'Yes!' Lola was clearly relieved she didn't have to deliver another no. 'He is on his way. One of the local wild parrots who annoy the hell out of me delivered the message. Can anyone tell me why Mother Nature came up with parrots? This one was so green it hurt my eyes . . . and his croaking! Only a donkey's voice is harder to bear! He named every bird who had been part of the message chain all the way from Indonesia. Please don't make me repeat them. But it seems Shrii will arrive in two days latest!'

That was good news for a change. They had saved Shrii two years ago, when Kraa, another griffin, had planned to kill him. Ben was sure Shrii was glad he could help them now in return. Not to speak of the danger that the griffins might cease to exist as well, if the Aurelia was threatened. Did Shrii know? Probably . . .

The sun was setting over the mountains, and Ben felt as if it was taking another precious chunk of time with it. Three more days until the Aurelia's arrival, and Eelstrom clearly had plans in place for an attack under water and one on the beach. While all they could do was to come up with some kind of defence . . . that was not a good feeling. Not at all.

'Maybe we can distract Eelstrom somehow?' he said. 'Is there anything that can make him forget about the Aurelia and turn his attention somewhere else?'

'Of course! Bait!' Freddie did a few excited dancing steps. 'We give him something he wants as badly as the pods. Bait! And when he tries to get it, *bam* –' he stomped on the table with his silver foot '– we catch him, and keep him captive until the Aurelia's pods are safely on their way! And of course until we have rescued the moss fairies and braidmaids!'

'And what bait would that be, brother?' Twigleg mocked. 'Didn't you hear that Eelstrom believes those pods will make him immortal!'

'Well, for example a dragon's heart!' Freddie exclaimed.

'For example.' Firedrake was standing under the trees. He had been at the pond talking to his family 'That's an excellent idea, Freddie.'

Ben stared at him in alarm.

'Thank you!' Freddie beamed. 'I'm sure Eelstrom won't be able to resist.'

'If this is a joke, it's a bad one! Stop this instantly, both of you!' Twigleg exclaimed.

Firedrake stepped closer to the porch. 'It might work.'

'What might work?' Sorrel stepped out of Mary's house, wearing strings of dried mushrooms around her neck. Mary had taught her how to dry them in her oven.

'Firedrake playing as bait for Eelstrom, so we can catch him!'
Freddie was even more pleased with his idea, since Firedrake had
given his approval. He was dancing excited circles on the table.

'Have you completely lost your mind, you little idiot?' Sorrel
exclaimed. 'Oh, but of course! Your brain has the size of a pea
and you're far more interested in your feet!'

'Sorrel!' Mary put a comforting hand around Freddie, who
looked quite devastated.

'I have to agree with Sorrel,' Barnabas said. 'Firedrake did
more than enough by rescuing us.' He turned to the dragon. 'You
are here for only one task: to receive and protect one of the
Aurelia's pods.'

'There are things we *want* to do and things we *need* to do,
Barnabas,' Firedrake replied calmly. 'We're running out of time.
Let's set a trap! Instead of just waiting and hoping that we can
somehow defend the Aurelia against Eelstrom's attack . . .'

Ben felt as if he was stuck in a bad dream. His dragon, the bait
for a man who'd have only one goal: to cut his heart out?

'It's decided. We've talked enough!' There was a growl in
Firedrake's voice. 'I'm a dragon, not a fragile child any of you has
to worry about. And if I have to fight Eelstrom to make sure
he won't threaten the very existence of us all – well, so be it. I
promise,' he added, with a glance at Ben, 'I have no intention of
giving him my heart!'

There are things we want *to do and things we* need *to do . . .*

Ben returned his dragon's gaze. Firedrake was right: they
couldn't act on fear. They would have to fight Eelstrom.

Sorrel, though, didn't agree with that at all. Her fur was
ruffled with anger.

'Did you forget that Firedrake is a father now?' she yelled. 'Yes,
his offspring annoys the death caps out of me, but I won't allow

them to become half-orphans on my watch! No! No, no, no!'

Firedrake lowered his head over the railing of the porch until he looked straight into her eyes. 'Is it better for them to just disappear? If Eelstrom threatens the Aurelia and takes us all with her, as we are her gift to this world? Don't you think this will be a very sad place without us? No more dragons or brownies, neither young nor old. Just Eelstrom's insatiable and maybe even immortal greed. Let's stop him. Let's stop him now.'

Sorrel gave a growl and turned her back on him. 'Whatever,' she snapped. 'Have it all your way. You always do.' Then she jumped off the porch and disappeared between the trees.

'I really don't know what to say!' Barnabas murmured. 'This is not what I do. I protect fabulous creatures. I don't use them as bait!'

'Nonsense, Barnabas.' Hothbrodd had been leaning silently under the trees. 'Firedrake and Freddie are right. This may work. And I really like the idea that Eelstrom will be the prey for a change.'

'So where should we set the trap?' Lola asked.

Freddie had climbed on to Mary's shoulder.

'What about Anacapa?' He pointed at the horizon. 'You can see the island from here. It is the smallest of the northern Channel Islands. We let Eelstrom know he can find a dragon on it, and when he gets there we catch him and lock him up! Maybe Firedrake doesn't even have to be there.'

'Yes, I do,' Firedrake said.

'Then so will I!' Ben said.

Which made his father look even more pale, but Barnabas was wise enough not to argue about it.

'Excellent! All good! Yes!' Lola licked some tomato sauce off her paws. Mary had served them excellent pasta. 'Now we just have to figure out how we let Eelstrom know that Firedrake is on that island! And what to do with the Copperman. I hope he won't bring his wasps!'

Twigleg stepped into the middle of the table. 'If you go, I'll go with you, master!' he said, in a trembling, but very determined voice.

'No.' Ben shook his head. 'No, Twigleg.'

'I was with you when we fought Nettlebrand!'

Ben shook his head again, although Twigleg's begging eyes broke his heart. 'No! I would be too worried about you. I'm sorry.'

Twigleg looked at his pointed shoes and frowned. Then he lifted his head and pushed his chin forward. (That was quite pointed too.)

'In that case I'll be the one to tell

Eelstrom there is a dragon on Anacapa. No one is more quali-
fied. I have more than three hundred years of training in the art
of deception. We all have to play our part in this, master!' he
continued, when Ben opened his mouth to protest. 'And don't
forget . . . Freddie and I will disappear too, if Eelstrom gets
his way.'

Ben just looked at him. He felt so much love for the
homunculus. And pride. And he was so scared at the prospect of
sending him to Eelstrom.

'There must be another way,' he said hoarsely. 'This may be
the most dangerous task of the whole mission, Twigleg!'

'But I will go with him!' Freddie exclaimed while running to
his brother's side.

'Well,' Lola said. 'That'll certainly make the whole mission a
walk in the park!'

CHAPTER THIRTY-THREE

NIGHT WATCH

'The Copperman is coming back.' Lola's voice broke off from time to time, but the line Hothbrodd had established between her headset and Ben's computer proved more reliable than even the troll had hoped. 'I'm sure he was up to no good!'

'Hothbrodd is on his way to the beach. He'll check on it.' Ben kept his voice low although Eelstrom for sure couldn't hear him. They all felt as if they were sitting in the plane with her, watching their enemy's mansion, flying rounds above it and the beach below. At least so far no wasps had shown up.

Barnabas was sleeping. He still didn't feel better, and everyone was quite worried. Mary had cooked a brew of every healing herb she knew. Sorrel had even brought him some of her mushrooms. But his father could barely eat and found it harder and harder to keep his eyes open. 'Maybe the stone has reached his heart after all,' Mary had said just an hour ago. 'I'm so sorry, Ben.'

It was hard to think about Eelstrom or the Aurelia, while his father was so unwell! But Ben knew Barnabas wanted him to take his place, so he tried his best. He'd even convinced Firedrake to get some rest. With Sorrel's help. 'What do you mean, you don't need rest?' she had snapped at the dragon. 'Do I have to remind you that you'll soon act as bait for a madman and his metal slave?' So Firedrake was sleeping in the moonlight under Mary's trees, Sorrel by his side – which was quite a beautiful sight.

Neither Alfonso nor Hothbrodd had been willing to look after two homunculi on a dark beach, so Freddie and Twigleg had stayed with Ben too. Freddie was dancing a melancholy dance amongst Mary's flower pots, but Twigleg seemed quite grateful to spend an eventless night on her porch. After all he had a terrifying task waiting for him once the morning came: to pretend to be a traitor to everyone and everything he loved, so Eelstrom would take the bait and leave for Anacapa. Ben reached over the table and the homunculus gladly accepted the comfort of his hand. He climbed up his arm and sat down on his shoulder, while Ben continued to listen to Lola's reports.

'The manticore does of course pose a threat for the humpelclumpusses,' she whispered. 'Eelstrom keeps him like a spoiled pet, which means he probably won't bring him to the island. But he looks very well fed – although sadly he did snack on some of my bugs – and Eelstrom usually allows him only in the front of the house so he can watch the street. So we should make sure the humpelclumpses come from the sea.'

Ben saw Twigleg swallow. A manticore. No, he didn't like it at all that Freddie and Twigleg were going to Eelstrom's lair.

'No other guards or henchmen,' Lola continued. 'Only the maid, who comes in during the day. On the island that metal man will definitely be our greatest concern! Even Hothbrodd wouldn't have an easy time taking him out, and we know dangerously little about the magic he can do.'

Maybe Eelstrom wouldn't bring him to the island? Of course he would. Ben frowned at his computer screen. If he only knew more about Coppermen and their abilities!

He'd been studying maps of Anacapa with Alfonso and a friend of Mary's who knew the island quite well. Together they'd chosen the spot where Firedrake would land and the place they'd lead Eelstrom to. They planned to leave shortly before sunrise: he, Sorrel and Firedrake . . . the old team. Except for Twigleg, who had his own part to play. It seemed like a lifetime ago that they had found the Rim of Heaven together. At least this time their enemy wouldn't show up unexpectedly like Nettlebrand. But Eelstrom was certainly the kind of enemy who was always good for a nasty surprise. The copper wasps had been proof of that.

Nevertheless, Ben preferred his mission to Guinevere's. To shapeshift into a seal and dive down into the wet depths of the ocean . . . no. Much better to be a dragon rider once again.

'Gilbert just texted me,' Lola whispered into his ear. 'There are reports that a Great Kraken was spotted in the Pacific Ocean. Let's hope that's Eight, and that he is on his way.'

Eight . . . his acquaintance was one of the many good things they had brought back from their last big adventure in Indonesia. The Great Kraken was the perfect Courier of Water, as Shrii, being the new leader of the griffins, would be the perfect Courier of Air. Ben couldn't wait to see them both again. Would this adventure grant them equally wonderful new friends? *For sure,* Ben thought.

Alfonso still hadn't told them whom he'd asked to be the Courier of Earth. 'She will be here in time,' was all he said. And they all knew by now that Alfonso Fuentes kept his promises.

'Nothing stirring here,' Ben heard Lola say. 'Everything calm, both at the house and at the beach. Cats' whiskers!' But suddenly she cursed.

'Lola?' Ben cast Twigleg a worried glance and Freddie stopped dancing.

They heard a hum, similar to a bumblebee's. And then Lola's voice again.

'All fine – it was a real wasp!' she whispered. 'Cats and skunks, I am getting quite paranoid!' They heard her yawn. 'I'll stay online until Hothbrodd is back from the beach. Then I'll take a short nap. But I'll make sure Twigleg has a full report, before he walks in there. Over!'

'Over.'

'If that manticore shows up, you break off the mission!' he said to Twigleg.

But the homunculus shook his head. 'Don't worry, master! Eelstrom will not be interested in feeding us to his pet monster. After all we're going to tell him where to find a dragon.' There was only a slight hint of doubt in his voice.

'I completely agree!' Freddie called up from under the table, where he was practising a few new steps the bluelings had taught him.

Don't worry . . . Ben looked to where his dragon was sleeping, as Mary walked out of the house and sat down at the table.

'How is my father?'

Mary shook her head. 'He doesn't eat and barely drinks. He says his eyelids are made of stone. I hope Alfonso learns something from the Chumash.'

Twigleg gave Ben's shoulder a comforting pat with his little hand. 'He'll be fine, master,' he said. But he couldn't hide the concern in his voice.

They hadn't let Vita and Guinevere know the plan yet. And he would soon leave for Anacapa!

'I'll be here to take care of your father!' Mary said. 'And Alfonso and I will keep searching for a remedy!'

'Hello! Hellooooo!' Lola's voice shrilled out of the radio's speakers. 'A seagull just let me know that Elewese has organised transport for the humplecumplusses!' Lola hissed. 'A pelican will deliver the two to Eelstrom's balcony, as I can't drop them off without raising suspicion. The bird promised of course not to eat them.' Lola giggled.

'Excuse me? A pelican?' Twigleg jumped up so abruptly that he tumbled from Ben's shoulder. Ben caught him just before he hit the table.

'I'm sure Elewese picked a bird he can trust, brother!' Freddie didn't look worried at all. On the contrary, he was beaming with anticipation. 'How cool a ride is that!' he exclaimed. 'We'll arrive at Eelstrom's lair in style, brother!'

Twigleg's face gave away the fact that – not for the first time – he doubted his brother's sanity. 'In style?' he repeated. 'I wonder what style you have in mind, Freddie. Pelican snack style?'

CHAPTER THIRTY-FOUR

HOLES ON THE BEACH

Hothbrodd didn't like sand in his boots. Not at all. There was no sand in the forests of this world, and forests were the only surroundings a troll considered appropriate. But . . . since Barnabas Greenbloom had once saved him from a gang of night trolls, Hothbrodd went where Barnabas asked him to go – though sometimes moaning and swearing. Trolls aren't exactly the most positive species, and they welcome any excuse to swear. They have developed swearing into an art form over millennia. The curses Hothbrodd was mumbling as he walked down the beach with Alfonso referenced a lot of intestines, blood, bowel movements – and many old Viking gods.

'Do you like sand?' he growled, when Alfonso stopped behind the rocks, where Vita had talked to the Ears of the Ocean.

'No,' Alfonso replied. 'But it's better than mud.'

'Is it?' Hothbrodd frowned, pondering that unfamiliar thought, and stared at the waves that covered the sand with white whispering foam. The moon was almost full. It drew a wide silver path on to the waves, and the stars looked like silver coins someone had thrown into the night's face. Well, to Hothbrodd they looked like that. Trolls are not very romantic.

They had inspected the beach inch by inch since Lola had reported that the Copperman had spent some time there. But so far they hadn't found anything suspicious. Nevertheless . . . Hothbrodd would never have doubted anything Lola Greytail reported. The flying rat was an annoying know-it-all, but she was an excellent and very reliable scout.

'I suspect whatever Eelstrom has waiting for the Aurelia is hidden deep under the sand,' a voice behind them said.

Yes, leprechauns moved silently, but Hothbrodd was very proud of his hearing, and he was sure, this one used magic to show up that unexpectedly.

Derog Shortsleeves's sharp-toothed smile couldn't convince the troll to like him any better than the sand in his boots. In fact, Hothbrodd liked leprechauns even less. He didn't like dogs either, and the one sniffing at the wet sand just a few steps away looked to him like a walking bread bun. Or a potato on crooked legs.

'Your dog can be glad I'm a day troll, leprechaun,' he growled. 'Night trolls eat dogs.'

'I am very aware of that,' the leprechaun replied. 'And leprechauns make boots from troll skin – if they have to.' His eyes were frosty green as he gave Hothbrodd another smile. 'The Copperman made sure my selkie friends were out hunting when he came down here. Those metal men are terribly strong and great magicians. They can alter animals and plants into completely new life forms with just a bit of spit or touch. But,' he cast a fond glance at his dog, 'luckily he mistook Mannanan for a normal dog.'

Mannanan lifted his back leg, peed on the spot he had sniffed, and walked on.

'That was the third one,' Shortsleeves said. 'I asked him to mark every spot where the Copperman stopped for a while. Let's see how many more there are.'

He nodded at them and strolled after his dog.

Hothbrodd walked towards the spot, where Mannanan's pee had left a dark mark in the sand.

Deep under the sand . . .

'Elewese!' The troll heard Alfonso call over the waves.

A figure emerged from the water. Hothbrodd had imagined the starfish-man to be smaller. When Elewese stepped out of the water he looked even more impressive. He was almost as tall as Hothbrodd, and his armour-like skin was something the troll really envied him for. Not to mention all those arms. The things he could have built and carved with them! All the tools he would be able to hold at the same time!

Elewese smiled when he walked towards him, as if he read the envy from the troll's green face. But his face turned grave when he looked up at the mansion where Eelstrom was staying. They for sure all wished the moon hadn't been that full and bright. It felt as though someone was shining headlights on the beach, but the windows of their enemy's lair were dark. Which didn't mean much, Hothbrodd thought. Coppermen lived underground so they could for sure see very well in the dark. Especially when the moon was a *forbannet* lantern in the sky!

'I think it's fine if they see us,' Alfonso said. 'They know now that the spell on the Greenblooms was broken. My men saw the Copperman up at the camp. And why not make them a bit nervous?'

He looked up at the house. 'Yes, I am sure someone is watching,' he murmured. 'Let's make sure they only see what we want them to see.'

'And that they can't hear us!' the starfish man added.

The ocean was all roar and hiss and rush, when they stepped so close to the waves, that they soaked Hothbrodd's boots. No, he didn't like the beach.

'I watched the metal man from the rock over there,' Elewese said. 'Being a starfish has its advantages.'

'When he is fully transformed he isn't much bigger than your fist,' Alfonso explained, when Hothbrodd cast Elewese a bewildered look.

'Maybe even a bit smaller,' Elewese smiled. 'The Copperman brought a metal container. I think it opened at the bottom when he put it on the sand because when he picked it up again there was a big hole in the sand, big enough for you –' he pointed at Hothbrodd with one of his arms '– to crawl in.'

The troll cast a glance down at his huge shape.

'The metal man took his time to erase any trace of what he'd done. He did it so well that not even I could tell where the hole had been after he'd left.'

'He dug at least three holes,' Alfonso said, 'if the leprechaun's dog is to be believed. I don't like this. But . . .'

'. . . if we start digging now, our enemy knows we're on his track,' Hothbrodd growled. 'So let's pretend we have no clue. Otherwise they may plant new devilish things. I suggest we come back for the hunt shortly before the Aurelia arrives.'

'Any idea what we'll hunt?' Elewese asked.

'Worms,' Hothbrodd replied. 'That's what Lola's bugs heard.'

'That doesn't sound too bad,' Elewese said.

'It sounds pretty bad to me, starfish man,' Hothbrodd replied. 'I've met worms that bite your head off as playfully as you crack a mussel.'

On the balcony of Eelstrom's mansion a dark silhouette appeared. The moonlight showed it quite clearly. It was the Copperman. He stared at them. Then he stepped back and melted into the shadows, the roof cast.

'Three spots,' Alfonso murmured. 'Let's hope the dog finds them again once it's time to dig for what the Copperman planted.'

They all stared at the moonlit sand.

Until Elewese grabbed Alfonso's hand with one of his arms and with another dropped a few empty snail shells into it. 'These are for your sick friend. Grind them and have him drink a brew of the powder. The merpeople say it helps their limbs to get light.'

Hothbrodd cast Alfonso a quizzical glance. 'Barnabas?'

Alfonso nodded.

'I'm sorry to hear that Greenbloom is unwell,' Elewese said, while he stepped into the waves. 'He is a good man. But sadly that's often more of a danger than a protection in this world. I see you on Anacapa. Good luck with that plan!'

Then he dived into the waves.

Oh, yes, Hothbrodd envied him for all those arms.

He cast a glance at Eelstrom's mansion. He would use them all to strangle the Copperman, and his master with them.

CHAPTER THIRTY-FIVE

FAR OUT ON THE OCEAN

The fishing boat Alfonso had organised was fast. Ricardo, who was steering it, was the youngest in Adolfo's crew. He had coloured his raven-black hair coral-red and was softly singing to himself as he navigated the waves – in a language that didn't sound like Spanish to Guinevere.

'What language were you singing in?' she asked, when Ricardo fell silent and they all just stared at the moonlit sea that was melting around them into the night, landless and eternally moving.

'Zapotec,' Ricardo replied with a smile, 'which if you take it literally means "person of the place of the sapodilla". One of our most important fruit trees. I come from Oaxaca, like Alfonso, but we speak many different languages there.'

Oaxaca . . . the name tasted of adventure, of trees and animals so different from the ones Guinevere had grown up with. One life would never be enough to see everything she wanted to see. 'I'm sure we have many lives, Guinevere,' her mother had once said to her. 'So don't rush through this one just because you believe you have to get everything done that you wish to do.'

Tonight she would definitely be doing something she had always wanted to, and she was so glad it was happening in this life. Ever since Guinevere Greenbloom had been a little girl, she had dreamed of being a fish-tailed maid of the sea – despite that sad fairy tale about the Little Mermaid, and despite the dangers the merpeople who came to MÍMAMEIÐR talked about. Guinevere was a decently good diver, not half as good as her mother, but still . . . she'd seen the world waiting under the surface of the oceans. Only through protective goggles though, with an oxygen tank on her back and a suit that both protected and separated her from the underwater realms she was so eager to explore. To feel that water on her skin, to see with eyes that didn't fear the deep, to breathe without a metal tank . . . she had imagined it so many times in her dreams. Would it feel the way she had imagined, when she slipped into the selkie skin?

Guinevere saw the same question on her mother's face – and the same impatience to find out. But soon the vastness of the ocean and the night sky above them made her forget about time. After a while Guinevere was not even sure it existed any more, except as an endless space open in all directions. How did the Aurelia sense time, having lived for so long with no end in sight? Would she be able to ask her?

'We're close.' Ricardo's whisper brought back time as Guinevere knew it – so fast, counted in minutes, hours, days. Not in centuries or eternities.

The dawn was breaking and they were still not sure Lizzie had received any of their messages. The selkie the leprechaun had sent out had not returned, and neither had the dolphins Elewese had asked to tell Lizzie they were on their way. So all they'd navigated on were Gilbert's calculations of the Aurelia's path, based on the birds and Lizzie's one message.

Guinevere had expected to see the Aurelia's light in the water below when Ricardo stopped the boat. She had asked her mother many times to tell her all she knew about her. But obviously the Aurelia was careful and still far deeper down than they had expected. The water was dark, and there was no proof that they were at the right spot.

'I guess we just have to try,' her mother said.

Ricardo looked at the dark water and shook his head. '*Muy peligroso,*' he murmured. 'Far too dangerous!'

'Maybe we'll sense the Aurelia once we're wearing the skins!' Vita said and unrolled her selkie fur. 'We'll come back to the boat, if we can't sense her!'

Ricardo still looked quite doubtful. But Guinevere agreed with her mother. They had to try.

'Let's just hope Hawaiian merpeople talk to selkies,' Vita said. 'In the Northern Seas they fight each other.'

Guinevere decided not to think about that. She pulled the seal fur over one arm, as the leprechaun had explained.

Derog Shortsleeves had told the truth. The moment she slipped her hand into one of the flippers, the magic happened all by itself. Suddenly she was on her belly, and the world looked so different – and the railing was an obstacle she hadn't thought about at all! But selkies are strong.

That was her first lesson. It was easy to pull herself up. Her mother was already diving into the waves as Guinevere was slipping over the railing. And then – she hit the water.

Oh, what a feeling! To suddenly have a body that was made for the waves and yearned for them! Guinevere swam loops and circles and jumped out of the water just to feel it embrace her again like a long-lost friend. Vita had to remind her at some point what they had come for.

Yes! She could hear her mother's voice in her head. She felt her words like a tinkling in her fur, and read her flippers like the writing of a pen. Oh, this was deep magic! Guinevere had felt such enchantment the last time she was on the back of a Pegasus, and when holding the young dragons. Though maybe this was even better, because for the first time she *was* a fabulous creature. She was truly one of them!

Deeper and deeper and deeper they swam, until there was no trace of the pale morning light, just darkness. But all around them the outlines of fish emerged, drawn by coloured lights. They glimmered on scales and fins and were everywhere. Some fish made a hasty escape when they saw the two selkies – a living reminder that seals were ferocious hunters – and a few times Vita pointed at the silhouette of a shark or squid and waved Guinevere close to her side.

This was so different from what she had imagined.

It was so much better.

Overwhelmingly, breathtakingly better.

And then . . .

There was light below them and song and beauty, with a thousand arms.

CHAPTER THIRTY-SIX

DRAGON RIDER

Ben felt Firedrake's silver scales beneath his hands, although thanks to Mary's potion his dragon was as invisible as he himself. Ben felt the wind in his face and the strength of fire and air carrying him through the clouds. No. There was nothing compared to this.

Dragon rider.

Ben wanted to yell his joy up to the fading stars, but that didn't go well with the mission to make their way in secret to Anacapa. So he kept the joy inside, a warm glowing light deep inside his heart, stronger than the apprehension he felt thinking about what lay ahead, the worry about his father – and about Twigleg, who was getting ready to once again play the traitor.

Dragon rider.

Each time he climbed on to Firedrake's back Ben felt like never climbing down again. Each time those silver wings spread beside him, he imagined doing this for the rest of his life, this and nothing else – to fly his dragon, to become one with Firedrake's strength and beauty, his wisdom and knowledge about the world. No human could ever feel as much at home in this planet's mountains and above its oceans the way the dragon did. No human could ever talk all the tongues heard in this world. Firedrake did. He understood the whispers of the trees and the murmur of the waves, the chirping of the birds and the hissing of a snake.

Dragon rider.

Sorrel was supposed to come with them, but she'd decided to eat a mushroom Mary had warned her about. She'd been throwing up all night and hadn't even had the energy to protest when Firedrake had decided that in such a weakened state she couldn't come on such a dangerous mission. Was this whole mission cursed? First Barnabas, now Sorrel? 'I don't think poisonous mushrooms count as curses,' Lola had commented on that thought. 'And neither does the greed of brownies.' Probably not. But anyway, just he and Firedrake had taken off to fly to Anacapa.

Ben was still worried about his dragon being the bait, but he agreed by now that this was their best chance to put an end to Cadoc Eelstrom's devious schemes. And he had to admit he liked the prospect to take revenge for what their enemy had done to his father.

On the waves below the moonlight gave way to the first red blush of the rising sun, and Ben could already see the silhouette of Anacapa on the horizon. It resembled the back of a giant turtle rising from the sea.

Would Twigleg play his part well enough to lure Eelstrom to the island? And how would it feel to confront the man who'd turned him and his family into stone and wouldn't hesitate to cut Firedrake's heart out of his breathing chest to become invincible?

Good! Ben thought. *It will feel good.* He leaned over Firedrake's back and felt his warmth and strength under his hands.

Dragon rider.

Mary would grind the snail shells Hothbrodd had brought back last night, which they hoped would finally beat the stone in his father's blood. What if those didn't work either? What if nothing worked? But he couldn't allow himself to think about that now. 'Promise me,' Barnabas had said, 'you'll only concentrate on your task. And on your safety. Forget about me! If it gets too dangerous, you run – save yourself and Firedrake! Look at me, son! I want you to swear it on your dragon's life!'

He had. And he would try his best to forget how weak his father's voice had been – so grey with the stone.

Firedrake let himself sink deeper.

'What does he look like?' Ben had asked Lola before he'd left.

'Like a skinny blonde boy not much older than you,' she had replied. 'With eyes like blue glass, a very determined mouth above a receding chin and quite a thin neck. According to your father he claims that the birthmark behind his ear was caused by a fairy who spat in his crib and was at some point sure he was a changeling and the child of an immortal elf. Well,' she had added with a giggle, 'it seems he's finally realised he's mortal. Why else would he want that pod so badly?'

A changeling . . . weren't they soulless clay creatures that elves supposedly left in the cradles of human children they stole, and who mimicked humans until one day they revealed their true nature?

Ben shuddered as the wind pressed him harder against Firedrake's back spikes.

No, he was quite sure Cadoc Eelstrom was human. And it was time to finally meet him eye to eye. He had spent far too many hours imagining his face.

Beneath him the barren surface of Anacapa came closer. The island didn't look very welcoming. Ben saw nothing but low bushes and just a few scattered trees. Not a place where a dragon could hide easily, that's for sure, but they hadn't come here to hide. Mary's potion would keep him and Firedrake invisible for another few hours, but the dragon's paw prints would leave a track, and once it had brought Eelstrom to where they wanted him the potion would probably soon cease to have an effect. But by then their enemy would be welcome to see them. For they had certainly not come to hide on this island.

Ben cast a glance back over the ocean, while Firedrake slowed his flight and got ready to land. Hothbrodd and Alfonso would be on their way as well, as soon as they could be sure Twigleg had succeeded in sending Eelstrom off to the island. The others would wait for Shrii. Including Sorrel. Ben really hoped she wouldn't kill herself one day with a mushroom.

He felt how Firedrake dug his claws into Anacapa's rocky ground and heard him fold his wings. The dragon and his rider were in place. Now everything depended on Twigleg.

CHAPTER THIRTY-SEVEN

AN EXPERIENCED TRAITOR

No. Riding in a pelican's beak was not an experience Twigleg had ever wished for. The beak that carried him and Freddie through the air was slippery and dark and stank of raw fish. He would never get rid of that stench! Not to speak of all the bruises their carrier's bumpy flight technique gave them! And what if he didn't deliver them to Eelstrom's balcony, but to the hungry beaks of pelican offspring? 'His name is ShadowOnTheWaves, *Señor* Twigleg!' Alfonso had introduced him. 'And he is a lord amongst the pelicans of this area. It's a great honour that he will carry the two of you.'

An honour. Sure. As long as that Bird Lord didn't eat them.

Freddie slung his arm around his shoulders and squeezed him affectionately. 'I can't wait to see you at work, brother!' he whispered into his ear. 'So far I only heard about your skills as a double agent! How you tricked the mountain dwarf... amazing! What was his name again?'

'Gravelbeard.'

The pelican took a dive that pushed Twigleg's stomach up his throat. This was worse than Lola's plane! And yes, fooling that dwarf had actually been fun. But this time he was not conning a mountain dwarf of average intelligence. Eelstrom had delivered impressive proof of how perfidiously cunning he was, and the Copperman . . . No, this wouldn't be easy. The fact that he smelled of fish would certainly not support his credibility. *And if you succeed, Twigleg, your master and his dragon will be the bait.*

No. Forbidden thought. Definitely.

'The enemy is in his living room,' he heard Lola say through the radio he carried. 'If the bug tells the truth. I feel quite guilty that I didn't warn them more sincerely about the manticore. Well, what happened happened. Give the pelican the signal.'

The signal.

Twigleg knocked against the beak hull that surrounded him and felt how ShadowOnTheWaves changed direction. *I feel quite guilty that I didn't warn them more sincerely about the manticore.* Great! Did Lola have the same sentiment when it came to him and Freddie?

'Don't forget to leave the radio and the earplug in the beak, humclopus!' she shrilled.

Of course. Twigleg hastily pulled the plug out of his ear and placed the radio in the bottom of the beak. It would have been comforting to be able to communicate with Lola, but he had watched too many crime shows with his master to perform this task with a wire. The rat had promised to stay nearby and keep an eye on the events unfolding – and to call Alfonso for help if it was needed.

There.

The bird had landed. Twigleg heard the rustling of feathers as the pelican folded his wings. Then darkness turned into light. The huge beak opened and Twigleg gazed at windows blackened by dark blinds. Great – Eelstrom might not even notice their arrival!

'Hello?' Twigleg called. 'Hello, Mr Eelstrom?'

The wind blew so strongly from the sea below that it tore the words from his lips and nearly pushed Freddie out of the open beak. Twigleg managed to grab his arm just in time.

This was off to a great start! Maybe it was better to forget about the whole scheme.

But just when Twigleg was considering this option, the huge glass sliding door they were staring at was pushed open and the Copperman stepped out. He was even more impressive than Twigleg had imagined. His presence was like a shiver in the air, and his shimmering metal eyes seemed to look right through them. Even Freddie stepped back as far as the pelican's beak allowed.

'Two homunculi. So that was the smell I sensed near that strange little house that the Greenbloom boy tried to protect.' The Copperman's voice rang like a bell. 'What do you want? Mr Eelstrom doesn't like visitors. Even when they're as small as you. And neither does he like big birds sitting on his railing.'

The pelican received the comment with an unimpressed glance. *You are good at this, Twigleg! You have lied and spied for centuries!* the homunculus reminded himself, while he took a deep breath and climbed from the relative safety of the beak on to the railing, which was luckily quite wide. Once Freddie had followed him, the pelican closed his beak, but he stayed on the railing. Which was quite a comforting sight, Twigleg had to admit.

The Copperman gave the huge bird a look that was both admiring and disapproving. Then he ignored him and focused on his passengers.

'I haven't seen your kind for at least two hundred years!' he said. 'Who made you? A witch? An alchemist? An elf?'

Twigleg swallowed all the questions those comments provoked in his mind and warned Freddie with a glance to do the same.

'We are here to talk to Mr Eelstrom!' he yelled into the wind, trying hard not to lose his balance on the railing.

'About what?'

Calm, Twigleg. He cleared his throat. 'We will only tell him that in person.'

The Copperman gave them a long thoughtful glance – so long that Twigleg began to worry that he was trying to make up his mind whether to throw them into the waves below, or just break their necks. But finally he turned and disappeared through the sliding door. The wind was so fresh that Freddie sought shelter in the pelican's plumage and Twigleg felt like a frozen chicken leg by the time the Copperman returned.

'Mr Eelstrom grants you ten minutes of his time. It worked to your advantage that he's never seen a homunculus. You may not want to wake the wish in him though to explore your species in more detail.'

That warning made Twigleg swallow. *Calm, stay calm,* he told himself. *They are not as bad as Nettlebrand.* Though he was not at all sure of that.

The Copperman didn't lend them a helping hand as they climbed down the railing. He just watched them without expression and, once they finally had made it down, waved them through the sliding door into the house.

The room they stepped into was as huge as the house suggested, and darkened by the closed blinds. The only light came from two lamps that framed a sofa. Cadoc Eelstrom was sitting on it, and yes, he looked indeed not much older than Ben.

Twigleg's eyes searched for traces of all the years the moss fairy dust had erased, but he couldn't find any. Eelstrom clearly preferred more formal clothes than his master.

A white shirt buttoned up all the way to the long thin neck, a well-tailored dark blue jacket, leather shoes instead of the trainers Ben mostly wore. There was a coldness in the pale-blue gaze that made Twigleg's tiny heart shiver. He was looking at someone who only and exclusively cared about himself. The tense face said it, and so did those cunning eyes. Of course he would steal the Aurelia's pods – even if that meant death for every fabulous creature in this world.

Oh, his master would have to be very careful, although he was with his dragon.

'You have ten minutes, homunculus.'

His voice was as young as his face. He must have killed thousands of moss fairies by now. Twigleg had to fight the urge to clench his fists.

When Eelstrom got up, something stirred behind the sofa. Oh no! Freddie cast Twigleg an alarmed look. The manticore. What was he doing here? Hadn't Lola sworn he was always just in the front part of the house? His master clearly enjoyed the fear on their faces. But the manticore only cast them a bored glance, and sneaked with annoyingly slow paces out of the room. Maybe he was used to better food than two skinny homunculi. Or their scent was not to his liking. Whatever it was, Twigleg's heartbeat only slowed down once the beast's scorpion tail had disappeared through the door.

'You are lucky. I just fed him.' Eelstrom walked towards them until he was standing just a step away. 'Did Barnabas Greenbloom send you? Of course. Who else would send such small fry with a filthy bird as his messengers?'

He looked down at Freddie with a contemptuous frown. 'Heavens. One of you is even damaged goods. That's so Barnabas.'

Freddie answered that insult with an angelic smile, tapping the wooden floor gently with his silver foot. *Let's get him, brother!* he tapped in perfectly clean Morse code. Twigleg was very proud of him.

'My brother Freddie did indeed lose his leg, Mr Eelstrom,' he said. 'Be assured, it had no effect on the clarity of his mind. Neither does his size.' Twigleg was surprised how calm his heart was now beating. The years in Nettlebrand's service had done him some good after all. 'It was torn off by another monster – in that case not the human kind.'

Eelstrom stared down at him, as if he wasn't sure whether to take the monster reference as a compliment or an insult. Would he have them stare up at him for the whole conversation? Probably.

'To answer your question: no, Barnabas Greenbloom didn't send us,' Twigleg said. 'He would in fact be very upset if he knew we are here. We came to offer you a deal. Or a form of collaboration if you prefer that term.'

Freddie nodded in confirmation. They had practised this conversation quite extensively. His time to talk would come.

Cadoc Eelstrom picked a manticore hair from his sleeve. His shoes were clearly the work of a leprechaun. *One step forward,*

Twigleg thought, *and he will crush me under them.* He could feel that pale-blue gaze like a scalpel. Did Eelstrom imagine taking them apart to understand what made a homunculus breathe? Probably. Or maybe he wondered whether their hearts, boiled or ground, had any positive effect on his lifespan?

'I'm trying to place your accent, homunculus,' Eelstrom said, frowning down at them. 'It is not American. But of course . . . you were made in the Old World.'

'Indeed.' Twigleg's neck began to hurt from staring up at him. 'In northern Italy, to be exact.' That brought back the memories of another human monster: the alchemist who had made him. *No! Concentrate, Twigleg!*

'We are here to offer you information, Mr Eelstrom.' He straightened his shoulders. 'Information that I'm sure you'll find very interesting. We know where Barnabas Greenbloom hides his dragon.' There it was.

Cadoc Eelstrom tried his best to conceal his surprise. But he couldn't fool the homunculus. Good. They had surprised him once. Hopefully they would do it again.

'So good old Barnabas *does* have a dragon.' Eelstrom chose his words slowly – a common trick to hide one's excitement. 'I must admit, I didn't believe those rumours.'

'Oh, yes, he does.' Twigleg began to enjoy himself. 'And that dragon is actually quite close.'

Eelstrom didn't take his eyes off him. He knew all about the art of lying, Twigleg was sure, and he was waiting to detect the signs. But Twigleg's life had depended for more than three centuries on his ability to lie without giving it away.

'Well, then why shouldn't I find him myself? Dragons are of quite substantial size, I guess?'

'You would never find him. Barnabas Greenbloom is a smart man. He knows how to hide his greatest treasure.'

Eelstrom was silent for a few moments as if he had lost himself in a memory. Had Barnabas outwitted him before? Yes. Twigleg saw the humiliation still on Eelstrom's pale face.

'What about his son?'

Twigleg breathed in. And out. 'What about him?'

'Is he a dragon rider? Barnabas is too old, but a dragon always longs for a rider.'

Twigleg wondered whether he knew that from Barnabas's stolen notebooks.

'Yes,' he replied. 'Ben Greenbloom and the dragon are very close.'

Cadoc cast a glance at the Copperman, who was still standing next to the sliding door. 'That's how they broke the spell! Dragon fire! You could have seen that!'

The Copperman's face showed no emotion. 'How? The last dragons were extinguished long ago.'

'Well, obviously not,' Eelstrom snapped, so sharply that the huge man bent his head. 'And of course Barnabas wants to use the dragon as the Courier of Fire . . . Who'll stand in for Air, Earth and Water?'

They'd expected that question. 'Greenbloom is very secretive about that,' Freddie chirped.

Go, brother!

'He always treats us like that!' Freddie exclaimed. 'Like

foolish little dimwits who can't know about the great Greenbloom's plans! We are over four hundred years old. Together we speak more than a hundred languages. But Barnabas Greenbloom despises us because we were made by a human, unlike all the creatures he loves. He treasures every filthy gnome more than us, and we're tired of it. So tired!'

'Enough!' Twigleg snapped at his brother, although he felt the urge to hug him.

Freddie pulled his head back between his shoulders and smiled at Eelstrom apologetically. Oh, he was good at this. Really good! Though, of course, not quite as good as his older brother.

'So what if I want that info about the dragon?' Eelstrom wiped a few manticore hairs off his dark sleeve. 'What is your price?'

'We . . .'

Twigleg felt the glance of the Copperman. There was something in his face . . . a longing. A longing for what?

'We want one of the pods. The ones you and Greenbloom came here for. Just one. And don't think you can betray us! Once we have the pod, we are willing to share one more piece of info we suspect you'll find at least as interesting as the one about the dragon. But only once we have the Aurelia pod.'

'And what piece of information would that be?' Eelstrom looked down at them with mocking bemusement. It was at times of great advantage to be small. One could be sure to be underestimated.

'We know the location of MÍMAMEIÐR, Greenbloom's sanctuary for fabulous creatures.'

The pale-blue eyes darkened for just a second, and Twigleg felt Eelstrom's hunger to exploit the magic in this world like tiger teeth that tore his heart out of his small chest.

'They may of course all be gone soon,' Freddie piped. 'All of them . . . dragons, brownies, gnomes, mermaids . . . and me and my brother too. If you make the Aurelia angry . . .'

Twigleg forgot to breathe. That had not been part of their plan. For sure not. What was Freddie doing?

He beamed up at Eelstrom as if they were talking about whether he liked chocolate as much as Freddie.

Eelstrom bent down and gave Freddie a frosty smile. 'I never believed in these apocalyptic tales,' he said softly. 'And there is always a certain risk that comes with great endeavours. I find this one acceptable. Don't you agree, little runt?'

For a moment Twigleg was sure Freddie wouldn't be able to swallow the hatred he must feel. But he did. With a smile.

'Absolutely!' he piped back. 'I just wanted to make sure you know about this risk. And your servant –' he turned to the Copperman '– as well.'

The Copperman returned his gaze. 'I am aware of it, homunculus,' he replied calmly.

His master was still staring down at the homunculi.

'What do you and your brother want the seeds for? You have a very long lifespan.'

Twigleg detected a hint of suspicion in his voice.

'But we have already lived more than four hundred years!' Freddie exclaimed. 'We worry every day that our clock may run out! With the pod we never have to worry about that any more.'

Cadoc Eelstrom gave off a mocking laugh. 'I will share my immortality with two homunculi. Oh well, nothing is perfect. Where is the dragon?'

CHAPTER THIRTY-EIGHT

TO THE RESCUE

Yes! The humclopusses had done a magnificent job! Lola flew a few celebratory loops before hiding her plane in a palm tree to watch the Copperman pack their hunting equipment into a helicopter. He packed worryingly little, Lola thought, for hunting a dragon. Which of course brought her to the conclusion that they intended to use magic. Not good. After the events with the petrifying monster they had of course expected that. Still . . . while Lola was watching the Copperman she was not so sure any more that she still liked the dragon bait plan.

Alfonso and Hothbrodd were on their way to Anacapa, after she'd given them the green light. And no, they hadn't taken the humclumpulusses with them. Too small! The troll hadn't dared to bring up that argument with her. But he'd convinced her that she would be needed here.

Agreed.

The first task was almost done. She had planted tracking devices on the Copperman and the helicopter. The wasps had tried to get in the way, nasty little buggers, but Lola had equipped her plane with a scent device that caused them to fly erratic loops and kept them away from her. Her own invention, she was pleased to say! As were the tracking devices that looked like thistle seeds to the suspicious eye. It was immensely useful to have tiny clawed hands. The naughty little things would send a signal to Hothbrodd's and Ben's phones. She had been slightly worried they wouldn't stick on the Copperman, but so far they did. Only three more quite important ones needed to be placed.

There.

Cadoc Eelstrom – or the Anti-Greenbloom, as Lola liked to call him – stepped out of the pompously big house to walk to the helicopter he had chartered. Lola placed the device in a bamboo cane, took a deep breath and aimed at Eelstrom's deceptively boyish shoulders.

The tracker got stuck right between them. It really looked like nothing but an innocent plant seed. Not bad, Lola!

She placed another one in their enemy's short blonde hair, and number three – one couldn't play this one too safe – on his trousers. He was dressed like a rich lion hunter in an old Hollywood movie. Oh yes, he was going on a hunt. Without a clue that this time he was the prey.

Hopefully.

Lola made sure he and the Copperman were in the helicopter before she turned her plane towards the house. There were some moss fairies to be rescued. And hopefully she would find the braidmaids too! They had all agreed that it would be safe after all to try the rescue already, as the mission on Anacapa either resulted in Eelstrom's capture, or there would be red alert anyway.

She had spotted an open window on one of her rounds. On the upper floor, facing the less glamorous view of the near highway. It nearly threw her plane against the wall when the helicopter took off.

Good luck, dragon rider!

Lola shared the Greenblooms' dislike of weapons. But the Copperman was really giving her a headache – right between her ears. Mary's invisibility potion would only make the flight and the first few hours on the island safe for Firedrake. But he was a dragon after all. So enough of the worries.

Lola whistled a little tune while she dived with her plane through the open window. 'Rats rule'; she had written that one herself too. As she had hoped, no alarm went off. She used a cloaking tool for all her indoor missions. Hothbrodd had developed it from some kind of tree sap and so far it had proved to be reliable with all alarm systems. The window led into one of those tiled rooms humans built to flush away whatever their bodies got rid of, with huge amounts of water. Not a very reasonable thing to do, but alas, they weren't the most reasonable species!

Luckily the door of the room stood open. Doors could cost a lot of precious time. Usually she had to land and lasso the doorknob to open it. But this time the gap was even wide enough to just fly through, and Lola hummed happily to herself while she buzzed down the long corridor that opened up in front of her. It was very white, like the rest of the house. Quite a strange colour choice, considering the effort it took to keep it clean. But, once again . . . humans . . .

Of course, Lola had memorised the floor plan of the massive mansion to make sure she wouldn't get lost: past three doors to the left, then down the corridor branching off on the right and behind the second door she would hopefully find the moss fairies and the braidmaids. If the bugs had got that right. The ones who had survived the manticore had by now crawled out of the house, so at least she wouldn't have to collect them as well. She still felt quite guilty that the mission had turned out to be so deadly. Shame!

Lola made it without any problems into the second corridor. But alas, just when she was heading for the right door, she heard a voice – quite a strange voice, half-human, half-catlike. It sounded as if it was talking to itself.

'Quite a strange scent!' Lola heard it murmur as she hastily landed her plane on a fan that was drawling its rounds under the ceiling. 'Is it rat? No. There's something else. Hmm.'

The fan was luckily not moving fast. But it wasn't the best of hiding places, as it didn't grant a steady view down into the corridor. Alas, it was the only one available in all the whiteness.

And there he came, the mumbler with the strange voice, on soft but murderous paws – the scorpion tail stinging the stale air, the bearded and almost human face scanning the corridor in search for the source of the scent he was commenting on.

The manticore. Of course. Lola had expected to run into him. After all, the homunculi had encountered him too, not to mention the bugs. Manticores were not the most pleasant of fabulous beasts, and this one seemed also to be some kind of mutation, as his fur had the colour of freshly polished copper. Except for the chattiness, Lola couldn't spot much of a difference though. As far as she could detect, he was just a plain mean, nasty manticore.

'Rat and motor oil?' He bared his two rows of shark-like teeth. Yes, they definitely looked bigger and sharper. 'What does this mean? Did the filthy rodent take a bite of the wiring in the master's cars?'

Filthy rodent . . . nice. Lola was very tempted to fly her plane into the vain and arrogant face below her. But that wouldn't serve the purpose of her mission so she just enjoyed picturing how such a collision would go. Manticores were constantly concerned about their appearance. They were said to spend hours combing their beards. This one for sure looked very coiffured.

There. He cast a glance up to the fan. The circling blades hid Lola well. But her scent . . . sadly all that circling air carried it down to the manticore's very efficient nose.

'Perfume?' he murmured. 'Lavender with a hint of rose. Cadoc prefers much more musty notes. This doesn't make sense! A rat wearing perfume?'

By now he was sitting right under the fan, his scorpion tail neatly wound around his lion claws. Heavens, she should have held back on the perfume this morning. She would never get to that door! Manticores did not only have the body and eyes of a very big cat. They also had their patience.

'I think I see a tail,' she suddenly heard the manticore purr. Damn, her tail. She always forgot about that.

'Oh, yes. It is a fat rat! Female, probably,' the manticore purred. 'Yes, quite fat. That note of motor oil is unfortunate, but the lavender may cover it enough. Otherwise I'll take her to the kitchen and ask the cook to soak her in olive oil before I eat her.'

Olive oil? That was too much. Definitely.

The manticore licked his teeth.

She had to be fast. Very fast. Even though she would run the risk of crashing on the floor. She resisted the temptation to spit into the blasé face staring up at her and started her engine.

The cat eyes widened as she swooped down. Lola hit the manticore right on the head with her left wing; luckily it didn't break, thanks to the enforcements Hothbrodd had done for her. She sent a heartfelt thank-you to the troll as the manticore collapsed. Lola managed to pull the plane up just in time before it hit the tiled floor. It was still so fast that it shot past the door she had come for and down the corridor, but Lola was able to slow it down before it reached the end. The manticore was stretched out on the floor when she returned, but she was sure he would be on his paws again worryingly soon. All the more reason to be quick.

The door wasn't locked – at least she was not completely out of luck! But the door had a knob that needed to be turned and Lola lost precious time landing and climbing up there to open the latch. Oh, she should have accepted Freddie's offer to accompany her! Well, too late! She saw the manticore's scorpion tail twitch as she closed the door behind her with a push of her paw. Yes, he would be waiting for her.

The room she was in was quite small considering the size of the house. But so were the ones who were kept locked up there. Lola landed right next to the cage in which six quite miserable-looking moss fairies were hunched together. The cage was conveniently placed on a big table, and – hurrah! – the aquarium holding four braidmaids was placed right beside it. The fairies were in such bad shape that they barely lifted their heads, but the braidmaids were fierce creatures who looked like they might be able to take care of themselves. As soon as Lola pushed the glass on top of the aquarium aside just a bit, they crawled out and jumped off the table.

'Wait!' she hissed down to them as they headed for the door. 'How about *Thank you, rat*? And I wouldn't open that door unless you wish to end up as manticore snacks.'

'Thank you, rat!' one of them hissed back and mocked her with a bow, while the others just stared at her with grim faces, as if she had been the one who'd trapped them. 'We can handle that cat. Is the metal man around?'

'No.' Lola resisted adding that they obviously hadn't been able to handle *him*.

The fairies were still not moving as she climbed up the cage and opened the door. Curse Eelstrom, he must have squeezed the dust out of them so often that there was not much life left in them. Hopefully they could still fly! She certainly wouldn't be able to take them all in her plane.

The braidmaids had made it to the door on their spindly legs, but they failed miserably at getting up to the handle. Well, maybe that would teach them some gratitude.

One of the fairies had finally opened her pale-golden eyes.

'Who are you?' she murmured. 'You look like a rat.'

'That's because I am a rat,' Lola replied. Moss fairies were not very bright. 'Can you all fly?'

The others had opened their eyes as well. 'We can try!'

They all began to flap their wings, their tired faces bright with hope. Well, this was looking good. The braidmaids were still trying to get to the handle, climbing on top of each other, but they collapsed like a house of cards just when the last one had made it to the top.

'Silent!' Lola hissed as they untangled their limbs. 'All of you! We'll only get out of here together!'

It seemed that truth had dawned on the braidmaids as well by now. They actually fell silent and Lola had a chance to listen for

sounds from outside. She didn't hear the
manticore mumble to himself,
but he was on the hunt now,
and even manticores knew that
required silence. Anyway . . . that
was a problem they would
deal with once they opened
that door. For now, she had to
focus on the fairies.

'Listen!' she said, while one fairy after the other fluttered out
of the cage. 'As soon as we manage to open that door you follow
my plane! Fly as high as you can. I'm sure the manticore will
jump at us, and if you're not careful he'll have you between his
teeth before you can say Ouch! Understood?'

They all nodded.

Catmint and cheese, they did look exhausted. And it was a
long way back to that open window. But they'd still have a better
chance of survival than with Eelstrom.

Lola climbed into her plane.

'We won't give him a chance to jump at you, rat!' one of the
braidmaids hissed. 'Right, sisters?'

The others nodded and bared their teeth. Lola had to admit she
was quite impressed by them. After all, they were half her size!

'If you say so,' she whispered back. 'I can come back and check
on you?'

'No need,' they hissed back. 'But tell us where to find the
metal man.'

Nosedive and rusty propellers! They were tough. Impressive.
'He won't be back all day,' Lola replied. 'He left to hunt a dragon.'

That shut them up.

'You can help me open the door,' she whispered to the fairies, who had gathered around her. 'Try to turn the knob until the latch snaps open, and then pull while I fly towards the opening door! You all have to follow me, before the door shuts again.'

Both the braidmaids and the fairies nodded, though two of the fairies looked quite scared. They were fragile little things. Lola was very glad she hadn't been born as a fairy. Or a braidmaid. It would have driven her nuts to constantly have to keep tangling and untangling her legs! No, rat was perfect.

The fairies did a good job and Lola flew through the opening door, followed by all of them – and the braidmaids.

The manticore was waiting, as expected. He came for them the moment Lola's plane shot out on to the corridor. But he hadn't expected a ferocious attack from four very angry braidmaids.

His screams and howls followed them down the corridor, and when Lola cast a quick glance back she saw the braidmaids clinging to the manticore's legs, digging their teeth into his fur.

One. Two. Three. Four. Five. Six. Yes! Lola was very relieved when she saw all the fairies had made it, and were swarming after her down the corridor. The door of the tiled room was still open and the fairies had already fluttered through the window when the braidmaids came tumbling into the bathroom, covered in manticore hair, their tiny claws red with its blood. They managed to get to the window without Lola's help by climbing up a pipe. So she let them do their thing and followed the fairies, as the wind outside whirled the little things all over the place. Lola herded them in like sheep, and with a lot of breaks in oak and eucalyptus trees, she patiently guided them towards the safety of Mary's mountain.

CHAPTER THIRTY-NINE

FROM BLUE TO RED

Guinevere only noticed the merpeople when she and Vita were already surrounded by them. The Aurelia had made them both forget everything – even what they had come for. Lizzie . . . they had to find her father's old friend and warn her of Eelstrom's squid!

But the merpeople who had surrounded them didn't look like they had any intention of letting them go. Their scales were sparkling with hostility, and there was no hope of peacefully escaping the circle they had formed around them.

'More selkies? What do you want?' The mermaid who swam towards them with a firework of signals was stout and dark-haired, and she clearly didn't like selkies. Guinevere felt her signals like angry fingers on her fur, and although they were hostile she was thrilled she could decipher them as easily as the flipper signals of her mother.

'Selkies cause nothing but trouble!' a merman with bright red hair signalled. 'Send them away, Laimomi!'

'No! Wait!' The mermaid who pushed through the circle

looked different from the others. Her face was almost human and by her side swam a huge fish that glowed like a Halloween pumpkin. Was that the lantern fish the leprechaun had mentioned?

'What if they bring another message?' the mermaid signalled. 'Let us hear what they say!'

'Lizzie?' Guinevere saw the widest selkie smile spread across her mother's face. 'It is you, isn't it? I'm Vita, Barnabas's wife, and this is his daughter, Guinevere!'

Lizzie looked at them both with an incredulous smile.

'Vita? Guinevere? So Barnabas married a selkie?'

Both Guinevere and Vita burst into laughter. It surrounded them with yellow bubbles.

'No!' Guinevere signalled with her flippers, as she was not sure Lizzie could hear her thoughts. 'We borrowed the skins from the selkies. My father doesn't even go near the water, since . . .'

'. . . since he thought he couldn't save you from drowning,' her mother completed the sentence.

Lizzie's face turned grave.

'That was a dark day,' Guinevere heard her voice in her head. 'Well, as you see, I didn't drown. I am sorry I never tried to contact you all. For years I didn't know how. I was also worried Cadoc would learn about the merpeople settlement through me. And then the years just went by, and I lived such a different life that my old life and even my old friends seemed unreal. Like a dream I once had. But tell me: Barnabas is well and his old wonderful self, I guess?'

Guinevere exchanged a glance with her mother. 'He's actually not that well.' Lizzie gave her the courage to talk with just her thoughts. 'Eelstrom woke a monster that cast a petrifying spell on us. Father took it the hardest, as he tried to protect us. But our friends are looking for a remedy. And my brother and his dragon will try to trap Eelstrom and lock him up until the Aurelia is safe.'

'And his dragon?' Lizzie's eyes widened. 'It seems we have many tales to tell.'

All the merpeople were flashing excited lights. Even deep under the sea a dragon meant great magic.

Lizzie slung her arm around the mermaid who had first confronted them. 'May I introduce the friend who saved me from drowning? This is Laimomi. I will spare you the others' names as they're all Hawaiian. You may find them hard to remember – I know I did when I first came here.' She smiled at Guinevere. 'Barnabas has a daughter! I am so glad to meet you!'

'I'm very glad to meet you, Lizzie!' Guinevere replied.

I just want to be *you!* she almost added. A mermaid. Humans could turn into mermaids? How? But there was no time to ask.

'We came to warn you!' Vita pointed past the Aurelia, where the silhouettes of five big squid were barely visible in the dark. 'Those squid are Eelstrom's creatures. We fear they will try to steal the Aurelia's pods.'

The other merpeople flashed red in alarm.

'We were already worried about them,' Laimomi signalled. 'And we came up with a plan to find out what their intentions are.'

Lizzie nodded. 'You arrived at just the right time,' she said.

'Let's find out together.'

Guinevere felt as if she had known her all her life when she once again smiled at her. She followed Lizzie closely, when they all made their way to the dark waters, where the squid were moving. To live under the sea! Surrounded by merpeople friends, followed by a glorious lantern fish, riding seahorses ... yes! Guinevere was sure Lizzie and Laimomi were doing that all the time. Could there be a better life? Away from all the noise of the upper world, surrounded by creatures and plants most human eyes would never see, probably living in a shipwreck, whose wood creaked with stories from many centuries ...

Around her the merpeople had slowed down.

The creatures lurking where the light from the Aurelia didn't reach were definitely not regular squid. At least they weren't any species Guinevere had heard of. Each one was at least five metres long, their eyes placed right underneath their lean triangular hoods. The right eye was much bigger than the left, as with normal squid, but there was nothing normal about their skin. It was pale red. *Like copper*, Guinevere thought as she followed the others. Their hoods even had a metallic shimmer, like helmets of ancient knights, and their tentacles were unusually long and thick. Guinevere counted twelve, in contrast to their natural cousins' eight. Did they have the deadly beak hidden between their tentacles that squid were feared for? It pushed poison through their prey's shell – not strong enough to harm humans. But what if the Copperman had made these squid as poisonous as an octopus, whose sting paralysed the breathing?

Lizzie had heard her thoughts.

'It may be that strong. We watched them hunt,' she signalled. 'They kill fast. Even huge prey, so be careful!'

A shoal of blizzard fish drifted past one of the dark silhouettes, and for a second Guinevere felt the gaze of a huge eye. Then suddenly one of the tentacles shot forward and all the blizzard fish were gone.

'Did you see?' Guinevere swam closer to Lizzie's side. 'We found out that they have claws hidden between their tentacles! Huge shimmering claws, similar to a lobster's.'

Lizzie shuddered. 'Just the thing to—'

'—cut the pods off the Aurelia's arms,' Guinevere finished. 'That's Eelstrom's plan! The squid steal the pods just when she gets ready to release them, and before anyone else has a chance to receive them.'

'But where did he find those squid?' Laimomi had joined them. 'I've never seen the like.'

'He caught a Copperman,' Vita answered as they peered at the squid through floating algae and shoals of fish. 'He can alter creatures with his magic.'

Lizzie's shook her head. 'I was always worried I would have to deal with Cadoc's evil schemes again. I tried so hard to forget that he is still out there doing terrible things. How foolish of me!'

Laimomi grabbed her arm. 'Even more reason to test whether the sepia fog works!'

'Sepia fog?' Guinevere noticed that the lantern fish had come closer. He had such a wonderful face. She shyly reached out with her flipper, and was very happy when he allowed her to touch him.

'Yes,' Laimomi replied. 'We need a way to disorientate the squid, to give the Aurelia time to get away or defend herself, in case they attack her.'

'Did you try to talk to her?' Vita asked.

Lizzie shook her head. 'No. I can't even communicate with whales. I think they find everything we think or worry about quite foolish. We don't understand their world and they don't understand ours. Imagine how much more that's true of the Aurelia. Her song just gets louder when we get closer, and her light makes us so dizzy that we have to turn around. I'm sure those arms of hers can be deadly, though so far we haven't seen her use them.'

Vita looked at the others. 'Do they all know what may happen if she gets angry?'

'That these may be the last days for all of us, if we can't prevent that? Oh, yes.' Laimomi said. 'In our tales the Aurelia is not only called the Great Singer. We call her also the Bringer of Life and Death. If those squid take her pods, her anger will be the end of many things – and all of us.'

Her anger . . .

Guinevere looked back at the huge shimmering shape of the Aurelia. She seemed to be made of nothing but light, woven from blues and purples and golden sparks. What did her anger look like?

She would soon find out.

Looking back at the squid Guinevere felt almost blind. Their darkness seemed to filter all light out of the water.

There.

Lizzie gave a signal with her tail, and from behind the merpeople hundreds of tiny sepia squid appeared and slowly drifted towards the copper squid.

Of course! Lizzie and the others hoped that their ink would work like underwater fog!

But Laimomi suddenly grabbed Lizzie's arm. 'Two are missing!'

She was right! There were only three. Where were the others? Guinevere searched the water with her eyes.

There! Two squid were heading for the Aurelia and her glimmering veil of arms. Why did they attack now? The pods were of no use until they were ripe – which if the tales could be trusted would only happen when the Aurelia reached the coast. Guinevere saw the same helpless question on the others' faces while they were all swimming frantically towards the Aurelia. The pods were so big by now that one could detect them easily on four of her shorter arms.

Guinevere desperately tried to make her new body swim faster, as did Vita, but the merpeople were far ahead. They swam with breathtaking speed, but the two squid were getting closer and closer to the Aurelia's arms.

The merpeople began to form a chain, grabbing each other's hands. Sparks rose from their tails, more and more, until a cloud of them floated towards the squid and attached themselves to their copper skin. They clearly irritated them. They slowed down and tried to wipe the sparks off their bodies. One stopped and whipped his skin in a frenzy. But the other one continued, slashing at the sparks with his tentacles. The merpeople sent more and more after him, but despite their efforts the squid reached the Aurelia – and dived into the maze of her arms.

Guinevere felt her heart stop when a shiny claw protruded from the squid's tentacles. She heard the merpeople scream in her head as the claw opened and cut the tip off one of the shimmering arms.

The Aurelia turned as dark as if all her lights had been swallowed by the water. Then a red shiver ran over her enormous body and gathered in the injured arm. It began to glow like a burning candle wick, and the squid who'd just left the veil of her arms behind caught fire and dissolved in the water. The other one hastily made his escape, still covered with the merpeople's sparks. He glowed between the others like an illuminated Christmas tree as he joined them in the dark.

When Guinevere finally dared to look back at the Aurelia, she was once again all light and colours, drifting through the water as peacefully as if what they'd just watched was nothing but a bad dream. There was only a hint of red on her shortened arm, but it disappeared soon, like the embers at the end of a match.

The merpeople had let go of each other's hands as Vita and Guinevere caught up with them. Why had the squid attacked the Aurelia? Guinevere heard that question from all sides. He hadn't even tried to get a pod!

'They were testing whether their claws can cut her arms,' she heard her mother say. 'And now they know they can.'

Yes. That made terrible sense.

And they had learned what the Aurelia would do. They all had seen it. The tales were true. She would burn everything near her, and her pods would be lost for ever. Then the rest was probably true as well. All fabulous creatures would disappear, for the Aurelia would take back all the gifts of life that she'd brought over the centuries.

Where would they go? Would she give them to another world? Where her gifts were received with gratitude instead of greed?

Please! Guinevere thought. *Please! It's only Cadoc Eelstrom who's attacking you. And we're fighting him! My brother will risk his life to protect you!*

Lizzie was staring into the darkness where the other squid were lurking.

'They will try again,' she said.

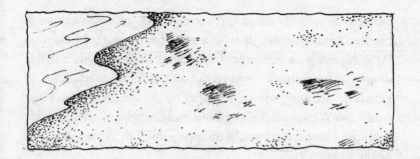

CHAPTER FORTY

ANACAPA

Ben had fought the beak of a griffin with Firedrake and Nettlebrand's claws and teeth. But so far he and his dragon had never faced human weapons. Would Eelstrom use them? Lola's report didn't sound like it. After all, he knew for sure what Barnabas had assured Ben of before he left: 'Dragon scales can't be penetrated easily,' Barnabas had said. 'Not even by modern bullets. They'll actually get firmer the older Firedrake gets. And have you forgotten all the old tales about how difficult it is to kill a dragon?'

'But they nearly extinguished them nevertheless,' Ben had replied.

'Because there were so few of us and so many of your kind,' Firedrake had added. 'Don't worry about me, dragon rider.'

That was easier said than done. Like Lola, Ben feared that as Eelstrom knew about the firmness of Firedrake's scales he would make use of the Copperman's magic. But while Firedrake was leaving paw prints for Eelstrom on Anacapa's stony ground Ben finally felt the calm determination he'd sensed before when facing evil with his dragon. It seemed such an outdated word, but Ben couldn't come up with a more fitting one for Eelstrom. Wait. *He is also an idiot*, he thought, while following his invisible dragon and erasing his own tracks on the way. For what would Eelstrom do with his immortality, if he succeeded and the Aurelia took back all the magic she had brought into this world? Even the Copperman would disappear. Well . . . that might not be the worst part.

Mary's friend had recommended a narrow beach on the western side of the island as the place where the dragon would await his enemy. It was surrounded by steep rocky cliffs with a cave cut deep into them. Hothbrodd and Alfonso were already hiding in there. Ben erased their tracks as Firedrake lay down in the sand. He was still invisible – Mary's potion would probably last another hour. Ben hoped that Eelstrom would arrive earlier, so that he wouldn't see Firedrake right away. 'Why do you hope for that, dragon rider?' Firedrake had asked. 'If I have to fight with him, I want him to see me.' Yes, Ben understood that. If he was honest, he wished for Eelstrom to see him as well.

Nevertheless . . . Firedrake's track was very visible all along the beach, but Ben had erased it close to the dragon. Let Eelstrom guess where exactly he was.

Ben raised his head. There. Was that a helicopter?

He crouched down behind Firedrake, finding his invisible body with his hands.

'Yes. I think they are coming.' The dragon was, as always, so calm that Ben felt that calm in his own heart. And yes, he heard them too. His hearing had indeed sharpened. And not only his hearing. All his senses were beginning to pick up things in a different way. Not only sounds and scents . . . even the wind had a taste by now and there was a strength in his body that felt as if Firedrake was breathing within him.

Dragon rider.

Yes, he was ready to face Cadoc Eelstrom. He actually couldn't wait.

But the first one who showed up was the Copperman. Ben saw him appear high above them on the cliff. He looked huge even from a distance, as he stared down at the track of paw prints. He seemed to not quite believe what he saw.

Ben felt Firedrake stand up, though all he saw was the sand trickling off the dragon's body. 'I've never seen anything like him,' he growled. 'He looks like those metal-clad knights who used to chase us.'

'Yes,' Ben murmured. 'I just wish he would carry visible arms like them.'

This felt too easy.

He threw a pebble into the cave – the signal for Hothbrodd and Alfonso that their enemies had arrived.

The Copperman began to climb down the cliff – and there came his master.

Cadoc Eelstrom just stood still for a few moments and stared down at the tracks on the beach, before he followed the Copperman.

It was true – he really did look barely older than Ben. He seemed to be nothing more than a lanky boy with short blonde hair and expensive sunglasses. It seemed absolutely impossible that he had gone to school with his father! He climbed down the steep cliff with the light steps of a fourteen-year-old. Only his clothes gave a hint at the truth – he was dressed as if he had walked out of an old movie about lion and elephant hunters. That and the boyish face sent an eerie warning. Yes, Cadoc

Eelstrom looked like a moody teenager, but they would be fighting magic – magic he had stolen from fabulous creatures. Fabulous creatures like Firedrake.

The two had reached the beach. The Copperman stopped and Eelstrom stepped to his side and stared at where the tracks ended. He definitely noticed the cave. He probably would expect Firedrake to hide in there.

The dragon rose to his feet. Ben did the same.

Eelstrom turned his head, listening.

Come closer, Ben thought, *come closer, Cadoc. My father is still sick and weak from what you did to him, and even I remember the stone in my chest. Let's get this over and done with!*

Ben was still surprised their enemy had only brought one helper to hunt a dragon. But by now he felt the threat that huge body exuded. Not even a dozen men would have felt half as threatening. The Copperman gazed to his left and to his right and cast a watchful look at the ocean, before he followed his master towards the dragon they couldn't see.

He certainly sensed Firedrake. Even Ben felt his dragon's presence like something that almost took his breath away – so much strength, so much life, flesh holding fire. It was easy to read Eelstrom's face while he followed the metal man. His pale face was stiff with desire and every step was a strange mix of haste and hesitance. The Copperman in contrast walked through the sand as if he approached something sacred.

They both stopped at Firedrake's last paw print, and only now did Ben notice the bag the Copperman carried over his shoulder. It was the only thing he had brought, and Ben didn't like the look of it.

'It's new to me that dragons make themselves invisible!' Eelstrom called towards what he couldn't see. 'Did Barnabas teach you that? Or one of those creatures he surrounds himself with? He is such a trusting fool. Two of his fabulous friends came to me and told me you're here.'

Firedrake shook himself one more time. The sand surrounded his invisible shape like golden mist.

'Barnabas Greenbloom a trusting fool? You prove you're a fool if you believe that.'

A dragon's voice has a power of its own. Ben saw the Copperman shiver, as if his metal skin had suddenly felt the wind. Even Cadoc Eelstrom lost the arrogant smile and took a step back. But he recovered quickly.

'I'm sure everyone listens to that voice,' he said. 'Shame one probably cannot cut it out of you as well.'

He tried hard to hide the fierce desire that had brought him here – and the fact that Firedrake's presence indeed had an impact on him. He tried to cover it up with an uneasy laugh and bent down to wipe the sand off his dark leather shoes. Then he straightened up and stared once again at where Firedrake was standing.

'I guess you are one of the silverscales? I heard rumours that some of them survived the dragon hunts. I admit I never believed them. Those knights were also after your hearts, I guess. Invincibility was, in those days, as desirable as now. Who knows, maybe you can live without a heart! Some people say I am heartless, and look at me. I think I look just as young as your dragon rider. Is he here too?'

Ben felt Firedrake stir by his side. And that he was angry.

'You like the sound of your own voice, Cadoc.' Ben stepped out behind Firedrake before he could stop him. 'Of course I am here. A dragon and his rider are like one.'

Eelstrom stared in the direction he heard his voice come from with a mix of curiosity and . . . Ben was not quite sure. Jealousy? Fear?

'I guess you're not all grey and stony any more. Shame. I should have just broken you into pieces!'

Firedrake gave off a deep growl. He became visible, slowly still, but enough to make Cadoc take another step back. The Copperman though didn't move. He just kept staring at those silver scales one by one emerging, the long neck, the powerful tail, the wings folded.

'The two homunculi betrayed Firedrake because we asked them to,' Ben said. '*We* can trust our friends. Can you? No. I guess you don't have any.'

'What for? Friends are vastly overrated,' Cadoc replied, his eyes on the dragon, who by now was fully visible. 'I'm surprised your father didn't come himself to stop me. Does he leave all his business to you these days?'

'He would be here, if you hadn't nearly killed him.'

Cadoc smiled the meanest smile Ben had ever seen. 'I am thrilled to hear that.' He stepped closer to the Copperman and put his hand on the bag he carried. 'Get out of the way, dragon rider.'

Ben answered him with just a smile. To their left Elewese had emerged from the waves. The dolphins surrounding him turned to Chumash men the moment they stepped out of the water.

'That's him?' Elewese's arms all pointed at Eelstrom. 'He's just a boy. Let's get him.'

Cadoc had spun around, while the other Chumash surrounded the Copperman. 'It gets better and better,' he snarled. 'A starfish and some dolphin men. I wonder what your hearts can do when ground up.'

'Even a night troll would consider your heart indigestible.'

Hothbrodd had stepped out of the cave with Alfonso and three of his men. 'This was easier than expected. Let's tie them up.'

'Trolls, fishmen, dragons . . .' Cadoc cast them all a mocking glance. 'This is without doubt a Greenbloom mission.' He cast the Copperman a commanding glance. 'What are you waiting for? More strange creatures to show up?!'

But the Copperman seemed to not even hear him. He had only eyes for Firedrake.

'Free me, Lord of the Dragons!' he exclaimed, while he fell on his knees. 'Free me with your fire!'

'Take his bag, Elewese!' Ben called out, but Cadoc was faster.

'Treacherous piece of metal trash!' he yelled, pulling the bag from the Copperman's shoulder.

Both Hothbrodd and Elewese tried to hold him back when he reached inside, but it was too late. The thing Eelstrom threw against the cliff looked like a rusty egg. It burst open the moment it hit the stone. The creature it released was first barely as big as a sparrow, but it grew with breathtaking speed into a huge reptile. Its copper-coloured wings ended in claws, and its beak was as long and sharp as a rapier.

The Copperman buried his face in his hands as the creature he had brought to the beach became two, then four, then eight creatures, each uttering a piercing scream as they attacked the dragon.

Ben was already on Firedrake's back when he spread his wings to meet them in the air. His fire destroyed three, but one of the attackers drove his beak into his shoulder, right beneath his wing, and Ben felt Firedrake's pain as sharp as if it was his own.

Below them Hothbrodd had thrown Eelstrom face down into the sand, and the Chumash had bound the Copperman, who was still on his knees and didn't resist them. From the crushed egg though more and more of the sabre creatures hatched, growing even bigger than their predecessors. Ben wished for a sabre himself as he tried to kick them away from Firedrake, but all he had were his feet and his arms. His skin proved indeed to be almost as resistant to the beaks as Firedrake's scales but from time to time they tore a wound nevertheless. The screams escaping the beaks pierced his ears, unwelcome proof, how much more sensitive they were by now and though he felt Firedrake's strength and fire in his limbs, there were just too many attackers.

Hothbrodd was staring up at them in despair, while Alfonso's men were gathering stones and throwing them at the reptiles. The creatures were a dense swarm by now, enveloping Firedrake and Ben, although the dragon still melted dozens with his fire and tore them apart with his claws and teeth. So many. Too many.

'A Greenbloom doesn't kill!' Ben believed he heard Barnabas's voice. 'We'll make ourselves into the monsters they are.' But when another beak pierced his skin he imagined driving that same beak into Eelstrom's heart. Although Hothbrodd had tied him up and was pressing him into the sand, he looked up at them in triumph while his creatures covered Firedrake and his rider with bleeding wounds . . .

He should have taken that bag! Firedrake should have grabbed him by his thin neck! He—

Another scream pierced Ben's ears. But this one sounded different. It came from jungles far away.

The shadow that darkened the beach was huge and winged like the attackers. It came down from the blue sky above them. Ben saw feathers in all colours this world knew, and joy melted all the despair in his heart. Even the wish to kill.

Shrii, the king of the last griffins, landed on Anacapa like a storm. His feathers filled the sky as if the rainbow had come alive. He grabbed the sabre-beaked creatures and crushed them in his claws. Firedrake welcomed him with a roar, and side by side the dragon and the griffin ploughed through the swarms of attackers until the beach was covered with sharp beaks and copper feathers.

Had they been living things? Ben wondered. Or just artificial things the Copperman had made from living creatures? *Well, Twigleg is an artificial thing, Ben Greenbloom*, a voice whispered inside him, as he wiped the blood off his hands and felt the wind from Shrii's wings on his hot face. The world was such a complicated place and it was so hard to figure out what was right and wrong.

The griffin's claws dug deep into the sand as he landed just a few metres away from Firedrake and folded his enormous wings.

'At just the right time, my friend,' Firedrake said, while he bent his neck to greet Shrii. 'I've never been happier to see you.'

'I'm glad I didn't come too late,' the griffin replied, picking the remains of a beak out of his plumage. 'I had to fly through quite a few storms on my way. And when I arrived everyone seemed so worried that I decided to check on you here. I thought we were only here to receive a few precious gifts from the ocean? Instead of fighting sharp-beaked enemies?'

'That is the task we're here for.' Ben's knees were shaking with exhaustion as he walked towards the griffin. 'But there is some-one who wants to steal those gifts, and we had to make sure that doesn't happen. We might have failed without you.'

Hothbrodd dragged Eelstrom to his feet and shook him like a captured rabbit. 'Thought you'd get his heart, right?' he growled at him. 'Well, guess what. I feel very tempted to feed yours to the seagulls! But they'd probably fall dead from the sky.'

'You stink, troll!' Cadoc hissed at him. 'And I will for sure not miss your kind. Or those freaks,' he nodded at the dolphin men and Elewese. 'I will upset the Aurelia just to see you all drop dead! And first of all—!'

He tried to kick the Copperman, but Hothbrodd dragged him back.

'I am sure you also wouldn't mind if the leprechauns vanished,' Ben said. 'We received a gift from one, just for you.' He nodded at Hothbrodd.

The troll reached with a grim smile into one of his huge pockets and pulled out a belt.

'No!' Ben saw for the first time a glimpse of fear on Cadoc Eelstrom's face. 'Get your hands off me, all of you! You'll regret this, dragon rider!' he yelled. 'I will eat that dragon's heart and take that griffin's golden eyes to make myself see every treasure in this world!'

'Can you lend me a hand, Elewese?' the troll growled, while his captive wiggled in his grip like a fish.

The starfish man stepped closer and wrapped his arms around Eelstrom. 'There are rumours in the water that you have creatures resembling squid following the Aurelia,' he said 'and that they cut off one of her arms. She nearly burned us all. Call them back.'

'Never!' Cadoc hissed. 'You'll all be history in just a few days!

And I'll have all eternity.'

'He can't call them back.' The Copperman was still on his knees. 'No one can. He had me make them that way.'

'Well, there goes your last chance.' Hothbrodd began to sling the belt around Cadoc's waist.

'Tell your father I killed the last unicorn, dragon rider!' Cadoc yelled while he desperately tried to escape the belt. 'Barnabas always looked for them. They are gone! And their magic was a big disappointment!'

Ben felt the blood leave his face. Unicorns. Yes, his father had always wanted to find one.

Cadoc spat into Hothbrodd's face as he closed the leprechaun's belt. But that didn't spare him.

The next moment Elewese dropped a shabby shoe into the sand.

'Look at that,' Hothbrodd growled as he picked it up. 'All that he is now. I thought the shoe would be all shiny like his clothes and his boyish face. I forgot leprechaun magic reveals the true nature of things.' He pulled another belt out of his pocket. 'Your turn, metal jaw.'

'Wait!' Firedrake said.

The dragon walked slowly towards the still-kneeling Copperman and looked down at him. 'What did you mean when you asked me to free you?'

'Only a dragon's fire can break the spell Eelstrom put on me,' the Copperman replied.

'Don't, Firedrake,' Hothbrodd growled. 'He built them all. The creatures who nearly killed you and Ben. He called the monster that made Barnabas sick, and those following the Aurelia.'

The dragon was still looking down at the Copperman. 'They came from Eelstrom's mind, Hothbrodd,' he said.

Then he took a deep breath and wrapped the kneeling man in his blue fire.

The Copperman tore the rope they had bound him with the moment the dragon stepped back. He pushed Elewese and Hothbrodd away without effort when they tried to grab him. But then he sank on to his knees again – not in front of Firedrake, but in front of Ben.

'I can't call back the creatures Eelstrom made me create, dragon rider,' he said. 'But take this as a gift for my freedom.'

Without flinching he broke the little finger off his left hand and held it up to Ben.

'This should heal your father. Tell him I am very sorry. Eelstrom told me to aim the monster's rage at him. But if you melt this copper and shape it into a ring for him to wear on his shortest finger, the rage that hurt him will leave, and the ring will protect him from now on against such spells.'

Ben looked at the finger in his hand. He didn't know what to say. It looked like someone had broken it off a metal sculpture, so perfect in itself, and yet filled with a strange kind of life that he had not sensed before.

The Copperman slowly rose to his feet and wiped the sand from his metal shins.

'I may also be able to help with the creatures I planted on the beach,' he said. 'But I have to warn you. They are quite fierce.'

CHAPTER FORTY-ONE

EIGHT

No, Guinevere didn't want to give that selkie skin back. Not ever. Though maybe she would have exchanged it for a mermaid's tail. And some hands. Hands were quite useful, she had learned in this short time having to make do with flippers. The merpeople had by now accepted her and Vita as friends – mostly thanks to Lizzie, Laimomi and Koo, who more and more often swam by Guinevere's side. 'Koo usually doesn't like seals,' Lizzie had told Guinevere with a wink. 'I think he has a slight crush on you.'

Guinevere was certainly in awe of the big lantern fish. And of Lizzie. She so wished she had always known them. She had by now asked Lizzie a million questions about the merpeople's life, and she seemed to never get tired of answering. Well, there was not much else to do, of course, while they were following the Aurelia. The copper squid hadn't tried anything since that last attack. But there was nothing they could do to chase them away, not even all together. The only thing they could do was to form a dense shield of merpeople and sea creatures of all kinds around the Aurelia and hope that they'd somehow be able to keep the aggressors at bay. For if they didn't – the squid's attack had proved that – her anger would burn the oceans and everything near her. And no, Guinevere didn't want to remind herself that in her anger the Great Singer might take all her fabulous friends with her. Nevertheless . . . each time she looked at Koo or Lizzie or Laimomi she imagined them vanishing right in front of her eyes. Like a beautiful dream that disappeared with the first morning light. Would she disappear with them, as she was wearing a selkie fur? Guinevere almost wished for that, as why would she want to live in a world without all her fabulous friends? Without Firedrake and Sorrel, Twigleg and Freddie, Hothbrodd, Lola (yes, Lola definitely counted as a fabulous creature) and all the others, who filled MÍMAMEIÐR with magical life. No, she hoped she would disappear too, and she was quite sure her parents and Ben felt the same. She cast a look at the merpeople and smiled at Koo: yes, they would either beat Eelstrom, or fade together.

Guinevere was deep in those grim thoughts, when Koo suddenly looked like a swimming hedgehog and blinked so feverishly, that Guinevere couldn't translate that fast.

The message he had received was obviously good though, as Lizzie hugged him so fiercely, that it brought a very pleased look to Koo's face. He had a wonderful face.

'Good news!' Lizzie sparkled, all fireworks. 'Such good news, my friends!!' She swam a somersault and hummed with joy like an underwater bee. 'Your brother and his dragon – they caught Cadoc!'

Guinevere's heart turned into a feather in her chest. Ben had done it! The Aurelia would be safe! Though . . . Guinevere cast a glance at the squid. They were still there.

Would they act
without their master
telling them?

Lizzie had turned,
and for a moment
Guinevere thought
she was looking at the
squid too. Koo and
Laimomi had turned as
well, and all the merpeople were
staring into the darkness beyond
the Aurelia's light and song. Were the
squid attacking once again? Guinevere
saw something moving in the dark
waters. Something huge. But it wasn't
one of the copper squid. The silhouette
was bulkier and swam very differently,
though also with many arms.

'Oh, this is bad!' Laimomi flashed, all

alarm. 'It's a kraken! A Great Blue Kraken! Maybe he's coming to help the squid!'

Koo turned blood-orange red, and the merpeople gathered in alarm around Laimomi. But Guinevere exchanged a relieved glance with her mother. Vita had of course recognised the new arrival as well.

'No worries!' she signalled with her fins. Like Guinevere she still didn't quite trust the telepathy talks. 'This is a very good friend of ours!'

'You have a Great Blue Kraken as your friend?' Laimomi sounded impressed. 'You two seem to be more at home under-water than I thought!'

'My parents asked Eight to be the Courier of Water,' Guinevere signalled while waving at the kraken with her other flipper.

Eight waved back with all his arms, but the merpeople still watched his approach with great worry. Many of them had lost relatives to octopuses, and a Great Kraken had the strength of hundreds of his smaller relatives.

Vita waved Guinevere to her side and together they swam towards Eight to prove to their friends that there was really nothing to worry about. Lizzie and Koo were the first to follow them. Then Laimomi approached the Great Kraken as well. But the others were still watching from a safe distance.

Guinevere was for a moment worried that Eight might mistake them for normal seals, even though he had waved at them. But the kraken had obviously heard about their mission. He stretched out two of his arms towards them, gently wrapped the tips around them and lifted them up to his eyes.

'Well, look where we meet again! Who would have thought!' Guinevere heard his booming voice in her head. (Krakens are brilliant at using telepathy.) 'The white rat sent word through some singing snails that you are dressed in selkie skins. I think he was worried I would eat you by mistake. Gilbert always forgets I'm vegetarian! Right, Eugene?'

The tiny crab that was sitting on the kraken's huge head winked at Guinevere with its four eyes. Eugene and Eight had helped FREEFAB with quite a few missions by now. They were inseparable – though a few months ago Eugene had fallen in love with a Norwegian crab called Maureen and had even considered staying in the MÍMAMEIÐR fjord for her. But Eight had found the Nordic waters to be awfully cold, and finally their friendship had proved stronger than love.

'Eight, may I introduce you to Lizzie, Koo and Laimomi?' Guinevere signalled.

Koo came closer, but the two mermaids still kept their distance. Eight reached out with another two arms and gently dipped the tips against their chests. The other merpeople blinked in alarm, and Koo bared his teeth.

'Be calm, Little Ones!' Eight's voice boomed very gently in all their heads. 'I only attacked merpeople once in my life, when two of your kind stole my companion's eggs. It caused her and me great pain. But that happened more than seven hundred years ago.'

Guinevere was not sure those words calmed the merpeople's worries, but Eight had forgotten about them anyway. He even let go of Guinevere and Vita. He had spotted the Aurelia.

'Eugene, look at her!' the kraken boomed, while his arms began to move in the rhythm of the Aurelia's song. 'The Singer from the Deep, the Bringer of Light! I would never have thought I would see her with my own eyes!'

The crab had to run left and right to stay on the kraken's head when his huge friend began to hum softly and dance with all his arms. But suddenly Eight turned and stared into the dark, where the copper squid were barely visible.

'What are they doing here?' he boomed. 'Those are very strange creatures. There is something wrong about them.'

'Yes, very wrong, Great Kraken!' Lizzie signalled. 'Can you protect the Aurelia from them? They already cut into one of her arms. They will try to steal her pods once they are ripe.'

The kraken stared into the darkness.

'Four great squid,' he murmured. 'That's a lot to fight even for me. And what are they hiding under their tentacles? Are those claws? Let me think about this. Strength alone will not be enough, I fear. Do you agree, Eugene?'

'Absolutely!' his crab friend clattered back. 'I sadly agree full-heartedly, though I have the greatest respect for the strength of yours, as you know. Any direct attack might result in you losing

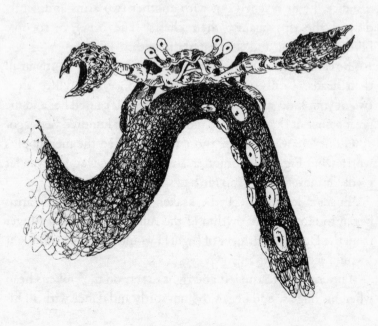

a few arms. Which would not only be very bothersome in the future but also endanger the mission we came for.'

'True, true!' the kraken boomed. 'But if they succeed in stealing the pods, Eugene, there won't be a mission!'

No, there wouldn't. Guinevere suddenly felt the water around her like a great weight. The others had succeeded in catching Eelstrom. But if they failed to keep the Aurelia safe in the water, everything accomplished on land would be in vain.

CHAPTER FORTY-TWO

A COPPER RING

Things were actually not yet all safe on land. Not at all.

Cadoc Eelstrom was just a shabby shoe that Hothbrodd held very firmly in his hand, when they came back to Mary's house. But they all still felt the fear they had experienced on Anacapa, and the squid were still out there, following the Aurelia, determined to attack, with no way to stop them. Had Cadoc Eelstrom won, although they had defeated him?

Ben couldn't help but ask himself that question. Hothbrodd threw the boot with vigour into a metal wardrobe where Mary kept a few things safe from the fires that regularly swept her mountain. 'You're sure he's safe in there?' Ben asked.

'Well, he's a boot, but he can't walk away, can he?' the troll replied with a grim smile as he shut the wardrobe. 'Stop worrying. Leprechaun spells are very reliable. We beat him dragon rider! And now have Mary look at your wounds. I'm impressed how well your human skin held up against those beaks. And you're getting stronger. Everyone saw it on that island. You *are* turning into a little dragon, Ben Greenbloom.

Firedrake, you and Shrii may have saved all our lives.'

Ben felt the blood rush to his face, and he mumbled something like, 'Nonsense, it was all of us.' And, 'We still have to protect the Aurelia.' But the troll's words made him very happy, and his heart hadn't felt that light for a long time.

His father was sleeping when he walked into Mary's guest room with Twigleg on his shoulder to check on him. Barnabas looked so peaceful that Ben didn't wake him. He just bent over him and whispered: 'We caught him. And we brought something back that will hopefully make you feel better soon!'

Mary and Alfonso were checking on Firedrake's wounds as he stepped back on to the porch. They were healing already, as did Ben's. 'Dragon skin!' Twigleg whispered into his ear, while Mary added a tincture from Alfonso's village to her modern bandages and antiseptics. 'Firedrake's magic is in you by now. Maybe I don't have to worry about you that much any more.'

The Copperman was standing silently under Mary's trees, watching them all with a longing on his face that spoke of loneliness and the wish to once again be with his own kind. They had of course told the others why they had brought him back from Anacapa. But Lola, Freddie and Sorrel (who was still throwing up from time to time) were watching him with unveiled hostility, since he had climbed out of the helicopter that Hothbrodd had insisted on flying back from Anacapa.

'Okay, everyone's wounds have been bandaged,' Lola shrilled when Mary put away her first aid kit. 'And Eelstrom has been leprechauned. Hurrah for that. But can we now talk about the wasp-maker?' She pointed at the Copperman who silently returned her glance. 'I still can't believe you all made peace with him! Did you lose your mind on that island? I just freed the braidmaids and moss fairies he caught for his master, and what about Barnabas? He can still barely move a limb!'

Freddie nodded in support, and even the bluelings snarled from the roof, where they were cleaning Mary's gutters.

The Copperman had lowered his head, while Lola called out his sins, and when Ben opened his mouth to defend him, he lifted his huge hand – the hand where the finger he had broken off, was missing.

'It is all true, rat,' he said, his eyes still lowered in shame. 'It is the curse of my kind, that we have to serve any mortal who notices us in our underground world. Some of us are lucky and someone like him,' he nodded at Ben, 'crosses their path. I was not lucky.'

'So what happens if you don't play their obedient slave?' Freddie walked down the railing of the porch until he was standing right in front of the Copperman. 'Like you, my brother and I served an evil master, but we are very small. You are not. You even have magic!'

The Copperman still hung his head. 'It is impossible for us to resist, once the spell is cast, homunculus, and we can't use our magic against our enslavers. It's as if he is inside us and even rules our bodies. Some of us kill themselves to escape. But I have three children and a wife waiting for me – if they still believe I am alive. I couldn't bear the thought of never seeing them again. That's my guilt to carry.'

'But with your help your master would have caused them to vanish too!' Lola shrilled. 'Did you ever think about that when you created the creatures he asked you for?'

'Every moment, since I knew about that risk, rat,' the Copperman gave back. 'But Eelstrom threatened to find and enslave them too if I were to end my slavery by killing myself. And there was always the hope that we might survive his deeds.'

Lola set out to reply to that but she fell silent when Ben stood up.

'Did you notice there is a finger missing on his hand?' he said. 'He broke it off himself, to save my father. If that doesn't work, you can judge him.'

The finger melted on Mary's stove, and the Copperman reached into the hot liquid metal and formed a ring from it. As soon as Ben pushed it on to Barnabas's little finger, his father began to breathe freely, and after a few minutes he sat up in his bed and looked first at the Copperman and then at his son.

'I guess you have to explain a few things to me, son,' he said to Ben. 'Does his presence –' he nodded at the Copperman, who was standing behind Ben in the open door '– mean we are Cadoc's prisoners?'

'No,' Ben said, taking his father's hand with a smile. 'Not at all. Actually Cadoc Eelstrom is our prisoner. The plan on Anacapa worked, and so did the leprechaun's belt. Oh yes, and Shrii arrived! Just in time.'

Barnabas looked once again at the Copperman and then at the ring he was wearing. 'Definitely a lot of things to explain,' he said. 'And I see you are clearly doing very well without my help.'

CHAPTER FORTY-THREE

HIDDEN UNDER THE SAND

Everyone tried to convince Barnabas to stay on Mary's mountain while Alfonso, Hothbrodd and the Copperman got ready to go down to the beach. It was time to deal with the creatures hidden under the sand. But Barnabas shook his head and held up the hand with the copper ring.

'I'm as good as new!' he said. 'In fact, I haven't felt this well for years! Whatever this ring does, I like it. So let's go to the beach!'

It was true. Barnabas felt as if the Copperman had wrapped a bit of magic around his finger, and that along with the fact that Cadoc Eelstrom was a boot in a closet, made him feel almost like a young man again. The only thought that still weighed on his shoulders, as Alfonso drove them down to the beach, was that Guinevere and Vita were deep down in the ocean and that the squid the Copperman had made were still not under control. *Trust in them, Barnabas!* he told himself, as Hothbrodd parked high above the sand that would soon welcome the Aurelia. *Look how well Ben did without you! Why shouldn't Vita and Guinevere succeed as well? And hopefully they'll have Lizzie by their side.*

Shrii was already waiting with Lola on the beach. Lola still frowned at the Copperman, but she was so thrilled the griffin had joined them that she had left her plane behind to ride on Shrii's back.

'Feathers and plume!' she shrilled, as she climbed down his wing and jumped into the sand. 'That bird is strong competition for my plane. What a ride!'

'I take that as a great compliment from such an accomplished pilot,' Shrii said. 'The rats of our island never ask for a ride on our backs.'

He was an impressive sight, with his eagle head and his lion body. His coloured plumage shone in the light of the almost full moon and made him very visible on the pale sand. But it was past midnight and the beach was deserted. Barnabas caught himself looking up to Eelstrom's mansion nevertheless, just to remind himself that it was deserted. Except for the manticore. Should they just release him into the wild, once the seeds of the Aurelia were safe?

The Copperman had followed his gaze.

'You are sure the leprechaun spell will hold?' he said. 'Why didn't you tell your dragon to kill Eelstrom?'

Barnabas didn't get to explain that he didn't believe in killing, and that Firedrake usually agreed with him on the matter.

'A griffin. Very impressive,' a familiar voice said behind them. 'You continue to surprise me, Greenbloom.'

Derog Shortsleeves appeared as suddenly as always, his dog by his side. 'My magic is very reliable, Copperman,' he said. 'No worries there. But have you really stopped serving your master?'

The Copperman returned his gaze calmly. 'The knife he stole from your father is under his pillow. I am sure a leprechaun doesn't need a key to get into a human house? And maybe your dog will like the manticore. I won't go back there. I'll help you with the creatures I hid on this beach, and then I'll go find my family.'

'You would never see them again if I didn't know you *had* to serve Eelstrom, when he caught my brother,' Derog Shortsleeves said. 'Humans may forgive, especially when they are called Greenbloom. But a leprechaun wants revenge.' He pointed down the beach. 'Mannanan detected four unusual visitors under the sand. Is that correct?'

The Copperman shook his head. 'I buried six of them.'

'Indeed? Well.' Derog Shortsleeves shrugged his shoulders. 'Shame. I intended to exchange Mannanan's sniffing services for the shoe my belt turned our enemy into.' He looked at Barnabas enquiringly. 'What will you do with it?'

Yes, what would they do with it? Barnabas frowned. He had no answer for Shortsleeves. The boot would turn human again with the next new moon. Or whenever someone polished the leather. That's how this kind of leprechaun spell worked. But they couldn't let Cadoc go, knowing that he would soon hunt and harm the next fabulous creature.

'The Copperman is right.' The moon lined Shrii's rainbow feathers with silver. 'There are six of them. Fierce worm-like creatures. I hear them moving.'

They all stared at the sand under their feet, but they could neither see nor hear what Shrii's ears picked up.

'We need to watch all the spots while we catch the first worm,' the Copperman said. 'For it will alert the others.'

'Catch?' The leprechaun chuckled. 'I guess they'll be too big to put them in a jam jar. They're supposed to snap up the Aurelia's pods and deliver them to Eelstrom, so I imagine them to have quite spacious jaws?'

'Don't worry, leprechaun,' Hothbrodd growled. 'We'll make

sure they're the right size, once we've caught them.' He grabbed into the sack he had brought and placed the two bluelings on Barnabas's shoulders.

The leprechaun eyed them suspiciously, and his frown deepened when they stuck out their blue tongues at him. Hothbrodd meanwhile pulled six loaves of bread out of the sack and placed one at each spot Copper led him to. The loaves were as big as the troll's fists and smelled of fish and Mary's buckwheat flour.

Hothbrodd sniffed the last one with disgust before he put it in the sand. 'You really think we got the taste right?'

The Copperman just nodded. Alfonso, Barnabas, Hothbrodd, the Copperman and Shrii . . . There was one spot left when they had all taken up their posts. Lola admitted that she couldn't offer much help with this task and crawled into Hothbrodd's pocket.

'I'll call Elewese,' Alfonso said, but the leprechaun stopped him with an impatient gesture.

'All right, all right!' Shortsleeves growled while he strolled to the last unguarded spot. 'Let's try it the Greenbloom way. But if that worm makes a run for the sea Mannanan will definitely not just catch him in a jar.'

Mannanan was clearly hoping for that. He was licking his snout while he sat down next to his master. The bread Hothbrodd had placed near it didn't interest him at all, but Barnabas tried not to worry about that. After all, the creatures they were waiting for didn't resemble dogs in the slightest. Not even dogs like Mannanan.

The Copperman had agreed that the griffin should lure the first worm out, as he would find it easiest to catch them with his beak.

Shrii bent his head and listened.

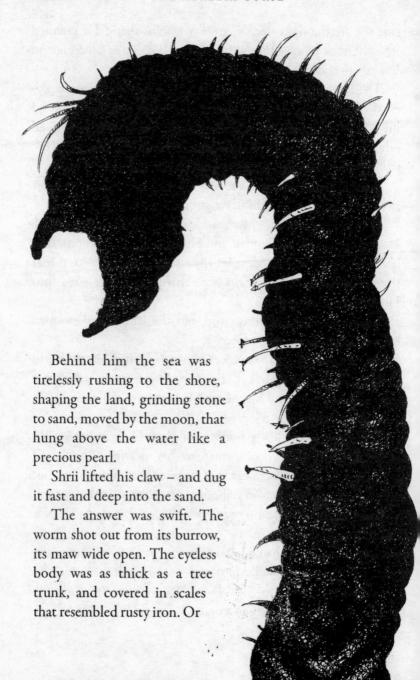

Behind him the sea was tirelessly rushing to the shore, shaping the land, grinding stone to sand, moved by the moon, that hung above the water like a precious pearl.

Shrii lifted his claw – and dug it fast and deep into the sand.

The answer was swift. The worm shot out from its burrow, its maw wide open. The eyeless body was as thick as a tree trunk, and covered in scales that resembled rusty iron. Or copper. The griffin stepped back, his beak ready to grab the worm if it tried to escape, but it closed its toothless gums around the loaf of bread as they had hoped. It had swallowed only half of it when it went limp.

Barnabas and Hothbrodd smiled at each other, and Shrii was just pulling the rest of the motionless body out of its hole, when Alfonso shouted out in alarm. The worm whose burrow he was guarding shot out and grabbed his arm with its toothless gums. It held on so fiercely that even the Copperman, who rushed to Alfonso's aid, couldn't free him from the worm's grip. They were still wrestling with it when the worm Barnabas was guarding shot out of its burrow as well. Hothbrodd managed to shove one of the loaves down its throat, just before it swallowed Barnabas's head – and spun around just in time to see his own worm break out of the sand. But that one luckily swallowed the bait without hesitation. The Copperman had just managed to free Alfonso's arm and to shove another loaf into the attacker's huge maw, when the last worm made its appearance right in front of Mannanan's paws. The dog snapped it in two, like a pair of scissors and Derog Shortsleeves cast Barnabas a glance that without doubt could be translated as 'isn't this so much easier?'

It wasn't. The two halves were very much alive. One even grew another head and slithered towards Mannanan. Barnabas managed to grab the little dog by the tail, before he fully disappeared in the worm's maw. While the Copperman came to Barnabas's and Mannanan's aid, Shrii closed his beak around the other half. But both were wiggling so fiercely that it took Alfonso's and Hothbrodd's additional help to feed them each some of the remaining bread. Even Lola climbed out of Hothbrodd's pocket to help – although there was not much she could do.

Even Hothbrodd and the Copperman were breathing heavily, when the two halves finally went as limp as the other five worms and all lay side by side in the sand. They looked like huge copper cables a giant had left behind. The longest worm measured three metres and its maw could have swallowed Barnabas with ease.

The bluelings ran their hands over the scaled bodies and a few minutes later the creatures they had fought so hard resembled a bunch of garden worms that got lost on the beach.

'You see, leprechaun?' Hothbrodd said, while he dropped them one after the other into an empty jam jar. 'There's no problem with the size. And who knows. Maybe they eat plastic and Barnabas can use them to clean our oceans from all the garbage his fellow men throw in there.'

The bluelings were celebrating their successful operation by having a sand and shell battle with Lola. Mannanan took part by barking at all of them. And the Copperman took a handful of sand and wiped the worm saliva off his metal hands.

'I hear you are a kind man, Greenbloom,' he said. 'But don't ever let that kindness convince you to let Cadoc Eelstrom go. His heart is rotten through and through.'

Then he was suddenly gone as if the night had swallowed him, and all Barnabas could do was stare at the spot where he had disappeared.

Hothbrodd put his hand on his shoulder.

'Nothing needs more strength than kindness, Barnabas,' he growled. 'But let's hope that one day we won't regret that we let that copperhead go.'

Let's hope . . . would hope be enough?

Barnabas walked towards the waves and stared over the ocean, along the silver path the moon was painting. He ran his fingers over the ring on his finger. He still felt its magic. They had had unexpected helpers.

Alfonso stepped to his side.

'The whales won't come. They lost too much to the humans these past few years. But Elewese is gathering all the help he can find for tomorrow.'

'What about the squid?'

Alfonso shook his head. 'Elewese says the whole ocean speaks of them. In very worried songs. But it seems the Great Kraken you called has joined the Aurelia. Let's hope he can fight them when they go for the pods.'

'Let's hope . . .' Barnabas stared at the shimmering waves. What about his wife and his daughter? Who would protect them? *Who are you fooling, Barnabas?* he thought. *They won't look for protection. They will defend the Aurelia, for if we can't there will be nothing left to protect or defend.*

The waves washed up to his shoes and left foam soaked with moonlight on the withered leather.

'Lizzie!' Barnabas called over the water. 'Take care of Guinevere, won't you?'

Only the waves answered him with their restless murmur.

CHAPTER FORTY-FOUR

ROTTEN

Ben was not sure what woke him. Firedrake was sleeping next to him, numbed by the same exhaustion he felt himself since the fight with the beaked birds. One more day. Ben had to admit he couldn't wait for this all to be over and to finally climb on Firedrake's back to receive the Aurelia's pod.

One more day.

But what if it will be the last one for Firedrake, Twigleg and all the others? something whispered inside him. *What if the next new moon will free Cadoc Eelstrom from the leprechaun's spell, and all that's left of the magic the Aurelia brought into this world is a pod that will make him immortal?*

Nonsense! Ben told himself off. If the Aurelia claimed back everything that she brought into this world, Cadoc's squid would definitely not be able to keep one of her pods safe from her rage!

Or would they? The night bred gloomy thoughts like that easily and Ben decided to chase them away by going into the house to find the ointment Mary had left out for him to use on his wounds. Twigleg and Freddie were snoring away in their house. At least it offered them some protection on Mary's wild mountain, and Twigleg had insisted on sleeping close to him. Was Freddie dreaming of the moss fairies? Ben wondered as he got up silently, making sure he didn't wake the homunculi or Firedrake. Twigleg's brother had a serious crush on one of the fairies, and the bluelings were very taken by them too. Only Twigleg seemed to be immune to their charms. Had his homunculus ever been in love? Ben pondered as he walked towards the house. A few months ago he himself had developed a serious crush on one of Guinevere's friends. It had been so embarrassing. Being a dragon rider was much less challenging.

Ben was surprised to see the flickering light of a candle behind Mary's living-room window. But he still didn't suspect anything when he walked up the porch steps. The Copperman was with the others at the beach, catching worms, and Eelstrom was nothing but a boot in a fireproof wardrobe.

'Mary?' He opened the door and walked into the dark house.

'Look, who's here. The dragon rider.'

Cadoc Eelstrom was standing next to Mary's dining table with a burning candle in his left hand and a small brown shoe in his right hand. At his feet, Ben spotted the remains of a mushroom on the floor, with Sorrel's tooth marks in it.

'I have to say, these belts are fabulous,' Cadoc said in a low voice, as he mocked Ben with a smile. 'That brownie looks so much more pleasant this way, doesn't she? All that furry fuzz gone.' He lifted the shoe up and scrutinised it with contempt. 'If she hadn't walked in, I would have tried the belt on the old lady, but that would have been so much less enjoyable! Don't look so surprised! Not even Copper knows that every New Year's Eve I have my cook serve me the hearts of twenty-three red squirrels. I can only recommend it. They make humans quite resistant to most spells. The Copperman always looked rather tormented when I made him catch them. What did you do with him? Let me guess. You took pity on him and let him go, right?'

Ben just stared at the shoe that had once been Sorrel.

'Give her to me!' he said hoarsely. 'Give her to me, you rotten—'

'Rotten? That's all you can come up with?' Eelstrom mocked him with a smile. 'How about cunning? Devious? Cruel? Your father called me a monster once. But then he decided that would be an insult for all the monsters in this world. Of course I took it as a compliment.' He ran his hand over the small brown shoe. 'I wonder what you gain when you eat a brownie's heart. Can you find the rarest mushrooms?'

He laughed.

'Give her to me.' Ben stretched out his hand. 'If she stays here, I won't get in your way.'

'Get in my way?' Eelstrom pushed the boot into his rucksack. 'I'll tell you what happens now, dragon rider.'

He slipped the rucksack back on and held the candle threateningly close to Mary's tablecloth.

'I'll leave this miserable place, and you'll stay where you are. Fires burn very fast in these mountains, even in winter, and I locked the old lady's bedroom door – which may be a problem for her.'

He walked slowly backwards to the entrance door, keeping his eyes on Ben, who felt paralysed by all the thoughts rushing through his angry mind.

'Tell the dragon he can come and give me his heart in exchange for his brownie. But only once I have the Aurelia seeds.' Eelstrom pushed the door open. 'If you try to follow me, I'll throw this shoe away and the coyotes will chew it up before the next new moon will break the spell.'

He held the candle against Mary's curtains. 'See you, dragon rider. Let's see how you deal with fire!'

The flames lit up immediately. They climbed up the window, growing, spitting sparks and embers, as Eelstrom disappeared into the night. With the shoe that had once been Sorrel.

Ben tore down the burning curtains. The flames didn't singe his skin and he managed to extinguish them before they set Mary's house on fire. *The fire won't be able to hurt you*, he heard Firedrake's voice in his head. Not even when he pressed his bare hands on the embers burning on the floor. But it still took much too long before he had extinguished them all. He stumbled to Mary's bedroom door and unlocked it with shaking hands. Mary was standing behind it in her nightgown, her eyes wide with fear.

'Cadoc escaped!' Ben gasped. 'But I put out the fire. He has Sorrel.'

Then he ran outside. Firedrake and the homunculi were still sleeping. Ben hadn't even noticed that he was sobbing until he knelt down at his dragon's side.

'Firedrake! Wake up!'

The dragon lifted his head and opened his eyes. They were cloudy with sleep.

'Eelstrom has Sorrel! And I let him go!' Ben was shaking. With fear. With anger. And with contempt for himself. 'I . . . I didn't know what to do! He had a candle and . . . and he threatened to . . .'

Firedrake was on his paws so swiftly that he nearly threw Ben off his feet.

'Sorrel? He has Sorrel?' He looked around and sniffed the cold night air. 'Get on my back!'

He spread his wings while Ben was still climbing up his flank.

'He used the leprechaun belt on her! And he said if we follow him we'll never find her.'

Twigleg and Freddie came stumbling out of their house and stared up at them, their little faces white with terror.

Firedrake gave off a roar. 'Of course we'll find her. And him!' A flame, red with rage, escaped his nostrils.

'You two go back into your house!' Ben called out to Twigleg from Firedrake's back. 'The coyotes are out!'

He saw Twigleg pull Freddie with him, while the dragon rose into the air with a few swift wingbeats. Ben could feel Firedrake's anger in every scale of his body. He couldn't remember ever having seen him so angry before.

'Eelstrom didn't see where we took him!' Ben yelled. 'He doesn't know his way around, but I'm sure he'll try to get to the road.'

Firedrake didn't answer. He was flying very low to the ground to catch Eelstrom's scent. He soon had his track, Ben could feel it. Cadoc had run towards the road and then turned left, where it wound down the mountain towards the sea.

He didn't get far.

Firedrake caught up with him when he'd barely reached the next curve of the narrow road. Cadoc reached for his rucksack the moment he heard the dragon's wings behind him, but Firedrake grabbed him before he could make another move. He landed, and threw Eelstrom on to the concrete of the road, hovering over him, his nostrils raining sparks on to his clothes and face.

'You know nothing about a dragon's heart, human!' Firedrake growled. 'Or you wouldn't have touched the brownie.'

'Let me go, fireworm!' Cadoc tried to sound threatening, but his voice was little more than a squeal. He was still trying to get to the rucksack. Ben climbed down from Firedrake's back and pulled it off Eelstrom's shoulders. He tried to fight him but the dragon's claws pressed him on to the concrete of the road.

'Or what?' Firedrake growled, lowering his head until Eelstrom felt his breath on his face. 'I was never more tempted to crush a man. It would be so easy. As easy as shaking the dust out of those poor moss fairies. But I don't enjoy killing. I never did. It leaves a shadow on the heart, and I certainly don't want your shadow on mine.'

Eelstrom moaned, his face stiff with rage and terror, as the dragon closed his claws even more firmly around him.

Firedrake looked enquiringly at Ben.

He pushed his hand into Eelstrom's rucksack and searched for the shoe. Yes, it was still there. Ben pulled it out and showed it to Firedrake. Just a small brown shoe. 'She'll be fine,' he said. 'I promise. The leprechaun told us to just polish the leather.'

'Yes. No need to be upset!' Cadoc gasped. 'I think she looks much better as a shoe!'

Firedrake brought his teeth so close to his face that they touched Eelstrom's nose. 'One more word and I will kill you. With pleasure,' he growled. 'Do you hear me, human?

Firedrake was terrifying in his anger. Even Ben felt the shadow of it when he climbed back on to the dragon's back.

Firedrake lifted Eelstrom from the concrete with his claw and spread his wings.

'Yes, here's a dragon's promise human . . .' he said with a threateningly calm voice. 'Your life will end tonight, if Sorrel was harmed because of you. And not even Barnabas Greenbloom will be able to save you.'

CHAPTER FORTY-FIVE

BLISTERING FUNGUS

Mary was waiting on her porch when the dragon brought back the man who had tried to burn her house down. Lola, Twigleg and Freddie were sitting by her side, and her burned curtains lay at her feet.

'It's those fairies, master!' Twigleg stammered, when Firedrake landed in front of Mary's porch. 'Their dust makes me all woozy. That's why I didn't wake!'

'It's all fine, Twigleg,' Ben said, though he wasn't quite sure of that yet. 'We need ropes.'

Twigleg argued with Freddie over which knots to use, while Mary and Ben tied Eelstrom up. He didn't fight them. He just stared at them, his pale-blue eyes dark with anger. Firedrake didn't take his eyes off Eelstrom until he was wrapped in rope like a cocoon.

'Hopefully there aren't any hearts he can eat to escape ropes!' Twigleg whispered to Ben, as they locked their enemy into the metal shed where Mary stored her farming equipment – after they'd removed anything that might help him escape.

'Oh no, Firedrake will kill him if he tries to run again,' Freddie said.

'Yes, I think Eelstrom knows that as well as you, Freddie.' Mary said, and went into the house to get some cloth to polish the shoe that would hopefully become Sorrel again. Ben had left it on the porch table.

Freddie walked over to the boot, and pressed his ear against the leather. Then he looked at Firedrake. 'Ohhhhh . . . she is even angrier than you!'

That brought a smile to Firedrake's worried face. 'I'm sure she is, Freddie.'

When Mary came back, one of the moss fairies fluttered out of the house with her. Freddie gave her a wide smile when she sat down next to him, but Twigleg cast her a suspicious glance, while Ben sat down on the edge of the table and put the small shoe on to his lap. *She will be okay.* He was quite nervous as he began to polish the brown leather. What if Sorrel had been harmed by the spell? The grief would tear Firedrake's heart to shreds! And Ben would not stop him if he killed Cadoc Eelstrom for that. *If you ever kill, Ben*, he heard Barnabas say, *it will harm your heart as well. And you will plant the same evil that you are trying to fight.* But what then? Would they build a prison for Eelstrom at MÍMAMEIÐR? That was a terrible thought.

The leather he was polishing began to shine. It began to feel warm under his hands. Ben even felt it shiver. Firedrake was watching him, his face stiff with worry.

'Now!' Freddie said.

Twigleg had drawn a circle with a stick on the dry ground right in front of the steps that led up to Mary's porch. Firedrake stepped closer when Ben quickly placed the shoe in the centre. It was shivering. Yes, it was. Fur sprouted from the leather, and they heard a familiar voice.

'Blistering fungus! Stinkhorn! Cleft-foot amanita! Northern tooth and mock orange!'

A whole alphabet of smelly mushrooms escaped the shoe while it slowly morphed into the shape of a brownie girl.

Firedrake grabbed Sorrel by her furry neck the moment she got on her feet. He dropped her between his front paws and sniffed her from head to toe, over and over again until he was finally sure she was really back.

'What?' Sorrel exclaimed, when the dragon turned her around once again and inspected her from the back. 'What's going on? What, chanterelles and redheads, are you looking for? Fleas? That's outrageous! I am a very tidy brownie! I'm . . .'

'You were a shoe, Sorrel!' Ben stated.

'Excuse me?' Sorrel looked down at herself, as if she was worried she'd missed something.

'Eelstrom kidnapped you,' Firedrake said. 'He was able to break the leprechaun's spell and used the belt on you! But we caught him.'

Sorrel frowned, and looked at him and Ben very warily. But then she saw Mary nod as well. And Twigleg, and Freddie. Even the fairy nodded – whose name by the way was Shokoanna.

'Ah!' she murmured. 'Well, I thought I felt something around my waist when I was checking on the mushrooms Mary was dry-ing on—' She put her paws on her belly and on her hips, as if she suddenly felt the belt there.

Then she bared her teeth.

'Where is he?' she hissed. 'I will bite off his nose. And his ears. I'll show him not to mess with a brownie!' She turned to Ben. 'What kind of shoe was I?'

The question came so suddenly that Ben burst into laughter. It took away all the fear and anger that the recent events had left like soot in his heart.

'Not sure you would have liked it. Quite a small one actually,' he said. 'Small and brownish.'

'Hmm.' Sorrel scratched her ears. 'I think I'd regret biting his nose off. All that evilness he carries around would probably kill me. But what should we do with him?'

Yes, that was still the question. Neither Barnabas nor Hothbrodd had an answer to it when they came back from the beach with Lola, and heard about the events that had unfolded at Mary's house.

'Well, I hope no one is suggesting letting him go like that Copperman!' Hothbrodd growled, when they were all sitting around Mary's dining table. There hadn't been time to wipe up the soot around the window, and there were still a few shreds of burned curtain on the floor. Ben looked at his hands. Not one blister, although he remembered the heat of the flames very well. They had licked his skin like fiery dogs. Dragon rider. He hadn't told the others yet. There were too many other things to talk about.

'No, we're definitely not letting Cadoc Eelstrom go!' his father said looking at the sooty walls. 'And I am so sorry, Mary. We are terrible guests! A candle! Something so useful and beautiful, spreading light in the dark. But Cadoc uses it to burn curtains and start a fire. Of course.'

He looked at Ben. 'I hear he doesn't look much older than you.'

Barnabas hadn't cast one glance at their prisoner yet. He hadn't been anywhere near the shed, as if he was worried about what he would do if he met his old schoolmate.

'Yes, you would probably guess he's fourteen like me, or even younger.' Ben shuddered. 'But he doesn't have the moss fairies any more, so his true age should show soon.'

They could hear Eelstrom swearing in the shed, even though they were inside.

'He's been yelling pretty much the same since we locked him up,' Ben said. '*Give me one of the Aurelia pods or you'll regret it! It's only your fault if the squid hurt her and all your fabulous friends disappear!* On and on and on. But he's getting hoarse.'

'I still wouldn't mind if Shrii or Firedrake ate him,' Hothbrodd growled. 'The world would be a better place for sure.'

'They'd probably both die from the poison circling in his blood!' Lola shook her head. 'No. That fairy shaker won't turn us into executioners. But what do we do with him? We can't even prove his crimes!'

'They wouldn't be considered crimes, Lola, as his victims aren't human.' Freddie had climbed on to Hothbrodd's shoulders. He loved to be high up. 'The moss fairies would never be accepted at your courts as witnesses to his cruelty!'

'We can decide later what to do with Eelstrom,' Hothbrodd growled. 'The Aurelia will be here soon. As soon as the pods are safe, we decide what to do with Eelstrom.'

Barnabas frowned. 'Yes,' he sighed. 'She is almost here. Still no news from the courier Alfonso recruited for Earth?'

'Panther and spit mushrooms! I completely forgot!' Sorrel exclaimed. 'She is supposed to show up tomorrow morning. A gopher asked me to tell you.'

'A gopher?' Ben had to smile. He hadn't even known what a gopher was, until he had seen a few peek out of the holes they were digging all over Mary's property. They looked like very small furry men wearing white gloves.

'*She?* What is she?' Hothbrodd grunted. He was still upset he hadn't been at Mary's house when Eelstrom made his escape. 'Did the gopher tell you that?'

'Nope,' Sorrel replied, while she inspected her fur, as if she was worried there was still some leather left. 'He was back in his hole before I could ask.'

Outside Eelstrom had fallen silent.

'Let's get some sleep,' Mary said. 'We have a big day ahead of us.'

CHAPTER FORTY-SIX

THE COURIER OF EARTH

It is hard to concentrate when you are holding your worst enemy captive just a stone's throw away from you. Even when the task in hand may decide whether you lose most of your friends! Eelstrom began yelling again the moment Hothbrodd got off the porch where he'd been sleeping and walked over to Mary's pond to splash some water on to his face. The troll didn't need much sleep, but today they were all up early. Two of Alfonso's men were already standing guard in front of the shed, and the coyotes Alfonso had asked to watch the house at night were strolling off into the mountains, because Lola was not the only one still worried about the Copperman.

Hothbrodd had searched the prisoner for any communication devices, but he had only found a remote control for a car.

'What are you looking for, troll?' Eelstrom had mocked. 'A remote for the squid? How stupid do you think I am? Yes, those squid are far more advanced than your pathetic homunculi. You've chosen the wrong human friends! You will disappear and I'll be immortal!'

Ben was surprised Hothbrodd hadn't punched him for that.

'Yes, he would have liked that,' the troll had growled. 'The stupid troll, who throws a fit when you insult him. No, that rotten little maggot isn't worth a troll punch.'

Barnabas had still not paid Eelstrom a visit. Ben had seen him walking towards the shed several times. But Barnabas had always stopped and turned shortly before he reached it.

'If you want to confront him, I'll make sure he won't get to you,' Hothbrodd said at some point.

But Barnabas had shaken his head. 'No,' Ben had heard him say. 'It would just make me angry. We have far more important things to do.'

And then he had helped Ben and Hothbrodd to load Alfonso's truck with the equipment they'd use to block all access to the beach once the sun was setting. Hopefully no ranger would come by and wonder what construction works made it necessary to put up barriers and close the two winding paths leading down to the sand. Alfonso and his men would patrol the car park to make sure no one watched from up there, and the leprechaun was, at this moment, placing a few bits of enchanted leather into the trash cans to instill an irresistible wish to go home in anyone who came close to them. Yes, they would be well prepared, at least on land.

'Your son will regret that he and that stinking dragon chased me like a hare! Do you hear me, Barnabas?' Cadoc Eelstrom was very hoarse by now, but his voice still carried far.

Ben felt his father's concerned look.

'I'm not worried Dad,' he said. 'Hothbrodd is right. Let's forget about him until the Aurelia pods are safe!'

Ben could almost sense Eelstrom's hatred on his skin by now. And something in him whispered that he and Firedrake hadn't chased Cadoc Eelstrom for the last time. But he didn't tell his father about that.

He was walking over to the house with Barnabas to get some water when a shadow fell on him from behind. Ben thought it was Firedrake at first, but when he turned, there she was. He knew immediately that, despite her enormous body, they didn't have to fear her.

The Courier of Earth . . .

Alfonso couldn't have picked a more impressive one. Her fur was black, with a hint of blue and brown and green, and the claws on her huge paws were golden on the left and silver on the right. They gave away what she was, even more than her enormous size. She was Bear, but not just one of the black bears who, although almost extinct still roamed these mountains. She was the spirit of bear, a fabulous creature, who had probably seen thousands of years. Freddie had lent Ben an audiobook of tales which he had listened to flying over from Norway. Many of the

tales on there had talked about her. Some tales claimed that she could make the mountains shake with one roar and that water sprang where she dug her claws in the ground. Ben believed them all when he looked into those wise, golden eyes. They were mischievous too, and Ben had learned from the tales that the Native Americans believed her to have a weakness for pranks.

'El Brujo asked me to come here, Greenbloom.' Her voice was deep, so deep, and so warm and soft at the same time. 'And you,' she looked at Ben with amber eyes, 'you are the boy who rides the Fire. I smell it on you.'

Ben saw Firedrake and Shrii look in his direction. Both spread their wings.

Bear's fur caught in the wind the griffin and the dragon brought when they landed just a few steps away from her.

Ben felt so small amongst those three, and at the same time so at home. He saw on Barnabas's face that he felt exactly the same. In the distance, Eelstrom was yelling his threats but Bear didn't even turn her head.

'I am so glad you came,' Barnabas said. 'So very very glad.' His glasses got misty and he took them off to polish them with his shirt, a happy smile on his face. Behind him, Ben saw Mary step on to her porch with a pot of fresh coffee – and freeze when she saw the huge furry visitor. Next to the dragon and the griffin. Fire, Air and Earth.

'Tonight.' Shrii said just the one word, while a warm breeze ruffled his bright feathers.

'Tonight,' Bear repeated, so dark against the griffin's colours and the dragon's silver. 'And she will bring beginnings or an end. But I hear that will be decided by the Water.'

'Earth, Air and Fire will be there as well.' Firedrake bent his head, while he stepped closer to Ben's side, as if he was not quite sure whether he needed to protect his rider. 'All four or none.'

'All four or none,' Shrii repeated.

'That's how it will be.' Bear bowed her heavy head, first at Firedrake and then at Shrii. 'I will meet you at the beach. And you as well, young rider of the Fire,' she added with a smile to Ben.

Then her huge body turned into a million particles of black soil and the wind and the rays of the sun carried Bear away.

'How many more magical guests will you bring to my house, Barnabas Greenbloom?' Mary asked when she poured coffee into the mug Barnabas held out to her. 'I've seen the great bear only once so far, in my dreams. I think I was seven years old.'

'I also brought you a very sinister guest,' Barnabas replied, 'who burned your curtains and wouldn't have minded burning you alive as well.'

'Well.' Mary shrugged. 'There is currently so much light in this house that some shadow had to show up. And we all know: the brighter the light, the darker the shade. Any news from Vita and Guinevere?'

Barnabas shook his head. Ben slung his arm around his shoulders.

'They are fine, I'm sure.' He tried to comfort him, but he had to admit that he was worried too by now. They all were. Lola had asked the Ears and the braidmaids and Elewese. Nothing. As if the sea had swallowed his sister and his mother for good.

'They will all be gone!' they heard Eelstrom's, by now very hoarse, voice yell. 'All your fabulous friends. Gone! Like the dodo and all those other beasts you only meet in books! And you can close that ridiculous shelter place of yours!'

Barnabas frowned.

'Don't listen,' Shrii said. 'Don't make it happen in your mind already, any of you!'

'Don't tell me I didn't warn you!' Cadoc Eelstrom yelled. 'You can still give me that pod and—'

The rest of his threat was drowned out by music. Very old music, as Twigleg and Freddie had chosen it. Mary's yard was suddenly filled with cembalos and violins and violas da gamba, creating sounds that belonged to a different time and a different continent.

Freddie came running across the yard, adding a few dance steps on the way.

'I hope you lot don't mind!' he piped. 'Twigleg and I couldn't bear his yelling any more. Hothbrodd was quite annoyed too, so he helped us set up the speakers. He suggested some heavy metal music. I quite liked that idea, but Twigleg said that would wreck his nerves even more.'

Ben had to smile, despite the fact that Eelstrom's yelling still came through the violins from time to time. And his father started humming softly.

Freddie knew the old Scottish tune of course. He began to tap-dance around Barnabas, while adding the words to his tune:

'When "Friendship, Love, and Truth" abound!
Among a band of brothers,
The cup of joy goes gaily round,
Each shares the bliss of others.

'Yes!' Freddie exclaimed, while spinning on his silver foot. 'We'll always believe in friendship! Do you hear that, Eelstrom? You will never take that away from us!'

Cadoc Eelstrom's answer was drowned out by music.

CHAPTER FORTY-SEVEN

JUST A SMALL, PALE FISH

No one had heard from Vita and Guinevere because the black fish had come. Thousands of them had joined the Aurelia, and the shoals of tiny ink-black bodies, swallowed any signal Koo sent out. The lantern fish was quite upset. He had blown himself up to his greatest possible size to strengthen his signal and get it past the shoals. But they were everywhere, and when Koo had, yet again, got lost amongst them for hours, Lizzie asked him to stay close. After all, the black fish were also the best possible camouflage for the copper squid.

They hadn't attacked the Aurelia again. But why should they? They had learned what they needed to know, and they were clearly aware that the pods weren't ripe yet. That moment would come very soon though. Guinevere saw them glowing on the Aurelia's arms like coloured pearls pulsating with the life they held within – and still they had no idea how to protect them. Despite the merpeople's warnings, and although Eugene had pinched him to express his fierce protest, Eight had made an attempt to chase the squid away. And the kraken had actually managed to rip the claws off the biggest one. But it had nearly cost him an arm, and they had all finally convinced him that the risk of losing another was just too real.

The waters around them were changing. They all felt the currents that signalled there was a coastline nearby. Lizzie guessed that they had barely ten hours left until the Aurelia would reach the shores of Southern California.

The ocean was resonating with her song, and her lights now painted symphonies of colour, even amongst the black fish. The Aurelia didn't seem worried about the squid, despite their attack. Did she not mind losing those four pods, because she lived for ever and knew there would be others? Did she trust in her ability to fight?

Guinevere saw the apprehension on Lizzie and Laimomi's faces. Even Koo had turned a very dull brownish orange. Would

the fish disappear too? How many creatures owed the Aurelia their lives? Nobody knew, as they couldn't ask her.

They were about eight hours away from the coast when Lizzie and Laimomi gathered them all at a safe distance from the squid.

'We have an idea,' Laimomi said. 'It may be foolish, but I hope you all agree that we have to try something – before our only options are being torn to shreds by the squid or vanishing to Neptune knows where. There are millions of sea creatures following the Aurelia by now, some of them we know nothing about. Maybe one of them is able to help us! It could be tiny, but . . .'

'But what?' one of the mermen signalled. 'Maybe it can sting the squid to death?'

'Maybe!' Lizzie replied. 'Or blind or shock them the way some of the rays can attack us? We don't know! So let's find out! We suggest each of us look for fish we don't know and find out what they can do!'

'What are you waiting for? Go!' Laimomi signalled, when everyone just stared at them. 'We have barely eight more hours and four squid to deal with!'

So off they went. Vita joined Laimomi, and Lizzie took Guinevere along, because approaching most fish looking like a seal could be quite a challenge. Guinevere felt incredibly ignorant when Lizzie kept pointing them out to her: shovelnose guitarfish? Would she have believed they existed, had she not seen them swim by, following the Aurelia's shimmering trail of arms? There were blue striped fangblennies, butterflyfish, leopard and angel sharks, lizardfish, flatheads, triplefins and green jacks, Pacific bumpers and bat rays, giant hawkfish, hornyhead turbots, seahorses, pipefish, hairtails . . . and they all looked so different, in shape, size and colour! Compared to the dwellers of the sea the creatures on land suddenly seemed quite limited in their variety. But each time Guinevere asked Lizzie whether any of them might be of use against the squid, she only shook her head.

None of them looked hopeful when they gathered again. Not even Eight, who held a wide selection of sea creatures in his arms.

No, the angel sharks wouldn't be a match for the squid, nor would the rays be able to challenge them. It would cost dozens of them their lives if they tried to shield the Aurelia. Guinevere's seal heart felt like a stone in her furry chest. The others had managed to trap Eelstrom! How could they now fail in the very waters the Aurelia was swimming in? She felt terribly helpless. All the enchantment that filled her heart since she'd slipped into the selkie skin was erased by the fear that the squid would attack once the Aurelia reached the shore. *Before our only options are being torn to shreds by the squid or vanishing to Neptune knows where* . . . Fire and death . . . would that be all the Aurelia would bring, instead of beauty and life and hope? Guinevere wanted to grab Cadoc Eelstrom with her seal teeth and . . .

'I think I found someone who could help!' The mermaid who came forth had silvery hair and dark-blue scales. A pale, almost transparent fish was swimming by her side. She was tiny and didn't look impressive at all.

'That's Haumea,' Lizzie whispered to Guinevere. 'She knows more fish species than any of us. She speaks hundreds of their languages.'

Haumea pointed at the tiny scaled creature by her side. 'This is Zishhh. She is a licker fish. Almost three thousand of her kind are following the Aurelia, and I think they may be able to help us.'

The others watched with very doubtful expressions as she held up two big, empty shells. Zishhh hesitated for a moment, but then she swam to the left one. Her orange lips left a soft silvery shine on the surface when she licked at it with her thin pointed snout. Zishhh licked the right shell as well – and hid shyly behind Haumea's back.

The mermaid smiled at the others and pressed the shells together.

'Eight!' she signalled the kraken. 'You're by far the strongest of us. Try to tear these apart.'

Eight carefully took the shells from Haumea's small hands and pulled. He used two, then four and finally all eight arms, but the shells stuck firmly together.

Guinevere saw smiles emerging on all the faces around her.

'Their claws!' Lizzie signalled. 'We glue their claws together! Brilliant!'

'But Zishhh and the other licker fish . . . will have to get so close to the squid. Won't they kill them?' Guinevere asked.

Zishhh peeked out from behind Haumea's back. 'We can spray our glue,' she declared with a shower of white lights. 'And we're very small. They will not even notice us.'

'But there is one problem.' Haumea's lights dimmed. 'To make the glue stick, the squid will have to close their claws after the licker fish have sprayed them . . .'

The smiles disappeared.

'So we have to give them something to snap at,' Lizzie signalled.

They all looked at the hooded shadows looming in the dark.

'Well . . .' Laimomi said. 'There are four squid, we are ten merpeople . . .'

'No!' Guinevere wrote with her flipper. 'No! It can't just be you! I want to help! We should be many to confuse them. They shouldn't know where to snap first – so they get really hectic and clamp their claws shut firmly!'

Vita was not happy about her suggestion – Guinevere saw that, although it is not easy to read a seal's face. But her mother didn't protest, for there was a rule in the Greenbloom household, since Guinevere and Ben had reached the age of fourteen: if either of them wished to be involved in a rescue mission, their parents wouldn't forbid it.

'Looks like we have a plan,' Lizzie signalled.

They found many creatures who wished to help. Eight was quite upset when Lizzie asked him to stay behind. 'So sorry, Eight,' she explained. 'But if you come, the squid may focus on you and we need them to snap wildly in all directions to glue their claws.'

Guinevere counted ninety-six helpers, as they headed towards the shadows where the squid were lurking. They split into six groups, progressing slowly as they wanted their enemies to watch them coming. Those huge eyes needed to be on them exclusively – otherwise they might notice the licker fish trying to come from below.

Guinevere looked out for the brave little fish while she was following Lizzie. But she only caught a glimpse of something pale – so vague that she wasn't sure whether the tiny glue fish were really closing in on the deadly claws. By now, some light was seeping through the countless wet and salty layers of the ocean. The Aurelia was rising higher as they were getting closer to the land, and Guinevere was able to see the squid more clearly for the first time: their huge eyes, their metallic skin and the claws that betrayed them to be altered beings. They looked so terrifying that her heart sank. But neither Lizzie nor any of the other helpers showed any hesitation as they slowly, but steadily, made their way towards the monsters.

Distract them! Make them snap at you! Drive them crazy!

Laimomi's directions had been very clear. She hadn't had to mention how deadly this task might turn out to be for some of them. All those approaching the clawed hunters were willing to sacrifice themselves for the shining pods the Aurelia was carrying. With this mission, each one of them proved that they considered life itself to be more valuable than their own.

How strange, Guinevere thought, while she parted the water with her flippers and once again admired how smoothly her new body moved. How very strange that humans claim to be the most advanced creatures on this planet but at the same time don't care about all the others.

In front of her Lizzie slowed everyone down. The licker fish needed time. There were many claws to spray.

Slowly, they approached . . . while the Aurelia was singing behind them.

Slowly . . . while the squid were watching them with their huge eyes.

'The small one for looking down, the big one for looking up,' Lizzie had explained, when Guinevere had asked why they had different sizes. 'One searching the darkness below, the other the lighter waters above, that's why they're so different.'

Two of the copper hats were already pushing their claws out from under their tentacles. Guinevere's selkie heart was racing. Had the licker fish reached them? Would their glue really hold?

They would soon know.

'Don't forget,' Laimomi had warned, 'even if we succeed in disabling their claws – their beaks and arms will still be very dangerous.'

Yes, Guinevere had watched how the one whose claws Eight had ripped off had killed a shark as effortlessly as a human kills a fly. She exchanged a glance with her mother. No, Vita definitely didn't like her being there, and Guinevere wished for some of those bright yellow lights Lizzie flashed when she said: *I'm fine!*

Then suddenly – so suddenly that for a moment it paralysed Guinevere – one of the squid went for its prey. His claw shot forward to grab a leopard shark. But . . . it didn't open. Neither did his second claw. The same happened with the other squid. They were furious. They grabbed their tentacles with their arms and tried to open their useless claws with their beaks.

'Retreat!' Laimomi signalled.

But the squid followed them, furious and out for murder. Many creatures perished in their beaks, others were killed when they used their glued claws like clubs, swinging them with terrible force. Some panicked and came too close to their suckers. It was Eight who finally saved them. He came down on the squid with a cloud of bluish ink that blinded them. And then he grabbed them. This time they didn't have claws to cut his mighty arms. The Great Kraken tied their tentacles together until they floated helplessly in the water, and catapulted them into the abyss below. One after the other. When Eight noticed that the squid whose claws he had ripped off was missing, it was too late. A telescope fish spotted him in the distance, and a school of sharks went after him. But neither they nor the squid came back.

And the Aurelia was less than six hours away from the Californian coast.

CHAPTER FORTY-EIGHT

NO PEACE

The sunset was just a few hours away – and they still hadn't heard from Lizzie or Vita and Guinevere. What if the squid stole the pods before Firedrake and Shrii could grab them? What if they attacked Eight? What if Bear would be sinking her huge paws into the waves in vain?

What if?

Ben just couldn't stop thinking these foolish thoughts, as he helped Alfonso to lift the last barriers on to his truck, and check one more time whether they had all the constructions signs and chains to block the beach entrances with. Not that they had seen many people down there in the past few days. At least the Aurelia had chosen to come in winter. As for the windows of the few houses that were facing the ocean . . . they could only hope that no one would look out to the waves in the middle of the night, as the light of the Aurelia was sure to be visible. Elewese had asked all the birds to swarm around the houses when she rose, and Lola and Hothbrodd had prepared some kind of fog machine that they would place on the cliff to further obscure the view.

Several elephant seals had joined the protective ring Elewese and the dolphin men were preparing for the Aurelia. The pelicans would watch over her arrival from the air, as would the cormorants.

'Not so sure about the seagulls,' Lola had said. 'They are robbers by nature and not really into saving things.' It all felt like adding one puzzle piece after the other to guarantee a peaceful welcome for the Aurelia. But if just one piece was missing . . . just one . . . disaster would creep through that hole. And there were still quite a few missing.

'Gone! Gone! Gone! They'll all be gone!' Eelstrom was chanting in his improvised prison. 'But she didn't make my squid so they will stay and they'll cut the pods off her arms! Snip-snap!'

He was so hoarse by now, that his chanting was more of a croaking. The 'Gone! Gone! Gone!' was a regular by now, mixed with threats, mocking insults and outpourings of rage. Mary had brought the prisoner food nevertheless, closely watched by Alfonso's men, but Eelstrom had thanked her by spilling hot tea on to her hands.

'That son of yours, Barnabas, did you realise he'll disappear too? The little fire I started didn't harm him at all. He has so much dragon in him by now that he's a goner for sure!'

'Barnabas, don't!' Hothbrodd growled, when this latest outpouring made Ben's father finally turn and march towards the shed. 'He's playin' you!'

'Hothbrodd is right,' Ben stepped into his father's way. 'Let me go in there! Before –' he winked at Barnabas '– I disappear.'

His father looked at him, for what seemed like a long time.

'I guess I have to get used to the fact that my two children are quite grown up by now,' he finally said. 'Okay. You talk to him, but Hothbrodd and I watch.'

Firedrake followed Ben with his eyes as he walked towards

the shed, but his dragon didn't try to stop him. Rogelio, who was watching the door, cast an enquiring look at Alfonso before he unlocked it.

Cadoc was sitting on a crate at the back of the shed. He blinked as the light fell in and Ben stepped through the door. His father waited in front of the door, along with Hothbrodd.

'You try anything, Eelstrom,' the troll growled, 'and I break your neck like a straw.'

Eelstrom just gave him a hostile look.

'Hello, Barnabas,' he snarled with his sore voice. 'Long time no see. Well, I did see you, but you were made of stone.' He laughed and nodded at Ben. 'Hiding behind your son? Did you say good-bye to him and all your fabulous friends?' He turned his gaze to Ben. 'Did you explain to them that they'll all vanish because of you? The noble Greenblooms – their saviours and destroyers! Heavens! I only want one pod!' His hoarseness didn't make it easy, but he tried his best to purr like a tame kitten. 'I swear! Just one. Grant me that and I'll call the squid back. I'm sure there's a way.'

Ben heard his father take a deep breath behind him.

'Your stolen face is showing the first lines, Cadoc,' Barnabas said, his voice strained with the effort to keep it calm. 'You'll age fast without the moss fairies . . . I'll leave him to you, son.' Then he walked away, while Hothbrodd kept standing guard in front of the open door.

'You cannot seriously think we believe one word you say, right?' Ben calmly said, although he heard his own blood rushing in his ears. 'So, what's all that yelling about? No one can call those squid back. The Copperman made that very clear. But we'll find a way to protect the Aurelia from them. So spare your voice and our ears.'

He stepped back, without taking his eyes off Eelstrom. He wasn't someone to turn one's back on.

'I agree with my father,' Ben said. 'You do look wilted. I wonder how old you'll be when we get back from the beach.'

'Shut up!' Eelstrom's pale skin had reddened with anger. 'You won't come back, dragon rider,' he hissed, as he felt his face for the lines Barnabas had mentioned. 'And neither will your fireworm.'

'Oh yes, we will be back,' Ben said. 'Just to see your wrinkling face.'

Cadoc bared his teeth like an angry dog.

'If you come back, you won't enjoy it for long. I will hunt you. You and your dragon. Until my cook serves me his heart on a platter.'

'My dragon?' Ben took a step back into the shed, although Hothbrodd gave off a warning grunt. 'That's how you see the world, right? Everything is property, yours or whoever is fast enough to grab it. I warn you: if you ever go after my father again, or threaten my mother, my sister or any of my friends, I will find you, and Firedrake and I will chase you like a rabbit once again. And then we'll put you in a cage, as you did with those poor fairies, and you can get old in there. Really old.'

Cadoc came for him, his fists clenched. But Ben just pushed him back into Mary's fruit tree nets and empty flower pots. He felt his strength like a sleeping beast inside, as Cadoc struggled to get back on his feet – it was a sensation both comforting and frightening.

'You were right. There's a lot of dragon in me by now,' Ben said. 'So don't try that again. I'll see you in the morning.'

'You're dead, dragon rider!' Eelstrom yelled after him as he walked out of the shed. 'You and your filthy dragon. I'll destroy you! I'll destroy everything you care for! I'll find your fireworm and have you watch while I rip his heart out! I'll find that sanctuary and I'll burn it to the ground! No, wait! I'll give a basilisk the scent of your sister!'

Hothbrodd locked the shed door, before Ben could turn and walk back in.

'Enough, dragon rider,' he growled. 'You can punch that *søppel* once those pods are safe.'

'*Søppel?*'

'Trash. In Norwegian,' the troll explained.

'*¡Vamos, amigos!*' Alfonso called from his truck. '*Tenemos que dar la bienvenida a un invitado muy importante.* Three of my men will be watching the prisoner. And a pack of coyotes and . . .'

'Hey! There's a rattlesnake in here!' they heard Eelstrom yelling. 'She just crawled out of a pot! You trying to kill me?'

'*¡No se preocupe!*' Alfonso called over to the shed. 'I left her there. Her name is Hutash and she won't harm you. Unless you harm her. Or try to escape.'

Silence answered him. But it was drenched in Cadoc Eelstrom's hatred for them all.

CHAPTER FORTY-NINE

BACK

The black fish wouldn't leave. They definitely planned to be part of the Aurelia's rising. So both Lizzie and Vita agreed that one of them should go ahead – to tell Barnabas and the others about Eight's defeat of the squid and whatever else those waiting at the beach should know. The Aurelia was slowing down with every mile that they approached the coast, as if the pods were now eating up all her energy. Even her lights had dimmed, whereas the four pods were glowing brighter with every minute.

'As she is going so slow, each of us can easily reach the beach at least half an hour before she does,' Laimomi signalled. 'So who should go?'

Clearly none of the merpeople wanted to leave – especially as most of them had never communicated with humans. The mere mention of land and shore brought back frightening memories for many of them.

'We go!' Vita said, when she saw the hesitation even on Lizzie's face. 'Guinevere and I are still quite clumsy in the water and we'll be much more helpful on the beach.'

Lizzie gave her a grateful smile, but Laimomi shook her head firmly. 'It's still quite a way to the shore and it's getting dark up there. You won't be able to find your way alone. You may have a selkie fur but you don't have a selkie's mind yet. No. It's better I bring you!'

'Nonsense, Laimomi, both you and Lizzie are needed here!' The mermaid who came forward had only one arm. 'I'll show them the way. I can't help much with the squid, but I'm still a fast swimmer.'

'Yes, you are, Flick,' Lizzie said. 'And you two –' she gave Vita and Guinevere a firm hug '– will be very safe with her, because no one senses danger earlier, or knows this ocean better. Flick is quite a traveller.'

The one-armed mermaid accepted these compliments with a guarded smile. Then she waved to Vita and Guinevere to follow her, while the others spread out again to help guard the pods. All the fish, eels, sponges, snails and turtles that followed the Aurelia were gathering around them by now. When Guinevere gazed back, they looked like living veils, formed by thousands of bodies, small and tall, and she felt her heart sink at the prospect of leaving this all behind and once again being an earthbound creature, feeling the pull of gravity on her feet. No ups and downs, no floating above undersea mountains and forests. She would no longer be wrapped in the song of the Aurelia and the constant movement of the sea, no Lizzie in her life, no Koo nor

Eight placing her on his head from time to time (although Eugene didn't like that at all) – and she hadn't even seen the mer-people's dwellings!

Flick was indeed a very fast swimmer, despite her lost arm. They learned she had lost it to dynamite used by humans for fishing. Guinevere's own swift selkie body felt heavier and heavier though, with every flipper stroke. *Of course*, something whispered inside her, *because you're going in the wrong direction, Guinevere Greenbloom!* What was wrong with her? She would soon see Firedrake and Shrii, her father and her brother, Hothbrodd, Lola, Twigleg and Freddie! She loved them all so much, even Mary and Alfonso, whom she hadn't known that long! And still . . . all she wanted was to be down there, amongst all those creatures who talked without words, sang strange songs and lived in a world without sky or earth, where one felt gravity so much less, and the heart was filled with a thousand new songs.

When they broke through the surface of the water, the sun was already setting and they could see the shoreline in the distance. It was strange to take a deep breath above water for the first time in days, and to feel the wind and the last light of the sun, to see the sky above and the full moon.

Flick stayed with them until they reached the rocks that framed the beach, where the Aurelia would release her pods. Guinevere saw her father and Ben and Hothbrodd in the distance. She couldn't see Firedrake or Shrii yet. They were probably waiting for the night to hide them. Who would be the Courier of Earth? She wanted to know the answer, but all she could think of was what she had left behind.

'You're fine from here?' It was the first time Guinevere had heard a mermaid's voice. It was as soft as water.

'Yes,' her mother said. 'Thank you so much, Flick!'

The mermaid nodded and turned.

'Wait!' Guinevere saw her brother lift his head, as if he had recognised her voice, although it was still a seal's. Flick turned, and Guinevere looked at her mother.

'I want to go back with her,' she said. 'Please, Mum. I want to be with the merpeople when the Aurelia rises.'

She knew the answer her mother wished to give. But Vita Greenbloom was a very good mother.

'Go!' she said. 'But stay close to Lizzie and the others.'

Then she turned and swam towards the shore. Guinevere knew why she turned so abruptly. Vita didn't want her to see how hard it was for her to let Guinevere go back.

'Why?' Flick was watching her with both curiosity and surprise. 'Why are you going back? You're not even a good swimmer.'

'I'll get better,' Guinevere replied.

That made Flick smile. 'Yes,' she said. 'Yes, you will. Although a selkie body will always be less fun than a mermaid's.'

Then she disappeared in the darkening waves with a flip of her tail. Guinevere cast a last glance at the beach – and followed her.

CHAPTER FIFTY

WAITING

Waiting. That was all they could do now. Ben heard Mannanan's bark from the car park – which told them that no cars were left up there. The barriers and the enchanted trash cans had done their work, and up on the cliff more and more birds were gathering on the roofs of the houses. They were waiting too – for a first glimpse of light beneath the waves. But the ocean was still as dark as the sky, except for the silvery light spilled by the moon.

Firedrake and Shrii were hiding right under the cliff, with Sorrel, Lola and Hothbrodd, while Bear was standing next to Alfonso and Mary, her huge shape resembling the rocks that broke the waves to their right. The Courier of Earth was smaller than the dragon and the griffin, but Ben felt her strength as clearly as the wind and the rush of the waves.

His parents were sitting just a few steps away side by side in the sand. Everyone could see how relieved his father was that Vita was back – and at the same time how worried that she hadn't brought his sister. Ben couldn't wait to hear the tales

Guinevere would bring back from the deep but he would have to wait for them for quite a while as he would go with Firedrake when he carried the Aurelia's pod to Scotland. The weeks in the dragon cave and the fight on Anacapa . . . both had taught Ben that he couldn't be separated from Firedrake any more. The dragon rider had to be by his dragon's side – even though he would miss his human family. Very much so, in fact. He was indeed changing. As if something had opened inside him that wouldn't close again. As if every ride on his dragon made them both more and more part of each other. Where would that lead? He couldn't wait to talk to Guinevere about it. She had experienced a change even more profound by shifting shape and living in another body! Would he ever dare to try that? Maybe. Though not with a selkie skin for sure. Some of the Native American tribes were believed to turn themselves into hawks and eagles. That would suit him better. *Of course!* He could hear Guinevere laugh. *You are Fire and Air, brother.* And she . . . would she be Water and Earth?

Waiting . . .

Derog Shortsleeves hadn't come down to the beach yet. He was probably still watching the car park. Ben was sure that the leprechaun enjoyed scaring unsuspecting visitors away from the steps that led down to the beach.

'The Aurelia should be here soon, don't you think?' he asked Twigleg, who was shivering on his right shoulder.

'Very soon, master.'

Freddie was dancing on the moonlit sand to a song only he could hear. Or maybe he was dancing to the murmurs of the sea? With Freddie one never knew. He danced to the sound of rain against a windowpane, the bubbling of water in the kitchen, or the rustling of pages when Twigleg was reading a book. Maybe the alchemist had made Freddie with the life spark of a cricket!

Ben heard the steps of big paws behind him. Very familiar steps.

'I just said goodbye to your parents,' Firedrake said. 'Maybe you should do that now as well. We'll leave as soon as the Aurelia releases her pods, and we'll be gone for a long time. First Scotland, then the Rim . . . unless you have changed your mind and would like me to drop you off at MÍMAMEIÐR before I head home.'

Ben shook his head. 'No, I haven't changed my mind. And I told them already that I'll go with you. But yes,' he cast a glance at Barnabas and Vita, 'I should probably say goodbye now.'

Twigleg cleared his throat. Which usually meant he was about to make an, in his opinion, important announcement – or was nervous about what he was going to say. 'I will of course come with you, master!'

'You're sure?' Ben wrapped his scarf around the homunculus. It was a windy night. 'I have no idea when I'll be back. And it's winter in Scotland. Not to mention the Himalayas. You will be cold most of the time.'

Twigleg shook his head vehemently, though Ben saw that he definitely wasn't looking forward to Scottish and Tibetan cold. 'You're a dragon rider. I'm the dragon rider's homunculus.'

Ben couldn't help but smile. 'What about your brother?'

'Oh, he is fine!' Twigleg sighed. 'Freddie is always fine!'

That was true. But Freddie would miss Twigleg – maybe more than Twigleg believed.

'We could take him too.'

'No!'

'Don't be so jealous!'

'I'm not jealous at all!'

Ben knew it made no sense to continue this discussion.

His parents were staring at the waves when he walked over to them. Hothbrodd was sitting by their side. There was still no light except for the silver the full moon cast on the waves.

'I came to say goodbye. If all goes well, I guess there won't be time once the Aurelia arrives.'

It was very hard to say those words. So many memories flooded Ben's heart – his first encounter with Barnabas in the Arabian desert, Vita at the dragon rider's tomb, Guinevere at the monastry in the Himalayas . . . and then the sudden warmth it had brought to his life to have a family again . . .

'Of course!' Barnabas got up. 'There won't be time. You're right.'

He pulled Ben close and hugged him fiercely. His mother got up and did the same.

'If all goes well,' she whispered into Ben's ear. 'It will! Let's just believe in it. And you'll have a fabulous time with Firedrake. I'm sure you won't miss us at all!'

She smiled at Ben, but he saw the same tears in her eyes that he felt in his own. Barnabas wiped one off the tip of his nose as well.

'Heavens, these are very emotional times,' he murmured. 'Take good care of yourself. Promise, dragon rider!'

Ben nodded. Hothbrodd squeezed him so hard that he wouldn't have been surprised if some of his ribs had cracked. 'Here!' he growled and picked up a long shaft of wood that was lying in the sand behind him. 'I made this for you. Just in case. I know you all don't like weapons, but after that fight on the island I thought a dragon rider may need a lance from time to time.'

The point was sharpened, and the shaft was light when Ben weighed it in his hands. 'Thank you, Hothbrodd!' he said. And turned to Vita.

'Can you tell Guinevere I'm so sorry I won't get a chance to hear all the tales she'll bring back?'

What if she didn't . . .? No. He wouldn't allow that thought. He'd probably miss his sister the most. He had never realised it as clearly as on this moonlit beach: his heart would always be in two places. He missed Firedrake when he was in MÍMAMEIÐR and he would miss his family when he was staying with Firedrake. But he knew he had to be with him. Their bond only got stronger – with every day he drew breath.

'Looks like both our children are spreading their wings, Vita,' Barnabas said. 'Well, their flippers in our daughter's case.'

'And it may not be too long a farewell this time.' Vita smiled up at Ben. 'I still haven't seen the young dragons. Maybe you'll find us at the Rim when you come back from delivering the seeds. If this all goes well! And yes,' she added with a smile for Twigleg, who was sitting on Ben's shoulder, 'we will look after Freddie, Twigleg. And he will look after us, if I know him.'

She looked to her right. Alfonso came walking towards them.

'The pelicans have spotted her,' he said. 'The Aurelia is coming.'

CHAPTER FIFTY-ONE

THE ARRIVAL

The Aurelia had fallen silent. Her lights faded, one by one, and she was suspended in the water, her arms floating around her like a robe. Only the pods were still glowing, like fallen stars, and the four arms that held them drifted slowly into position. Three floated upwards, the fourth one sank down, until it pointed into the depths the Aurelia had come from, the pod on it shimmering like a pearl as blue as the sky.

Guinevere was with Lizzie, Koo and Laimomi when the Great Singer announced the end of her journey in this way. All those who had travelled with her watched wide-eyed as the Aurelia slowly began to rise, pulsating with a pale blue-green light, as if the breath of the ocean had taken shape in her. Above her, the water was soaked with moonlight and in it Guinevere saw Elewese and all the ocean dwellers who'd gathered to guard her arrival. The Aurelia stopped when she had come so close to the surface that she could have reached up with her arms. The pods began to glow – so brightly that Guinevere wished her flippers were long enough to shield her eyes. Most of those who'd followed the Aurelia had to lower their gaze and when they finally dared to look at her again, the pods had come loose.

Three were drifting towards the surface. The blue pod was sinking into the depths, where Eight was waiting. The kraken caught it as gently as if it was a bauble blown from the finest glass. He was just wrapping another arm protectively around it, when a shadow dived up from deep below and shot towards the pods that were slowly floating up to the surface. An all too familiar shadow . . .

Three merpeople tried to block the copper squid's path, but he whipped them so violently with his tentacles that they drifted away with lifeless limbs. Guinevere, Lizzie, Koo and Laimomi all swam faster than ever before in their lives. But they were on the other side of the Aurelia, and when they had passed her veil of arms the squid was already high above them, going for the pods that had by now almost reached the surface. They floated towards it like balloons, red, green and violet-brown, each covered with a different pattern of lines, holes and spikes. The squid had opened his beak, obviously planning to swallow at least one.

But the Aurelia had noticed him.

And a hundred eyes and a thousand arms turned as red as fire.

No. No, this couldn't happen! Guinevere desperately pushed through the water with her flippers. From everywhere, alarmed helpers rushed forward, those who'd waited and those who'd come all the way. The Aurelia's arms began to glow like burning coal, one after the other. A school of dolphins was attacking the squid. They managed to delay him for a few moments, but they couldn't stop him. Something clung to one of his terrible tentacles. Someone . . . Elewese! But even his starfish strength was nothing compared to the squid's, who the Copperman had created. He shook him off so violently that Elewese was thrown against the dolphins, while the squid once again headed for the pods, his beak wide open. He had to let go.

Lost! Everything was lost. Guinevere waited for the Aurelia's flames to burn her, for her body to dissolve, and for Lizzie and

Laimomi to disappear.

But just then a shadow fell on to the water from above.

Silver claws broke the surface.

Firedrake.

The dragon dived down, as swiftly as a dolphin clad in moonlight scales. Guinevere felt her heart melt with relief, but then she saw Sorrel and her brother on Firedrake's back. Ben had a lance under his arm. No! They would drown! She wanted to swim towards them, but Lizzie held her back. The squid sank his beak deep into Firedrake's paw, while the dragon shielded the pods from him with his body. But Ben hit the squid with his lance, and the dragon drove his claw into the monster's hood, and tore him loose from his paw so fiercely that he finally let go and tumbled into the deep.

The pod! Guinevere saw it shimmering in Firedrake's paws when he rose back to the surface, his riders on his back. The Aurelia's red was fading and she shone instead with all the colours of the rainbow. Guinevere couldn't take her eyes off her and only realised how close she herself had come to the surface when she broke through the water.

Above her, Firedrake rose into the night sky, his wings bright with the light of the moon. One of his front paws was dripping blood from the wound made by the squid's beak, but he held the red pod firmly between them nevertheless. Ben threw his lance into the sea and waved – yes, those were their parents on the beach! And on Ben's shoulder . . . was that a very wet Twigleg? Guinevere barely recognised Sorrel behind her brother, she looked so different with her soaked fur. Guinevere's heart burst with love for all of them, while the dragon and his riders rose higher into the air, carrying what the sea had given eastwards. Of course! Ben would go with Firedrake to sow the Aurelia's seeds. She wouldn't see her brother for a very long time! That realisation stung like a stingray's barb.

But then she remembered the other pods. She turned with a start, and looked into Lizzie's face.

'It's all good!' Lizzie pointed to Shrii, who was circling above the water, his colours blackened by the night, the green pod safely in his claws. He was surrounded by swarms of pelicans and cormorants – all the feathered helpers who had gathered to welcome the Aurelia.

The griffin screamed, his voice rich with triumph and joy. Then he turned and flew over the water, towards the open sea, heading back to the thousand islands he called home.

Three. Three were safe. But where was the fourth? It was the purplish-brown one and had drifted on to the shore like treasure from a sunken ship. The creature who picked it up was huge and furry, and her paws looked strong enough to hold the moon. It was a bear, but unlike any Guinevere had ever seen. Bear picked the pod up and looked at it. Then she covered it protectively with her other paw and walked away, slowly, until her dark silhouette dissolved into the night.

'They're all safe! All four!' Laimomi appeared next to Lizzie and hugged Guinevere so fiercely that it made her really miss her own arms. Even Koo came close to the surface and brushed her back with his fin. A circle of merpeople formed in the waves, while below them the Aurelia was slowly sinking back into the depths she had come from. Guinevere followed her with her eyes. She would miss her. She almost dived down again just to hear that song for a little while longer, but Koo pushed her up and swam circles around her, until she joined the others. Yes, he was right. It was time to celebrate. Underneath them the Aurelia's light still illuminated the water, and the ocean's surface was made from moon silver, while the merpeople danced in the waves. For yes, of course they can dance! Around them, fish and snail and sponge were swirling around each other. And on the beach . . . on the beach Barnabas and Vita Greenbloom were waiting for their daughter.

'Your father hasn't changed at all,' Lizzie said to Guinevere. 'Though I am sure he doesn't use moss fairy dust! Let's say hello to him. It's been too long.'

CHAPTER FIFTY-TWO

OLD FRIENDS

The sea was breathing stars. Tiny sparks were emerging from the waves, millions of them, as if the Aurelia had left some of her light behind. The waves were washing them on to the sands and the wind was carrying them up into the sky. They attached themselves to Guinevere's once-again human skin and hair, and made the world look all new. And maybe it was. Maybe the creatures who'd emerge from the Aurelia's seeds would bring a magic they couldn't yet foresee. It was a beautiful dream, and on this night one almost dared to believe it. All was well. The world hadn't lost all its fabulous creatures to the greed of a never-aging boy. There would be more of them, and Guinevere would try her best to meet them all.

She smiled, and looked over to her parents, who were sitting next to her with Lizzie amongst the shower of sparks. They were laughing, hugging, talking, listening to each other and then . . . hugging each other again. Guinevere touched the sparks that had attached themselves to the selkie fur on her lap. They made her fingertips glow. Would she ever have a friend like Lizzie when she was as old as her father? Of course Barnabas wasn't terribly old, but forty-five sounds as far away as the North Pole when you are fourteen. Who would she miss at forty-five as much as her father clearly missed Lizzie Persimmons? Guinevere was not sure she had found a friend like that yet – except for her brother. Yes, she was sure she would miss Ben. She was missing him already. To imagine that one day she wouldn't know where or how he was, was unbearable.

Her father laughed out loud. He looked so young in his happiness, despite his grey hair and his wrinkles. Why was it so hard to imagine one's parents the same age as oneself? Guinevere had to smile again . . . no, with her parents it wasn't actually that difficult.

'Yes, isn't it incredible?' she heard Barnabas say. He sounded quite proud. 'Our son is a dragon rider, Lizzie! Do you remember, how I dreamed of one day meeting a dragon who'd carry me around the world?'

Guinevere hadn't known that about him, but Lizzie nodded. 'Of course I do! All your walls were covered with pictures of dragons. While I dreamed of having my very own Pegasus!'

'Guinevere saved the offspring of the last living Pegasus!' Barnabas exclaimed. The proud smile he gave her melted Guinevere's heart.

But Lizzie's face had turned grave. 'Barnabas!' she said. 'I know we don't even want to think about him. But we have to discuss what we'll do with Cadoc.'

Barnabas immediately looked his age again.

'We don't know, Lizzie,' Vita said. 'We've locked him in a shed for now. He's been yelling threats and insults since we caught him. He looks barely older than Ben, thanks to moss fairy dust.'

'Yes, I'm sure dozens of them lost their lives so Cadoc Eelstrom could still look like the boy who went to school with us. We're keeping him locked up at a friend's house in the mountains, so –' Barnabas cast a glance at Lizzie's fish tail '– if you want to see him . . .'

'She cannot see him.' Hothbrodd was standing behind Barnabas, with Lola on his head and Freddie on his shoulder.

'He escaped!' Lola shrilled. 'I had this strange feeling all night, so once the pods were safe I flew—'

'*We* flew,' Freddie added.

'Correct,' Lola said. 'We flew up to Mary's to check on the shed. Alfonso's men were still guarding the door. But . . .' she sighed.

'The shed was empty,' Hothbrodd growled.

Lizzie looked up at the troll as if he had torn out her heart with his message and eaten it. 'But how? Who could have freed him? That Copperman Barnabas told me about?'

A loud bark made them all turn around.

Derog Shortsleeves was standing in the sand, Mannanan by his side. He kept a safe distance from Hothbrodd's fists.

'Mr Eelstrom is in my care now,' he said, while Mannanan sniffed at the sparks glowing everywhere in the sand. 'As I mentioned on another occasion – I'll have my revenge. And a leprechaun always keeps his promises.'

'No wall built by humans,' Guinevere quoted the *Encyclopedia of Fabulous Creatures*, 'can hold back a leprechaun and his kind.'

She exchanged a look with her parents. They had both risen to their feet.

'Yes, no walls and clearly no sheds,' her father said. 'I should have considered that.'

'Where is he?' Lizzie was beating the sand with her tail fin. 'Tell us, leprechaun!'

Derog Shortsleeves gave one of his sharp-toothed smiles. 'You should ask what is he, mermaiden.'

He pulled a small bottle out of his pocket. It was a whisky bottle, of quite a fine Scottish brand. Something was moving behind the clear glass. Swimming, actually. It got quite upset when Derog pulled the glove off his right hand and tickled the bottle with his claw.

'There is a rare and very powerful leprechaun spell,' he purred. 'Very few know about it. Eating a few red squirrel hearts does not protect against it, that's for sure.' He shook the bottle, which made the inhabitant bounce around like a cork.

'Come on! I'm sure you can't wait!' Hothbrodd grunted. 'Tell us what kind o' magic that is.'

Derog Shortsleeves held the bottle in front of his green cat eyes. 'We call it the *make them their own judge* spell. You let your enemies talk. You let them curse and insult you . . . and so choose their future shape themselves.' He shook the bottle one more time. 'Mr Eelstrom proved to be quite creative. He called me a miserable wiggling worm living in the scum. So that's what he is now.'

He winked at Barnabas. 'I also said I won't kill him. As I mentioned before: a leprechaun always keeps his promises.'

'Without doubt.' Vita said and handed him the selkie skin he had loaned her. 'You proved that very impressively, Mr Shortsleeves. Your help was indispensable.'

The leprechaun received the fur and the compliment with a nod, but when Guinevere tried to hand him her fur as well, Derog Shortsleeves shook his head.

'Consider it a present, Guinevere Greenbloom,' he said. 'Its owner entrusted it into my care many years ago when she felt her end was near. She was a very good friend. And she would like you.'

Then he took a deep bow – and he and Mannanan were gone.

Guinevere read from her parents' faces that they were not sure whether they felt relief or regret that the leprechaun had freed them from the task of dealing with Cadoc Eelstrom. She felt guilty about it, but all she could think about was the selkie fur.

Lizzie stayed for another few hours, until her green-scaled skin began to itch for the sea. She said goodbye to Barnabas and Vita. Then she waved Guinevere to her side.

'So you have your own selkie skin now, little sister,' she whispered. 'Which means you have no excuse not to visit me. I'm not sure you'll convince your father to come too, but let's see.'

'I think I would like to come alone,' Guinevere whispered back.

'Then that's set!' Lizzie replied. 'Once you're back in Norway, be ready for an invitation from the sea. I am sure Koo will be delighted to send it to you. Mermaids keep their promises too.'

Guinevere very much hoped so.

She was still staring at the waves long after Lizzie had gone.

CHAPTER FIFTY-THREE

EPILOGUE

Many weeks later, Guinevere stood with her parents at the Rim of Heaven awaiting the return of Firedrake, Sorrel and her brother. And Twigleg of course. Freddie had been breathless with excitement for days, and he began to dance wildly on Guinevere's shoulder when Firedrake's silhouette appeared between the peaks surrounding the Eye of the Moon. Each of the Greenblooms held a young dragon in their arms. The smaller ones still liked to cuddle. Firedrake's offspring however were now rowdy – and so big that not even Hothbrodd was able to lift any of the three.

'Scales! Thorny! Moondance!' Guinevere called into the cave. 'Your father is back!'

They all shot out of the cave so swiftly that they reminded Guinevere of the pelicans she had watched shoot down for fish in California. When their mother appeared in the cave entrance, her three children were already flying circles around their father.

'I am so glad he is back,' Maia sighed as she stepped to Guinevere's side. 'It is time for me to go on an adventure.' She

pushed her nose gently into Guinevere's back. 'Maybe I could fly you back to MÍMAMEIÐR?'

'I would love that!' Guinevere replied, leaning her head against Maia's chest.

Her scales had a hint of gold in them, quite different from Firedrake's. Their glow reminded Guinevere of the Aurelia. She had told Maia and the dragonlings all about her – in the breaks between just lying on her back and following the young dragons with her eyes as they flew through the cave, getting bolder and bolder with every day. Vita and Barnabas had done pretty much the same. While Lola and Freddie had practised dragon riding on whoever allowed them on their back. The dragonlings had clearly made Hothbrodd their favourite, although he often growled at them. Sometimes half a dozen followed him, and when the troll stretched his mighty limbs out on the cave floor at night, it wasn't long until several young dragons were sleeping next to him.

The world was filled with wonderful

creatures. And Guinevere couldn't wait to find out which new friends the seeds of the Aurelia might grant her one day.

When Firedrake landed in front of the cave entrance, his three children were still fluttering around him. Ben waved at Guinevere and their parents, while Sorrel was greeted by Burr-Burr-Chan and the other brownies. Freddie climbed up Firedrake's scales to welcome his brother, and Twigleg looked very happy when he embraced him.

Yes. All was well.

WHO'S WHO

Human Beings

Mary Bright, close friend of Alfonso Fuentes, whose house serves as FREEFAB headquarters in this adventure.

Cadoc Eelstrom, former classmate of Barnabas Greenbloom and a fierce enemy since their schooldays. Cadoc hunts, captures and kills fabulous creatures to steal their magic and use it for his own, usually devious, purposes. Barnabas has saved many creatures from him over the years – often risking his own life.

Alfonso Fuentes, old friend of Barnabas, lives in Malibu.

Barnabas Greenbloom, Ben's adopted father and co-founder of FREEFAB, an organisation for the conservation of endangered fabulous creatures.

Ben Greenbloom, aged fourteen, lives with his adopted family, the Greenblooms, at MÍMAMEIÐR in Norway, and helps to study and conserve the fabulous beings of this world. Ben has a very special friend, Firedrake the silver dragon, whose dragon rider he became two years ago.

Guinevere Greenbloom, Ben's adopted sister. She was mainly concerned with the water creatures of MÍMAMEIÐR. Until she met the last Pegasus . . .

Vita Greenbloom, wife of Barnabas, mother of Guinevere and adopted mother of Ben. Co-founder of FREEFAB and expert on winged fabulous creatures.

Kahurangi Ngata, another old classmate of Barnabas and, like him, a passionate protector of fabulous creatures. He is Māori, one the indigenous people of New Zealand, and lives there.

Lizzie Persimmons, another close friend of Barnabas since school. At the beginning of this story Barnabas is sure Lizzie died many years ago. See also Fabulous Creatures of Water.

Fabulous Creatures of Land

barkgnome, small fabulous creature whose skin resembles tree bark.

Bear, fabulous creature who represents Earth when the Aurelia delivers her seeds.

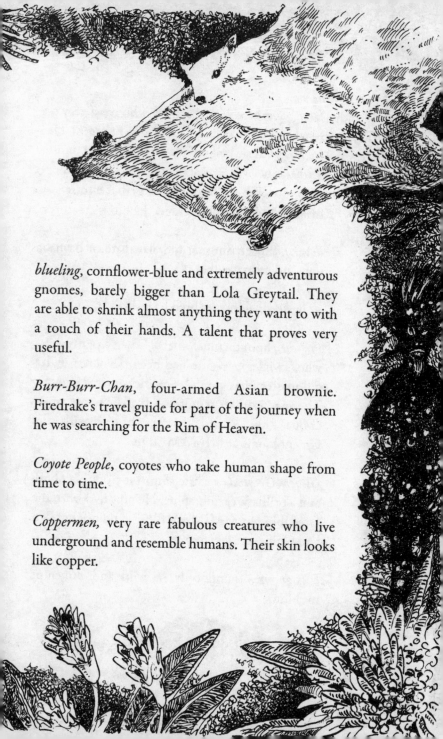

blueling, cornflower-blue and extremely adventurous gnomes, barely bigger than Lola Greytail. They are able to shrink almost anything they want to with a touch of their hands. A talent that proves very useful.

Burr-Burr-Chan, four-armed Asian brownie. Firedrake's travel guide for part of the journey when he was searching for the Rim of Heaven.

Coyote People, coyotes who take human shape from time to time.

Coppermen, very rare fabulous creatures who live underground and resemble humans. Their skin looks like copper.

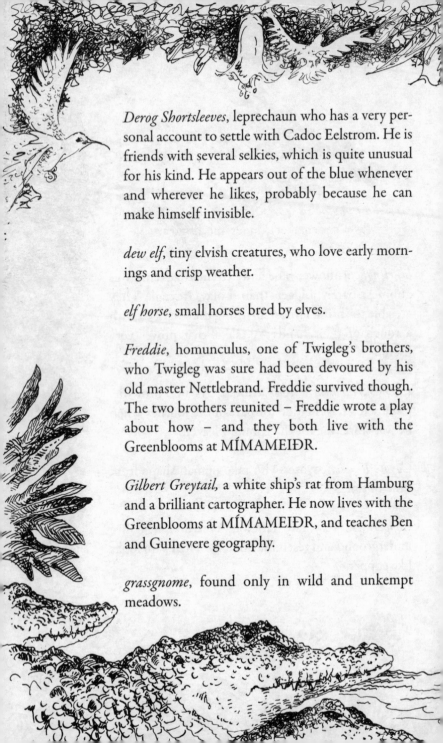

Derog Shortsleeves, leprechaun who has a very personal account to settle with Cadoc Eelstrom. He is friends with several selkies, which is quite unusual for his kind. He appears out of the blue whenever and wherever he likes, probably because he can make himself invisible.

dew elf, tiny elvish creatures, who love early mornings and crisp weather.

elf horse, small horses bred by elves.

Freddie, homunculus, one of Twigleg's brothers, who Twigleg was sure had been devoured by his old master Nettlebrand. Freddie survived though. The two brothers reunited – Freddie wrote a play about how – and they both live with the Greenblooms at MÍMAMEIÐR.

Gilbert Greytail, a white ship's rat from Hamburg and a brilliant cartographer. He now lives with the Greenblooms at MÍMAMEIÐR, and teaches Ben and Guinevere geography.

grassgnome, found only in wild and unkempt meadows.

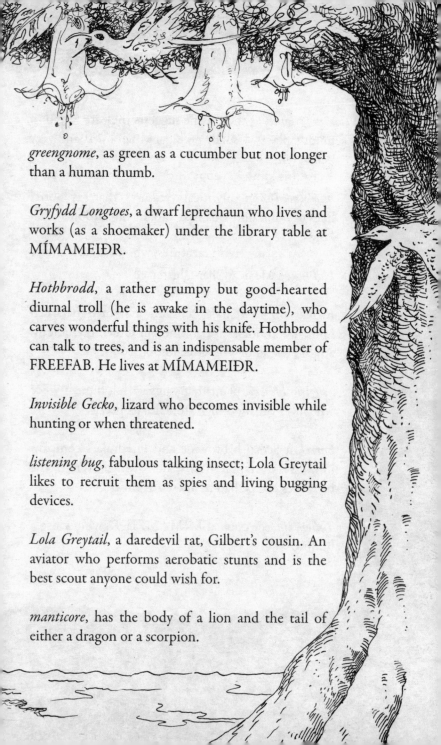

greengnome, as green as a cucumber but not longer than a human thumb.

Gryfydd Longtoes, a dwarf leprechaun who lives and works (as a shoemaker) under the library table at MÍMAMEIÐR.

Hothbrodd, a rather grumpy but good-hearted diurnal troll (he is awake in the daytime), who carves wonderful things with his knife. Hothbrodd can talk to trees, and is an indispensable member of FREEFAB. He lives at MÍMAMEIÐR.

Invisible Gecko, lizard who becomes invisible while hunting or when threatened.

listening bug, fabulous talking insect; Lola Greytail likes to recruit them as spies and living bugging devices.

Lola Greytail, a daredevil rat, Gilbert's cousin. An aviator who performs aerobatic stunts and is the best scout anyone could wish for.

manticore, has the body of a lion and the tail of either a dragon or a scorpion.

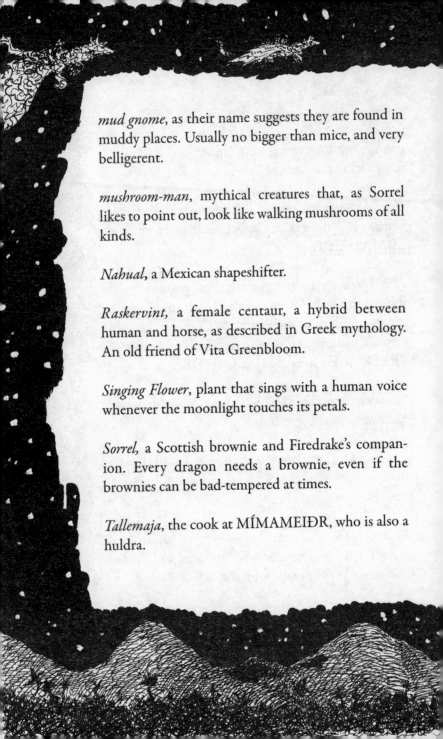

mud gnome, as their name suggests they are found in muddy places. Usually no bigger than mice, and very belligerent.

mushroom-man, mythical creatures that, as Sorrel likes to point out, look like walking mushrooms of all kinds.

Nahual, a Mexican shapeshifter.

Raskervint, a female centaur, a hybrid between human and horse, as described in Greek mythology. An old friend of Vita Greenbloom.

Singing Flower, plant that sings with a human voice whenever the moonlight touches its petals.

Sorrel, a Scottish brownie and Firedrake's companion. Every dragon needs a brownie, even if the brownies can be bad-tempered at times.

Tallemaja, the cook at MÍMAMEIÐR, who is also a huldra.

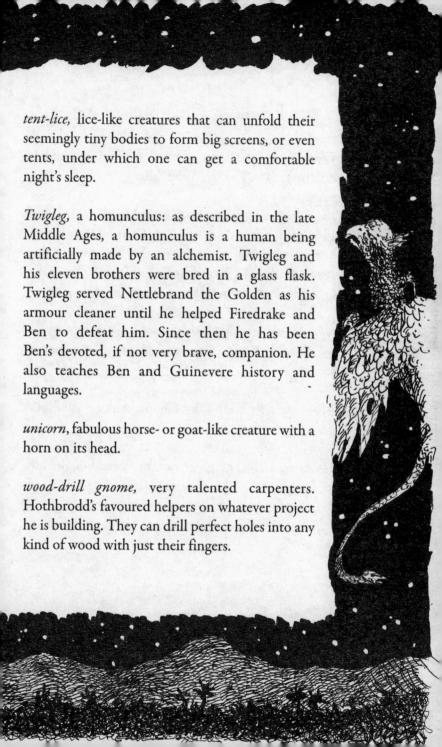

tent-lice, lice-like creatures that can unfold their seemingly tiny bodies to form big screens, or even tents, under which one can get a comfortable night's sleep.

Twigleg, a homunculus: as described in the late Middle Ages, a homunculus is a human being artificially made by an alchemist. Twigleg and his eleven brothers were bred in a glass flask. Twigleg served Nettlebrand the Golden as his armour cleaner until he helped Firedrake and Ben to defeat him. Since then he has been Ben's devoted, if not very brave, companion. He also teaches Ben and Guinevere history and languages.

unicorn, fabulous horse- or goat-like creature with a horn on its head.

wood-drill gnome, very talented carpenters. Hothbrodd's favoured helpers on whatever project he is building. They can drill perfect holes into any kind of wood with just their fingers.

Fabulous Creatures of Air

Chara, one of the Pegasus foals Ben, Guinevere and the others saved in *The Griffin's Feather.*

cloud dragon, a dragon that resembles drifting clouds and lives for thousands of years. Their bodies are most likely made from wet mist and they are said to never touch the ground. Barnabas Greenbloom believes that lightning is often, in fact, the fire of cloud dragons.

copper wasp, very aggressive wasps, created by Copper, the slave of Cadoc Eelstrom, to guard his master's secrets.

copper starling, created by Copper for the same purpose.

Firedrake, a silver dragon from the Scottish highlands. In *Dragon Rider,* he and Ben defeated Nettlebrand, the dragons' worst enemy, and found a refuge in the valley of the Rim of Heaven for the last dragons in the world.

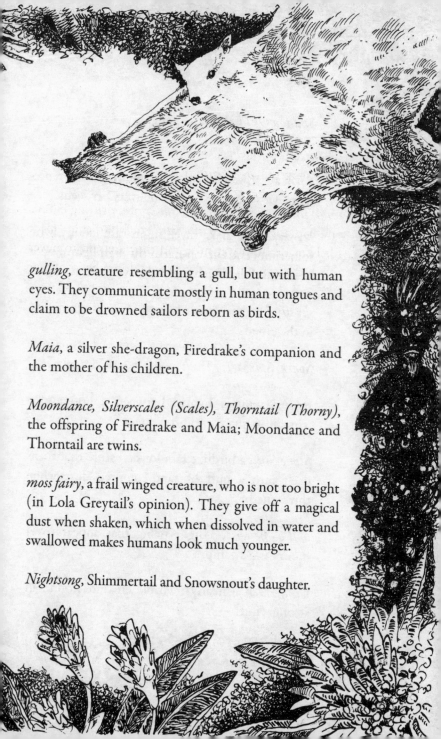

gulling, creature resembling a gull, but with human eyes. They communicate mostly in human tongues and claim to be drowned sailors reborn as birds.

Maia, a silver she-dragon, Firedrake's companion and the mother of his children.

Moondance, Silverscales (Scales), Thorntail (Thorny), the offspring of Firedrake and Maia; Moondance and Thorntail are twins.

moss fairy, a frail winged creature, who is not too bright (in Lola Greytail's opinion). They give off a magical dust when shaken, which when dissolved in water and swallowed makes humans look much younger.

Nightsong, Shimmertail and Snowsnout's daughter.

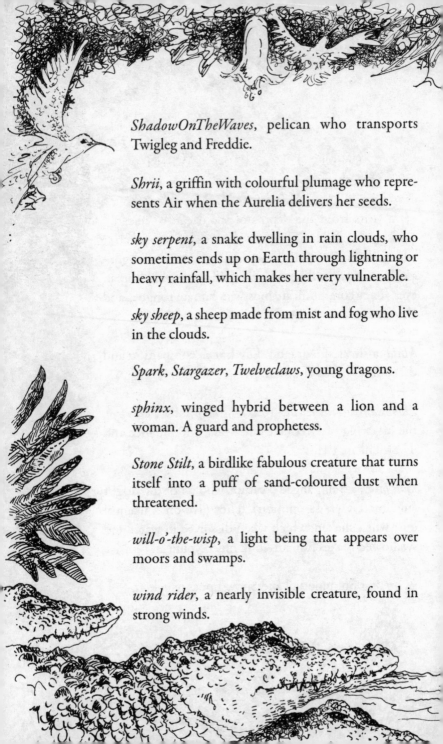

ShadowOnTheWaves, pelican who transports Twigleg and Freddie.

Shrii, a griffin with colourful plumage who represents Air when the Aurelia delivers her seeds.

sky serpent, a snake dwelling in rain clouds, who sometimes ends up on Earth through lightning or heavy rainfall, which makes her very vulnerable.

sky sheep, a sheep made from mist and fog who live in the clouds.

Spark, Stargazer, Twelveclaws, young dragons.

sphinx, winged hybrid between a lion and a woman. A guard and prophetess.

Stone Stilt, a birdlike fabulous creature that turns itself into a puff of sand-coloured dust when threatened.

will-o'-the-wisp, a light being that appears over moors and swamps.

wind rider, a nearly invisible creature, found in strong winds.

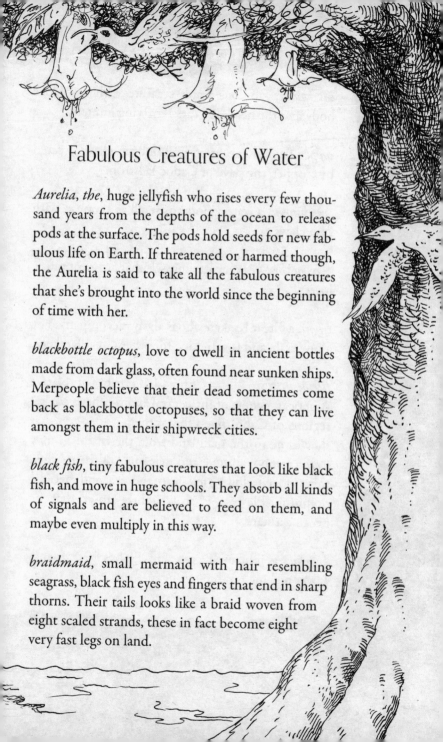

Fabulous Creatures of Water

Aurelia, the, huge jellyfish who rises every few thousand years from the depths of the ocean to release pods at the surface. The pods hold seeds for new fabulous life on Earth. If threatened or harmed though, the Aurelia is said to take all the fabulous creatures that she's brought into the world since the beginning of time with her.

blackbottle octopus, love to dwell in ancient bottles made from dark glass, often found near sunken ships. Merpeople believe that their dead sometimes come back as blackbottle octopuses, so that they can live amongst them in their shipwreck cities.

black fish, tiny fabulous creatures that look like black fish, and move in huge schools. They absorb all kinds of signals and are believed to feed on them, and maybe even multiply in this way.

braidmaid, small mermaid with hair resembling seagrass, black fish eyes and fingers that end in sharp thorns. Their tails looks like a braid woven from eight scaled strands, these in fact become eight very fast legs on land.

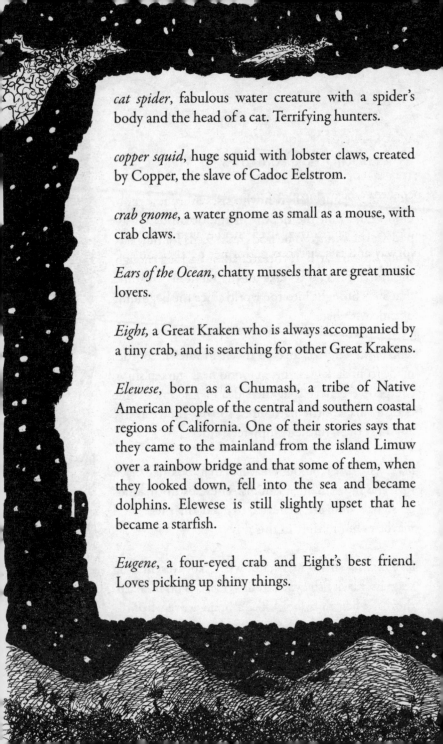

cat spider, fabulous water creature with a spider's body and the head of a cat. Terrifying hunters.

copper squid, huge squid with lobster claws, created by Copper, the slave of Cadoc Eelstrom.

crab gnome, a water gnome as small as a mouse, with crab claws.

Ears of the Ocean, chatty mussels that are great music lovers.

Eight, a Great Kraken who is always accompanied by a tiny crab, and is searching for other Great Krakens.

Elewese, born as a Chumash, a tribe of Native American people of the central and southern coastal regions of California. One of their stories says that they came to the mainland from the island Limuw over a rainbow bridge and that some of them, when they looked down, fell into the sea and became dolphins. Elewese is still slightly upset that he became a starfish.

Eugene, a four-eyed crab and Eight's best friend. Loves picking up shiny things.

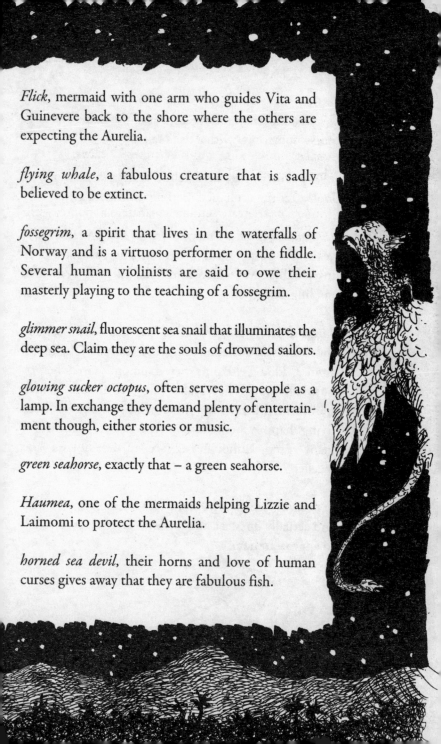

Flick, mermaid with one arm who guides Vita and Guinevere back to the shore where the others are expecting the Aurelia.

flying whale, a fabulous creature that is sadly believed to be extinct.

fossegrim, a spirit that lives in the waterfalls of Norway and is a virtuoso performer on the fiddle. Several human violinists are said to owe their masterly playing to the teaching of a fossegrim.

glimmer snail, fluorescent sea snail that illuminates the deep sea. Claim they are the souls of drowned sailors.

glowing sucker octopus, often serves merpeople as a lamp. In exchange they demand plenty of entertainment though, either stories or music.

green seahorse, exactly that – a green seahorse.

Haumea, one of the mermaids helping Lizzie and Laimomi to protect the Aurelia.

horned sea devil, their horns and love of human curses gives away that they are fabulous fish.

kelpie, a supernatural water spirit in the shape of a large horse, sometimes with a fish's tail.

Koo, a lantern fish who helps Lizzie and Laimomi to look after the orphaned merlings in their care.

Laimomi, Hawaiian mermaid who saved Lizzie many years ago from Cadoc Eelstrom. The two have been inseparable ever since and take care of orphaned merlings together.

Lizzie Persimmons, friend of Barnabas since school, she nearly drowned freeing the mermaid Laimomi from Cadoc Eelstrom's net. Laimomi saved her by pushing one of her scales into her mouth, which transformed Lizzie into a mermaid too. She has been living happily with the merpeople of Momi for many years – although her face still resembles a land dweller.

man-eating sea pig, resembles an underwater wild boar and actually does eat humans who are reckless enough to approach them.

merling, child of the merpeople. Makana, Haimi, Bane, Kona, Leilani and Ahonui are orphans and live under the care of Laimomi and Lizzie.

merpeople, term for sea dwellers whose upper body resembles humans while the lower body is a fish tail.

mud nix, love to camouflage themselves with mud.

nymph, female water spirit with a love of dancing and music.

nixlings, tiny merpeople.

pebble fish, in fact not fish, but living pebbles who dwell on the bottom of the ocean.

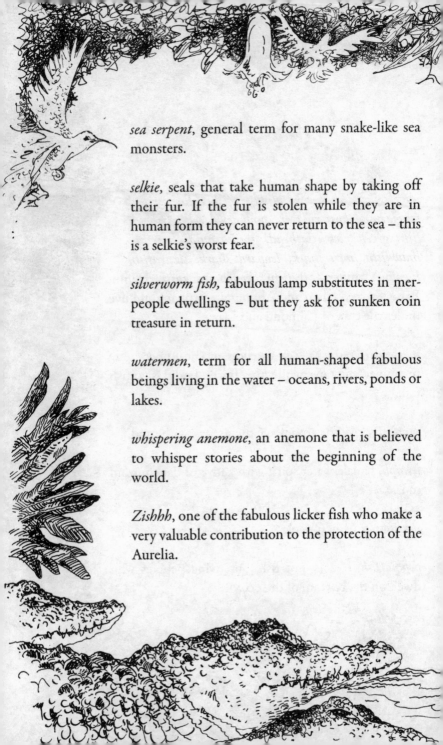

sea serpent, general term for many snake-like sea monsters.

selkie, seals that take human shape by taking off their fur. If the fur is stolen while they are in human form they can never return to the sea – this is a selkie's worst fear.

silverworm fish, fabulous lamp substitutes in mer-people dwellings – but they ask for sunken coin treasure in return.

watermen, term for all human-shaped fabulous beings living in the water – oceans, rivers, ponds or lakes.

whispering anemone, an anemone that is believed to whisper stories about the beginning of the world.

Zishhh, one of the fabulous licker fish who make a very valuable contribution to the protection of the Aurelia.

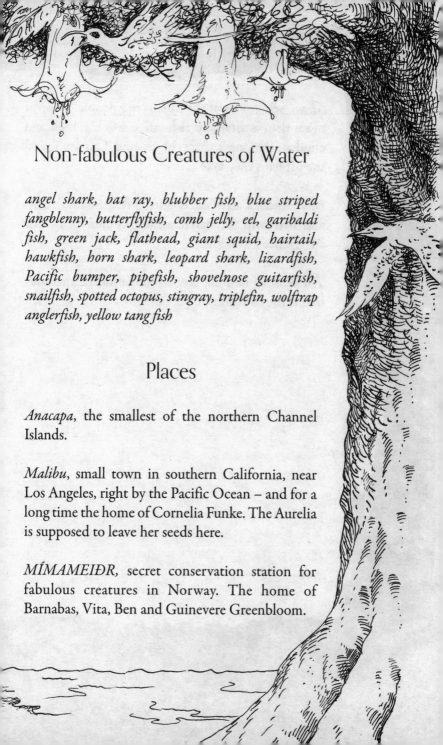

Non-fabulous Creatures of Water

angel shark, bat ray, blubber fish, blue striped fangblenny, butterflyfish, comb jelly, eel, garibaldi fish, green jack, flathead, giant squid, hairtail, hawkfish, horn shark, leopard shark, lizardfish, Pacific bumper, pipefish, shovelnose guitarfish, snailfish, spotted octopus, stingray, triplefin, wolftrap anglerfish, yellow tang fish

Places

Anacapa, the smallest of the northern Channel Islands.

Malibu, small town in southern California, near Los Angeles, right by the Pacific Ocean – and for a long time the home of Cornelia Funke. The Aurelia is supposed to leave her seeds here.

MÍMAMEIÐR, secret conservation station for fabulous creatures in Norway. The home of Barnabas, Vita, Ben and Guinevere Greenbloom.

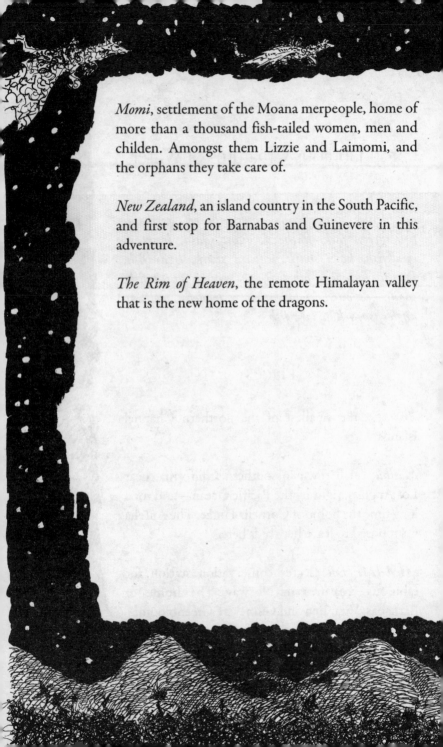

Momi, settlement of the Moana merpeople, home of more than a thousand fish-tailed women, men and childen. Amongst them Lizzie and Laimomi, and the orphans they take care of.

New Zealand, an island country in the South Pacific, and first stop for Barnabas and Guinevere in this adventure.

The Rim of Heaven, the remote Himalayan valley that is the new home of the dragons.